JESSICA STEELE

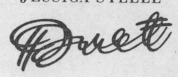

FAREWELL TO LOVE

FAREWELL TO LOVE

BY
JESSICA STEELE

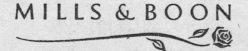

MILLS & BOON

MILLS & BOON LIMITED
ETON HOUSE, 18-24 PARADISE ROAD
RICHMOND, SURREY TW9 1SR

MILLS & BOON, the Rose Device and Duet are trademarks of the publisher.

First published in Great Britain 1989 by Mills & Boon Limited

© Jessica Steele 1989

Australian copyright 1989 Philippine copyright 1989 This edition 1995

ISBN 0 263 78954 3

Set in Times Roman 10 on 12 pt. 19-9502-55154 C

Printed in Great Britain by BPC Paperbacks Ltd

CHAPTER ONE

WAS ever a girl so happy? Meredith caught sight of herself in her full-length bedroom mirror, and could not help smiling at the young woman in bridal attire who smiled back. Today was her wedding day. Today, only a few hours ago in fact, she had married Ryan Carlisle.

A sudden movement drew her attention to her great-aunt Evelyn, who had come to her room with her for the traditional purpose of helping her to get changed into her going-away outfit. Not that she and Ryan were going away, for he was a very busy man, and, with everything happening so fast, it just was not convenient for him to leave his business at present.

'Are you all right, Aunty?' Meredith queried, and realised that the shimmer of tears in her great-aunt's eyes came only from her loving thoughts of the moment.

'I've never seen you look so happy,' Miss Evelyn Simmons sighed softly.

'I've never felt so happy,' Meredith replied gently— though she quickly qualified that lest she should have unintentionally wounded her great-aunt. 'Not that I haven't been happy living here with you and Uncle Porter all these years, and with Grandfather too, when he was alive,' she smiled.

'I know, dear, I know,' Evelyn Simmons said sweetly. Though her misty-eyed look had vanished when, being realistic for one of the very few times in her life, she added, 'Your grandfather would have been proud of you this day.'

Meredith, having lived in the Simmons household from the age of five, knew exactly what she meant. Grandfather Simmons had been a hard man, a man who worshipped money and a man, it seemed, who had been entirely without sentiment. Had he been alive today he would have been more proud to have witnessed that she had married herself to a man of some wealth than that she was happy to marry the man she loved—and the man who loved her. Not that Ryan had ever said he loved her, but Meredith knew he did—why else would he have married her?

She turned her back on a small moment of disquiet and, smiling at her great-aunt, observed signs of tiredness in the face of her dear old-fashioned seventy-nine-year-old relative. 'I can manage on my own, Aunty,' she told her quickly, and, indicating the small bedroom chair, suggested, 'Why not rest for a few minutes?'

Miss Simmons began to waver, but it was soon apparent that she was more concerned over her brother, her junior by two years.

'Tessa should have been here to help you,' she stated, bringing out Tessa's name somewhat begrudgingly, for she had never approved of the way Meredith's friend had gone to live with Duncan Smith without benefit of a marriage ceremony. 'If you're sure you can manage, though, I shouldn't at all mind going to keep an eye on Porter. He's not at all used to strong drink, but I'm sure I saw him helping himself to a second glass of champagne. What with his heart and...'

'You go, darling,' Meredith urged, having previously explained why Tessa could not be with them at such short notice. Feeling saddened for a moment when she thought of how tragically Duncan had died eighteen months ago, Meredith placed an arm about her great-aunt's shoulders and walked to the door with her. 'You worry too much about that brother of yours,' she told her, aware herself that her great-uncle Porter might, in his seventy-seventh year, have something of a tired heart, but also aware that he was not above playing on his 'heart condition' when he wanted his own way about something. 'I'll be down as soon as I've changed,' she smiled to her aunt.

Meredith's head was filled with thoughts of Ryan Carlisle once her aunt had gone. 'Ryan Carlisle, my husband,' she breathed out loud. 'Meredith Carlisle,' she added, savouring the name; already Meredith Maybry, her maiden name, seemed light years away. Suddenly Meredith gave a self-conscious laugh, and hastened to her wardrobe to extract her going-away suit.

The smile was back on her face as she stepped from her white wedding dress. The wedding arrangements had been made so fast that there had been no time to shop for a wedding gown, but she was glad now that Aunt Evelyn had insisted she find time.

Meredith was brimful of happiness as she donned the blue suit which brought out the bright blue colour of her eyes. The new suit had been another 'must' that her aunt had insisted upon. Even when Meredith had told her that she did not really need a going-away outfit, since with no time for a honeymoon she was only taking a half-hour journey across London to Ryan's apartment, her aunt had again insisted.

'I'm not having the neighbours seeing you leave home in something they've seen you wearing a dozen times before,' Evelyn Simmons had said firmly—at which Meredith had hardly been able to prevent herself from laughing.

'But we only have one near neighbour!' she had protested. Mrs Peplow, next door, was the same seventy-

nine years as her great-aunt, and was a lady Meredith
had known since she had come to live with her mother's
kin, seventeen years ago. 'And besides being your friend,
she's more family than...'

'Lilian Peplow may be my very good friend as well as
our neighbour,' her aunt interrupted, 'but that's by no
means any excuse for allowing our standards to drop.'
Rather than upset her dear aunt, Meredith had somehow
found the time to do as she wished.

Once that suit she had purchased was neatly zipped
up and buttoned, however, Meredith was glad that her
aunt had insisted the way she had. For suddenly she was
feeling slightly nervous and on checking her appearance
she saw, without conceit, that the blue of the two-piece,
as well as enhancing the colour of her bright blue eyes,
seemed to give an added something to the creamy complexion of her skin, and to the shining blonde of her
hair.

With a mixture of emotions bombarding her at the
thought of going down the stairs to join her new
husband, and of leaving the home she had known for
most of her life, Meredith needed a minute or two in
which to collect herself. The man she had that day
married was a man of some sophistication and, at pains
not to seem unsophisticated to him, she seated herself
in the chair which she had earlier suggested her great-
aunt might rest in, deciding that a few more minutes
spent in calming herself would do no harm.

Though, as she began to feel more calm about the one
issue, she began to have qualms about leaving her elderly relatives. Suddenly, now that the time had come to
leave her home, and them with it, she was starting to
feel guilty that she had ever for a single moment experienced an occasional if firmly held down urge to do

something different with her life. More frequently of late, she owned, up until the time she had met Ryan, she had known an out-of-character restlessness within herself—a restlessness that had pushed her to want to leave home. But to leave the home she shared with her aged great-aunt and great-uncle had been out of the question then.

Not that she had never been away from home. She had—once. That had been the dreadful time a year and a half ago when Tessa's Duncan had died. She had gone straight away to be with her friend in Derbyshire and to be what help she could. But she had only been able to stay a week, because Great-Uncle Porter had suffered one of his 'heart turns' and she had been summoned urgently home again.

Meredith sometimes thought that her great-uncle must have the most remarkable heart, for countless were the times when he would have them all believe that he was at death's door, but each time he recovered.

It was because of him, and his dicky heart, that she did not have a permanent job. Her thoughts drifted back to how, on the death of her parents in an accident when she was five years old, she had been taken to live with the two brothers and one sister—her mother's only relatives. As she had been brought up most strictly, however, with every word her grandfather uttered being law, it was not until after his death when Meredith was fifteen that there had been any lessening of the stern atmosphere. Her uncle Porter was inclined to be a shade domineering at times, it was true, and was growing more like his brother Ogden every day, but both he and Aunt Evelyn were kind to her, and in due time had even allowed her to go to art college with her great friend Tessa Wallace—something which would have been unthinkable in her grandfather's day.

Tessa was a born artist, while Meredith accepted that she merely had flair. She had worked hard, though, and, while Tessa went on to specialise in painting landscapes, she had gone on to specialise in design.

But, for all their training and talent, Tessa found it difficult to scrape a living out of painting landscapes and she moved to Little Haversham, on the outskirts of Derby, with Duncan, while Meredith eagerly sought a job in which she could use her training.

Her spirit was undaunted when no job seemed available, and she applied for a job as a window-dresser, to discover that window-dressing was where her real talent lay.

Unfortunately, while Uncle Porter had made no objection to her going to art school, it appeared that he had a good many objections to her going out to work. They were not wealthy by any means, and lived modestly on money left to them by Meredith's great-grandfather—money which might have been a vast sum once, but which over the years had dwindled and dwindled in value. But just the same, when Meredith was called home twice in her first week at her window-dressing job because Uncle Porter was having pains in his chest, and three times in her second week for the same reason, she felt that she could do no other than give in her notice before her employers gave it for her.

When the next two window-dressing jobs she applied for and got had to be given up because of her great-uncle's repeated bouts of illness, Meredith was forced to give way. Clearly Uncle Porter frowned on her going out to work. All she was doing by attempting to carve out a career in the window-dressing world was getting herself a bad name for being unreliable.

For once, though, Meredith experienced a strange feeling of rebellion and, acting on that feeling, she had put her name down on a register for temporary work, should any become available. Which—her eyes grew dreamy—was how she had come to meet Ryan.

The agency had rung her a week before that fateful day. Montgomery's, a mammoth new store which had been under construction for an age, was at last almost ready for the grand opening day. Everyone was frantically busy, because with a top-class celebrity booked, nothing could halt the store's being opened next Friday—nothing at all. A large hiccup had occurred in the build-up to next Friday, though, in that half the preparation staff had suddenly gone down with some tummy bug and, although there were dark mutterings about canteen food, dark mutterings were not going to get the job completed in time.

'Can you help?' implored the harassed woman from the agency, having had to find a good many workers from window-cleaners to carpet fitters.

'Do you think I'm good enough?' Meredith asked doubtfully. Montgomery's were an upmarket firm and, thanks to Uncle Porter, she felt she could in no way be called professional yet.

'You won't be working on your own,' the woman assured her. 'And I can promise you that any pair of artistic hands and artistic eyes will be more than welcome.'

'Then I'll be pleased to do it,' Meredith told her.

She had been too. She had put up with Uncle Porter's sour looks when she had told him where she was going, and she'd had a quiet word with Mrs Key, their daily help, and asked her to keep an eye on him for her. And, after a back-breaking week, she was quite pleased with her window-dressing efforts.

So, too, was the chief window-dresser, for he had thanked her very much, and said that she must come along to the store's opening the next day.

Almost, she had not gone. Had it not been for the Shakespearean actor who had been engaged to open the store, and whom Meredith had admired for his acting when she had seen him on TV, then she would not have gone. Nor would she have ever met Ryan Carlisle. Not that she was introduced to him, for as far as she could make out, when on Friday morning she stood tucked in with the rest of the staff, no one as lowly as a window-dresser had been invited to be part of the VIP party.

At that point, though, she had no inclination whatsoever to rub shoulders with the top brass. But although she, along with nearly everyone else, was eager for a sight of the Shakespearean actor, suddenly she lost all interest in him. 'That's Mr Montgomery,' she heard someone say. 'The white-haired, sprightly-looking chap.'

All eyes turned to see Mr Montgomery, and as Meredith took in the impeccably dressed white-haired man, her glance strayed to the tall, well-to-do-looking man standing talking to him. Her glance stayed on him. Indeed, she felt incapable of taking her eyes off him. And suddenly her heart was beating faster so that she almost had to gasp for breath. For, just as suddenly, though she had never seen the dark-haired man in her life before, though she did not so much as know his name, Meredith knew that she was in love. Feeling unable to take her eyes from him, Meredith, with a fast-beating heart, took in the fact that he appeared to be somewhere in his mid-thirties, that he was as impeccably dressed as his companion, and also that she had not a hope in the world that a man of his sophistication would ever notice, far less fall in love with, anyone such as her.

She managed to take her eyes from him as the opening ceremony got under way, and gave herself the sternest lecture on being such a crazy idiot as to imagine that she had fallen in love at first sight, and with a complete stranger. But she only had to flick a glance at him, as she did every now and again while the actor cut a wide ribbon and made a speech and then Mr Montgomery made a speech, to feel that same never-before-known emotion.

'Are you coming, Meredith?' another window-dresser asked, making her realise that the opening ceremony was over.

'I—er—think I left something in the staff-room,' she quickly and equally crazily invented.

On reflection, though, Meredith decided that perhaps her invention of the moment was not so crazy after all. For 'with all hands on deck', so to speak, now that the general public had been let into the store, it was pretty near guaranteed that the staff-room was empty.

Realising that she needed to be alone to try and get herself together from the shattering experience she had just undergone, Meredith said a hurried farewell to her window-dresser acquaintance and went as hurriedly to the staff-room.

Much good did it do her, though. Because although the staff-room was empty, and there was no one there to interrupt her train of thought, Meredith still didn't know quite what had hit her half an hour later.

It was ridiculous, she reiterated, trying to summon up the saner part of her. Why, she didn't even know the man's name!

She was still in the staff-room when, five minutes later, one of the salesgirls dashed in. 'It's bedlam out there!'

she told her, changing her high heels for a more practical pair of shoes and dashing out again.

Guessing that other staff would dive in from time to time and that she could not hope to have the staff-room to herself for much longer, Meredith prepared to go home. What was the point of staying, anyway? she thought as she made for the staff lift. She wasn't going to see him again, she wasn't going to speak to him ever, and, since there seemed to be something very active about him, he had probably left the Montgomery building already and, for all she knew, was at some other opening ceremony.

She had reached the staff lift and had just pressed the call button, though, when, to prove that he was not at some other opening, and that indeed he had not even left the building, the man she had so instantly given her heart to came and stood next to her. Suddenly, as her heart set up a tremendous clamouring, Meredith's legs at the same time felt so weak that she had no idea how she was going to step forward into the lift when it came. For, grateful for the smallest crumb, she saw that it seemed she was going to travel down in the lift with him—just the two of them!

Striving hard to keep her sense of mental balance, for this man had the oddest effect on her, she guessed that he had chosen to take the staff lift out of the store as the quickest route.

The lift arrived and, ready to admire the least thing about him, Meredith admired the courteous way he waited a second for her to precede him into the lift. 'Thank you,' she murmured politely. She admired him more when, with his finger over the ground-floor button, he looked at her enquiringly.

She nodded, and had the bonus as he went to turn from her of catching sight of the name-tag which store security had insisted that every visitor, bar customers, wore before the start of proceedings that morning, and which, now he was leaving the store, he had started to remove. Not, though, before she had read, 'R. Carlisle, Carlisle Electronics'.

He had pocketed the name-tab and the lift had started to descend when, in sheer desperation, acting totally unlike the normally reserved person she believed herself to be, Meredith heard her own voice suddenly blurt out, 'I have interests in the electrical field too!'

'It's—a small world,' he replied smoothly, and Meredith knew, just *knew*, that he was thinking, 'Liar'.

'I truly have,' she said earnestly, and became enormously aware that she was going to have to make a bigger fool of herself than ever. Because she felt obliged to confess, 'My father left me thousands and thousands of shares in Burgess Electrical.' Standing that close to him, she could not miss the sudden surprised look he gave her; and, grabbing at what pride she could, she got in first before he could beat her to it. Feeling even more stupid, she had to add, 'But, as you no doubt know, Burgess Electrical shares aren't worth the paper they're written on.'

The gods were merciful to her when at that point the lift reached the ground floor. R. Carlisle of Carlisle Electronics was still looking at her as though it was not every day that some lying window-dresser accosted him in a staff lift. When the lift doors opened, this time wanting to be as far away from him as she could, Meredith shot through them as though her heels were on fire.

The next afternoon she was in the sitting-room with her great-aunt and great-uncle and was still going through agonies about her actions yesterday. Oh, where, she inwardly mourned, had her customary reserve been then?

She only realised that she had sighed when her aunt looked at her. But just then the phone, which was always placed on a table near to Uncle Porter, rang.

He picked it up. 'Hello,' he said, sounding a trifle grumpy as he did sometimes. There followed a few moments' pause, during which Meredith started to wonder why he should begin to look as grumpy as he sounded, and then she heard him ask bluntly, 'Who wants her?' He looked more disgruntled than ever when, to her absolute stupefaction, he held the phone out to her and said, 'It's for you! He says his name's Ryan Carlisle.'

'For...' Meredith said croakily, and even while her mind quickly translated the 'R. Carlisle' she had been thinking about for the past twenty-four hours into Ryan Carlisle, she just could not credit that he could be on the other end of the phone! But her great-uncle was starting to look cross that she was not coming to take the phone from him and, because she realised that her thinking had been all haywire since yesterday anyway, so that it was nothing but plain coincidence that a Ryan Carlisle was ringing her about something, she went and took the phone from her uncle. 'Hello,' she said.

'Hello, Meredith,' said an absolutely sensational voice which she just knew belonged to none other than the man who, unbeknown to him, had kept her sleepless last night. 'We met yesterday, in a lift,' he reminded her, when there was absolutely no need. 'After the Montgomery store opening,' he added.

'Oh—yes, I—I remember,' Meredith replied, fighting with all she had to keep her voice even.

'I wonder if you're free to have dinner with me to-night,' he queried.

Scarcely believing that she was hearing what she was hearing, Meredith knew that if she did happen to have a previous engagement—which she didn't—she would have broken it. 'I—should like that,' she told him honestly.

'I'll call for you at seven-thirty,' he told her, and rang off.

Which, had he but known it, left Meredith in a flat spin. Though before she could deal with her own doubts and fears she had to deal with her relatives.

'Who was that?' Uncle Porter demanded to know.

'A—friend,' Meredith told him. 'He's taking me out to dinner tonight.'

'Why, that's lovely, my dear,' said her aunt, as if she had only just realised that her great-niece seldom if ever went out in the evening.

'What about *my* dinner?' Uncle Porter questioned, at his demanding worst.

'You're not helpless, Porter,' his sister told him shortly. 'Besides, Meredith deserves a night out with her young man. And anyway, I helped her prepare a casserole for dinner this morning, so you won't starve if...'

'Her young man!' Porter exploded, forgetting his stomach as he exclaimed more or less what Meredith had been thinking.

Her young man, she thought when later up in her room she looked with dissatisfaction at the contents of a wardrobe with which yesterday she had been perfectly satisfied. Oh, what was she going to wear?

By seven-fifteen, having changed several times from one dress to another, she was finally ready. Attired in a smart black dress which was neither too revealing nor too modest, she sat in her room and went through agony after agony as she wondered—had he been serious?

He had sounded serious, she remembered, not wanting to start believing that because she had been so idiotic as to tell him of those worthless shares yesterday he thought—having recovered from being so accosted—that he would play a little game with her.

It couldn't be some game he was playing to teach her not to try and get into conversation with unknown men in a lift, could it? Meredith discounted the idea when she recalled thinking that he looked an active sort of man. Her impression of him was that he was a man who would have no time to waste on inconsequentials. Which made it certain that he would not have gone to the trouble of finding out her telephone number if all he wanted to do was to play some game. Surely, if her impression of him was correct, it must mean that, since he had gone to the trouble of finding her phone number, he must be interested in her—and not ...

Her heartbeat went into overdrive again. Was Ryan Carlisle interested in her? It seemed so. As she sifted through everything it came to her that, since her phone number was listed under the name of Simmons, and not Maybry—the name he must have remembered from seeing her security name-tag yesterday—he must have asked more than one question about her. For a start, he would have had to make an enquiry of the chief window-dresser. Then, having got the information that she worked for an agency, he would have somehow had to inveigle her phone number from them. And that was not all. Since her name-tag had given only her initial 'M', and he had called her 'Meredith', he must have found out her first name; and not only that, but somehow, since he had said, 'I'll call for you', he had found out where she lived!

For the following ten minutes she didn't know whether to believe that Ryan Carlisle really did know where she lived, or was just having her on. When at the end of those ten minutes the front door bell sounded, she could have cried with relief. Not wanting her great-aunt to disturb herself to answer the door—and it was a certainty that Uncle Porter would not move to answer it—Meredith, with butterflies fluttering madly in her insides, hurriedly left her room.

Ryan Carlisle, when she pulled back the door, was every bit as tall as she remembered him, and every bit as appealing. He had a strong face. His firm chin, his firm if well-shaped mouth, his straight, aristocratic nose and high, intelligent forehead all spoke of a man who knew where he was going, and, since she guessed that he was the owner of Carlisle Electronics, she guessed too that he had already got there.

'H-hello,' she greeted him on a husky note, her blue eyes meeting grey eyes that seemed to have taken in her firm chin, her shapely mouth, dainty nose and smooth forehead in return. 'Will you come in for a moment and meet my family?' she asked him politely, knowing full well that Uncle Porter would chase after her, clutching at his heart, if she dared to leave the house without first introducing her escort for the evening.

Great-Aunt Evelyn was sweetness itself when Meredith introduced Ryan. Meredith wished she could have said the same of her great-uncle.

'What time are you bringing her back?' he demanded to know of Ryan.

'What time would you like to come home, Meredith?' Ryan turned to her to enquire, enchanting her further by not turning a hair at her great-uncle's rudeness.

'Any time after dinner,' she said as easily as she could, bearing in mind that she felt embarrassed to death and for once exasperated with her demanding relative, feeling that she could just as easily at that moment have told her uncle that she was never coming home again.

The mood passed the instant she and Ryan were outside, but once he had settled her inside his sleek car which simply purred away from the kerb it became clear to her that Ryan Carlisle missed nothing.

'Have you lived with your great-aunt and uncle for very long?' he enquired.

'Since I was five,' she told him openly, having quickly discovered that it was no figment of her imagination that she truly had fallen in love with him at first sight, and loving every moment of this, her most unexpected time with him. 'My parents were killed in an accident when I was five,' she explained, and, beginning to feel that she was being a chatterbox but knowing that nerves had something to do with it, for she was most reserved as a rule, she told him, 'My grandfather was alive then, and Grandfather had a strong sense of duty. So...' She paused to take a gulp of breath. Although she really believed she must be boring him out of his skull, she discovered that she could not stop talking. 'So, naturally, it was unthinkable that I should go to live with anyone but them. Not,' she added, 'that there was anyone else to go to.' Determinedly, she closed her mouth and bit down on any more words which would have bubbled to the surface.

To her relief, though, Ryan did not appear to think her garrulous tongue out of the ordinary, but commented, 'It seems you've inherited your grandfather's strong sense of duty.'

'Oh,' she said, and, not sure what he meant by that statement, she asked, 'Why do you say that?'

'I rather gained the impression that you'd as soon not return to your home tonight,' he replied.

About to quickly tell him that her great-aunt was a dear, and that her great-uncle really was not as bad as all that, Meredith suddenly had the most ghastly feeling that Ryan Carlisle thought her much more modern-minded than her old-fashioned upbringing allowed her to be. Suddenly, she had the most awful feeling that he thought she was in the habit of staying out all night with whoever her dinner companion was—and that he was sounding her out on that score!

She felt no end disappointed in him, though she guessed that he had not lived to be in his mid-thirties without a little experience of some of his dinner companions returning to his place for a nightcap. But, since it had been she who had tried to engage him in conversation to start with and who might thereby have given him the wrong impression of her—albeit that her remarks to him had been totally innocent—she nevertheless thought she should get it straight, right here and now, that she was not the 'sleeping-around' type.

'Oh, I always go home every night,' she told him, and for good measure, she added, 'without fail.' And then, having got that message across, she found she was babbling again, as she went on to qualify, 'That is, except when I went to stay with my very good friend Tessa Wallace in Little Haversham...'

By the time Ryan Carlisle was pulling up outside a smart-looking hotel, Meredith had told him all about

her artist friend in Derbyshire and about the sadness of
her losing her much-loved Duncan.

As Ryan escorted her into the restaurant of the hotel
and the head waiter, clearly valuing him as a favoured
customer, led them to a well-positioned table, Meredith
was thinking in terms of not opening her mouth again
for the rest of the evening. Nerves, pure and simple, were
responsible for her having suddenly become this prat-
tling female, and she hated the fact that Ryan was not
seeing her at her best.

For, even if she didn't know what her best was, she
wanted him to see her in a good light so that, if the gods
were really, really kind to her, he might ask her for another date.

Aware that she was being greedy in the one respect of
wanting to know more and more of him, Meredith found
that she had hardly any appetite for food. Though, when
Ryan looked at her after she had spent long enough
studying the menu, she decided that, since she had accepted an invitation to dine, it would be the height of
bad manners to say she felt she could not eat a scrap.

'I'll have the Stroganoff, I think,' she told him, and
found she was going off again when she added, 'I made
it once at home, but Uncle Porter said he didn't want
any more of "that foreign muck", so I haven't eaten
any since.' Firmly then she closed her mouth. But to her
relief, not to say joy, Ryan smiled at her as though her
related anecdote about her grouchy uncle had amused
him.

From then on, Meredith began to relax. She rather
guessed that Ryan's manner had a lot to do with that.
For he had a good line in funny anecdotes too, and as
the meal progressed she fell more and more under his
spell. She also became more and more relaxed, so that

the next time she became talkative it seemed to her to
be not babbling this time, but more two adults having
a conversation—even if the conversation they were
having centred on the shares which her father had left
her.

How they had got on to the subject of her worthless
shares, she could never afterwards remember. Although,
since she had died a thousand deaths each time she recalled the way she had blurted out to Ryan in the lift
yesterday, 'I have interests in the electrical field too!',
she was fairly certain that she had not been the one to
bring the subject up. But such was Ryan's charm that
she felt no embarrassment when she told him that
evening, 'Of course, the shares weren't as worthless then
as they are now. But then, the shares were never that
important. It was the chance to get back at my grandfather that mattered.'

'Your father purchased them to spite your grandfather?' Ryan queried, keeping up with her very well,
she realised, since she was not explaining this too
brilliantly.

'Sort of,' she said, and could see nothing for it but to
go back to the beginning. 'I don't think my grandfather
ever wanted my mother to marry and thereby get away
from his domination. Although, if he couldn't prevent
her from marrying when she reached twenty-one, he was
determined that she was certainly not going to marry
any penniless office worker.'

'But she did?'

Meredith nodded, and quietly she told him all that
over the years her great-aunt Evelyn had confided. 'Apparently my parents very nearly didn't get married at all
because of the hell my grandfather gave them over my
father's lack of finances.'

'Obviously they did marry, though,' Ryan smiled encouragingly.

Meredith smiled back. 'They did,' she said. 'But my father never forgave Grandfather that, through him, he so nearly lost the woman he loved. According to Great-Aunt Evelyn, the two were for ever afterwards at loggerheads.'

'You sound as though you're not totally convinced of that,' Ryan commented.

'Oh, I am,' she assured him quickly. 'But in any case, there's written proof in the way my father left his will.' For once she could see that Ryan was not keeping up with her, and, feeling comfortable with him, she went on to explain fully. 'It took my father some years to get on his feet financially, but by the time I had arrived he had his own department and was well able to keep a wife and family. He then began investing heavily in shares— the Burgess ones,' she smiled, and resumed, 'Aunt Evelyn believes that it was purely to infuriate her brother Ogden that my father took great pleasure in showing him the will he made on my fifth birthday. In his will, I was to inherit the shares when I was twenty-five but, should I marry before my twenty-fifth birthday, on the day I married the shares were to go to my husband. It was my father's way of telling Grandfather that he was determined I wouldn't suffer should Grandfather become my guardian and frown on any penniless suitor who came calling.'

'This way, your father would have seen to it that on your wedding day your husband became a wealthy man.' Ryan this time caught on straight away.

'That's right,' Meredith beamed at him. 'Of course, my father never dreamed that I'd be orphaned only a few months later. Though he'd had the tremendous satisfaction of infuriating my grandfather over the way he'd left his shares...' Her smile had gone when, quietly, she told Ryan, 'My father never knew that his hated father-in-law had the last laugh when the value of those shares started to decline until they became absolutely worthless.'

Just then the attentive waiter came again to their table to see if they required more coffee, and with a start of surprise Meredith saw that she had disposed of one decent-sized cupful without having the smallest memory of having done so.

'Yes, please,' she told the waiter, not because she wanted more coffee, but because she never wanted this evening to end, and she knew that once they left the restaurant Ryan would take her home and she would never see him again.

It delighted her when he too said he would have another cup, just as though he too did not want the evening to end. And her heart just flipped when, suddenly, she caught him looking at her hard and long. He smiled, though, when he saw himself observed, and a little while afterwards he settled the bill and they left the restaurant.

They were almost at her door and Meredith was aching for some way to extend the evening. But there was no way, and all too soon Ryan was escorting her from his car and up to her front door.

Almost then she asked him in for a cup of coffee, only to realise that she had missed out on the chance of that sounding like a natural invitation since, through her greed in wanting more time with him back at the restaurant, they were already swimming in coffee.

'Thank you for a very nice evening,' she told him politely as he handed her key back after he had unlocked the front door.

'Thank you, Meredith,' he answered smoothly, and although she wanted with all she had to stay talking to him, she somehow found the will to do just the opposite.

'Goodnight,' she said, and swiftly she put herself to the other side of the door.

In bed that night she hit the highest peak of her existence as she recalled that once or twice Ryan had seemed amused at a reference she made here and there—while at other memories she hit the darkest trough. Oh, my hat, she thought, I must have bored him silly with my prattle about my father's will!

She was still cringing over that when she began to feel uplifted, for there had been no need for her to feel at all disappointed in Ryan for having ideas of taking her to his bed. Moments later, though, she was accepting that what did disappoint her was that he had not even so much as tried to kiss her.

By the following morning, Meredith was keeping very much to herself her disappointment that Ryan Carlisle had not only shown no inclination to kiss her, but no desire either to want to take her out again—or even so much as hint at a second date.

'Did you have a nice time, dear?' her great-aunt asked at breakfast.

'Very nice,' Meredith replied, and she smiled, and Great-Uncle Porter grunted. Somehow, though, the fact that her uncle had chosen this morning to throw a fit of the 'moodies' barely impinged on her consciousness.

By Monday Meredith just knew that she was never going to hear from Ryan Carlisle. Which made her very surprised when that evening, as she was on the way to the dining-room for her evening meal, she darted into the sitting-room to answer the phone en route and heard Ryan on the line.

Her surprise was total, and was perhaps the reason for her quite spontaneous exclamation of, 'I didn't expect to hear from you again!'

'It's your shares I'm after,' he teased, and, hearing a smile in his voice, Meredith loved him all the more that he should make the way she had bored him over those shares seem to be their own private joke. 'I know I've left it late, but I'm still at the office. Can you have dinner with me in an hour?'

Swiftly Meredith thought of both her aunt and uncle already seated round the dinner-table, just waiting for her to join them before they began their meal. Against a mental picture of Uncle Porter's dark displeasure if she did not join them, though, she put her feeling that Ryan Carlisle was not a man who asked again, once refused.

'Yes,' she said, and wasted no time once he had put his phone down before racing to the dining-room to tell her relatives to start without her.

Then, having left Aunt Evelyn dealing with Uncle Porter's cross, 'Well, I call that the giddy limit!' she hurried back upstairs to view her wardrobe with renewed displeasure, knowing that she just could not wear the black again.

There were a few minutes to go before Ryan called for her when, having opted for a mid-calf skirt of gold with a matching waistcoat and cream silk blouse, Meredith realised that her throat just called out for a fine gold chain to complete the outfit.

Since Uncle Porter insisted that her jewel case—not that she had too much in it—should be covered with

clothing and left to repose in the bottom drawer of her
chest of drawers, it took only a moment for her to stoop
to retrieve it. As she did so, however, her eyes lighted
on the buff-coloured folder which had lain there for some
while now. On impulse Meredith took the folder with
its contents from its usual home.

When a minute later the front door bell sounded, the
fine gold chain was secured around her throat and, as
she went quickly to leave her room, she took with her
the folder which she had taken out on impulse.

'I shan't be late back,' she called to her relatives, who
were now in the sitting-room. And, since they had already
met her escort, she saw no reason to ask Ryan in—he
must be starving anyway—and went sailing on to meet
him. 'I thought you might like to see my share certificates,' she told him with a grin, when his glance encom-
passed the folder she had in her hands—and so began
the second most wonderful evening of her life.

She was less garrulous on that dinner-date than she
had been on the previous one, but she had still done her
fair portion of talking when, with the time nearing midnight, Ryan took her home.

'Thank you,' she said as he drew the car up outside
her home and cut the engine.

'Thank you, Meredith,' he said, and she knew that in
the darkness he was smiling.

When Ryan helped her from his car and walked with
her to her front door, her heart was going like a trip
hammer. He had sounded as though he had enjoyed the
evening too—would he ask her out again?

He did not ask her out again, but what he did do was
to take her by the arms, and gently kiss her.

She sighed blissfully as he broke his brief kiss and let
go of her. Her sigh, though, seemed to halt him, and

his voice sounded just a trifle curt when he demanded, 'Hell's bells, was that your first kiss?'

Meredith rapidly came to, to realise that somehow or other through the evening Ryan must have picked up a hint that she did not have very much experience. Her naïve response to his kiss just now must have shown that too, she guessed. 'Of course it wasn't,' she told him, however, not wanting her marvellous evening with him to end on a sour note. 'Why, Aldo and I . . .'

'Spare me the details,' Ryan cut her off, and, taking her key from her, he unlocked the front door and pushed it wide. 'Goodnight,' he said, and strode back to his car.

Meredith sighed again as she climbed the stairs to bed. This time, though, her sigh was anything but blissful. Her trouble was, she realised, that she had barely any experience of men, and, living with her relatives the way she did, with Uncle Porter playing up on the few occasions she did go out, she did not see how she was going to gain any experience. She had just intimated to Ryan that she had experienced some degree of lovemaking with Aldo. But all she had received from Aldo, Tessa's older brother by four years, was an experimental kiss which she had not liked very much at all.

Wishing that she had been out with dozens of men, and that she was smart and sophisticated, Meredith climbed into bed, blushing under the bedclothes when she realised just how gauche she must seem to Ryan. So much for her enthusiasm in greeting him with, 'I thought you might like to see my share certificates'—he had not even glanced at them!

Realising that she had been so taken with her marvellous evening that she had forgotten to retrieve her buff folder from Ryan's car, but had left it here, Meredith

silently groaned as she also remembered that a copy of
her father's will lay inside it too.

'Oh, grief!' she murmured in anguish, and, remembering how she must have bored the socks off Ryan on
Saturday when she had spoken in detail of her father,
her grandfather and that wretched will, she hoped with
all she had that the folder containing both share certificates and the will had somehow managed to slide under
the luxurious carpet in Ryan's car—well out of sight.

She got up the next morning knowing that if she was
ever lucky enough to see Ryan again—though she was
firmly of the opinion that two dates with her had been
sufficient for him and that there would not be a third—
then never ever was she going to mention again the word
shares, nor the word will.

Against all her expectations, though, she did see Ryan
again. For he rang her that same afternoon, and, to her
great joy, asked her to dine with him that evening.

'I'd like that,' she told him, the understatement of the
year, she thought, and put down the phone to have to
face her demanding uncle.

'You're not going out with that man again tonight,
are you?' he questioned her grumpily, and when she said
that she was, he was at his most miserable, and contrary
with it.

'Ignore him—he's got a touch of the Ogdens,' her aunt
advised.

But a fractious Uncle Porter was difficult to ignore
and, run ragged by an over-demanding uncle, Meredith
was not skilled in hiding her feelings when Ryan arrived.

'What sort of a day have you had?' he asked percep-
tively once they were seated in his car.

'Oh, to get away from it all!' she replied, and, having
meant her words to come out jokily, she was appalled

when it sounded as though she had just about had enough of her elderly relatives. Quickly she put a smile into her voice, and brightly bounced a cheerful question back at him. 'What sort of day have *you* had?' she asked.

That dinner followed the same pattern as her dinner date with him last night. Ryan was a witty conversationalist and countless were the times he made her laugh. In no time at all, she had forgotten every bit about how grouchy her great-uncle had been.

When the time came for Ryan to drive her home, Meredith was feeling so much at ease with him that, not wanting the evening ever to end, she asked him if he would care to come in for a coffee.

'Yes, I should,' he replied without hesitation, but, to her everlasting delight, he seemed to be more interested in her when he followed her into the kitchen. And no sooner had she picked up the coffee jar than he took it out of her hand and placed it down on a working surface. 'What a lovely creature you are,' he murmured, and, while her heart started to thunder so loudly that she was sure that he must hear it, he reached for her and gathered her into his arms.

His first kiss on her mouth was warm and gentle. But, not wanting the evening to end on the same curt note as the previous evening, so that he should know that she was not some naïve miss, Meredith put her arms around him and clung to him.

His reaction, though, stunned her and made her aware that neither she nor her old-fashioned upbringing were yet ready for this. For his kiss changed to become ardent, and as he pulled her body close up to his, while part of her wanted to respond madly and she leant against him, one of his hands caressed from her back and came to cup her left breast in a tender hold.

With her body beginning to tingle with an emotion entirely new to her, Meredith gasped and pulled back out of his embrace, some part of her brain registering that her great-uncle would have a heart attack which would prove fatal if he chanced this moment to come down the stairs.

'I...' she gasped, wanting most urgently to be back in Ryan's arms, while at the same time needing time to adjust to this intimate side of loving. 'I...' she repeated, wanting quite desperately to say something that would nullify any curt word of parting he had for her.

But, to her gratitude, when she looked at Ryan's expression it was to observe that he did not appear to be curt or angry at all, but more good-humoured than anything.

Proof that he had indeed stayed good-humoured was to be seen in the way he touched a finger under her chin and, referring to what she had begun to say last night drawled softly, 'Whatever went on between "Aldo" and you, my dear, it didn't go beyond a few kisses.' And while Meredith had started to tingle anew, Ryan shattered her completely when, swamping her with his charm, he said, 'It seems to me, little virgin, that since I'm not to be allowed my "wicked way" without marriage, you'd better marry me without delay.'

'You—want—t-to marry me!' Meredith choked incredulously.

'Without delay,' Ryan repeated, his eyes watchful on hers.

'Oh, Ryan!' she cried, and just had to ask, 'You love me?'

His answer was to take her into his arms and gently kiss her. And she had all the proof she wanted that he loved her, for when a man like Ryan said 'without delay' he meant just that. Already he was sweeping her off her feet by telling her that with a special licence they could be married by the weekend.

Thrilled in a way she had never in her twenty-two years experienced, Meredith was ready to agree to anything he said. Years of living with her great-aunt and great-uncle, though, were not so easily discarded.

'I can't be ready by then!' she just had to tell him, and she itemised, 'I have to tell my aunt and uncle, then I'll have to fill up the freezer and see to it that they...'

'So, OK, I'll give you two extra days,' he conceded, and thrilled her yet again when he said firmly, 'But I insist, Meredith, that you don't make me wait longer than next Monday.'

The sound of the front door opening brought Meredith out of her reverie. For here it was, Monday, and here she was in her going-away outfit, and she should have gone downstairs ages ago.

With her heart overflowing with happiness, she hurriedly left her seat to go swiftly from her bedroom for the last time. Her attack of nerves was over, and more than anything she wanted to be with Ryan, her husband.

Already as she sped silently along the landing she could hear his voice as he saw his friend and best man, Monte Montgomery, on his way. She had known that Monte Montgomery had an appointment later, and it vexed her that she had stayed in her room so long when she should have been by Ryan's side to say goodbye to their guest.

A moment of shyness took her, however, and when she was about to round the landing and go down the stairs she paused. And that was when Monte Montgomery's voice took over from Ryan's and floated up the stairs. And that was when her world came crashing down about her.

For, 'My stars, Ryan, you must be the jammiest devil I know,' she clearly heard his friend say jovially. 'Not only do you get those shares you've wanted for so long— but the woman you have to take with them just happens to be beautiful!'

Stopped dead in her tracks when she would have gone on, Meredith was bewildered by what Monte Montgomery was saying. But when it quickly dawned on her that he was saying that Ryan had married her not because he loved her but because of the shares, she stayed where she was, sure that Ryan would put his friend right in no uncertain terms.

But her husband of a few hours did not put his friend right. To the contrary, Meredith, in utter disbelief, actually heard Ryan—*agreeing* with him!

'It takes the edge off having to marry at all that my bride just happens to be beautiful,' she heard him admit, and, as the colour started to drain from her face, she heard him add, 'But to own those shares I'd have married her had she looked like the rear end of a horse.' Meredith was clutching on to the stair-rail as though her life depended upon it when he tacked on cheerfully, 'It's a bonus, of course, that she's a biddable little thing, and...'

At that point, Meredith could not bear to hear any more. With pain tearing away at her insides, she returned to the bedroom as noiselessly as she had come from it. The small wedding party was waiting for her to join them downstairs, but, with her heart starting to break, she needed to think.

CHAPTER TWO

WITH her world falling apart around her, Meredith was so distraught by what she had just heard that, having fled to her bedroom, needing to think, she discovered that any chance of clear thinking was impossible. The words '... to own those shares, I'd have married her had she looked like the rear end of a horse' were spinning around in her head, and all she knew for sure was that Ryan Carlisle had not married her because he loved her, but because to marry her was the only way in which he could get his hands on her shares. Why he should want her worthless shares was not important to her just then. All that was important was that Ryan, her husband, the man she loved so very much, did not love her.

Some noise from downstairs broke into her unhappiness and panicked her into going to the door of her room. Crazily the notion passed through her mind that, if she did not soon show herself downstairs, Ryan might come looking for her. Why, in the light of what she had just learned, she should think he would do that, she was unsure, but she was not yet ready to face him on a one-to-one level, and so quickly she left her room.

She was at the door of the sitting-room when she realised that she did not want to see anyone else either. But Mrs Key, who was there that day partly as a guest and partly to dispense food and drink, suddenly came from the direction of the kitchen.

'You look almost as lovely in your going-away suit as you did in your wedding dress,' their daily help crooned when Meredith, spotting the tray of tea in her hands, opened the sitting-room door for her.

Somehow, because it was expected of her, Meredith managed to pin a smile on her face as she stood back to allow the tea-carrying Mrs Key to go into the room first. Somehow, too, she managed to hold that smile in place as her glance flicked past Ryan, who was in conversation with their elderly next-door neighbour, Mrs Peplow, and went to where her great-aunt Evelyn appeared to be having a few cross words with her brother Porter.

Uncle Porter's colour was much too high, Meredith thought, though whether from too much champagne or too much excitement, she could not tell. In her view, though, he'd had enough excitement for one day. She would do him no good at all, she realised, if she suddenly gave way to the hurt that was screaming away inside her and created a scene.

'Shall we go, my dear?' Ryan's coming silently to her side and asking the cool, relaxed question brought Meredith down from a hysterical pitch. She had never created a scene in her life, for goodness' sake, so she wasn't likely to start now—and certainly not in front of her aged relatives!

Which fact, although she had been undecided what she should do, or where she should go, finally brought her the answer. For the sake of her great-aunt's peace of mind, and out of respect for her great-uncle's dodgy heart, she would go with her husband. What happened after that she had not quite decided.

'I'll just say my goodbyes,' she told Ryan quietly, and went first to have a word with Mrs Key, having previously arranged with that good lady that she would ring her at her new home if she was at all worried about either of her relatives. Next, and because she had known Mrs Peplow nearly all her life, she went and kissed her goodbye, and then she went and said goodbye to her aunt and uncle.

'I suppose we're never going to see you now that you're married,' her uncle said grumpily, the champagne he had consumed not improving his temper.

'Don't start, Porter!' his sister warned him, and motioned to Meredith to go now, since it did not look as though his manner was going to get any better.

'I'll—be in touch,' Meredith told her aunt huskily, giving her a swift hug. And in the early evening of what was turning out to be the worst day of her life, she went quickly out to where Ryan's car was standing at the kerb.

There had been a brief let-up in the hurt and pain screaming away at her as she had said her goodbyes. But as Ryan got into the car beside her and began to drive off, the pain and hurt he had caused her returned in full force.

'You're very quiet,' he said when they had been driving for some minutes and she had volunteered not a word.

Uncertain if he was saying that it made a pleasant change to have her quiet after the chatterbox she had occasionally been prone to being, Meredith swallowed down more hurt. 'It's been a busy day,' she told him evenly.

Busy was not the word for it, she thought as she recalled how prior to that day she had raced around like a mad thing because she had thought Ryan impatient to marry her. Oh, he'd been impatient to marry her, true enough, but not because he loved her. Oh, what a fool she had been!

All the while she had dashed around—shopping for the home, shopping for herself, cooking for the freezer—

she had believed he loved her. Willingly, wanting to marry him as much as she had thought he wanted to marry her, she had done the hundred and one things that had to be done in order to be ready for today. In the belief that he loved her, and with no time to spare in which to go to see the inside of his apartment—her new home—she had happily packed a suitcase of her favourite clothes. And Ryan, with every appearance of looking forward to this day as much as she, had taken the case to his apartment for her.

But he *had* been looking forward to this day, she suddenly realised. Not because he was impatient for her, but because he was impatient to get his hands on her shares.

He had wanted her shares so badly that he had been prepared to marry her had she looked like the rear end of a horse, she recalled painfully. He had not wanted to marry at all, though, really—she did not have to look past his 'It takes the edge off having to marry at all that my bride just happens to be beautiful' to know that.

Suddenly then, though, Meredith was recalling what else Ryan had said, and as she remembered how cheerfully he had said, 'It's a bonus, of course, that she's a biddable little thing,' she started to get angry. And, having left the restraints of her upbringing, she began to feel less and less *biddable* the nearer she got to her new home.

She welcomed the feeling of anger. The pain was still there, but to feel angry too was a great help. She had grown up knowing that she did not possess a temper but, dammit, there were limits!

The locale where Ryan had his apartment was salubrious-looking, and expensive. As they went in he introduced Preston, the smartly uniformed hall security man, and then, having referred to her as 'my wife', he was escorting her over to the lift.

But Meredith did not feel the thrill which she would have felt an hour earlier to be spoken of as 'my wife'. She did not feel like a wife, and as they stepped out of the lift and Ryan unlocked the door of his apartment, and her anger went up another notch, she decided that she was not going to be a wife to him.

She knew that for certain when, having closed the door to the outside world, and just as though he believed it was expected of him, her new husband made as though to take her in his arms.

With her expression stony, Meredith evaded him. To show how concerned he was *not* by her actions, she saw him shrug as his arms fell back to his sides. Nor did he make any attempt to take hold of her again, but he allowed her to cross over the hall and walk down the three thickly carpeted steps into his large, thickly carpeted and luxurious sitting-room.

And it was there, in the middle of his sitting-room, that nerves, anger, and hurt all fused into one within her. Without a glimmer of a smile on her face, Meredith turned, and, while she was quite well aware that he had no idea she had overheard him in conversation with Monte Montgomery, she asked shortly, 'Why did you marry me?'

She saw the alert look in his eyes, but he was cool, and appeared still in a fine good humour, drawling, 'It seemed a good idea at the time.'

But Meredith could see nothing to be good-humoured about, and silently she stared at him with her brilliantly blue eyes. To his credit, though, Ryan was not a man who would look away from trouble. And after waiting a minute longer for her to follow up if she was going to, he took the initiative from her.

'I refuse to begin our marriage with you going into a fit of sulks over some imagined slight,' he told her bluntly, good humour nowhere to be seen.

'*Imagined* slight!' she exclaimed, part of her idiotic enough to want him good-humoured with her again, while the saner side of her was ready to be up in arms that he should dare to accuse her of having a fit of sulks.

'Something's been festering away in you ever since we left your aunt and uncle's home,' he went on brusquely, and while she was giving him ten out ten for perception, he was ordering, 'So out with it—let's have it all!'

Meredith had a brief struggle with the person inside her who wanted Ryan to stay in a good humour, and a short tussle with the one who was trying to stay in the well-mannered—and biddable—mould of her up-bringing. But the mould had already started to crack, and she was discovering in herself a pride which refused to allow her to stay quiet and pretend that nothing had happened.

'How about—and I quote,' she began coolly, '"To own those shares, I'd have married her had she looked like the rear end of a horse"?'

She saw it register with him that she must have overheard his conversation with Monte Montgomery. But not by so much as a flicker of an eyelid did Ryan look as though he felt he had said anything to be ashamed of. Indeed—and she was watching him intently—it seemed to Meredith that he thought she had a fine cheek in listening to his conversation anyway!

He wasted no time, however, in squashing completely any lingering hope she might have that she had got it all wrong and that there must be some simple explanation, when, as bluntly as before, he told her quite openly, 'Of course I married you for those shares—if that's why you're sulking.' And, while she was taking that on the chin, he went on, 'So all right, perhaps I should have told you that your shares in Burgess Electrical, far from being worthless, as you thought them, have shot up in value in recent months, but...'

'My sh...the shares—they aren't worthless?' she questioned, still not very interested in the shares, but not wanting him to see how his unfeeling confirmation that he had not married her for love was rocking her foundations.

'Not now,' he told her, and, openly still, he went on, 'Not now half the electronic firms in the business, mine included, are waiting their chance to take Burgess Electrical over.'

'Firms—your firm—want to take them over?' she queried in surprise. She had never had a head for business, but even with her limited comprehension of what went on in big business, it did not seem to her to be a very good investment. 'Burgess Electrical have been ailing for years and years—to the point of extinction not too many years ago,' she told Ryan, though she now realised he probably already knew that anyway. 'So wh...?'

'So why want to take them over?' he finished for her, and, again openly, he told her, 'On account of the most minute piece of antiquated equipment which they manufacture. A piece of equipment which was dismissed as obsolete, but which, it's now been discovered, can cut production costs by huge amounts for whoever can get hold of it. Unfortunately, Burgess Electrical hold the patent, and are unwilling to sell it.'

'Which means that you, along with everyone else,' Meredith worked it out, 'are buying up Burgess Electrical shares as fast as you can.'

'Past tense,' Ryan grunted. Since she had been bright enough to stay with him this far, he went on, 'Everyone's already bought—there just aren't any more available. That is there weren't, until...'

He did not have to continue, for not only was Meredith keeping up with him, she had gone streaming on to work more out for herself. 'My godfathers!' she exclaimed. 'You must have thought you'd hit the jackpot that day in that lift when I told you that my father had left me thousands and thousands of Burgess Electrical shares!'

'I couldn't believe what I was hearing,' he admitted, and further owned, 'Nor could I believe my eyes when a look at the share certificates showed that your father was obsessed with buying more and yet more of them.'

'Nor could you believe your eyes, I suspect,' Meredith said acidly, 'when a sight of my father's will confirmed what I'd already told you—that those shares became the property of my husband should I marry before I reached my twenty-fifth birthday.'

'What are you complaining of?' Ryan queried, giving her a sharp look on hearing acid in her tones for the first time. 'I married you, didn't I—which was what you wanted?' And while Meredith immediately lost her acid feelings and was instead mortally wounded that he should so uncaringly refer to the love she bore him, he went on to startle her when he rapped, 'Be honest, Meredith. You couldn't wait to leave home. All you needed was a good excuse—and I provided it.'

For ageless seconds she just stared at him. She had received shock upon shock since marrying him, but as her wounded heart bled a little more, so her intelligent

brain quickly grasped what he had said and she grabbed
at the chance he had given her to keep her pride intact.
By the sound of it, Ryan had no idea how very much
she loved him. As far as he was concerned, she began
to see, her eager response to his few kisses, and her
eagerness to rush around doing all she had rushed around
to do, including giving him a packed suitcase, all
stemmed from her impatience to get away from her aunt
and uncle!

'You're right, Ryan, of course,' she got herself sufficiently together to drawl, and, having remembered that
she had a suitcase here somewhere, with some vague
notion of collecting it and getting out of there, she asked,
'Can you tell me where you put the suitcase I gave you?'

'It's in a spare bedroom,' he replied, and unwittingly
gave her a moment or two to get over yet more hurt.
Quite clearly, she realised as he led the way back up the
three steps and turned right along the hall to where the
bedrooms were, he had never meant them to have a
proper marriage anyway.

Suddenly, though, as she followed him to one of the
spare bedrooms, Meredith realised the impossibility of
returning to her old home. Oh, lord, she thought in
anguish: apart from Aunt Evelyn's having a thing about
what the neighbours would say, her aunt was of the
school which believed that a woman, once married,
stayed married, and remained with her husband no
matter what.

The spare bedroom which Ryan took her to was completely furnished, and, glancing at the bed, Meredith felt
all at once exhausted and as if she could sleep for a week.
It was then that she saw she needed some time to make
some sort of plans. It was then also that she saw that it

was a bit late to think of checking into a hotel while she considered what to do.

'Is it all right with you if I make use of this room for...'

'Suit yourself,' Ryan cut her off, and sounded so uncaring that she knew she had been right when she had thought it had never been in his head for them to have a proper marriage. Though she was to wonder if she had got that quite right when, his good humour quite obviously returned, he murmured, 'It might have been interesting to teach you a few things, but you're your own person now. It's for you to decide what you want...'

'I can do without the lecture,' she told him shortly, and when he went from the room without another word she went over to her suitcase which was by the window and bent down to unlatch it.

She twisted round, though, and straightened up when, carrying bedlinen and towels, the man she had married came back into the room. 'That should cover the sleeping arrangements,' he said, placing his cargo down on the bed. 'There's a bathroom through there,' he added, pointing to another door in the room. Meredith suffered a weak moment and realised that, had he been—coaxing—and not matter-of-fact as he was, she might, even knowing what she did, have been persuaded to 'let him teach her a few things'. But even as she realised that, he was saying easily, 'I'll leave you to it. That is, unless you want anything to eat or...'

'I want nothing, thank you,' Meredith told him firmly, and while she had the strength she turned her back on him and knelt once more to her suitcase. There followed a taut moment of silence, then, quietly, the door was closed. Swiftly she jerked around to check, but she was alone.

Ashamed of her wanton feelings of a moment ago, she went and switched on the small bedside light, and then switched off the centre light in the room. Then she moved the linen Ryan had brought in from the bed and, kicking off her shoes, lay down on the coverlet. Once or twice just recently she had thought she had been a bit of an idiot, but as the seconds and then the minutes ticked by, and then the hours started to pass, she recognised that she had been more than plain idiotic.

No wonder she had experienced the occasional moment of disquiet when thinking of the love she'd believed Ryan had for her! Some sixth sense must have been at work trying to tell her she had got it all wrong. Not that she would have listened anyway, she realised. She had wanted to believe he loved her, and she would not have heeded any logical voice that insisted on asking why a sophisticated man like him should be interested in unsophisticated her.

Oh, Meredith Maybry—Meredith Carlisle, she corrected herself—however could you have been such a fool as to allow yourself to believe, just because you had fallen in love with him at first sight, that he had done the same?

Life was just not like that, she realised, and suddenly she found she was in the painful process of growing up overnight. A stray tear or two could not be held back as she now accepted Ryan's words for the truth they had been when he said, 'It's your shares I'm after.' Oh, lord— had she been green!

And how very worldly he had been, she realised. She was dry-eyed when, as dawn approached, she began to break free of the placid mould she had been in all her life. The swine, she thought angrily: he had known what he was about the whole time!

Too angry suddenly to lie there any longer, Meredith
got up from the bed and, sorting through her suitcase,
extracted fresh underwear, trousers and a sweater, and
took them with her to the adjoining bathroom. She grew
more angry than ever with the man she had yesterday
married as she quickly removed her going-away outfit
and set about having a wash and changing her clothes.

Like a lamb to the slaughter, she had not only presented him with the proof he needed that she did have
share certificates for thousands upon thousands of
Burgess Electrical in her possession, but she had also
given him free access to her father's will!

Why, she'd like to bet that both the will and the share
certificates had been handed over to his lawyers the very
next morning to see if there was any loophole that would
see him married to her for nothing.

She drummed up more anger against him when, since
she could not see him taking anything at face value, she
thought it highly probable that he had again contacted
the agency she had worked for, this time to check that
she had not yet reached her twenty-fifth birthday.

When the small voice of fairness arrived to point out
that Ryan had believed he was doing her something of
a favour, in that by marrying her he had given her a
chance to know something different in life from service
to her aging relatives, Meredith deliberately turned her
back on it. That altruistic he wasn't! If it hadn't been
for those shares he would never have phoned asking her
out to dinner in the first place. Ryan Carlisle had known
exactly what he wanted, and had gone straight for it.
He might be too busy to go away on honeymoon—not
that he'd had any such intent—but he would not be too
busy to have those shares transferred to his name, would
he?

Daylight had filtered through the early April morning when a trouser- and sweater-clad Meredith returned to the bedroom. Packing the clothes she had just changed from into her case, she fastened the locks and hefted it up.

She opened the bedroom door, remembering the way she had left her family home out of concern for her great-uncle's dicky heart. She made her way to the main door, having no clear idea of where she was going, but knowing only that, while it was unthinkable that she return to her old home, for the moment anyway, it was equally unthinkable that she should stay on here—where, most obviously, she was not wanted.

Meredith had thought her feelings were frozen over as she put her suitcase down prior to unlatching the main door of the apartment. But when Ryan's voice abruptly addressed her, startling her into turning around, she knew from the sudden pounding of her heart that, though she had grown up rapidly in these last hours, she still loved him.

'Where in hell's name do you think you're going?' he barked, as on bare feet he strode along the hall from his bedroom towards her.

Meredith was more familiar with seeing Ryan clean-shaven and immaculately turned out, but as she noted the stubble on his chin and the way his hair was ruffled as though he had been fast asleep when some sound had disturbed him, he seemed more dear to her than ever. But her heart had led her astray before, and while it did the most peculiar things to her insides to see from the short robe he had thrown about him that he must have little else on, she hardened her heart. Even as it dawned on her that for him to ask where she was going must mean that he had been prepared to let her carry on living there for a while, Meredith was denying every one of her weaknesses.

Spurring on hate against him, for the first time in her life she used sarcasm, as she told him loftily, 'I'll let you have my forwarding address.'

She could see from the slight narrowing of his eyes that he did not care very much for her manner, nor for this hint that she had changed somewhat from the docile female he thought her.

His voice had taken on a definite degree of coolness, at any event, when, fixing his eyes firmly on the blue of hers, he drawled, 'I take it that you're not returning whence you came?'

He *is* a swine, she thought as, reading his comment for the sarcastic offering it was, she started to grow angry. For as she recalled their most recent conversation, it did not take much for her to realise that his belief that she would not return to her old home in a hurry stemmed from his certainty that all she had wanted had been some good excuse to escape from it in the first instance. Her anger was doubly fired as she realised too that Ryan did not care a snap of the fingers where she went. It did not matter a jot to him what she did, now that he had got control of those shares.

'You know quite well that I shan't be returning to my family!' she told him sharply as her anger against him began to peak. She was aware that her emotions were getting out of control, but she held on tightly to the one fact that Ryan believed she had married him to get away from her family.

Unable to concentrate on more than her desire not to give him any idea that to return to the safe, if dull, haven of her old home had quite some appeal, Meredith found that she could no longer keep her buffeted emotions under control when Ryan, at his most arrogant, aloofly drawled, 'Then, my dear, I insist you allow me to provide for you.' It was not offensive enough that he should use the same endearment which had once thrilled her but which most clearly he did not mean, but Meredith's already weakening grip on her emotions was lost when, sarcastically, he added, 'What sort of a husband would I be if, having saved you from your...'

What adjective he would have chosen to denigrate her family, Meredith did not wait to find out. But, certain that he was about to say something of a derogatory nature about her great-aunt and great-uncle, she remembered how he had referred to her confidently as a 'biddable little thing' and suddenly she was inflamed. In a flash she had sent her right hand arcing through the air and had caught him the most perfect, and to her the most satisfying, blow to the side of his face.

Nor was she repentant. That blow, she realised, had been on its way for some hours and had little to do with any remarks he might choose to use on her family. With yet more satisfaction, she saw how totally astonished Ryan was at this change from biddable to passionate. His chin jutted an angry fraction when she refused to look in any way sorry for her action, but then Meredith, with veritable sparks flashing in her brilliant blue eyes, suddenly observed something very much akin to admiration come to the grey depths of his eyes.

A moment later she was doubting that he admired any part of her—she had been fooled before—oh, how she'd been fooled! Which was why she acted quickly, before her imagination should lead her on a false trail which would undermine this new person she had discovered in herself. 'You'll never know, *my dear*,' she told him, 'just how much I enjoyed doing that!' With that she had the door open and, picking up her case, she left her husband of less than twenty-four hours.

In the lift her head was too full of Ryan for her to think where she was going now. But, as she stepped from the lift and Preston, who had been on duty when she arrived, came over and took her case from her, she realised that she had better do some thinking, and fast.

Whether he had been on duty all the while or whether he had been off duty and had come on again, she had no idea. But all her fast thinking brought her nothing other than the knowledge that it was too early for her to check into any hotel. She was therefore grateful to him when, just as though it had occurred to him on seeing her with her case that she had been called urgently away, he suggested, 'A taxi to the station, is it, madam?'

'Yes, please,' she replied.

He was already at his switchboard and on to the taxi service when, 'Which railway station would you be requiring, Mrs Carlisle?' he asked.

Meredith told him the only one she had used in London. 'St Pancras,' she instructed him.

CHAPTER THREE

THE one good thing about railway stations, Meredith mused glumly as she sat pondering what best to do next, was that one could sit, seemingly staring into space, at any odd time of the day or night, and no one took a blind bit of notice. To add authenticity to her façade of being a traveller, she had her large suitcase beside her.

She realised that she must have been searching for some kind of anonymity when she had eagerly grabbed at Preston's suggestion that she might want a taxi to the station.

Feeling exhausted and used up, she tried to concentrate on what she should do—dwelling over the past was not going to be any help. Tiredly she went over the options she had open to her. She could return to her great-aunt and great-uncle, but abruptly she shied away from the idea of doing that. She felt as appalled at the prospect of having to tell them that her marriage was over as they would be to receive such news. Besides, with all her hopes and dreams suddenly turned into ashes, she felt much too hurt inside to withstand any lecture from her great-aunt on the fact that, no matter what, her place was with her husband and not with them.

Meredith guessed that her lack of sleep last night was not conducive to her feeling any great enthusiasm for lugging her suitcase with her while she looked round for a modestly priced hotel.

She glanced at her watch and saw that it was a quarter to eight. For no reason, some quirk in her memory department prodded to remind her that it had been on this very station eighteen months ago that she had caught the quarter to eight train to Derby.

Her thoughts strayed to her good friend Tessa and to how yesterday she had wanted her there at her wedding. But for everything having been arranged at such short notice, Meredith knew that she would have been there. Tessa, though, had put some considerable time and energy into getting the elderly in the village of Little Haversham interested in art, and had got an art class running, and yesterday was the culmination of a year's efforts when they were having an exhibition of work.

'Oh, Meredith,' she had wailed when Meredith had excitedly telephoned her to ask her to be there, 'I can't come!' She had then sought round for different ways of being in two places at once, and they had both ended up laughing, as Meredith had told her, 'I'll send you a piece of wedding cake.'

How long ago that telephone conversation now seemed, Meredith thought, her only piece of good fortune being that Tessa had not been able to attend her fiasco of a wedding. The way things had turned out, the fewer people who witnessed it, the better.

Suddenly then, through her fatigue, Meredith all at once began to see that maybe to have recalled catching the train to Derby had not been any stray quirk at all. It was then that she began to see that there might be another option open to her. Indeed, the more she thought about it, the more it seemed to be the obvious option. What she needed more than anything right now was to get away to somewhere where she could take a long and, if possible, unemotional view of what had happened.

She knew without question that Tessa would offer her a warm welcome, but she hesitated. She'd had every intention of visiting her old home once a week at least, although, in the belief that she would be living with Ryan in his apartment, she had given Mrs Key his phone number in case of an emergency. Mrs Key was not the type to panic, and both Great-Aunt Evelyn and Great-Uncle Porter had seemed all right—was it only yesterday? Meredith recalled how she had meant to telephone to check on her family during this week, but she could as easily do that from Tessa's, she considered.

Anyway, she realised as she suddenly made up her mind and went looking for a telephone, she rather thought that, since this was supposed to be her honeymoon, they would not expect to hear anything of her for at least a week.

'Meredith!' Tessa squealed when she answered her phone and heard her friend on the other end. 'What the heck are you doing ringing me?' she exclaimed. 'You're on your honeymoon!'

'Actually,' Meredith said chokily, holding back sudden and unexpected emotional tears, 'I'm not.'

'You didn't... Didn't you get married yesterday, after all?' Tessa rephrased her question.

'I—did,' Meredith told her. 'But I—it's a long story,' she added raggedly, and on a shaky breath she asked, 'Can I come and stay?'

Meredith knew Tessa for a true friend when, after the barest pause while she assimilated what she had said and that she had used the singular 'Can *I* come and stay' and not *'we'*, plus her ragged, shaky tone, she did not ask any questions.

'Of course,' she told Meredith. 'Come and stay as long as you like. If you can get to St Pancras in time, there's a train which Aldo sometimes catches which leaves at nine—I'll meet you,' she added.

Meredith spent the hour-and-a-half train journey getting herself more under control. But she faced the fact that she was not anywhere near as tough as she wanted to be when she saw her long-skirted, stick-thin friend, with her waist-length hair waving in the breeze, waiting for her at Derby station.

'I've still got the old banger,' Tessa said cheerfully, having given her a hug and against Meredith's protests grabbed her suitcase from her. 'As it's such a sunny day, I thought we'd drive with the top down.'

'You're getting more eccentric than ever,' Meredith told her, and went with her to where Tessa had parked her Morris Minor tourer.

'Do you want to talk about what happened?' Tessa asked gently when they were out in the country.

'There's not a great deal to tell,' Meredith replied, and realised only then that there wasn't. 'I fell in love at first sight with Ryan Carlisle, and didn't stop to think when he asked me to marry him within a week of our meeting——' she broke off as she remembered that he had not so much as asked her to marry him, but had told her that she had better marry him, without delay '—that he might not have fallen in love at first sight with me in return.'

'You've since learned that his feelings for you weren't so immediate?' Tessa queried.

'I've since learned that he has no feelings for me whatsoever,' Meredith told her bluntly.

'Oh, love,' said Tessa softly. 'Are you sure?'

'Oh, yes,' Meredith told her. 'I'm sure.' Somehow she managed to keep her voice even as she revealed how she had heard her husband of a few hours in conversation with his friend Monte Montgomery, and how Ryan had done nothing to conceal a thing when, later, he had taxed her with going into a fit of the sulks.

'What he needs is horse-whipping,' Tessa told her as she pulled the Morris up outside her cottage. 'And what you need,' she said as they went indoors, 'is a jolly good howl.'

'Will it do me any good?' Meredith asked hopefully.

'Not a scrap, I'm afraid,' Tessa told her.

The next two days passed in something of a haze for Meredith. She was aware of doing various chores, of mechanically eating and drinking, and of going for long walks with Tessa, but her head was still full of Ryan and her disaster of a marriage.

When she went to bed on Thursday night, though, she was so drained from lack of sleep that nature took over and she slept fairly well. She awoke on Friday morning with her usual first thought: how her marriage had not lasted twenty-four hours and how she would have given anything for it to be otherwise. But she was starting to emerge from her shock, both actual and delayed, and, having caught up on some of her missed sleep, she discovered that she had pride and sufficient backbone to cope.

'I'll make the toast,' she volunteered as she went down and joined Tessa in her kitchen.

'Sleep better?' asked Tessa, taking a long look at her.

'Much better,' Meredith answered, and found a smile as, aware that Tessa supplemented her part-time teaching income by painting and selling her watercolours, she told her, 'If you want to go out sketching today, I could clear up for you.'

'So you don't like my brand of cobwebs, huh?' Tessa laughed, having more important things on her mind than to consider getting the vacuum cleaner out more than once every three months. 'I tell you what, though—I've an idea that Aldo might turn up some time after he's finished his stint at his advertising agency tonight—if you're feeling really like working, you could muck out the boxroom so I can put a camp bed in there for him if he shows.'

'He can have my room,' Meredith promptly asserted.

'He can *not*!' Tessa told her firmly.

'But he's your brother, and . . .'

'And you're my friend,' Tessa butted in. 'Besides, you were here first. And anyway, he may have resolved his differences with Caroline, his live-in girlfriend, and might not be giving Little Haversham a second's thought this weekend.'

Meredith sincerely hoped for Aldo's sake that he was having better luck in his love-life than she was having in hers. She did not want him to be hurt. She had always liked him and at one time she'd had a tiny crush on him. She had been completely cured, though, the instant he had kissed her that time. She did not know what she had expected—perhaps bells to ring, or something like that—but nothing in any way magical had happened, except that, having wondered what it would be like if he ever kissed her, she'd known then that she did not want him to kiss her again, and known also that she was over her crush.

As soon as Tessa had loaded up her car with her artist's equipment and had driven off, Meredith set to work on the boxroom. She felt better for having something to give her energies to, though she could not stop thoughts of Ryan from attacking.

The boxroom was small, and did not take long to put in apple-pie order. Finding homes for the clutter and impedimenta took longer. But, after she had stacked everything away neatly and tidily, it was still early when Meredith set about mucking out the rest of the rooms, with the exception of her friend's bedroom, which she considered private.

Discovering, however, that Tessa did not have a great deal in the way of cleaning materials, she decided to take a trip to the village's general store. While she was there, she would look for something tasty for dinner. Tessa had been a perfect angel ever since she had got here— to make dinner for her for a change would be the least she could do.

Taking her purse, Meredith was soon discovering that 'general store' did not begin to cover the emporium that served the village and anyone who happened to be passing through. Spotting one or two specialised items, she saw that the enterprising store owner had a range of goods to be purchased that was as wide as it was various.

Meredith had taken her self-service basket to the till, and the smart, businesslike woman was just reaching for the last of the articles from the basket when, with her mind on the Normandy chicken recipe they would have that evening, Meredith suddenly realised that she needed apple juice.

'Have you any apple juice?' she asked quickly, being unable to see any from where she was standing.

'Apple juice, Sidney!' the woman yelled, and from the sounds of flurried activity somewhere outside her vision, Meredith supposed that a carton of apple juice would soon be to hand. 'Are you journeying far?' the woman whom Meredith took to be the store owner asked, to pass the time while they waited.

'I'm staying with a friend in the village, actually,' Meredith smiled.

'Oh, you'll be Tessa Wallace's friend,' the store owner stated, and, while Meredith was still blinking as she wondered how the dickens she knew that, the woman was asking, 'Are you an artist too?'

Meredith shook her head, but even as she smiled as she realised that the village KGB didn't know everything, from the corner of her eye she spotted a part of a well-known financial paper peeping out from beneath some magazines on display. 'I'll take this too,' she said, pulling the paper out and, as a thin wiry man arrived with her apple juice, she thanked him for his trouble.

'That paper isn't today's—it's yesterday's,' the woman told her.

'I'll take it just the same,' Meredith smiled, and she left the store, thinking that there wouldn't be too much difference in the change in the price of Burgess Electrical shares from yesterday to today.

But from what Ryan had said, there must be a vast difference from the last time she had checked on them. Which, she realised, must be all of five years ago—if not longer.

While Grandfather had been alive they'd had a financial paper delivered every Saturday. But, since it had been only he who had read it, Great-Uncle Porter had cancelled it when his brother Ogden had died. The fact that Burgess Electrical shares were not quoted in the financial columns of the daily paper they took did not— since the shares had come to be virtually worthless— concern any of them.

When she got back to the cottage, though, Meredith knew a strange reluctance to check in the paper for the price of the Burgess shares. She knew quite well that she was using delaying tactics when first she set the kettle to boil, then put the cleaning materials ready to use later, and put the apple juice along with some chicken pieces she had bought in the fridge. Next she made herself a cup of coffee, and, the moment to be delayed no longer, she took up the paper and opened it out at the relevant page.

Some minutes later she was still reeling from the shock of seeing that the price of each share, multiplied by the many thousands she'd had in her possession, represented a small fortune!

By the time she had finished her coffee, though, Meredith was over her shock. She could not have laid claim to the shares for nearly another three years anyway. And, the way things seemed destined to be for her, she calculated that by the time she did reach the twenty-five years of age which her father had stipulated, the chances were that the shares would be worthless again anyway.

Not long afterwards she rinsed out her coffee-mug, and returned to her cleaning. She could not but be struck by the irony of the way things had turned out, though. For, while in making the will he had wanted purely to score a few points of her grandfather, in not changing it before he had died, her father had most definitely left things the last way in which he must have wanted them. Because of the hurt both he and her mother had suffered at the hands of her grandfather, her father, Meredith was sure, had intended that she should never suffer such hurt too. Although he had anticipated that the shares would increase in value, what he had not thought of when willing those shares the way he had—so that an impecunious suitor would become a wealthy man on the day he married her—was that that man might be more interested in marrying her for those shares than from love of her.

Not that Ryan was impecunious. He had been a wealthy man before their wedding day. He had... Oh, damn him! Damn him to hell, she thought angrily, and applied herself to her cleaning with renewed vigour.

'Fee-fi-fo-fum. I smell something delicious cooking,' Tessa said as, with her thin face serene from her day's work, she came in through the kitchen door that evening. Draping her jacket over a chair, she gave another appreciative sniff. 'Something, I should say, with a hint of...' she broke off. 'I say, have you been lacing whatever it is with polish?'

'I've *been* polishing,' Meredith confessed with a smile.

'So you've introduced yourself to my next-door neighbour,' quipped Tessa. 'Must have done—I'm sure I don't possess a tin of polish.'

'You don't—didn't. But I haven't borrowed any. I went to the shop in the village. Which reminds me—they know you have a guest.'

'They would,' Tessa said complacently. 'I told the milkman when I ordered extra milk.'

'Ah,' Meredith murmured, and asked, 'Do you want to eat now, or shall we wait and see if Aldo turns up?'

'Is there enough for three?'

'Ample,' Meredith replied.

'We'll wait awhile if you like. But since I only had a bar of chocolate for lunch, I'll have some bread and cheese to be going on with.'

Meredith knew her friend lost count of time when she was working, so together they made some sandwiches and a pot of tea, while Meredith made a mental note, if Tessa was going sketching again tomorrow, to pack her some sandwiches to take with her.

Drinking tea while her friend took the edge off her hunger, they talked idly of one thing and then another, with Tessa bringing Duncan's name into the conversation. 'He was so very special to me,' she said quietly, and while Meredith noted that the pain that had once been in her friend's voice when she spoke of Duncan had gone, Tessa went on to reveal, 'At one time, though, I thought I should never want to go out with any other man as long as I live—but that passed.'

'You've dated other men since Duncan died?' Meredith asked gently.

'A couple of times,' Tessa nodded. 'And it hasn't been anywhere near as bad as I expected.'

They fell into idle conversation again, then, as Meredith went to check that her efforts in the culinary department was not drying up in the oven as they waited to see if Aldo would come, Tessa went to have a wash and brush up.

Having checked the meal, Meredith returned to the kitchen table and, with her thoughts taken over entirely by Ryan, she was soon oblivious to her surroundings. Then Tessa silently returned.

'Perhaps he'll call,' she suggested gently.

'He won't,' Meredith replied, realising that she must have been staring into space, but not pretending that she didn't know whom Tessa was talking about. 'Apart from anything else,' she said, forcing a grin, 'he doesn't know where I am.'

But knowing for sure that she was never going to hear from Ryan Carlisle again did not stop Meredith's heart from going into her mouth when, not long afterwards, they heard a car draw up outside.

'Aldo, scorning the use of British Rail,' announced Tessa, and as she went to the door to let him in, sanity returned to Meredith

'Meredith!' her friend's brother exclaimed as he came into the kitchen, looking, to her eyes, older, sadder and wiser.

'How are you, Aldo?' Meredith smiled, finding that the hand she extended to shake his was taken, but also that he bent forward to plant a kiss of greeting on her cheek.

'Fine,' he replied, but it became very plain over their meal, when all he could talk of was Caroline and how she had walked out on him, that he was feeling far from fine.

Meredith was grateful to her friend that not a word did she say to indicate anything of her recent emotional upset. Though, since Aldo seemed to be suffering agonies, if not exactly in silence, Meredith doubted that he had any space for anyone else's problems.

At around ten, and just in case he wanted some private conversation with his sister, Meredith decided to go to bed. 'I'm afraid I've bagged the spare bedroom,' she told him, 'and...'

'And you have the honour of sleeping in the boxroom,' his sister chipped in. 'It's a bit cramped in there...'

'It doesn't matter,' he said, without much interest. 'I don't suppose I shall sleep anyway.'

Meredith went to bed vowing that for Tessa's sake she was going to be at her most cheerful in the morning. Not that she could remember going around with the long face which Aldo wore.

She was first up the next morning, and when Tessa came into the kitchen a short while later Meredith was bright and breezy as she said sunnily, 'I was going to bring you a cup of tea up.'

'Don't!' Tessa shuddered teasingly. 'I can't take such heartiness first thing in the morning!'

'Sorry,' Meredith smiled. 'Only it seemed to me that with both Aldo and me coming here and unburdening our...'

'Oh, for goodness' sake, Meredith!' Tessa cut her off. 'You're nothing at all like Aldo, if that's what's worrying you. Grief, part of his trouble is that he should have been an actor—surely you remember how dramatic he's always been about absolutely everything?'

'I must have fogotten,' Meredith murmured. 'But...'

'But nothing,' Tessa said firmly. 'You were here like a shot the time when I needed you, and I should be very hurt if you'd thought of going anywhere but here when you needed a bolt-hole. Besides,' she added, with a sudden smile, 'I like having you here.'

'If you put it like that,' Meredith smiled back, 'I'll—er—make the toast.'

They breakfasted together, with Tessa telling her wryly that, for all her dear brother had declared that he didn't suppose he would get any sleep, he must be finding the camp bed singularly comfortable.

When, as they cleared the table, Tessa went on to ask if she'd mind if she disappeared with her sketch-pad again that day, Meredith knew that they were true friends.

Having made some sandwiches for her to take, Meredith put them down on the corner of the solid kitchen dresser while Tessa got her things together.

'See you when the sun goes down,' grinned Tessa, and was off down the path, with Meredith chasing after her with the sandwiches Tessa had overlooked.

Meredith returned indoors with a trace of a smile about her mouth, realising again that, once Tessa had her mind on her work, she forgot about everything else. She hoped, though, that she would remember to eat.

Soon, though, Tessa had been replaced in her thoughts by Ryan. Knowing the futility of trying to keep him out of her head for very long, she let him stay as she washed the dishes and set the kitchen to rights.

He was still there in her head, and she was still trying to hate him, when she went into the sitting-room with her duster and did a general tidy around.

She was glad to see Aldo when, somewhere around eleven, he surfaced and came into the kitchen seeking a cup of coffee. She noticed his weak mouth for the first time, and wondered how on earth she had ever come to have had a crush on him, but she was still hopeful that conversation with him might take her mind off the man she had so foolishly married.

'How did you sleep?' she enquired out of politeness, and heard chapter and verse, interspersed with long, meaningful silences, about how insomnia was his soul-mate since Caroline had opted for pastures new.

Later on Meredith made him a snack lunch and listened while he talked 'Caroline' as she peeled potatoes and got everything ready for the evening meal.

She was brimful of Caroline, though, when at some time after three that afternoon the telephone in the hall rang. 'I'll get it,' she told Aldo quickly, and made her escape into the hall, knowing for sure that when it came to unburdening the soul, compared to Aldo she had been as if mute. Ready to take down any message for Tessa, Meredith went across to the telephone and picked it up. 'Hello,' she said. The wires seemed totally dead, for no one answered. 'I'm afraid Tessa's out,' she said, 'but...' The dialling tone in her ear told her that whoever was calling Tessa preferred to talk to her in person and had no wish to leave a message.

Putting the telephone back on its rest, Meredith took a deep breath and, on her way back to Aldo, she knew that, with the softest heart in the world, she could not take another basinful of 'Caroline'—not yet, anyway. Though if she took herself off for a walk, Aldo would no doubt suggest that he accompany her.

'I've got one or two jobs I want to do upstairs,' she popped her head round the door to tell him. 'Will you excuse me if...'

'I think I'll take a stroll—er—would you like to come with me?' he thought to ask.

'Oh, no, thank you, Aldo,' Meredith said quickly. 'I'll—er—I'll have a nice cup of tea waiting for you when you come back.'

His stroll did not take him long, but Meredith's strength had been renewed in his absence. Though at six o'clock she had formed the very definite view that if Aldo was staying longer than tomorrow, when next Tessa took herself off sketching, she was going to go with her.

Just then, though, she heard the sound of a car pulling up and, as relief entered her soul, she at first thought that it was Tessa returning. Somehow, though, this car sounded somewhat smoother than Tessa's car. When a short while later the front door bell rang, she knew positively that it was not Tessa.

But Meredith was ready to welcome their caller with open arms, whoever he or she might be, and she was first out of her chair as, with another, 'I'll get it,' this time she made for the front door.

Perhaps it was relief which was responsible for the smile she had on her mouth as she pulled back the door. But, even as her heart suddenly went crazy with joy, pride rocketed in to wipe the smile from her face. Because, though she had never expected to see him again, Meredith looked up and found herself staring straight into a pair of vividly remembered cool grey eyes.

Looking at him in disbelief, she recalled how she had told Tessa that the man she loved would not come calling because, quite simply, he did not know where she was. But the proof that he did know where she was was quite obvious as, striving hard for control, Meredith stared at none other than Ryan Carlisle.

She was still staring at him, solemn-faced, while her heart danced to see him, when that dance became a jig. For, even though his tone was as cool as his look, the words he smoothly spoke were, to her utter delight, the most beautiful words she had ever heard.

'Hello, Meredith,' he said. 'I've come for you.'

CHAPTER FOUR

MEREDITH'S wayward heart was singing. Ryan had come for her! He had just said so, which meant that there just had to have been a mistake somewhere. He must love her after all, she realised, and almost launched herself into his arms. Almost—but... Suddenly she was remembering the Burgess shares.

'You've—come for me?' she enquired, her tone cool as her common sense returned and she remembered in time how cool his tone had been. 'What on earth for?' she asked loftily, while her heart returned to a bitterly disappointed dull beat, and she wondered not only what all this meant, but how he had found her! 'There's nothing...'

'Your great-aunt rang,' Ryan cut her off shortly. 'Apparently her brother has been taken ill and...'

'Uncle Porter's ill!' Meredith exclaimed, although, in view of past experience of Uncle Porter, some of her alarm soon eased. She realised at once that this might be another instance of him playing to the gallery to get her to return to her old home, but even so, she knew that she could do no other than go to him. But, 'Why did my aunt ring you?' she asked Ryan snappily, refusing to slip back into the placid little mould she had inhabited before she had gone through a marriage ceremony with him.

'How the hell do I know?' he bit back, clearly not taken with this spirited young woman who seemed quite able to stand up for herself. Though his voice had changed, and had taken on a modicum of sarcasm when, silkily, he added, 'She probably rang me because you hadn't thought to let her have your forwarding address.'

She had not thought to let him have it either, Meredith thought crossly. But before she could ask him how he had found out where she was, she became aware that his glance had gone from her to somewhere over her shoulder.

Instinctively she looked back and, realising that she had forgotten all about Aldo, saw that he had come to see who she was talking to at the door. 'Er—this is Aldo Wallace,' she felt obliged to introduce him. 'Aldo,' she said, and, turning back to complete the introduction she saw that Ryan's eyes held chips of ice, and realised at once that he had no wish for her to introduce him as her husband. 'Aldo, this is Ryan Carlisle,' she said, having had no intention of telling Aldo that Ryan was her husband anyway. 'Come in, won't you?' she invited as suddenly Ryan's 'I've come for you' connected with him telling her that her great-uncle was ill. 'My uncle's ill,' she told Aldo as the three of them moved to the sitting-room, 'and Ryan has come to give me a lift to London.'

'Oh, I'm so sorry, Meredith,' Aldo said gently, and straight away offered, 'But I can drive you back to London. There's no need for...'

'There's no need for that,' Ryan cut him off curtly. 'I'll drive my wife to...'

'Wife!' Aldo exclaimed, and as he looked at Meredith in astonishment, and she coloured, for no reason other than that she experienced an absurd joy that Ryan was still referring to her as his wife. 'You never told me you were married!' Aldo added, and made it sound so much as if it meant something to him, and as if she should have told him the instant that she had greeted him yesterday, that Meredith felt the least Ryan would think was that the two of them were having some sort of an affair.

'There—was so much else to talk about,' she said weakly, and suddenly felt weaker still when all at once Ryan caught hold of her left hand.

'Had you used your eyes, Wallace,' he told him curtly, holding her hand in front of him, 'you'd have noticed that the lady wears a wedding ring.'

Abruptly Meredith snatched her hand back. She'd had enough! 'I'll go and get some things together,' she said shortly, and left them standing there.

Up in her bedroom, she packed her case and wished she'd had more about her than to sentimentally want to keep that wedding band on her finger. It meant nothing, for goodness' sake, and it was for certain that Ryan had not been sentimentally inclined when he had put that ring there.

She was about to take it off, just to show him that it did not matter, when she realised that he would notice its absence—just as he had spotted that she still wore it—and would most likely presume she had taken it off because of his reference to it.

Meredith carried her case downstairs with her wedding ring still on her finger. Her aunt, for one, would think her most odd if she was not wearing it when she saw her, and as yet, she realised that she was still not ready to tell her that her marriage was over.

'Will you tell Tessa that I'll phone her?' Meredith asked Aldo, as she found both men standing in the hall.

'Of course,' he answered, and, telling her that he hoped that things would be improved with her uncle when she saw him, he leaned forward and kissed her cheek. 'Bye, pet,' he bade her, and Ryan took her case in one hand and took a firm hold of her arm with the other, and escorted her out of the cottage.

'Where was your friend?' he asked as he set his car in motion.

'Out sketching,' Meredith replied. 'She went out early this morning.'

'Leaving you at home playing house with her brother,' Ryan stated—nastily, Meredith thought. 'I presume he's staying at the cottage too?'

'You presume correctly,' she told him stiffly, and spent the next silent half-hour sending hate vibes in his direction and wondering at the peculiarities of love, that she should hate him while she was with him, but not when she was apart from him.

After a half an hour of hating him, though, she was in love with him again. He need not have come up all the way to Derbyshire to collect her, yet he had. She had thought their parting final, but... Suddenly, a thought occurred to her and she found herself breaking into speech in a flurry of panic.

'You didn't tell my great-aunt that we've separated, did you?' she asked, knowing full well that her aunt was going to be mightily upset, appalled and disbelieving at the news. And, although she was not ready yet to break that news to her, Meredith could see that it would be better if she led up to telling her gently rather than having Ryan tell her straight out, the way he most likely would.

'You clearly haven't told her,' he replied tersely.

'Have you?' Meredith snapped.

'No!' he answered shortly, but seemed to relent as he added, 'I wasn't certain what you wanted your aunt and uncle to be told, so I left it for the time being.'

'They'll have to be told when we divorce,' Meredith commented, her thoughts bleak on that future prospect.

'You've divorcing me?' Ryan asked, that short note swiftly back in his voice.

As she had not given divorce a moment's thought, but was not likely to tell him that, Meredith's voice was cool as she replied, 'When I get round to it.'

She soon realised, though, that Ryan was a man who liked to be the one in charge of things when, most aggressively, he snarled, 'It's to be hoped that I don't beat you to it!'

'What possible grounds have *you* got?' she demanded, her ire fired as, very far from placid, she rounded on him.

'I'd say that you refusing to sleep with me on our wedding night might be fairly strong grounds, wouldn't you?' he asked loftily, and Meredith was back to hating him again.

She turned and looked out of the window. As she remembered it—for all his comment that, 'It might have been interesting to teach you a few things', he hadn't shown any signs of being desperate to get her into his bed.

All was silent in the car again as Meredith fumed against him, worried about her great-uncle yet wondering if Uncle Porter was really so bad, since it had been Aunt Evelyn who had telephoned Ryan, and not Mrs Key.

'What exactly did my aunt say?' broke from her lips when she had been determined not to say another word.

'Little, except that her brother had suffered another of his turns, and that he wanted to see you.'

That sounded fairly normal and very like every other time she had been called home, Meredith considered. But, thinking of those times and how, barring the other time she had been at Tessa's when the call had come, she had been back home within the hour, she just had to ask, 'Were you—er—able to cover for my not being at your place? The thing is,' she went on quickly, 'my uncle's had these attacks before and I've always...'

'Breathe easy,' Ryan instructed. 'I explained to your aunt that, as I'd a full afternoon of paperwork in front of me, you'd gone shopping and might not be back for hours.'

'I—er—thank you,' Meredith said, and they were nearly in London when she gave way to a question, this time one that had been concerning her for some time now. 'How did you know where to find me?' she asked suddenly apropos of nothing. 'I didn't tell you where I was going, and...'

'There's no great mystery,' Ryan cut in. 'You'd spoken of your friend Tessa Wallace who lived in Derbyshire. When Preston expressed the hope as I left for my office on Tuesday that you'd made it to St Pancras in time to catch your train, it didn't take a master brain to work out where you'd gone.'

Meredith refrained from telling him that she'd had no thoughts of going to Derbyshire when she had taken a taxi to St Pancras railway station on Tuesday. But, as she took in how easily two and two always added up to four for this man she had married, she went on to dot a few 'i's and cross a few 't's as she tried a little adding up herself.

'So, having remembered my telling you that Tessa lived in a place called Little Haversham, you motored up and stopped at the village store to ask where she lived.' It was not a question but, as Meredith made the simple calculation, a statement. When Ryan made a small movement of his head to indicate her conclusions were at fault, though, she had to accept that her powers of deduction would never be as accurate as his.

'Your friend's name and address is in the phone book,' he tossed at her casually.

'Huh,' Meredith grunted, and was silent for all of five seconds when suddenly, in connection with the telephone, she remembered something. 'Did you ring Tessa's number just after three this afternoon?' she enquired.

'I saw no point in driving out of my way had I got my facts wrong,' he replied coolly.

'Why didn't you say something when I answered the phone, then?' Meredith asked—she thought it was a perfectly natural question. 'Why drive all that way, anyway?' she went on before he had answered her first question. 'You could just as easily have given me the message that my uncle was ill and I could have taken the next train to London or...'

'Or have got your friend's kissing brother to give you a lift,' Ryan said curtly.

Quite obviously, Ryan had not taken to Aldo, Meredith realised, and she supposed that beside her husband Aldo did show up as being rather weak. But Aldo was kind and, ignoring the fact that the man she had married had been kind too, to have gone very much out of his way to come to collect her, she instead preferred to believe that he had not put himself out at all on her behalf.

'No doubt you had business in Derbyshire anyway,' she said stiffly, and realised that for once she had got it right when, after a moment's pause, he replied,

'I—had, as a matter of fact. Little Haversham is a bit off the beaten track, which is why I rang first. The reason I didn't speak when you answered the phone,' he went on after another pause, 'was because to do so would have given you a few extra hours of worry in the intervening period before my calling for you.'

The knowledge that Ryan Carlisle had thought to save her a few extra hours of worry made Meredith warm to him. Though suddenly she remembered how he believed she had married him only because she just could not wait to leave her home. And all at once it came to her that she must show none of the warmth she felt for him, if he was not to suspect the true reason why she had married him. At the same moment, too, she realised that, for someone who could not wait to shake the dust of her old home from her heels, she had reacted far too quickly by going to pack her case within a very short space of him telling her that her uncle was ill.

'You—er—must have realised,' she said slowly, 'that—er—despite everything, I love my great-aunt and great-uncle very much.'

'Of course,' Ryan replied promptly, and Meredith began to like him as well as be in love with him, when he added, 'I care for my relatives too—but I wouldn't want to live with them.'

Meredith knew the instant she saw her great-aunt that there was nothing faked about this, her great-uncle's latest 'turn'. 'How is he?' she asked when, seeing her Aunt Evelyn looking worried and drawn, she went and put her arms around her.

'It's been a bad do, Meredith,' her aunt replied. 'Though he seems much better since Dr Hastings came and gave him an injection. He's still as stubborn as a mule, though, and has refused point-blank to go to hospital.'

Hospital! Meredith thought, starting to get seriously alarmed. There had never been any talk of Uncle Porter going into hospital before!

'I'll go and see him,' she said quickly. 'I'll...'

'He's asleep at the moment. Dr Hastings has told me that he should be all right now, but not to hesitate to give him a ring if I'm at all worried.'

Making a mental note to have a few words with Dr Hastings herself, Meredith saw that she would be calling the doctor to her aunt before long if she wasn't careful.

'Have you eaten at all today?' she asked her as she guided her into the sitting-room and sat her down.

'I couldn't,' her aunt replied.

'Didn't Mrs Key come in today?' asked Meredith, wondering why her aunt and not the cheerful treasure of a daily help had telephoned Ryan. The Mrs Key she thought she knew was the salt of the earth, and was much more likely to have stayed on and waited with her aunt than to have left her to fend for herself.

'Mrs Key's son came off his motorbike yesterday,' Aunt Evelyn explained. 'The poor woman, she went quite to pieces when her daughter-in-law rang here to tell her. Anyway, Michael's going to be quite all right, but Mrs Key had to have today off in order to babysit while Michael's wife spends some time at the hospital with him. Lilian, from next door,' she inserted for Ryan's benefit in case he had not remembered Mrs Peplow at the wedding, 'has been in on and off through the day.

It was Harold, her son,' she again inserted for Ryan's benefit, 'who helped the doctor get Porter to bed.'

Unable to leave her aunt, who seemed to have a need to talk, Meredith grew anxious in the next thirty minutes about preparing her a snack meal. Suddenly, though, she realised that, as her aunt appeared to have eaten nothing at all that day, there was every likelihood that Ryan had not eaten a bite since lunchtime either.

'I'm making a cheese omelette for my aunt, but I can put some steak under the grill for you if you prefer,' she told him when, since he had made no move to return to his apartment during the last half-hour, she guessed that perhaps he thought for her aunt's sake that he had better act out his husband's role.

'A cheese omelette sounds fine to me,' he replied, just as though he feared, rightly, that the steak would have to be grilled straight from the freezer. 'Can I help?' he asked.

Meredith realised that he, like she, had seen that now was the worst possible time for either of them to acquaint her aunt with the news that their marriage was over, and she supposed she was grateful to him that he was playing his role to the full.

She was not grateful to him an hour later, though. She had been upstairs to check on her uncle and had returned downstairs, having left a small light on in his bedroom. Then, coaxing her aunt to go to bed, saying that she would keep an eye on her uncle, Meredith added that she would not return to Ryan's apartment that night, but that she would stay at her old home for a day or two.

But no sooner had she helped her aunt up out of her chair than Evelyn Simmons was turning to Ryan and was saying, 'You'll stay too, of course, Ryan.' And while

Meredith, in sudden panic, was seeking an immediate
excuse why he should not stay, her aunt was going on,
'I feel dreadful as it is that I interrupted your honeymoon the way I did. I shan't rest at all easy,' she declared, 'if I have to go to bed knowing that my actions
have parted husband and wife.'

With nothing brilliant coming to Meredith in the way
of a reason why Ryan should return alone to his home
that night, she looked to him for help. To her dismay,
though, not to say fury, he seemed to be in complete
agreement that his place was under the same roof as his
wife, and Meredith could cheerfully have killed him when
he told her aunt, 'I can't have you uneasy on my account, Miss Simmons. Of course I'll stay.'

'But—but...' Meredith butted in, and when two pairs
of eyes looked at her, one faded blue pair, and a pair
of cool grey—and, if she was not very much mistaken,
amused—ones, she prepared to lie her head off. 'But
I've already pulled you away from your paperwork,
Ryan,' she protested. 'I really don't think...'

'Don't give it another thought, darling,' he told her
smoothly. 'I can get up early in the morning, and carry
on with it then.' And, while she was silently fuming,
You pig! just as though he did not know what she was
thinking he calmly took over her job of aiding her aunt
up the stairs. Trailing after them, Meredith heard her
aunt telling him that it was a good job, with him being
so tall and everything, that Meredith's bed was a large
one.

Mutinying every step of the way, Meredith was just
thinking that were her bed ten feet wide, she still would
not be sharing it with Ryan Carlisle, when they came to
her great-uncle's bedroom. Her aunt left them briefly as
she went to take a look at her brother. She reported back

that he was asleep and they went on along the landing to the last door but one, which was the door to Evelyn Simmons' room.

'Find Ryan something to sleep in, dear,' she requested as the three of them halted.

'Like a shroud,' Meredith muttered, too low for her aunt to hear, but she got the shock of her life when, as she bent to kiss her aunt, she saw the most terrific grin split Ryan's features.

Angrily, as her aunt's bedroom door closed, she marched back to the airing cupboard. It had not been her intention to amuse him! Extracting sheets, pillow slips and towels, in much the same way as last Saturday he had done for her, she added one extra item to the bundle—one of her uncle's nightshirts. She knew that Ryan was not going to wear it, but since her aunt had put in the request, who was she to argue? Then she went back towards him and went on to the end of the landing to her old room.

Mrs Key had been at work, Meredith saw as she entered, in that there was no trace at all that up until a week ago the room had been hers. Oddly, though, for all the mutiny in her heart, Meredith had no wish to return to live in her old home, or to take permanent possession of this room. She had grown up, she realised. Maybe the hurt Ryan had inflicted on her was responsible for that. Feeling the sting of tears at the backs of her eyes, she abruptly dropped the linen she was carrying down on the bed, and headed for the door.

To her consternation, however, Ryan was blocking the doorway. 'Excuse me,' she muttered, keeping her head well down.

'What's wrong?' he questioned, and Meredith wanted to hit him.

'You have to ask?' she snapped, knowing that if he had gleaned that she had been upset, he would put it down to her being worried about her uncle, but feeling mightily relieved all the same that she no longer felt like shedding a tear.

'Your aunt says this present crisis is over.'

'So I'll say goodnight,' Meredith hinted as he continued to block her path.

'Am I to take it you aren't sharing that bed with me?' Ryan asked, and, wanting to hate him, Meredith fell deeper in love with him at the laughter that danced in his eyes.

'What? And risk ruining your only chance to divorce me?' she mocked. Pushing past him, she went quickly before the weak person he could so easily make of her won the day.

Putting thoughts of Ryan from her, she went back along the landing to her uncle's room. To her surprise, he was awake. 'I thought I was going to die,' he complained in greeting, showing no wonder at seeing her there, but just accepting that, if he was ill, she would naturally return from wherever she was.

'They only take the good ones first,' she replied cheerfully.

'Sauce!' he snapped, then asked, 'Can I have a banana sandwich?'

She was ready to humour him in whatever he wanted. Even if she did consider that a banana sandwich—something she could never recall him eating before, and at midnight—might give him roaring indigestion.

'I'll go and make you one,' she told him. 'Close your eyes and rest while I've gone.'

Going quietly to the kitchen, Meredith mashed all the indigestible lumps out of a banana and, adding a sprin-

kling of sugar to give him energy and on account of his
sweet tooth, she made her uncle a sandwich and returned upstairs with it, to discover that he had fallen
asleep again.

Finding a large handkerchief in one of his drawers,
she covered the plate and put it down on his bedside
table. Then she quietly pulled a chair up to his bed and
settled herself down. Poor love, he could be as cantankerous as the devil when the mood was on him, but
she could see his veins through the paper-thin skin on
his face—and, cantankerous or no, she loved him.

For the next three hours Meredith kept a watching eye
on her uncle while her thoughts floated to the other man
she loved. Though, she realised, she was more in love
with Ryan than loving him. True, she had today discovered that she was beginning to like him—something
which there had been no time to discover, or even think
about, during their whirlwind courtship—if courtship
was the word.

Meredith felt good inside as she recalled how she had
seemed to amuse him. She enjoyed seeing him amused;
she loved that look in his eyes when all his habitual
coolness disappeared. He had been kind too. So what if
he had had business in Derbyshire? he need not have
taken on the responsibility—adding extra miles on to his
trip—of calling for her to bring her back to London.

She had thought she would never see him again, yet
he had known, before she had, where she would be. But,
since he had known he would find her in Little
Haversham, and had confirmed that by ringing Tessa's
number, he could easily have given her the bad news
over the telephone. But he had not. Really, Meredith
considered, the man she had married was rather a nice
person.

'What are you looking so smitten about?'

Her tender thoughts were rudely interrupted by her uncle who, unbeknown to her, had wakened a minute earlier and had lain watching her. Swiftly she changed course, to concentrate solely on a different male.

'Have a banana sandwich,' she suggested, only to find that he had woken in a crotchety mood and had gone off the idea of a banana sandwich.

'I'd like a cup of tea,' he announced.

Suspecting that he would be asleep again by the time she got back, Meredith hurried on tiptoe to the kitchen. While the kettle boiled she set a tray for two, and added some sweet biscuits, and a short while later she was returning up the stairs.

'How did you get here?' her great-uncle asked as she adjusted his pillows when he said he wanted to sit up.

'Ryan brought me,' she replied, swinging his mobile bed table round in front of him and placing his tea and biscuits down on it.

'Where's Ryan now?' he wanted to know.

'Asleep—in my old room,' Meredith told him, and added quickly, 'There's nothing seriously wrong with you. I'm sitting with you because I couldn't sleep, and so came to see how you were.'

'You usually go to bed in your day clothes?' he grunted, seventy-seven and as alert as ever he had been.

'Are you going to drink that tea or not?' Meredith, with no answer, put a question.

'Marriage has made a bossy woman out of you,' her uncle complained, and, just as she was going to apologise, 'I want to play chess,' he demanded.

Was there ever such a cantank...? Meredith remembered how she was going to humour him. 'Drink your tea first,' she suggested.

Just before seven, someone else walked into the bedroom, saw two figures asleep over a chessboard, and smiled.

Something touching her forehead brought Meredith awake. She looked up and saw her tall husband smiling down at her.

'Did you—did you kiss me?' she asked, something in her sleep-befuddled brain telling her that he had.

Ryan put a warning forefinger to his lips and looked to where her great-uncle slept on. 'I'm just off,' he told her in a low voice, and, as Meredith wondered why he should kiss her goodbye for her uncle's benefit when her uncle was asleep, she came fully awake to realise, with inner dismay, that Ryan was leaving.

'I'll see you out,' she whispered, and rising from her chair, she ignored the fact that sleeping in a bedside chair had made her ache in several places at once, and went with him down the stairs and along the hall to the front door. 'Thank you for—yesterday,' she told him politely when, wanting to do anything to delay his leaving, she stamped down the suggestion that she should cook him a man-size breakfast before he went anywhere.

'Any time,' he said and, looking down at her, he smiled, and because she liked his smile Meredith found she could do no other than smile back. And then joy was in her fast-beating heart, for with muttered words which sounded like, 'What a delight you are!' suddenly Ryan was reaching for her. 'Come here, Meredith Carlisle,' she heard him say more distinctly, 'and give your husband the time-honoured farewell.'

There was no thought in her head, as she thrilled to hear him call her by her new surname—his surname— to refuse to do as he bade. She had grown to like this man whose well-shaped mouth was now over hers. Her arms went up and around him. He was a nice man, a kind man, and she was in love with him.

Warmly Ryan kissed her, and as Meredith clung to him, his arms tightened about her. Then their kiss came to an end and, as Meredith tried with limited success to grab a cloak of sense about her, Ryan put her from him. His eyes stayed riveted to her eyes for about a second, then moved to take in her shy face and still-parted lips. Then, as if he needed some sort of control, he reached for the door-catch, glancing back, not at her, but briefly over her shoulder.

Then, as she tried not to let him see that there was a person inside her who wanted to implore him not to leave, so without another word he went from her.

Meredith stood stock-still when the door had closed after him. Just as she somehow felt that Ryan had been unable to stop himself from taking her in his arms and kissing her, so she had felt unable to do anything but respond to him when he had kissed her. And, just then, she did not regret that he could not have been unaware of her response to him.

Feeling forlorn that he had gone, Meredith turned, but, as she took one small pace back along the hall, she suddenly froze on the spot. For there, watching her, as she must have watched both her and Ryan sharing what must seemed a loving farewell, stood her aunt—and suddenly Meredith hated Ryan Carlisle.

Because he wasn't nice, and he wasn't kind, and he was a pig! Because she loved him and he didn't love her, and she had kissed him from love and he—he had only kissed her because he had known that her aunt had been watching.

CHAPTER FIVE

ON AND off throughout that morning, Meredith ran up and down the stairs fetching this, that or the other which her tetchy male relative demanded. But no matter how demanding her uncle was, or how irritable in his recovery, it did not stop her from thinking what a rat Ryan Carlisle was.

She was positive, as she carried a breakfast tray up the stairs, that Ryan had known her aunt had been in the hall *before* he had pulled her into his arms. She grew more annoyed when she thought of how she had determined that never again would he play her for a fool. So where had her brains been when his lips had met hers?

Meredith was taking a mid-morning warm drink up to her uncle when, unable to get out of her mind the willing way she had responded, she recalled again the idiotic way she had believed Ryan had been searching for some sort of control when he had glanced back over her shoulder and along the hall. For goodness' sake, as if she did not have enough proof of what a double-dyed rat he was! He had *known* her aunt was there! His glance had been merely to confirm that her aunt had observed the newlyweds taking fond leave of each other!

She was hurrying down the road to get the Sunday papers and some of her uncle's favourite 'Army and Navy' tablets when the obscure reason why Ryan should want her aunt to witness their 'lovers' parting became clear. Quite plainly he had seen to it that, were she now to tell Aunt Evelyn what a monster he had been over those shares, her dear old-fashioned aunt would smile and say, 'Well, you've obviously forgiven him, dear.'

The smooth-talking rodent, he knew perfectly well how very difficult she was going to find it to tell her family that her marriage was over! By kissing her—and, dammit, getting her full response—he had ensured that to tell her they had separated would be more impossible than merely difficult.

Meredith was coming back from the paper shop when the answer why he should want to make things so impossible for her broke through. Despite his telling her that she was her own person now, he had not liked it when she'd told him she would divorce him when she got round to it. Quite patently, he wanted any decision about divorce to be his prerogative alone.

Chauvinistic devil! she fumed; he was so used to being top dog that it was totally alien to him to allow any female to decide on anything which involved him. No female was going to tell him she would divorce him—*he* would make the decision as to when they would divorce.

She began to cool down when, as she was about to cross the road by the telephone box near to her old home, she suddenly realised that she would be more able to speak freely to Tessa if she rang her from the coin-box rather than the family sitting-room.

'Hello, Tessa, it's Meredith,' she said a few minutes later.

'How are things?' Tessa asked quickly. 'Your uncle—was it another of his false alarms?'

'It was more serious this time,' Meredith replied, and went on to reveal how Dr Hastings had wanted him to go into hospital, but how her uncle had refused. 'Uncle Porter is being particularly crotchety this morning,' she confided, 'so I'm hoping that that's a good sign that he's returning to normal.' Then she went on to speak of her aunt and of a few domestic matters, and then, and because Tessa was her very good friend and would not intrude unless invited, she enquired, 'I suppose Aldo told you that Ryan arrived to give me a lift?'

'That was—kind of him,' commented Tessa, sounding determined not to pry.

'He was in the area on business anyway,' Meredith told her, 'so it was no particular hardship for him to make a detour to Little Haversham,' and because she just couldn't help it, '... the rat,' she added.

'Which means that you still love him,' Tessa said gently.

Meredith returned to take the papers and her uncle's favourite sweets up to him, with her head full of this crazy business called love. How was it that, even when she knew her love for the swine he was, she should still love him? Logically, having learnt what she had, as instantly as she had fallen *in* love with Ryan she should have as instantly fallen *out* of love with him.

She sighed to herself as she prepared a light lunch in the kitchen. That was the trouble with falling in love—there was no logic in it.

Dr Hastings looked in shortly after lunch to see how his patient was, and, showing him up to her uncle's room to save her elderly aunt's legs, Meredith answered the doctor's questions pertinent to his condition, and asked a few of her own.

Allowing her uncle his privacy, she waited on the landing outside when the doctor went in. Her uncle's heart was growing weaker, he had told her, but with modern medicines he could go on for years yet.

'Is he always so charming?' Dr Hastings asked as he came from the room and together they went down the stairs.

At first Meredith thought the doctor was being sarcastic, but one quick glance at his face showed that his question was genuine and, as she realised that her uncle had chosen to give his seldom-seen angelic side an outing, loyalty to her aged relative made her say, 'He—er—can be a trifle—er—not so charming occasionally.'

A few minutes later she had understood that her uncle was much improved and could get up tomorrow. He could, Dr Hastings had said, carry on exactly as before, with the exception that it might be better if she could make a bedroom for him downstairs.

'Well, that's no problem, is it, Aunty?' Meredith said when she had seen the doctor out. And, being cheerful for her aunt's sake, 'We've ample room down here and...'

'Too much room, if you ask me,' Evelyn Simmons stated. 'This house is too big for Porter and me now that you've gone,' and before Meredith could get in a hint that she might be coming back she went on, 'I thought it too big while you lived with us, for that matter. There are so many rooms we don't use, and which have to be kept aired and heated. It's such a waste of good money.'

Meredith, who knew the ins and outs of their income well, knew that, although they were not in any way near as well off as they had been thirty years ago, her aunt spoke more from a feeling of thrift than from penury.

But, realising that since her aunt had been born and brought up in this large old house she had therefore absolutely no intention of leaving it, and was just letting off gentle steam, Meredith left the subject there.

'I think I'll go and get the vegetables cleaned ready for dinner,' she told her aunt, making her way to the door.

'I'll come and help,' Evelyn Simmons said, and although it had been Meredith's idea for her great-aunt to put her feet up for a while, she gave in gracefully. Whether Uncle Porter's being ill had anything to do with it she did not know, but it seemed to her that, as her great-aunt grew older, so she grew more independent.

Having spent most of the morning drumming up her hate against Ryan Carlisle, Meredith had simmered down and her equilibrium was far calmer than it had been as in the kitchen she chopped and inspected cabbage while her aunt peeled potatoes. Suddenly, though, her aunt dropped a question into the companionable silence, and in doing so, shattered Meredith's equilibrium entirely.

'Is Ryan coming to dinner?' she asked innocently.

'What...?' Startled, Meredith glanced at her quickly.

'You were dreaming,' her aunt teased, noting her startled look, and, smiling, she explained, 'I need to know if I should peel more potatoes than I normally do.'

'Oh! No! Er—that's fine, Aunty,' Meredith babbled. Then, getting herself more collected, outwardly at least, 'Ryan's got so much paperwork to catch up on...' she invented hastily, '...that he—er—won't want to break off to eat.'

Her aunt tut-tutted a little at the very idea of a man of Ryan's build not breaking off from work to stop for a three-course meal. But, having invented his 'fast' on the spur of the moment, Meredith had more serious things to think about. Suddenly she was battling to conceal her panic at the notion her aunt had just triggered off. Because, with Ryan Carlisle turning out to be a far more complex man than she had believed, she had

no idea if he might not only decide to come and join
them for dinner but—with his nerve—decide to stay the
night as well!

Blaming the fact that she had been so busy railing
against him for her not having seen this possible eventu-
ality until her aunt had prompted it, Meredith quieted
her panic by coming to a firm resolve. While anything
was possible where Ryan Carlisle was concerned, and
she had learned the hard way not to put anything past
him, she was most definitely not going to share her bed
with him. She fully realised that, with her uncle improving, she had no excuse for sitting up with him again
tonight and so keeping away from her bed, but if she
had to sleep on the landing outside her room that night,
she would.

It did not come to that, however. While part of
Meredith was too honest not to acknowledge the fact
that she was aching for a sight of him, the proud and
*un*biddable side that had been awoken in her began to
relax when dinnertime came and went with no sign of
him.

Going upstairs to collect her uncle's used dishes, she
accepted, having realised there was no logic where love
was concerned, that relief and regret about not seeing
Ryan were bound to mingle.

She spent a few minutes with her uncle, listening to
his complaints—the potatoes were floury and he hated
cabbage—and trying to jolly him along, then, promising
to return later to give him a game of chess, she took his
tray to the kitchen and washed up. Checking that the
kitchen was spick and span, she went to the sitting-room,
intending to keep her aunt company for half an hour
before she returned upstairs.

'Did Porter eat his dinner?' her aunt asked as she went in.

'Under protest,' she smiled. 'I . . .' She broke off as the phone rang. Since they did not receive too many phone calls, Meredith's heart went wild, but she was the nearest to her uncle's chair, so she went to answer it. 'Hello,' she said, just knowing that she was being stupid and that it was probably a wrong number, or Tessa, or Mrs Peplow next door. But the absolutely super voice of Ryan Carlisle came down the wires and Meredith was all relief—with not a scrap of regret in sight.

'I thought that, for appearances' sake, you'd like me to phone,' he said urbanely.

A smile started somewhere deep inside her. 'I'm—glad you did,' she told him, and realised that her tone must have been much too warm, though fortuantely he had found a different reason for that warmth.

'Your aunt's within earshot, I take it?' he enquired, and Meredith rapidly pulled herself together.

'Uncle Porter is much improved,' she stated, as she answered his question by making believe he had just made an enquiry after her great-uncle's health.

'So tell me . . .' Ryan began, and while Meredith expected him to say something along the lines of him hoping her uncle's improvement continued, he caused her to flounder when—quite outrageously, she thought— he enquired, '. . . why wouldn't you sleep with me last night? The warmth of your response when we kissed this morning belies the fact that you hate me.'

Meredith was aware that her colour was high from his remarks, but although she recognised that, even should their marriage be consummated, Ryan, the clever devil, would soon find some grounds to divorce her when he was ready, the newly awakened unbiddable side of her was coming to the fore.

'Of course I'll be all right,' she entirely ignored his tormenting observations to reply. 'I've known for ages that you have to catch a plane tonight and will be away for at least two weeks.' She noted her aunt's quick look of surprise as she overheard this piece of news, and she managed to inject an artificially warm note into her voice when she felt forced, for her aunt's benefit, to add, 'I'll—er—be home waiting for you when you come back.'

'And where—lying baggage—will you be if I come back in under two weeks?' Ryan drawled, and even as she thought that he seemed amused by her strong hint that he should keep away for two weeks, it registered that he was saying that he would, regardless, still turn up tomorrow if he felt like it.

'Goodnight—darling,' she said, and put the phone down.

'I didn't know Ryan was going away tonight!' Evelyn Simmons exclaimed the moment Meredith looked up.

'Didn't I say?' she hedged.

Her aunt shook her head, but Meredith wanted to crawl away into a hole when suddenly her aunt smiled understandingly, and observed, 'I should have guessed when I saw you hugging each other so tightly this morning that you knew you weren't going to see each other for a couple of weeks.'

In no time at all Meredith's great-uncle Porter was up and about. On Monday Harold Peplow dropped in with some magazines for her uncle, and it was with his help, and that of Mrs Key, that Meredith moved her uncle's bed downstairs. Her uncle grumbled, of course, but he otherwise seemed pleased with all the fuss.

On Tuesday Meredith did the washing. On Wednesday, she ironed it. On Thursday she did the shopping, and on Friday she and Mrs Key gave several of the rooms a good spring-cleaning. And on Saturday, when Meredith realised she was wishing she had never pretended that Ryan would be away for two weeks, she faced the knowledge that she was yearning to see him.

Sunday dawned dull and desolate, and when not so much as a wrong number disturbed the phone bell that day she realised that Ryan, having taken her hint, was behaving honourably and would not be contacting her. And Meredith did not like it one bit.

Who was he, that he should start acting honourably *now*? All that day, she tried to whip up anger against him. But when she went to bed that night Meredith had seen that it was not so much that Ryan was acting honourably, but more that he had better things to do with his time than to remember her.

Having slept badly, she got up on Monday and knew an urge to get away. Her thoughts strayed to Tessa and to Little Haversham, and suddenly Meredith knew that, if Aldo was back in London, she would very much like to return to Derbyshire.

Uncle Porter was back to normal now, and she thought the matter through as she bathed and dressed. Mrs Key's son Michael was well on the mend from his motor-cycling accident; Mrs Key was back in full harness and, as well as being more than willing to keep an eye on her relatives, was more than able to cope with any crisis which might arise.

The idea of returning to stay with Tessa had taken root by the time Meredith went down the stairs. The idea was still buzzing around in her head as she and her aunt prepared the breakfast. And, by the time breakfast was over and her great-uncle Porter had taken himself off to the sitting-room with his newspaper, Meredith just had to say something on the subject.

'Would you mind very much if I went and stayed with Tessa for a while?' she asked her aunt as they loaded the trolley to be wheeled back to the kitchen.

'You're missing Ryan, of course,' her aunt pinpointed, and surprised Meredith slightly when she added, 'I've noticed how restless you've been ever since he went away,' and with not so much as a sign of a sharp note in her voice when she spoke of Tessa—which was more usual ever since Tessa had lived with her Duncan out of wedlock, 'You go, dear. Tessa will be pleased to see you, I feel sure,' she said in gentle understanding.

Unable to speak openly on the phone about the last time she had stayed with her, when Meredith rang Tessa to ask if she could come and stay, she added, 'If you're on your own?'

'I haven't seen anything of Aldo for over a week,' Tessa laughed, and sounded delighted at the prospect of having her to stay again.

Meredith took the train to Derbyshire the next day, and Tessa was at the station to meet her and was every bit as pleased to see her as Evelyn Simmons had said.

'Things at home still the same?' Tessa enquired as they drove along, having heard from Meredith the day before about her great-uncle's recovery.

'Pretty much,' Meredith replied. 'Uncle played up a bit when I told him I was coming away, but Aunt Evelyn told him I'd be going anyway when Ryan returned from abroad.'

'He's overseas?'

'No,' Meredith replied, and explained how she had let her aunt believe that Ryan had flown abroad on business.

'How's Aldo?' she asked, to change what was a painful subject.

'Between you and me—driving me up the wall!' Tessa replied.

'He's still heartbroken over Caroline?'

'That's just it!' Tessa exclaimed. 'After giving you, I suspect, as well as me a wretched time of it over his ex—blow me if he didn't ring up last night—as happy as Larry, mark you—to ask if he could bring his new girl-friend to meet me.'

'He didn't!' Meredith gasped stunned, and as both she and Tessa burst out laughing, she added, 'The stinker!' Having recovered, though, she was serious when she asked, 'So he and his girlfriend are coming to stay this weekend?'

'They are not!' Tessa said firmly. 'Love him dearly though I do, that brother of mine is fine in small doses only.'

At Tessa's cottage, Meredith took her case up to the room she had used before. Then she went downstairs, where she and her friend spent a relaxing afternoon talking of nothing in particular, but nevertheless still finding plenty of things to discuss.

Because Tessa was filling in for one of the art teachers at evening classes who had gone off sick, they dined early. 'You're sure you don't mind me leaving you on your first night here?' Tessa checked before she went.

'For heaven's sake,' Meredith told her, 'I wouldn't have come if I thought I was going to disrupt things for you. Besides, I'm dying to start that book you've loaned me.'

'Oh, well, if you put it like that!' Tessa smiled. 'I'll see you later.'

Ryan was back in Meredith's head the moment the door had closed after her friend. He was still there an hour later, the book Tessa had lent her to read still unopened on her lap. Ryan was much in her mind as she went over yet again how, when she had overheard him in conversation with Monte Montgomery on her wedding day, her world had fallen apart. Her chin had tilted at an angry angle as she relived hearing Ryan state, 'It's a bonus, of course, that she's a biddable little thing', when she was suddenly startled out of her thoughts by hearing the phone ring.

Not knowing who might be calling, but not feeling apprehensive that it might be Aldo ringing his sister for a chat—Caroline must be a lady of the past now—Meredith went to answer Tessa's phone.

'Hello,' she said, and straight away received an earful from, by the sound of it, a very irate husband!

Ryan's voice, though still as fabulous as she had always thought it, was right now at its most disagreeable. 'What the hell do you think you're doing in Derbyshire?' he roared down the line.

'You—r-rang my home?' she queried, rendered almost speechless at hearing him so entirely unexpectedly.

'I rang your aunt pretending to be calling you from abroad,' he rapped furiously. 'The least you could have done was to let me know your movements!' And, while Meredith began to get over her astonishment at hearing from him so surprisingly, fairly violent emotions— prodded by her recent memory of him referring to her as 'A biddable little thing'—began to stir in her. 'Don't expect me to go in to bat for you if . . .' he barked.

'I never asked you to go in to bat for me!' a very unbiddable Meredith hurled spiritedly back at him.

'You sure as hell don't want it broadcast that our marriage is over!' he bellowed, and slammed down the phone before she could think of a suitable answer.

Swine! she fumed, and refused to cry. Pig, pig, pig, she silently berated him, but it was rather weakening to know that he could not be such a total swine, or else why would he have realised that her aunt might well have begun to wonder that he had not been in touch, and rung pretending to her that he was ringing from abroad?

It came to Meredith over the next few days that the time was drawing closer when she would have to confess to her aunt and uncle that her marriage was over. Somehow, though, no matter how many ways she thought up to explain to them the way it was, she never once thought of telling them the true reason why she and Ryan would not be living under the same roof. She was still thinking of the peculiarity of love on Friday, in that, while *she* could call Ryan a pig, and anything else that came to mind, she just found it beyond her to blacken his name to her aunt and uncle.

She and Tessa were sitting in the kitchen that evening, where the light was better, while Tessa practised her portrait skills for a village fund-raising event, when Tessa asked, 'Can I have a smile?' as her hand flew over her sketch-pad.

'Sorry,' Meredith apologised, and did her best to comply, even if she felt in not a very smiling mood as she cogitated on how best to break the news to her elderly relatives who believed that a marriage was forever.

'How's that?' asked Tessa as she tore the top piece of paper off her pad and handed it to her.

'Why, it's brilliant!' Meredith exclaimed, as she stared at the likeness of herself which her friend had just sketched. 'You'll make heaps for charity if you make all your sitters seem as carefree and full of life as you've made me look,' she said, as she glanced again at the drawing of the young woman who laughed back at her.

'It's more how I remember you looking when we were at art college,' Tessa told her as she took the charcoal-drawn portrait from her and studied it herself. 'It's how you'll look again, too, I've every confidence,' she told her.

'I can't wait!' Meredith grinned.

Later, when she went to bed, she could not help but wonder—would she? Somehow it seemed years away since she had last felt carefree. Yet it did not take her long to recall that the last time she had felt as carefree as that portrait had been that heady time when she had thought Ryan loved her.

'This morning,' Tessa announced at breakfast, 'I shall do some cleaning.'

'If you're serious, and with due respect I hardly believe my ears,' Meredith laughed, 'then I'll help.'

Tessa grinned as she detailed Meredith to 'do' the sitting-room while she herself 'sterilised' the kitchen. An hour later, though, Tessa had had more than enough and called through to the sitting-room, 'Shall we break for coffee?'

'It's only ten o'clock,' Meredith pointed out.

'Stick-in-the-mud!' Tessa jibed.

'Black or white?' responded Meredith as she went through to the kitchen to put the kettle on.

Tessa, although she tried hard, lost heart after that, and resumed work only briefly when she again called through to the sitting-room.

'I can do housework when it rains,' she said, and as Meredith joined her she began, 'The sun's shining,' but did not have to add more.

'Why don't you go and finish that bit of sketching you told me just wouldn't come right?' Meredith encouraged her. 'Perhaps you'll have better luck today.'

'Would you mind?'

'Of course not!'

'Come with me, then.'

Meredith thought of the books ready for dusting and which were temporarily all over the floor from her emptying the bookcase. 'Another time,' she told Tessa, and would have seen about making her some sandwiches to take with her, but her friend stopped her.

'If it all goes right, I should be through in about an hour,' she said, and made Meredith promise to cease all housework once she had the sitting-room back to rights. 'For my conscience's sake,' she pleaded.

'See you later,' Meredith called as she waved her off.

'I won't be long this time, I promise,' Tessa called as she got into her car. Meredith smiled—she had heard that before.

Once she had finished the sitting-room, and feeling a little grubby, she went and showered and changed into a full-skirted cotton dress. No matter what she did, though, Ryan kept her company.

When she was going to get him out of her head she had no idea, for he accompanied her to the general store when she decided to go and see what the store's refrigeration department had that might be interesting for dinner.

Returning from the general store, she made herself a lunchtime sandwich and a cup of coffee, and wondered what he was doing and where he was having his lunch.

She tried, without success, to oust him from her thoughts, but he refused to budge. He was still in her head an hour and a half later when she happened to glance out of the sitting-room window. And it was then that she thought that such constant thinking of him must have sent her over the edge, because she could have sworn she had just seen his car pull up outside.

Grief! she thought, as her heartbeat quickened, and, very much annoyed with herself, she took herself off to the kitchen. She would not give in to the temptation to go and look out of the sitting-room window a second time—she would not.

She had just set the kettle to boil for a cup of tea she had no particular interest in when a ring sounded from the front door bell, and suddenly everything in her went catastrophic.

It must have been his car! she thought. Only to at once counteract that thought by telling herself sternly not be ridiculous, there was more than one sleek black limousine around.

She was still having an inner argument when, with no idea of what she was going to say to him should it indeed prove to be Ryan and not wishful thinking—for in truth, she was aching for a sight of him—she went and answered what seemed a very impatient second ring at Tessa's front door.

'Oh, hello!' Meredith was inwardly delighted with herself that she had achieved such a surprised and even-sounding greeting.

'I thought you weren't in!' Ryan retorted uncivilly.

'I was in the kitchen,' she replied by way of explanation, rather than let him glean any idea of how she had gone to pieces when his first ring of the doorbell had sounded. 'Which reminds me,' she said, realising that she did not have to explain a thing, 'I've left the kettle boiling its head off. Er—come in,' she added, as she turned from him and made a dive for the kitchen.

'You're about to have a cup of tea?' he asked. Having switched the kettle off, Meredith looked at him and, spotting lines of tiredness around his eyes, went utterly weak.

'Would you like one?' she had offered before she had given herself time to think that it might be better if he made this visit as brief as possible.

'Thanks,' he accepted.

Meredith was not entirely sure how she felt at having him watching her as she warmed the teapot and popped in some teabags. 'If you'd like to take a seat in the sitting-room,' she hinted, and felt her ire start to rise when clearly he wanted to do nothing of the kind.

'What's wrong with the kitchen?' he enquired, and, as if hell-bent on watching her prowess as teamaker-in-chief, he pulled out a chair from beneath the kitchen table and sat looking on while she poured boiling water on the teabags.

Determined not to invite him to the sitting-room again, she set two cups of tea down on the kitchen table and pulled out a chair for herself at the other side. 'I expect you're this way on business?' she queried. But, remembering that the last time he had been in Derbyshire on business he had combined that trip with a detour to Little Haversham to tell her that her great-uncle was ill, she felt a sudden anxiety about her uncle.

Her anxiety was quickly quieted however when, with no sign of urgency Ryan drawled, 'I come this way once a year to visit a distant elderly relative on her birthday.'

'You've an elderly relative living...' this way, she would have ended, had he given her the chance, but, aggressive suddenly, Ryan had cut in to demand,

'Did you suppose you held exclusive rights in all elderly relatives?'

'No,' Meredith answered shortly. 'But you never told me about yours! Had you done so,' she went on a trace sarcastically, 'I'd have invited her to our wedding.'

'In the circumstances, it's just as well that she's too frail to travel!' Ryan tossed back at her caustically. And, while Meredith was feeling a rebirth of her recent face-slapping tendencies, he asked sharply, 'Where's your friend?'

'Tessa's out sketching!' Meredith snapped, nettled.

'And your other friend?' he barked abruptly.

'Other friend?' she queried curtly, not at all with him.

'Wallace, of the "Aldo and I" fame—the brother,' he elucidated in three different ways so that she could not help but know who he meant.

'He doesn't live here,' she retorted sourly, not liking the implication that she was dim not to know straight away who he meant. 'Aldo lives and works in London,' she added waspishly.

'So you haven't seen him this trip?'

With any other man, Meredith might have thought there was a suggestion of jealousy behind the question. But, since she knew little of men except one in par-ticular—the one she had married—and the idea that he might be jealous was laughable, she kept her head, biting out, 'No, I haven't!' And when suddenly, and to her immense surprise, Ryan burst out laughing, she chal-lenged hostilely, 'What's so funny?'

'It struck me that we sounded like some long-married couple,' Ryan answered. More because she preferred him in this better humour, Meredith had to smile—and then he made every one of her nerve-ends tingle when he gently touched a forefinger to the curving corner of her mouth, and murmured, half to himself, 'When did I ever consider you biddable?'

Such was his charm then that Meredith's backbone melted, and as she raised her eyes from his warm, smiling mouth to his warm grey eyes, she just could not keep a guard on her tongue. 'You look tired,' she told him.

'That's probably because I've been deskbound all week,' he replied.

'You find it more—stimulating—to be—er—up and doing, rather than locked behind your desk?' she queried, loving the fact that, for the first time ever, Ryan was allowing her to see a little of what made him tick.

'Much prefer it,' he answered openly, and, after a moment's pause, 'Which is why it was a pleasure to drive this way today.'

Meredith knew for sure that he could not be implying that he had found it a pleasure to drive to see her. Particularly she knew it when she recalled easily that his reason for being in Derbyshire that day was to visit an elderly relative. Knowing that, however, made it no easier to bear that she, his wife, must be an afterthought. Which, in turn, was perhaps responsible for her tone being a little tart when she told him, 'Riding around the country in a car isn't going to do you any good! What you need is some exercise in the fresh air.'

'You're suggesting we go for a walk?' he returned before she could blink.

'I wasn't, actually,' she said on a gasp.

'It's turned a mite chilly; you'll need a jacket,' he said, as if it was all settled.

'Are you this bossy at the office?' she countered, but she knew she would walk to the ends of the earth with him if he asked her—and that was before he smiled.

'Please,' he charmed her, and Meredith went to collect her jacket.

She thought she would never forget the enchantment of that walk. She later calculated that they were away from the cottage for about an hour. During that hour, though, she felt more at one with Ryan than she had ever been as they discussed any subject—barring their two selves—that came up.

Sadly, though, the harmony of that walk was not to last. They had turned round and were almost back at Tessa's cottage when Meredith, while marvelling at how in tune she and Ryan seemed to be, thought through a recent idea out loud. It went along the lines of her maybe renting a flat, and getting herself a permanent job.

'You're saying that, having made the break from your relatives, you now want to be totally independent?' Ryan queried, a dark frown coming to his good-looking features.

Meredith had not fully worked out her idea yet, but as it was burned on her brain that Ryan thought she had only married him to get away from her relatives, she was not going to disabuse him of the idea now.

'What's wrong with that?' she challenged him, and did not care that his frown deepened not only at her words but also her far from docile tone.

'I've already told you that I'll provide for you,' he told her sharply as they reached the cottage gate and stood glaring at each other, with Meredith suddenly cancelling out any notion she might have had to invite him in for some refreshment, and Ryan looking as though she'd have been wasting her breath anyway because the only place he was going was back to London. 'Where do you bank? I'll...'

'I don't need you to provide for me!' she flared hotly. 'I'm quite capable of...'

'It's my right to provide for you,' he cut her off
bluntly. 'I have a duty to...'

'Good grief!' Meredith cut him off this time, her new-
found temper getting well out of control that he, this
man she loved with all her being, should consider her a
'duty'. 'Really, Ryan,' she mocked, surprising herself as
much as him that her obedient self could sound so arrogant, 'you're just too old-fashioned for words!'

'Why, you little...' he began, and Meredith had a
feeling that he was close to wanting to put his hands
round her throat and throttle her. Only instead, some
movement behind her caught his attention, and as she
turned to see what it was she saw Tessa hurrying urgently
down the path towards them.

Meredith's temper disappeared instantly when, without
waiting for the niceties of introductions, Tessa said, 'Mrs
Key's been on the phone, Meredith. Your uncle's been
taken ill again—and this time it looks pretty bad.'

CHAPTER SIX

MEREDITH was grateful, as Ryan's car sped nearer and nearer to London, that he had been there to take charge. From the moment Tessa had said 'This time, it looks pretty bad', all animosity had vanished.

'He's in hospital?' Ryan had queried promptly, and fear had entered Meredith's heart when Tessa had replied gravely,

'He was in no condition to refuse to go, apparently.'

Vaguely Meredith was aware that she hadn't introduced the man she had married to her friend, but she rather gathered that Tessa had concluded who he was from the smart car which was parked by the kerb. Then Ryan was asking, 'Do you want anything from the cottage before we get off?' and, as her numbed heart overflowed with love for him that he, by the look of it, was prepared to take her back to London with all speed, she told him she would just go and collect her handbag.

Her anxiety grew greater as, whenever possible, Ryan kept his foot down, the quicker to get her to London. Mixed in with her worries for her uncle, though, was the anxiety of wondering how her great-aunt was coping.

'Do you want to go straight to the hospital or to see your aunt first?' Ryan enquired, just as if he knew what thoughts were going through her mind.

'Aunty will be at the hospital,' Meredith told him with conviction. And so it turned out to be.

Mrs Key was there too, and it was she who was outside the small side ward looking out for her. 'How are things?'

asked Meredith, hurrying towards her immediately she saw her.

'Not good,' Mrs Key replied, and added, 'Miss Simmons is with your uncle now.'

Thanking her for all she had done, Meredith went silently and quickly into the side ward where her tired and drawn-looking aunt was keeping vigil over her unconscious brother.

'I'm glad you're here,' she whispered as Meredith hugged her. 'Both of you,' she added as Meredith let her go and she observed that Ryan had come with her.

There was no change in Porter Simmons' condition over the next few hours, and as Meredith sat with her aunt at his bedside she was aware of Ryan there in the background, trying to make things easier for them.

It was he who brought them tea and sandwiches from somewhere, he who drove Mrs Key home when reluctantly she mentioned that she was baby-sitting that night, and Meredith was again grateful to him. It was Ryan too who, when a doctor came and checked on her uncle and declared that there was a slight improvement, drove them back to her old home.

Once there, she was staggered when she glanced at her watch and saw that it was nearly midnight. But, despite the fact that her aunt looked ready to drop, Meredith had to admire the way she remembered her manners as she told Ryan, 'You must have some supper.'

'I had something to eat at the hospital, thank you, Miss Simmons,' he told her gently, 'and . . .'

'And it's time you were in bed, Aunty,' Meredith took up. And, at her aunt's anxious look, 'The hospital will telephone us if—if there's any change in Uncle Porter's condition.'

'You and Ryan are staying the night?' Evelyn Simmons enquired.

'I—er...' Meredith began, feeling drained herself and for the moment stumped.

'Yes, of course,' Ryan replied, and Meredith was again grateful to him.

Though she was not quite sure how she felt when shortly afterwards, having locked up, he escorted both her and her aunt up the stairs. 'Goodnight, darling,' she bade her aunt gently as she kissed her cheek before coming away from her bedroom. Then Meredith, with Ryan right there beside her, went on to her own bedroom.

'Don't worry,' he said quietly when, with both of them inside her bedroom, she looked at him nonplussed.

Ryan could, she realised, have meant she was not to worry regarding her uncle. But, as common sense squeezed in through her tiredness, she realised that what he was saying was, Look, I couldn't do anything other in the circumstances than come along to your room. He was also saying, she realised, that as soon as her aunt was asleep he would go and sleep on the downstairs settee.

'I'm—not,' she said quietly, and, since she had left a suitcase of clothes in Derbyshire, she went to the chest of drawers and extracted a nightdress and a fresh cotton robe. Then, armed with both, she went to the small adjoining bathroom and washed and changed.

She felt only a little awkward when, nightdress- and robe-clad, she returned to the room. But Ryan, she felt, was the soul of tact when, turning from her to study a couple of out-of-date magazines on a small table, and keeping his voice down, he told her over his shoulder. 'Feel free to get into bed, Meredith, I'll be away shortly.'

She had hurriedly got into her bed, and had the bed-covers up to her chin when, with her eyes closed, she told him, 'Take your ease in the soft chair for a few minutes.' She heard the sound of him moving, then heard the creaking sound of the small bedroom chair as it took his weight. 'Goodnight,' she called.

'Goodnight, love,' he said softly, and Meredith had never loved him more. Because he was kind, and because when, her emotions ragged over her uncle, she had needed someone to say a kind word, Ryan had called her 'love'.

Somehow, with Ryan still in the room, she fell asleep. How that came about when she was aware of him in the same room as her with every fibre of her being, she did not know. Nor did she know that she had fallen asleep until two hours later when she awakened in the darkened room to feel someone getting into bed with her!

'What . . . !' she started to shriek, but Ryan was quick to calm her agitation.

'Shh!' he breathed. 'It's all right,' he soothed, and in a low voice, 'I tried to go downstairs, but your aunt has her bedroom door open and called out to me,' he explained. 'I was forced to come back and try to sleep in the chair. But that chair,' he said humorously, 'was made for a midget.'

Meredith owned to feeling slightly confused as she worked out that her aunt Evelyn must have left her bedroom door open with the intention of not missing hearing the phone should the hospital call. But, although every piece of intelligence was telling her she should tell Ryan in no uncertain terms to find somewhere else to sleep, somehow she could not do it. Aside from all the help he had been, the fact that he had sounded more amused than amorous, not to mention that he had perched himself right on the edge of the bed and could have been a mile away for all she could detect his presence, made it seem to her that to eject him was only being exceedingly petty.

'Goodnight,' she murmured and, turning her back on the other side of the bed, was soon drifting off to sleep again.

She slept only briefly this time, however, and awakened to find that at some moment in the intervening time, as she had turned over again to face her bed partner, so that bed partner had moved away from the edge of the bed to draw nearer to her.

Meredith was too disorientated to know how she felt when she began to appreciate that not only had they moved closer to each other, but she was now safely gathered up in Ryan's arms, and that her head was now— cradled on his shoulder!

Her body stiffened. It was all new to her, this lying in bed with a man. But, prompted a small voice, this man was her husband. This man was the man she loved. And suddenly all the stiffness went out of her body, and she rested against him.

She was still in his arms when she again awakened a couple of hours later. This time, though, she felt refreshed enough from sleep to make more clear evaluations and decisions.

Gently, in the early light of dawn, so as not to disturb him, she went to pull out of his arms with the purpose of leaving the bed and getting dressed. But she didn't get very far, because just as if he liked having her in his arms, Ryan's hold suddenly tightened—and Meredith knew that he too was awake.

'I'm g-getting up now,' she whispered falteringly as she raised her head and looked into the warm regard of his grey eyes.

'You don't sound very sure about that,' he murmured with a lazy smile, and suddenly, as he stretched out a naked arm to touch the arm that peeped out from her sleeveless nightdress, Meredith's heart began to pound.

'Oh—R-Ryan,' she said unsteadily, and was incapable of making or carrying out any decision when he moved to pull her tenderly closer to him.

'Relax, little love,' he said softly, and gently he laid his mouth over hers. And because she wanted his mouth over hers, Meredith relaxed as far as she was able and, with no thought in her head save for him, she stretched up to place her arms around his naked shoulders.

Again he gently kissed her, but as a flame surged into life in her at the touch of his nakedness, Meredith wanted more. Willingly her lips parted and, as his kisses became more ardent, she met his kisses with an ardency of her own.

She felt his hands warm through her nightdress at the back of her as he caressed her and traced tiny kisses down her throat. Then his warm hands were caressing to her front, and he had captured the throbbing, swollen globes of her breasts.

'Ryan!' she cried his name, and felt that fire burning in her for him begin to burn with an even greater intensity.

She clutched on to him, nevertheless, when, wanting to feel more of her silken skin, he went to remove her nightdress. 'No?' he queried, and she so loved him that, even when it must have been clear to him that she wanted him, it seemed he would have accepted a refusal from her.

'Yes,' she sighed, and she smiled as she whispered, 'I haven't—er—adjusted yet to being in bed with a—a man.'

'With your husband, my shy one,' he corrected her, and while his fingers busied themselves with her clothing, he tenderly kissed her.

A minute later he had moved her with him and they were both sitting in bed, without clothing. A minute later, he had captured her naked, silken, pink-tipped breasts in the most gentle of holds. 'Sweet love,' he breathed, 'sweet, untouched love,' and, with his naked chest tenderly pressing against the hardened peaks of her breasts, his lips over hers, he lay down with her. She felt his hands caressing her thighs and moaned in pleasure at what he was doing to her, and the wild emotion he was creating in her. She felt a moment's shyness when his touch became more intimate, but when she instinctively pulled back Ryan was there again to soothe her.

'Shh . . .' he gentled her. 'There's nothing to be afraid of.'

'I'm—n-not afraid,' she told him huskily, 'just . . .'

'I know,' he said understandingly, and kissed her and caressed her, until long minutes later, she felt tormented beyond enduring, and could think of nothing save that she wanted to be possessed by him.

'Oh, please!' she cried, in a fire of agony in her need for him, and she was lost to everything save him when Ryan called out her name—just as though he too was beside himself with desire—for her.

The next time Meredith awakened, a short while later, she was totally confused again. Earlier, there had been no confusion, just the clear knowledge that as Ryan had wanted her, so she had wanted him. But surely their making love with each other had to have more meaning than just the physical—or was she just being old-fashioned?

She realised that she was very probably being old-fashioned, though she doubted that she would feel any differently had she not been brought up in an old-fashioned household. In silence she gazed at the sleeping face of the man who had not so long ago been so infinitely gentle with her as he had led her step by tender step through to full womanhood. But as she gazed at him and her heart pounded again just from seeing him and remembering how it had been, Meredith knew she was never going to be able to think clearly until she had put some distance between them.

Being extremely careful not to wake him, for should he reach for her, she thought she might well again be lost, Meredith left the bed and, scooping up her robe as she went, tiptoed from the room.

Oh, how she loved him, she thought as she donned her robe outside on the landing, and was strongly pulled by a need to turn about swiftly and go and climb straight back into bed with him. But although it took some doing, she managed to resist that urge. She needed to think, not to give way to a natural instinct to feel his arms, strong and protective, about her.

She was not entirely certain what there was to think about as she went silently down the stairs and into the sitting-room. But, although she felt a mixture of clear-headedness and confusion, it was clear-headedness that won the day. For only a few minutes later she was able to realise that what lay at the bottom of her inner unrest was her knowledge that while she had given herself to Ryan in love, he had taken, not from love, but because he had to be the one to call the tune. It hurt that it was so, but there was no getting away from it. Ryan had wanted her biddable in his bed, and she—though she had determined that her days of being biddable were over—had given in totally, without a fight.

Her breath caught on a choky sound that she had been so unwary, so naïve, so—dammit—stupid as to listen to the dictates of her heart and her body instead of the intelligence of her head.

She had just finally decided that she was never going to be so weak as to allow Ryan Carlisle to make love to her again when, striking fear into her heart, the telephone rang. Instantly her thoughts were all for her great-uncle Porter. The clock on the mantel said twenty past six—who but the hospital would ring at this hour?

Conscious that if she let the phone ring much longer it would disturb her aunt, Mercdith, after a moment of frozen immobility, went quickly to answer it. It was the hospital. Gently she was informed that her great-uncle had died.

'Thank you,' she said quietly, and replaced the receiver to turn and find that a fully-clothed Ryan had come silently into the room. 'Uncle Porter has died,' she told him woodenly, and when Ryan came forward and seemed as though he was about to take her in his arms, she snapped icily, 'Don't touch me!' Hearing a sound on the stairs, she ignored the sudden lift of his brow at this change in her from the clinging, passionate and vibrant woman she had been a short while ago, and went quickly past him and out through the hall to where her dressing-gowned aunt was nearing the bottom of the stairs.

'Was that the phone?' her aunt asked.

Meredith nodded, and, there being no way in which she could dress up the bad news, began, 'Aunty darling...'

An hour later, and because her aunt wished it, Ryan drove them to the hospital. And, despite Meredith's coolness towards him, he seemed prepared to take them wherever they wanted to go.

Indeed, it was he who the next day escorted them to the necessary authorities they had to visit in having Porter Simmons' death recorded, and his funeral arranged. But not once, in the days and nights that followed, did he enter again the bedroom he had shared with Meredith.

And Meredith would not have wanted it any other way. At least, that was what she told herself at the beginning. Had Ryan attempted again to take her in his arms in those days prior to her great-uncle's funeral, then she was sure the sharp feel of her hand on the side of his face was the minimum reception he would have got from her.

But he attempted no such thing and, conversely, on the day after her great-uncle was laid to rest, Meredith began to see why. All too plainly, having made love to her, having had her malleable under his will, he had now lost all interest.

That knowledge hurt, and Meredith was grateful that she had plenty to keep her occupied when her aunt asked her to go through her uncle's belongings on her behalf, and to dispose of them as she thought fit.

Meredith was grateful, too, to Lilian Peplow who, since Great-uncle Porter's death, was spending more time in their home than in her own home next door. Initially she had called to offer her condolences, but her visits had grown longer and longer, and having her there to befriend her aunt as the two talked over old memories of the years seemed to help her aunt over her grief at losing her younger brother and daily companion.

Meredith's own friend Tessa had telephoned on the Sunday of her uncle's death to enquire how he was. 'Oh, I'm so sorry,' she had said when Meredith had told her. 'How's your aunt taking it?'

'Much better than I would have supposed,' Meredith said.

'How about you?' Tessa had then asked.

'I'm fine,' she had replied, but, able to talk freely for once, with her aunt having a lie-down upstairs and Ryan having gone to fill up his car with petrol, Meredith was this time completely and utterly unable to confide in her friend when Tessa enquired,

'Is Ryan still with you?'

Meredith had been feeling decidedly cold towards Ryan that day. But even so, it just seemed beyond her to revile him to her friend. 'He's very kind,' she told her.

'I'm glad,' Tessa commented quietly, and, save to ask if Meredith thought she should come to the funeral, she had little else to add.

Meredith could see no particular reason why Tessa should attend. It was not as though she'd known her uncle well, and most likely, had Tessa wanted to come, she would not have asked.

It was odd, the way things had worked out, Meredith reflected, as upstairs in her uncle's room she parcelled up clothes to take to Oxfam. Her aunt had quite logically decided, when she and Ryan had arrived at the hospital on Saturday, that Ryan's business abroad was completed and that he had been up in Derbyshire collecting her to take her back to their apartment when Mrs Key had telephoned to say what had happened.

Being gullible must run in the family, Meredith thought sourly a moment later, for her aunt had entirely accepted that, while Ryan was occupied with looking after them and the arrangements, he was not doing any work. She saw it as perfectly feasible that he should return to his own home each evening to catch up on his day's work.

Well, he can jolly well stay at his home each evening! Meredith thought furiously, not sure if the stray tear that escaped was on account of the harrowing job she was tackling or because Ryan had so tenderly taken her to the heights, only to drop her down to the cold, desolate depths.

And he need not bother coming round to her aunt's home again either, she fumed, as she stiffened her backbone. But the next second she was very near to wilting, because it was obvious to anyone with even half an eye that, with her uncle buried and with no more arrangements being necessary, Ryan would not be coming round to her aunt's home again.

Hiding her hurt at his obvious belief that, having slept with her once, once was quite enough, thank you, Meredith immersed herself in the job she had to do. She was still upstairs sorting out her uncle's clothing that afternoon when the front door bell sounded.

For once her aunt was paying a visit to Lilian Peplow rather than the other way around, and, believing that her aunt had dropped the latch but forgotten to take her key, Meredith went swiftly down the stairs to let her in.

When she reached the door and opened it, though, she discovered that she was wrong on two counts. First, it was not her aunt on the other side of the door. Second, as her heartbeats quickened and she sternly wiped any sign of welcome from her face, Meredith saw that she was mistaken in her belief that Ryan would not be calling at her aunt's home again. For the tall man who stood cool grey-eyed and scrutinising her was none other than he!

Almost Meredith closed the door on him without a word. Her pride had wanted her to do just that, she owned. But Ryan had indeed been as kind as she had told Tessa he had been, and she would be beholden to no one.

Without a word, she turned and walked along the hall to the sitting-room. She was aware that he had crossed the threshold and that he had closed the door and was following, but only she was going to know about the nonsense that was going on inside her.

'My aunt's next door visiting Mrs Peplow,' she turned round to tell him coolly. 'I'll go and fetch her if you'd like to...'

'It isn't your aunt I've come to see,' he grated, his eyes narrowing. Quite clearly he did not care for her manner.

'Then you must have come to see me,' Meredith clipped icily. Though she felt forced to go on by the sheer weight of his authority when, without saying a word, he stared grim-faced at her. 'Although why,' she added aloofly, 'completely baffles me.'

'You don't think we have something to discuss?' he bore her aloof manner to enquire coolly, and Meredith felt quite ill inside. As clearly as if he had just said the word 'divorce', she knew quite well what he was there to discuss.

'I've—nothing to discuss with you,' she told him flatly, as she inwardly panicked and her pride fought a battle with her love for him. The love said that no matter what, she needed time to get adjusted to the thought of them being divorced. But her pride began to win, and it was again aloofly that she told him, 'I shall stay here with my aunt, so you...'

'Naturally you'll stay here with her un...' He broke off. Then as Meredith struggled up from the depths of her unhappiness that not only was he stating categorically that he did not want her living with him, he was amazing her by his sheer nerve, when he added, 'I used to think—before we married—that you had some small feeling for me. Has that all gone, Meredith? Or was it all pretence from the start?'

'My, what a short memory you have, Ryan!' she drawled, constantly amazed at her own reserves of strength—or maybe it was just pride making her determined not to let him see that she felt like a whipped puppy inside. 'You surely remember that I'd have pretended to like the devil himself in those days when I had the notion that I wanted to leave home? Although,' pride spurred her on, 'should I ever have been so idiotic as to have begun to care for you, then you can be darn sure that it wouldn't have survived my finding out—on our wedding day—what a cold, calculating rat you are!' Meredith had to break off to pause for breath, but, as Ryan took all she threw at him, her pride had returned in full measure when, just before she sailed from the room, she told him impersonally, 'And now, if you'll excuse me, I'll return to the job of sorting my uncle's belongings.'

Her legs might have been feeling dreadfully shaky, but she made it to the upstairs landing without faltering. She only realised that she was holding her breath and listening, though, when, after what seemed an age of silence from downstairs, she suddenly heard the front door open and close as Ryan let himself out.

A dry sob shook her as she sucked in fresh breath. What more proof did she need that he had come that afternoon to ask her for a divorce? He had made no attempt to stop her when she had walked away from him—what more proof did she need that he did not care a scrap about her?

CHAPTER SEVEN

IN THE month that followed, Meredith thought over
countless times the way in which Ryan Carlisle had called
on her the afternoon when her aunt had been next door.
And each time she relived the way the conversation had
gone, she came to the same conclusion—that Ryan had
come to discuss their divorce.

Not that they had actually got around to talking about
their divorce. She thought over again, as she had frequently, the panic that had beset her when she had been
unable to face the finality of being divorced from him.
Thank goodness her pride had come to her rescue in
time, though, she mused, and she was again remembering how, mercilessly, in her opinion, Ryan had had
the nerve to refer to the 'small feeling' which she had
seemed to have for him.

She had since thanked her lucky stars that but for the
confines of her strict upbringing she might well have been
unable, in those days before their marriage, to refrain
from showing him just how totally enraptured by him
she was. Only by the skin of her teeth had she been able
to show just how 'little' she did care that afternoon. All
she hoped was that, if he ever got around to wondering
why, if she had no particular feeling for him, she had
given herself so willingly to him, he would think that
she had given herself out of sheer propinquity, having
found herself in the same bed with him, and from
weakness when confronted with the expertise of his
seduction.

Meredith got on with preparing the dinner that evening with Ryan still in her head. She did not know how to accept the thought of never seeing him again, but as she cleaned and sliced carrots it came to her that, not having seen him for a month, she had still pulled through.

She would pull through too, she determined fiercely. She had been fine before she had known him. Who was he anyway but...? Meredith set to work laying the table, aware that she was fooling no one but herself. She loved the rat, was in love with the arrogant swine; he was her world, and that was all there was to it.

It was over dinner with her aunt that Meredith was brought up short to realise that she was not fooling someone else on another front. She had previously explained that Ryan had suggested that, in these early days of her aunt losing her brother and companion of so many years, he thought it a good idea that she stay on at her old home for a while. But she was helping her aunt to some roast chicken that night when her aunt looked at her sharply, and told her, 'I think it's about time, Meredith, that you returned to your new home and began cooking dinner for your husband.'

'You don't want me to stay here any more?' Meredith took evasive action, having noted the no-nonsense look on Evelyn Simmons' face.

'It isn't that I don't want you here, child,' her aunt replied. 'Your presence in this house has brightened many a dark day. But,' she went on forthrightly, 'your place is with your husband.'

'I...' Meredith began, hesitated, and because she knew she could not go on avoiding this issue for ever, 'Actually, Aunty,' she got started again, 'Ryan and I—well, we're—er—not getting on too well at the moment.'

'How can you be getting on?' Evelyn Simmons questioned. 'You never see each other!'

'That's just it,' Meredith said quickly. 'We've decided on a—a trial separation.' The words, the painful words, were out. But as she looked at her aunt expecting to have to dash for the smelling salts, Evelyn Simmons surprised her by being more hardy than that. More hardy—and entirely disbelieving.

'Tosh!' she exclaimed. 'The two of you haven't had time to get beyond the honeymoon stage yet!'

'I made a mistake,' Meredith tried to tell her.

'Bunkum!' Her aunt refused to listen. And, heedless of what Meredith was trying to get across to her, she said bracingly, 'You're just not the sort to fall in and out of love every five minutes—you're too like your dear mother for that.' Having seen Meredith on her wedding day, and witnessed the stars shining in her eyes at the thought of being Ryan Carlisle's wife, she knew full well that her great-niece was heart and soul in love with him. 'Besides, Ryan is such a wonderful man, how could you fall out of love with him?' she asked, and, having never been married herself, she told her that the first year of marriage was always difficult, and spent the rest of that meal singing Ryan Carlisle's praises.

Wondering what her aunt would think of him were she to tell her that he had only married her to get his hands on the Burgess Electrical shares, and how—as simple as you like—she had fallen for it, Meredith left the table feeling mentally bruised and battered. Though no matter how mentally exhausted she felt from her aunt trying to get through to her that her husband was one in a million, it was utterly beyond her to be that disloyal to the man she loved.

They were in the sitting-room watching a programme
on TV which was doing nothing to lift her from the unhappy reverie she had fallen into when suddenly the
phone rang and, going over to answer it, she heard the
pleasant voice of her friend Tessa.

'I'll go and make a cup of tea,' her aunt said, on
hearing Meredith greet her friend by name.

'Sorry,' said Meredith when her aunt had trundled off,
'I missed what you were saying.'

'I was only asking how you were.'

'Fine,' Meredith replied.

'You don't sound it,' Tessa promptly came back, and
caused Meredith to apologise again.

'I've just tried telling Aunt Evelyn that Ryan and I
are separated. Aunt . . .'

'Heavens!' Tessa exclaimed.

'Absolutely. I'm afraid it didn't go down too well.
Aunty sort of thinks that Ryan's pretty special.'

'And you?' Tessa queried.

'As my aunt so rightly said while we were having
dinner—I'm just not the type to fall in and out of love
every five minutes,' Meredith confessed, but, suddenly
ashamed of being so weak, she asked brightly, 'How are
things with you? Any new commissions or any... Say,
I never asked how that fund-raising affair in your village
went! Did you make lots of lovely money for charity
with your "Portrait While You Sit" stall?'

'I did, and it was terrific,' Tessa told her enthusi-
astically. 'Luckily it was a super sunny day. Actually,'
she added after a moment's pause, 'I was thinking of
trying my hand at sketching sitters as a business venture.
Since I suspect that it's going to be a tough world to
break into commercially, though, and since that drawing
I did of you, having more time than at the fête, was one

of my best, not to mention the fact that you have more to recommend you than most,' she threw in lightly, 'you might do me a bit of good if you showed my artistic ability around.'

Tessa had gone on in the same light, joking vein to state that that particular portrait would be a splendid advert for her when, laughingly, Meredith interrupted her to state, 'If I had that sketch I'd be only too willing to show it around, but . . .'

'You haven't got it?' Tessa queried, but soon realised where the sketched portrait had disappeared to. 'Ah!' she said, and a second later. 'It's happened before; it must have happened again.'

'What . . .?' Meredith began.

'I must have left it on the kitchen dresser,' Tessa started to explain. 'The last time I did that—though that time it was a note for the coalman—I opened the sitting-room door a bit too quickly, and the draught wafted it off the dresser and underneath.' Meredith, remembering the heavy kitchen dresser, was mentally ahead of her friend when she said, 'Well, it'll have to stay there for a while; that dresser's so heavy, it only gets moved when I decorate. Come to think of it,' she added, 'it's never been moved.'

Feeling much happier than she had been feeling, Meredith was grateful to Tessa that she seemed set on cheering her up, and she briefly forgot her hurt about Ryan as they chatted on some more. Then suddenly she wondered how her friend's brother was faring now that he had a new girlfriend. 'How's Aldo?' she enquired.

'Don't ask!' Tessa sighed. 'His new girlfriend's chucked him, and he's fed up again.'

'Oh, dear!' Meredith sympathised.

'You can say that again,' Tessa murmured, and changed the subject to invite her to return to Little Haversham whenever she could. Shortly afterwards they said cheerio to each other, and Meredith went and shared a pot of tea with her aunt.

Meredith was out shopping the next afternoon when, with no salve seeming capable of healing her wounded heart, she paused to give thought to Aldo Wallace. He had appeared devastated when Caroline had walked out on him, and yet in no time he had taken up with someone else. True, by the sound of it that second relationship had barely got off the ground before his new girlfriend had thrown him over, but had he found some heart's ease during the brief period of dating someone else?

She returned home with her shopping and supposed that, to have considered how Aldo coped when his love-life went sour on him, she must have been seeking to find some way, some sort of an anodyne, to lessen her own pain. The way for her, however, she realised without having to think about it, did not lie through a new man-friend. Apart from the fact that she never went anywhere to meet someone new, the whole idea of dating anyone but Ryan was repugnant to her.

A smile curved her mouth as she let herself back into the house, however. She could just imagine what her aunt would have to say if she, a married woman, had any gentleman visitor come to the door for her other than the man she was married to.

'I'm back, Aunty!' she called as she went along the hall into the kitchen to unload her purchases.

'I'll put the kettle on.' Her aunt joined her in the kitchen. 'I've just had tea with Lilian, so I won't have a cup myself,' she said, but there was something in her voice which Meredith's sensitivity picked up as indicating that her aunt was worried about something.

'What's wrong, dear?' She halted in the middle of putting a bag of sultanas away, and turned to take in her elderly relative's disturbed expression.

'Nothing's wrong, exactly,' her aunt replied and, deciding to take a seat, she waited until her great-niece had decided that the stowing away of groceries could wait and had also taken a seat at the kitchen table; then she said, 'Harold came to see his mother on Saturday and, according to Lilian, he was quite sharp with her when she remarked how she'd been cleaning windows the day before. Anyhow, one thing led to another, and it ended up with Lilian saying that she wouldn't mind moving to a house that had fewer windows.'

'Mrs Peplow's thinking of moving?' Meredith enquired slowly, able to see immediately why her aunt was so disturbed. Mrs Peplow and her aunt had lived next door to each other for years. Mrs Peplow was part and parcel of next door, and Meredith could well understand her aunt's disquiet should her friend of so many decades think of moving.

'It hasn't got as far as that, but I'm sure it won't be long before the idea really takes root,' Evelyn Simmons said anxiously. 'Harold's already told her he isn't the least interested in inheriting the house. He's all for her selling up and buying something smaller and more manageable. According to him, she'd have the money over from the sale and would be much better off financially than she is now.'

By the sound of it, Harold was really putting the pressure on for his mother to sell up. But, because her aunt seemed so worried, Meredith tried the best she could to calm her fears. 'Perhaps when she's thought about it seriously she'll decide not to move,' she said gently. 'They're all large properties in this neighbourhood, anyway,' she inadvertently added fuel to the fire, 'so Mrs Peplow won't...'

'That's the whole worry of it,' her aunt butted in agitatedly. 'If Lilian wants to buy something smaller, she'll have to move out of the area and—and I'll probably never see her again. Oh, Meredith,' she said fretfully, 'I just don't know what I shall do if Lilian moves away!'

Meredith could have kicked herself for what she had said, and quickly she left her chair and went to put an arm about her great-aunt's shoulders. 'I'll still be here, darling,' she tried to make her feel better. 'And we can always take a taxi and go to see...' But her aunt had a very different viewpoint.

'You won't be here!' she interrupted her. 'Any day now you'll be returning to your husband—as you should have done before now. I don't know how you've managed to stay away from your married home for this long,' she went on, her tone growing disapproving, and Meredith realised that she might have got her aunt off the worry of what she was going to do if her friend and neighbour sold up, but only at the expense of her severest lecture so far on her duty to her husband, and her husband's home.

When Meredith finally got away from hearing her aunt's firmly expressed opinion on the sanctity of marriage, she escaped up to her room, and wondered why she should feel the loyalty she did to Ryan. He did not deserve that she should hold back from telling her aunt what a cold and calculating toad he was, and that he had not meant a word of the vow 'to love and to cherish' that he had made in that church. And yet she had taken a good half-hour of her aunt persistently, if quietly, hammering away, her main theme being that it would please her better if she went and kept her 'till death us do part' vow, rather than stay with her.

She braved going down the stairs again in the early evening when she realised that she couldn't leave it any later to make a start on the dinner. She knew in her heart that she was welcome in her old home, but that it was just that it went against everything her aunt believed in that she and her husband should live apart.

In the kitchen Meredith busied herself making a winter salad, which her aunt especially enjoyed, while she silently mused that she did not see how she could possibly leave her aunt anyway—particularly if Mrs Peplow was likely to be moving.

Tessa had invited her back to Little Haversham, she ruminated, but there was no way she could go and stay—not for more than a night or two, anyway—and leave her seventy-nine-year-old aunt on her own.

So how in creation was she supposed to leave the dear soul to go and live with that chauvinistic swine she had married? How, for that matter, could she tell her aunt that he would probably have bars and bolts fitted to his door against her, should she so much as hint that she might be taking up permanent residence in his abode?

Beating eggs for cheese omelettes, another of her aunt's favourites, Meredith could see no way out of any of her difficulties. It seemed to her, in a moment of dark despair, that life was being a bit of a pill just at present.

Which was perhaps why, when Aldo Wallace rang her most unexpectedly later that evening, Meredith, maybe seeking some sort of relief, acted in a way which she would not have considered earlier.

Dinner had passed with her aunt being pleasant but for the most part preoccupied. But, since Meredith was fairly certain that what occupied her aunt's thoughts must be either or both of the subjects which they had last discussed, she did not think that to invite a renewal of the discussion would be in anyone's interests. Nothing her aunt said was going to change the fact that she was living apart from her husband, nor would it do either of them any good. Nor, as far as she could see, would it help for her to suggest that Mrs Peplow might not sell up and leave when her aunt, having spoken with Lilian Peplow more recently than she had, better knew what her friend was more likely to do.

'I'll bring the coffee into the sitting-room if you like, Aunty,' she told her when they had finished the washing up from dinner.

No sooner had Meredith arrived in the sitting-room with a tray of coffee, though, than the phone rang. 'It's for you,' her aunt advised, having answered the instrument while Meredith set the tray down.

Instantly Meredith's heart was all of a flutter. Had it been Tessa on the other end of the phone, Tessa would have delayed her aunt to have had a few words with her. Meredith's heart settled to a dull beat, however, when she realised that the same could be said of Ryan. Somehow, and despite the many faults which she was prepared to attribute to him, she could not see him being so impolite as to ask to speak to her without first passing the time of day with her aunt.

Wondering why the heck she should think that Ryan might ring anyway, Meredith took the phone from her and said, 'Hello,' down the mouthpiece.

'Hello to you, Meredith, it's Aldo,' a male voice that was nowhere near as attractive as her husband's replied.

Since Aldo had never phoned her before and as far as she knew did not know the Simmons surname to look her up in the book, Meredith had to gather her scattered senses to latch on to who he was.

'How are you, Aldo?' she enquired, suddenly aware that, where before her aunt had afforded her every privacy, she was not making any excuse to do something in the kitchen in this instance of her being telephoned by some male who clearly was not Ryan Carlisle.

'About the same as you, by all accounts,' Aldo answered, and, getting to the point of his call, 'Tessa tells me your husband is away on business for some while, and that you need cheering up.'

'I don't!' Meredith denied, as she wondered what had prompted Tessa to tell him anything of the sort.

'Well, I do!' he said. 'Which is why, at enormous expense, I've managed to get hold of a couple of tickets for a musical which I know you're just going to love.'

'You're asking me to go with you?' she enquired, and caught her aunt's quick look at her.

'I certainly haven't rung to ask your aunt,' he replied, and asked, 'Are you going to come with me, Meredith, or have I thrown my money down the drain?'

'When are the tickets for?' she enquired, wondering why she was enquiring anything of the sort, because there was not one single item pencilled in on her social calendar and nobody used 'I'm washing my hair' as an excuse these days, did they?

'Next Tuesday,' he told her, adding, 'It was the earliest date I could get. Tessa's given me your address,' he went on, and as if it was all settled, 'I'll call for you in plenty of time.'

'Thank you,' Meredith murmured, and it seemed that the whole thing *was* settled, for Aldo rang off.

Slowly she returned the phone to its rest and realised that, for all she had laughed quite a bit during her last telephone conversation with Tessa, she had not for a minute fooled her friend about how down she truly felt. She suspected too that Tessa, by telling her brother what she had about her husband being away on business, was leaving it up to her to tell Aldo as much or as little as she wanted.

'Was that "Aldo" Tessa's brother?' her aunt, unable to contain her curiosity, broke in through Meredith's thoughts.

'Er—yes,' she owned, and, sensing trouble before she began, 'He's invited me to the theatre next Tuesday.'

'You're not going, of course.'

'I am, actually,' Meredith replied quietly.

'Do you think that's wise, dear?' Evelyn Simmons enquired as though trying really hard to get to grips with the thinking of the younger generation. 'I don't think your husband would take very kindly to you having gentlemen friends, do you?'

To Meredith's way of thinking, her husband would not give a tuppenny damn how many 'gentlemen friends' she had, but, out of respect for her great-aunt's years, she refrained from saying as much, but confessed to the truth of it as she answered, 'I don't consider Aldo Wallace as a man-friend, Aunty, but more the brother of a friend. It sort of puts him in a different category,' she added, and realised, when she later climbed into bed, that as far as she was concerned that just about summed up how she felt about Aldo. She had earlier that day felt the idea of dating any man but Ryan to be totally repugnant. But she felt no such repugnance about going to the theatre with Aldo, quite simply because, with him being her good friend's brother, she just did not look on him as a date.

The weekend had to be got through before Tuesday, though, and Meredith spent most of it telling herself— as though telling would make it fact—that she was really going to enjoy going to the theatre.

It turned out to be a wet weekend, with the rain hitting the window-panes non-stop, so any idea she might have had to go a short walk with her aunt to maybe take her mind off her worries about Lilian Peplow's moving did not materialise.

It was still raining on Monday, and Meredith had proof that her aunt was indeed worrying when shortly after lunch she announced that she had a headache and was going upstairs to lie down for a while.

'I'll mix you a couple of aspirins, shall I, Aunty?' Meredith enquired.

'I'll manage without, I think, Meredith dear,' her aunt, a staunch anti-pill taker, replied. 'Probably the weather has as much to do with it as anything.'

Meredith was not duped for a second. But she watched as her aunt slowly climbed the stairs and wished there was something she could do which would ease her worries. If Lilian Peplow did decide to leave, though, Meredith could not see that there was anything that she, or anybody else could do about it.

Wondering if it was too soon to have cheese omelettes and winter salad again, she went to the kitchen and was just thinking along the lines of having something special for dinner when the front door bell sounded.

As she went to answer it, her mind was more on what would please her aunt's palate than on who might be on the other side of the door. But when she pulled the door open, every thought of the meal that evening vanished.

'Good afternoon, Meredith,' said the tall, grey-eyed man pleasantly.

A smile began somewhere deep inside her. But even as that smile rushed upwards and her heart leapt with joy to see the man she felt starved for the sight of, her pride roared into action. Who was she, what was she, that after the way he had behaved she should greet him with open arms?

Her smile never made it, and when she spoke, her voice was far from welcoming when, not waiting for him to state why he was there, and in contrast to his pleasant manner, she coldly and abruptly told him, 'My aunt's lying down and doesn't wish to be disturbed.'

'I haven't called to see Miss Simmons,' Ryan clipped, her antagonistic tone clearly not going down very well. 'I...'

'If you've come to see me,' Meredith cut through whatever it was he had been about to say, 'then you've had a wasted journey. I want neither to see you nor to talk to you,' she told him spiritedly, and saw from the aggressive and sudden jut of his jaw that he had not reckoned on her having any spirit when he had married her.

'Damn your...' he began, but as if determined not to start a blazing row on her doorstep—for she was not inviting him in—he checked.

Looking into his suddenly cold grey eyes, Meredith wanted them warm for her. Even as she fired, 'And damn yours too!' she desperately wanted to feel his arms about her. Even as they stared hostilely at each other, she yearned quite hopelessly to rest her head against his chest, and felt, in an insane moment of weakness, that she would have given anything to have been able to do just that. But the days of her reacting instinctively to her feelings were long gone, and that weak moment dissolved as common sense reminded her how untrustworthy her instincts had been in the past.

But Ryan, having checked what he had been about to say, seemed to have found some control. 'Good afternoon, Meredith,' he began again. 'I've called to...'

'Waste my time!' she chopped him off—it was either that or be swamped by his charm. 'Well, I don't need you, Ryan Carlisle, now or ever!' she blazed. 'So you can...'

She did not get any further. Twice Ryan had tried to be nice to her. She rather thought that was a record. He was not, he made it abundantly plain, going to try a third time. 'You may be able to totally ignore your responsibilities,' he sliced sharply through what she was saying, 'but I'll not ignore mine. I've...'

'You look on me as a responsibility?' she flared aggressively.

Angrily Ryan glowered at her. 'Hell's teeth!' he snarled. 'You're so...' He broke off, and seemed to be searching all the while to keep a hold on his temper, which she seemed to be having the uncanniest knack of provoking. 'Dammit, Meredith,' he said, a tough note still in his voice, although his tone was quieter, 'you're innocent enough not to know your way around the big world. Y...'

'No, I'm not!' she contradicted him tartly, feeling that she was fighting for survival—she had been weak before, and look where it had got her. 'Thanks to you,' she went on acidly, 'innocent is exactly what I'm not!' For her sins, she discovered that she had triggered Ryan's anger again, though she hardly thought that the accusatory nature of what she had said bothered him one whit.

But, 'Saints preserve us,' he roared, 'you reckon one night in bed with a man makes you less innocent—less worldy-wise—than you were? You may have lost your virginity, but . . .'

'That's all I am losing!' Meredith yelled, her brilliantly blue eyes flashing as she glared into taken-aback-looking grey eyes, her new-found temper spiralling. How could he refer to what had been so beautiful in her memory in such a tough and uncaring way? 'If you have any respect for me whatsoever after—after that episode,' she blazed on, 'then you'll do me the courtesy of not calling here again!'

Meredith knew as those words left her that she was very close to hot, scalding and shaming tears. There was only one thing she could do. Without another word, she closed the door on him.

CHAPTER EIGHT

THERE was a secretive kind of look in her aunt's expression as they sat at the breakfast table together the following morning, or so Meredith thought. On this occasion, however, she did not enquire into her aunt's little secrets.

Having just spent one of the worst nights of her life, the restlessness she had experienced before was back again, and Meredith felt stifled and in need of going somewhere. Though because she had no intention of leaving her elderly relative alone for any great length of time, the best she could come up with to satisfy this calling to be off somewhere was to go clothes-shopping.

'I think I'll go and look for something a bit different to wear to the theatre tonight,' she remarked as she cut her toast in two.

'You do that, dear,' Evelyn Simmons replied, to Meredith's pleased surprise appearing to have accepted the truth of her telling her that she considered her theatre escort more the brother of her friend than in the 'man-friend' class.

'I might be some time,' she thought to mention, having no interest whatsoever in buying anything new, but feeling that if she stayed out until gone midnight she would still not have got rid of the restlessness within her.

'That's quite all right, Meredith, dear,' her aunt smiled. 'Have lunch out if you feel like it. Mrs Key will be here at nine, but in any case I want to go round and have a chat with Lilian later—it could,' she added mysteriously, 'take me some time too.'

Meredith left the house shortly after the daily help had arrived, and spent a morning going over and over again the many things that had kept her awake last night.

By her standards, that had been quite some slanging match between her and Ryan on her doorstep yesterday. She thanked goodness that their nearest neighbour, apart from Mrs Peplow who was a trifle deaf, lived quite some way down the avenue.

Not that Ryan Carlisle had seemed to bother who overheard them, she mused, as she went into one shop and browsed through a few clothes rails and came out again. Cheeky swine, him and his 'You may be able to totally ignore your responsibilities, but I'll not ignore mine'! She would not be his responsibility, she would not!

'I'm just browsing,' she smiled at an assistant who came forward as she entered the next shop, but her mind was again engaged elsewhere as she flipped through dresses on the various rails.

Nor, she fumed, as without buying anything she left that shop and went to have a cup of coffee, would she accept that she had any responsibility to him.

It had taken her an age when she had tried to work out what his 'You may be able to totally ignore your responsibilities' had meant. What responsibility had *she* ignored, for goodness' sake! But, since she did not think she had been remiss in connection with any responsibility towards her family, the only answer that would fit seemed to be that Ryan had been referring to the responsibility of being his wife!

Feeling emotionally drained, Meredith continued on her round of the shops and owned that she didn't think she could take much more. She had told Ryan that if he had any respect for her he would not call at her home again, but he was a law unto himself. Regardless that he evidently felt some sort of responsibility for her, he would do exactly as he pleased anyhow.

She had her lunch out as her aunt had suggested, but it was only as she made her way home that it came to her what she must do. She had been burying her head in the sand about the possibility of her and Ryan getting divorced, she realised. She had panicked, she admitted, when he had called that time before with 'something to discuss'—not that he now seemed in any particular hurry, or surely he'd have taken a different line when he had called yesterday? But she supposed she must have matured considerably over these past weeks, for divorce suddenly seemed to her to be the only clear-cut answer.

Rounding the corner into the avenue where she lived, she decided that nor would she try to hide from her aunt what she was doing. As soon as she arrived home she would come out into the open and tell her—gently, of course—everything that was happening. Aunt Evelyn was going to have to accept that not all marriages were made in heaven and that hers, for one, was giving her emotional hell.

Temporarily, though, all thoughts of a divorce and how she would set about telling her aunt left Meredith when, on entering the house, she saw a business-suited man she had never seen before in conversation with her aunt. She had noticed a car parked outside, but it had seemed to be more outside Mrs Peplow's house, and she had thought Mrs Peplow was the one with the visitor.

'Ah, there you are, Meredith!' Her great-aunt broke off from what she was saying when she saw her, but, too involved apparently to refer to the absence of any dress-shop carrier, she said, 'This is Mr Bartram from Tranter's, the estate agents. He's just doing a little measuring.' And while Meredith was trying not to blink as she wondered what in the name of goodness her aunt was up to, her aunt was giving her something else to think about when she told Mr Bartram proudly, 'This is my grand-niece, Mrs Ryan Carlisle.'

'How do you do, Mrs Carlisle,' Mr Bartram said, as he stepped forward to shake her hand. But by the time Meredith had recovered from the delicious thrill of being called Mrs Carlisle, both her aunt and Mr Bartram were in another room.

Half an hour later Mr Bartram, having been offered a cup of tea by Evelyn Simmons but having politely declined, was being shown out by her. Meredith still had no clue to what was going on, but, since it was her view that it would not hurt her aunt to sit down for a short while, she made a tray of tea and carried it into the sitting-room. Thirty seconds later, a rather amazed Evelyn Simmons joined her.

'I can't get over it,' she said, if shaken, then looking shaken in a pleased way.

'Can't get over what, darling?' asked Meredith, keeping a watchful eye on her aunt as she seated herself in her usual chair.

'You remember how Porter was always moaning about the value of our money going down and down?'

'I remember,' Meredith confirmed quickly.

'Well, what I'm sure he didn't know, or he'd have said, was that the value of our property has gone up and up! Why,' said Aunt Evelyn as she started to recover, 'my father paid only hundreds for this house, but according to Mr Bartram it's now worth thousands and thousands!'

'You've—had the house valued?' Meredith queried, and, following that with what seemed to her to be a logical question considering the recent demise of the only Simmons male, 'You need to have a value for probate or something to do with Uncle Porter's will?' she asked.

'Oh, there's no need for that,' Evelyn Simmons said contentedly. 'The house didn't belong to Porter, or to Ogden either. It was always mine.' And, while Meredith took in what she was hearing, now, for the first time, her aunt explained briefly, 'My father, your great-grandfather, was one of the old school. He didn't believe in women going out to work, so when it didn't look as though I was going to get married he left the house to me.'

'I didn't know that!' Meredith exclaimed.

'It was a sore point with both Ogden and Porter, so it made for peace all round if nothing was said on the subject,' Evelyn smiled. 'Anyhow, I always knew that Father intended there should be a home here for both the boys should they want one, and that his willing the house to me was just his way of seeing to it that I had some security. When Ogden's wife died and he was left with a ten-year-old daughter, your mother, it seemed only right that Ogden should move back here.'

'So you could help bring my mother up,' Meredith said gently.

'Oh, I don't know about that. Ogden had very strict ideas about your mother's upbringing and employed a governess for her. Anyhow,' Evelyn Simmons seemed to give herself a mental shake, 'who'd have thought that this house would be worth such a vast sum? I must ring Lilian to see how she got on!'

'Mrs Peplow...,' Meredith began, feeling a shade puzzled.

'Of course, I didn't tell you, did I?' her aunt smiled, and went on to reveal what the secretive look she had worn at breakfast had been about. 'You know that, with it being such a dreadful day yesterday, Lilian telephoned instead of coming round?'

'She rang just before lunch as I was on my way to the kitchen,' Meredith recalled.

'That's right. Well,' her great-aunt took a breath, 'what she rang to tell me was that Harold had made her see sense and she was selling up, and that Harold had fixed up for the man from Tranter's to come round and value her property today.'

'Mr Bartram has valued Mrs Peplow's property as well as yours today?' Meredith queried, recalling how worried her aunt had seemed after lunch yesterday.

'Yes,' Evelyn nodded. 'Of course I hadn't arranged then for Mr Bartram to come here too. But after Lilian told me what she did, and also how, while she didn't mind leaving her draughty old house, she was going to mind like billy-o not having me next door, I got to thinking.'

'You thought—that you might sell up too?' Meredith brought out that which seemed naturally to jell.

'I did,' her aunt agreed. 'As soon as I thought respectable this morning, I went round to see Lilian to enquire how she'd feel if I sold up too and we tried to buy new—and smaller of course—properties near to each other.'

'Mrs Peplow liked the idea?' Meredith queried, having thought that there was nothing new she could learn about her aunt, but discovering that, in certain circumstances, she was a speedy mover.

'She was extremely relieved at my suggestion,' Evelyn Simmons beamed. 'And in fact, she had a suggestion of her own to make: that instead of buying two small properties next door to each other, we might buy one large flat between us. We might even move to the coast,' she announced, and, with a smile beaming from her again, beamed, 'Isn't it exciting? I can see absolutely nothing wrong with the idea. What with Porter gone and you married and shortly returning to your husband, this house is far, far too big for one.'

'It—certainly is exciting,' Meredith nodded, but the last part of what her aunt had said had triggered off the thought that, for all she had sounded totally genuine, was this all some gigantic ruse of her aunt's to get her to 'return' to Ryan? Suddenly Meredith found that she was doing a rethink on her decision to bring her plans to end her marriage out into the open. And she kept them to herself still when she enquired tentatively, 'Would you still be thinking of moving if—er—Ryan and I were to—er—divorce?'

The change in her aunt's expression was dramatic, as she replied frostily, 'Yes, I should. Though it's to be hoped, Meredith that you would never shame the family by going through any divorce court!'

Meredith was upstairs getting ready to go to the theatre that night when she ceased wondering at her weakness in not telling her aunt her intention of ending her marriage. It was not so much weakness, she realised as she stepped into a stylish, silky-look dress of deep blue, but concern that her aunt had had a surfeit of excitement for the time being.

Going downstairs to wait for Aldo, Meredith had even begun to wonder if she and Ryan could be divorced without her aunt ever knowing. Aunt Evelyn had spoken of moving to the coast. Providing no newspaper reporter discovered the fact that Ryan Carlisle of Carlisle

Electronics was now divorced—and the signs looked good, for not one of them had picked up the information that he had married—Meredith thought that for her aunt's peace of mind she might be tempted to try it.

At all events, she realised that, with the house being sold, she would soon have to start looking for somewhere else to live. She had just seen that her one-time stated intention to find herself a flat—and a job—was coming nearer all the time when Aldo Wallace arrived to take her to the theatre. Meredith had just introduced the smartly attired man to Evelyn Simmons, and they were about to get on their way, when her aunt made her blink by asking, 'What shall I tell your husband if he rings while you're out?'

'Oh—just tell him where I am,' Meredith smiled at her as it all at once penetrated that what her suddenly wily aunt was about was to make certain that Aldo Wallace was aware—just in case he was not already— that his companion for the evening was a married woman.

It had crossed Meredith's thoughts to consider that Aldo might ask a question or two on the way to the theatre about her husband's absence. But, save for the remark, 'Life's a bind when the one you love isn't around,' which merely showed fellow feeling, the journey to the theatre consisted mainly of Aldo telling her how he was trying to get back with Caroline.

Respite from a repetition of what she had heard pretty well non-stop before came when they entered the theatre. 'You've managed to get some good seats,' she smiled to him as they were shown to their places in the stalls, and then, for the few minutes that were left before the curtain went up, she studied the programme which he had handed her.

At least, that had been her intention when she had opened up the programme. But suddenly, and without knowing at all why—for there was no reason for it—her eyes were drawn, as if compelled, upwards and over to the left. And that was when Meredith, her world falling apart for the second time, knew that Ryan Carlisle would not be ringing her home that night—not unless he did it in the theatre interval, anyhow. Though she could not see him leaving his stunning-looking companion on any such whim!

Somehow—foolishly, she admitted, since Ryan was every bit a virile male—she just had not thought of him dating other women. But as she stared at the one box whose occupants stood out from all the rest in the theatre, while she noted that there were four people in the box, the other two faded into insignificance. Only her husband and the person nearest to him—in age as well as physically—stood out, and Meredith saw for herself that he did indeed date other women, his date for this evening in particular being a most attractive and elegantly turned-out dark-haired woman.

But, as her eyes had been drawn to that certain box, so in those first few seconds of her world being turned upside down she realised that, just as she had spotted Ryan and his companion, he had spotted her and Aldo.

But even though she felt as if she had just been struck the most crippling blow, her pride was not dimmed. When coldness, not to say antagonism, seemed to beam a straight icy line down from Ryan to her, and not so much as a smile or a wave of acknowledgement did he give, Meredith was swift to think: well, two could play at that game. 'I didn't know she was in it!' She took her eyes off him to smile at Aldo, exactly as if she had just noticed that some famous personality was listed in the programme.

She was never more glad that at that moment the theatre lights began to dim. As well as not being able to show Aldo the fictitious person she had been referring to in the programme, she welcomed the darkness in order to get herself together.

She did not enjoy the performance. Though, as she truthfully owned, she had very little idea of what was going on on stage. She was overwhelmingly conscious of Ryan through the whole of the first half, and she never quite knew how she kept her eyes from going repeatedly upwards and to the left.

'Let's join the scrum and get a drink,' Aldo suggested when the lights went up again at the start of the interval.

Without hesitation Meredith left her seat. It was one thing to sit in the dark knowing Ryan was there, but quite another to sit in full view of him and try to pretend she had never felt happier—not that he was likely to stare down at her again.

As she waited with Aldo for the people further along the row to move out into the aisle, though, she just could not resist another look up. Her heart sank further down to the depths when she saw that the box Ryan had been in was now empty, proving he had better things to do than to sit staring down at her.

Step by small step, with Aldo in front, they edged their way out of the row and up the gangway of the stalls with the rest of the crush going for refreshments. Aldo was still in front as she went through the stalls entrance along with the masses and, to avoid the stairs leading down from the circle, took a sharp right turn.

Meredith had just stepped into an area at the bottom of the stairs, however, when suddenly a pair of strong masculine hands shot out and in one movement had plucked her into the only space where no one seemed to want to go.

'Do you mind?' she snapped, the fire in her angry words hiding the turmoil that was going on inside her from being this close with her tall, superbly suited and most definitely appealing husband.

To her undying gratitude Ryan let go the tight grip he had on both her arms, but his manner was as tough as his look as he demanded furiously, 'What the hell sort of game do you think you're playing?'

The jackal! The nerve of him! Incensed by his accusing tone, she denied her fast-beating heart. 'As sure as hell not the same extra-marital game you're playing—you can be certain of that!' Meredith, with veritable sparks spitting from her bright blue eyes, hurled at him. She saw his brow shoot up, though whether because she had just accused him of having an adulterous relationship outside of his marriage or because he had heard jealousy in her voice she was not stopping to find out. But before she left, and to make fully certain he knew he must be mistaken over any idea that she might be jealous, Meredith let go with an angry, 'I want a divorce,' and, noting that the crowd making for the bar had thinned out, she turned swiftly round and went as quickly as she could to catch up with Aldo.

The rest of the musical passed in a haze as far as she was concerned, and she was glad when it was time for Aldo to take her home.

'Thanks for a terrific evening,' she told him when, having apologised for not inviting him in on account of her aunt being asleep, she said her goodbyes to him.

'It was good, wasn't it,' he said, and with the words, 'We must do it again if your husband's going to be away for any length of time,' he watched her let herself into her home.

'Still up?' she enquired of her aunt, who was almost always in bed by ten.

'Was it a good play?' Evelyn Simmons countered.

'I'll lock up,' said Meredith, and despite the gremlins that were gnawing away at her she had to grin. Her aunt knew full well that the *play* had been a *musical*. 'I'm going to miss you,' she told her affectionately when the two of them went up the stairs.

'I don't expect, with that fast car of your husband's, I'll be very far away,' her aunt got one in before she turned into her room.

'I don't expect you will,' Meredith agreed, seeing no sense in upsetting her by telling her that she had, only a few hours ago, told her fast-car-owning husband that she wanted a divorce.

Having spent half the night lying awake being torn apart by a new and very dreadful emotion called jealousy, Meredith finally fell into an exhausted sleep in the early hours of Wednesday morning. The consequence was that she overslept and, even though she rushed around madly, she still didn't make the breakfast table for the usual time.

'Good morning, Aunty. Sorry I'm late—I overslept,' she said as she hurried into the breakfast room.

'I'll forgive you,' her aunt smiled. 'Although I should like to make an early start.'

'On what, darling?' Meredith enquired, blaming Ryan Carlisle for the fact that, though she was showered and dressed and had made it downstairs, her brain did not appear to have woken up yet.

'Why, on the packing, dear!' Evelyn Simmons exclaimed.

'Packing?'

'It won't do itself,' her aunt replied. 'And I've a collection of eighty years of living in this house to sort through.'

'Oh, I see,' Meredith said, and even though the estate agent's board had not been put up in the garden yet, much less a buyer having been found for the house, she enquired, 'Where would you like to start?'

'Attic or basement?' Evelyn Simmons seemed undecided.

'Attic,' Meredith opted, deciding that, since the basement was not the warmest place, she had better tackle that section of the house herself.

She was glad to be busy that day. She needed to be busy that day. But, as busy as she was, running up and downstairs with plastic bags full of waste which in due course she would have to coax the dustmen to take, she could not get Ryan nor his very attractive date of last evening from her mind.

And, in remembering his sophisticated female companion, Meredith's estimation of her own charms took a severe blow. How on earth, in those early days, those days before they had married, had she ever been so crass as to let herself believe he had fallen in love with her? With the evidence of the stylish women he went for etched in her brain, Meredith again died a thousand deaths to think that she had ever been such an idiot.

But having been so down, the only way then was up. It was around three that afternoon that, having persuaded her aunt that it might be an idea if she went and had a little rest, she discovered that her aunt would only agree to rest if she broke off too.

'I could do with taking a bath and washing my hair,' Meredith told her, having pulled, prodded and pushed boxes and cases around prior to carrying them to her aunt to sort through.

Ryan was in her head the moment she left her aunt, as he had been off and on since she had opened her eyes that morning. But this time, instead of her feeling defeated, mutiny had set in. So all right, she might not have the sophistication of his female 'friend' of last night, but Ryan himself had once called her lovely, and had also commented to Monte Montgomery that she was beautiful.

Who the hell was Ryan Carlisle, anyway? Having hit rock-bottom, Meredith had no mind to stay there. The nerve of that man! she fumed again as she bathed and then shampooed her hair. Who was he to demand, in that accusing way he had, 'What the hell sort of game do you think you're playing?'? For, no matter how many times she looked at his accusing question, she could see it no other way: he was daring to take her to task for being at the theatre with some other man!

She fumed even more when later her aunt went around to next door to have a chat with Mrs Peplow, and she set about preparing dinner and thought again of his colossal effrontery. Her heart gave a crazy leap of excitement, just the same, when the ridiculous notion came fleetingly to her that for him to act in such a—'possessive' was the only word that fitted—possessive kind of way surely had to mean that he felt he had some rights over her?

It *was* ridiculous, and she tossed the notion away. Ryan had no rights, nor did he want any. She remembered then how he had claimed that it was up to him to provide for her, and she was confused again at the complex man he was, and again she was briefly defeated.

She rallied, however, to rail silently against him again. The fact that he should actually have dared to question her the way that he had at the theatre while, figuratively speaking, he'd had that stunning-looking woman on his arm made Meredith wish she had said far more than she had.

The trouble was that one always thought of something brilliant and cutting after the event. Though perhaps there had not been very much to add after her final, 'I want a divorce.'

Her aunt looked quite pleased with life when they sat down to dinner, and was full of the plans she and Lilian Peplow were making. Which in turn reminded Meredith that she should be doing something about her own plans.

That evening she and her aunt washed up together while Evelyn Simmons chatted away, and Meredith tried to keep her concentration on what she was saying while wishing she could find some of her aunt's enthusiasm for finding somewhere else to live.

Meredith was loading up the coffee tray prior to taking it into the sitting-room when they heard the phone ringing. 'I'll go,' Evelyn Simmons said, and was on the way to the sitting-room as she added, 'It might be Lilian with some more information.'

Smiling quietly to herself that the two near-octogenarians were acting just like a couple of schoolgirls, Meredith finished loading the tray and followed in the direction her aunt had gone.

No sooner had she entered the room, though, than she at once knew that it was not her aunt's friend on the telephone. For, 'It's for you,' her aunt told her, and, saying the pleasantest goodbye down the mouthpiece, which at once told Meredith that it was not Aldo Wallace on the other end, she held out the receiver to her.

Meredith's mouth went dry as she took the phone from her aunt. Which she instantly recognised was absolutely stupid, since her caller was most likely going to be Tessa anyway. Perhaps though it was that something, something which she could not quite put her finger on, in her aunt's pleased look that made her dry-throated and wary.

Finding her voice, she said, 'Hello.' Then she promptly went weak at the knees when the most superb voice to her in all the world answered. Though the way he answered swiftly made her stiffen, and at once stung her into feeling mutinous again.

'Since you clearly don't want me in your home, you'd better come here to my place!' he grated, apparently suddenly given to ordering her around.

'Why the h...' she immediately started to respond, but just in time she remembered that her aunt was still in the same room '...dickens,' she amended quickly, 'should I?'

'I refuse to discuss our divorce in the street, on your doorstep, or in the foyer of some theatre!' Ryan rapped back toughly. 'I'm going away tomorrow,' he added sharply, and was the bossiest she had known him as he commanded, 'Come now!' and bang, his phone went down.

For several seconds after the line went dead, Meredith stayed gripping on to the receiver. At first she could not take in the fact that, in answer to her request that he do the courtesy of not calling at her home again—and clearly having taken exception to having their domestic matters discussed in front of a theatre audience—Ryan had telephoned to order her to come to his place. Then she was totally stunned that in response to her demand for a divorce last night, he had rung to agree that he too wanted a divorce.

Knowing deep in the heart of her that she did not want a divorce, Meredith replaced the receiver and was suddenly beset by raging jealousy. So much for her thinking that Ryan was in no hurry about getting a divorce! Screaming jealousy twisted unmercifully at her insides as she realised just then why Ryan was so agreeable to a divorce—and for him to ring so promptly must mean that he was now impatient to get the divorce under way. His reason, of course, being none other than the woman he had been at the theatre with last night!

'Is something wrong, dear?'

Her aunt, her voice sounding concerned, quickly brought Meredith to an awareness that she was not alone. 'No, no, nothing at all,' she answered as blithely as she could. But because she had no idea what expression she had worn, and supposed that some explanation was called for, she added, 'That was—Ryan,' and was so knotted up inside that she momentarily forgot that her aunt had answered the phone, so knew quite well who it was. 'He—wants me to go and see him—*now*—would you believe?' She tried to laugh scornfully.

But her aunt saw nothing to laugh at, scornfully or otherwise. Though to Meredith's frustration she did smile, apparently in total agreement with her great nephew-in-law's bossy edicts, as she replied, 'Then you'd better go, Meredith,' and added, 'Take a taxi, dear.' Meredith was staring at her, intending to do nothing of the kind, when happily Evelyn Simmons tacked on, 'There'll be no need for me to wait up tonight—you probably won't be back tonight anyway, come to think of it,' she said on a cheerful afterthought.

'I'll...' Meredith began, and realised that she had just been about to state that she would be back—when in actual fact she had no intention of going anywhere. Only, as her voice faded, she suddenly started to get mutinous again. Dammit, what was she afraid of, that she should refuse to go and see him? Being divorced could not be any worse than what she had now, for goodness' sake! 'I'll go, then, Aunty,' she heard herself say, and, the decision made, she picked up the phone, this time to ring for a taxi.

So he wanted a divorce, did he? she mutinied as she began to dial. Well, far be it from her to stand in his way!

CHAPTER NINE

MEREDITH was still mutinying against Ryan Carlisle when the taxi dropped her off at the smart apartment block where he lived. Nor was her mutiny in any way softened when Preston, the hall security man, greeting her as if he fully remembered her, said, 'Good evening, Mrs Carlisle,' and, as he smartly preceded her to press the lift call button, remarked politely, 'Mr Carlisle is expecting you, madam.'

The over-confident, overbearing swine! she fumed as the lift carried her upwards, her anger increasing by the second that Ryan had been so sure she would jump to his command that he had phoned down to tell security she would be arriving shortly.

She would not jump to his bidding, though, she would not! she thought angrily as she stepped out of the lift. She was here now because *she* wanted a divorce, and the sooner, the better. Ryan had said he was going away tomorrow—what was there to wait for? By the time he came back, she would have consulted her solicitor.

Fleetingly it passed through her mind to consider that perhaps their two solicitors would be the best people to consult rather than each other, but she brushed the thought aside. Before either of them consulted lawyers, they had to agree what grounds to use, didn't they?

A small flutter of nervousness unexpectedly seized her as she reached the apartment door of the man she had married. Angrily she pushed nervousness behind her and, stretching out a finger, even while aware that the efficient Preston had in all probability telephoned Ryan to say she was on her way up, she stabbed hard, and defiantly, at his doorbell.

A few moments later the door was opened. 'Come in,' he said tersely, his tone as uninviting as his look.

Without a word, her face as unsmiling as his, Meredith crossed over his threshold and waited politely, if stony-expressioned, for him to invite her across the hall and down the three steps into his sitting-room. The sight of him, tall and casually clad in a summer shirt and trousers, was already working against her mutiny, though.

Striving to get herself under control after the initial impact of seeing him, she began to distrust her emotions when, as his hand came out as though he would guide her down into his sitting-room, she felt a strange confusion. Deciding against allowing his touch to disrupt her emotions, she stepped smartly away from him and went down the steps.

'Take a seat,' Ryan invited coolly as he joined her near to one of the two couches in the room.

'This shouldn't take long,' she responded, her voice, she was glad to note, as cool as his. But, since it seemed sensible to do as he suggested, she took a seat on one of the couches. She watched as he lowered his length on to the one opposite, then began, 'You want a divorce, and...'

'I never said that,' he cut her off before she could finish.

For a second or two her heart behaved ridiculously, for Ryan appeared to be saying that he did not want a divorce. But, casting her mind back to what he had said, Meredith knew, since he had asked—no, ordered—her to come so they should discuss their divorce, that whatever he had or had not said, a divorce was what he wanted.

'Well, I'm not here for the good of my health!' she snapped tartly.

'Hmph, you've changed!' he grunted.

'Was I supposed to stay nice and biddable once I'd got what I wanted?' she retorted, not missing the way his eyes narrowed at her deliberate use of the word 'biddable'.

'You're saying that you really were the phoney I first took you for?' he challenged.

'What else?' Meredith kept a grip on herself to reply. It was something of a revelation to her that Ryan had distrusted her from the beginning. Although, she quickly recalled, it had only taken until their wedding day for the truth of what he believed to be revealed. Firmly she took herself in hand. Ryan must never know the true reason why she had married him. 'You knew I only married you to get away from my family,' she thought there would be no harm in reminding him.

'It doesn't appear to have done you much good, does it?' he rapped, for some reason which was completely obscure to her not seeming to thank her for the reminder.

'Not then,' she replied, and, her tone softening, 'Neither of us knew then that we would soon lose Uncle Porter. But,' she went on brightly, knowing he would remember who Mrs Peplow was, 'yesterday Aunt Evelyn and Mrs Peplow put their properties up for sale. They'll most likely move into a large flat together. Which,' she let him know, 'will leave me as free as air. So all's well that ends well.' She even managed a civilised smile. 'Now, what grounds shall we use for our divorce?'

Ryan did not return her smile. Indeed, it was more of a glower than a smile she got from him as he said shortly, 'You tell me!'

Which, Meredith thought, was very unfair in the circumstances. He had been around far more than she, so he must know how these things went. Her smile disappeared and she felt sorely like glowering at him in return, for, when she thought of how much more he had been around, it brought to mind that stunning creature he had been with last night. 'How about—adultery?' she was driven to ask—but only to be astonished by Ryan's reaction.

'*Yours?*' he snarled explosively, his expression suddenly murderous.

'Certainly not!' she hurled back in outrage. 'I meant *you*!' she said hotly, and was astonished yet again when not only did his murderous expression abruptly vanish, but he actually smiled.

'Certainly not me, Meredith,' he told her with some charm, and, to make her bones melt, 'I haven't looked at another woman since the day we met.'

'Oh,' she murmured, and did not even recognise that his charm had just rendered her ready to lie down and let him walk all over her until, just then, she remembered that it had not been Scotch mist he'd had for company at the theatre last night! 'Oh!' she said again, only this time it was said out of sudden fury, not only with him, but herself. 'Not much you haven't looked at another woman!' she lashed out waspishly, determining that never again would she be taken in by him. By no chance was she going to be led up the garden path twice! 'You'll be telling me next that your *friend* at the theatre last night was...' she spoke hotly, but was stopped cold

in her tracks when, with his grey eyes searching her
expression, Ryan cut her off.

'You sound—jealous?' he murmured thoughtfully.

Panicking wildly, Meredith scorned, 'Oh, for heaven's
sake!' every bit as if she had never shaken hands with
that green-eyed monster. 'I'm not jealous, I'm just angry
that you can tell such blatant lies when I've seen you
with other women with my own eyes!'

'Correction—woman, in the singular,' Ryan replied,
and, his expression serious, he told her, 'I didn't lie to
you intentionally,' he told her, 'It's just that, apart from
certain innate considerations, with Claudine Benetti
negotiating business with all the toughness of a man, it's
easy to overlook the fact that she's female.'

'Easy?' Meredith queried sceptically, positive, as she
recalled the stunning woman, that Ryan was playing her
for a fool. Before he could answer that question, though,
her recently acquired sarcastic tongue had found another
sceptical question. 'And what would the "certain innate
considerations" be, I wonder?' she scoffed.

Fully expecting him to come back with something short
and pithy on what she could do with her questions *and*
her sarcasm, she was surprised into believing him when
unhesitatingly he replied, 'More—common courtesies to
a female on the board of one of the overseas firms my
company deals with. Claudine had come especially to
do business with us,' he went on. 'When my PA discovered that she'd a liking for musicals, it was not only
courtesy but everyday working practice to entertain her
at the theatre when our business was satisfactorily
concluded.'

'You don't regularly take her to the theatre, then?'
Meredith queried, and wanted to bite her tongue out as
her enchantment at hearing that she had not the slightest

cause for jealousy faded slightly and she realised that for her sanity's sake she must keep her mind on the divorce.

'No, I don't,' he replied, and very nearly melted her bones again when, looking deeply into her eyes, he continued, 'Had my—er—reception—been more favourable when I came to see you on Monday, I'd have asked you to act as hostess for me at the theatre last night.'

'You came to see me on Monday to ask me to...' Her voice petered out, and almost she apologised for the way she had been with him. Almost, but not quite. She had to be tough, otherwise he *would* walk all over her.

'That was part of my reason for coming to see you,' Ryan agreed, without letting her know what the other part was. 'When you lost your temper,' he went on, for all the world as though he was a saint, 'there was nothing for it but for me to accede to your request not to call at your home again, and to ask one of my directors and his wife to make up a four.'

Meredith could not find fault there, or call him a liar, because there had been four people in the box, even if she had been so torn apart by jealousy and pain that she had no memory of what the other two had looked like. But, as her heart rejoiced that she had no need to be jealous of the woman who she now knew was called Claudine Benetti, so Meredith again had to find some toughness in herself. It had gladdened her heart that Ryan had called at her home because he had wanted her to act as his hostess. More, she was positively thrilled that it should have occurred to him to ask her. But was she to be such a weakling that she swooned with every magical, wonderful word that fell from his lips? His de-

vious, enchanting but entirely self-motivated lips, her
saner self prodded.

'Well, we both know that you'd do anything when it
concerns business, don't we?' she exclaimed acidly, and
only just held back from making some sarcastic reference to the fact that she would not be in his apartment
now, waiting to discuss their divorce, had he not prized
his business above his bachelorhood.

Ryan, though, had quickly picked up the acid in her
tone, and Meredith realised that she must not only be
stronger where he was concerned, but more careful too,
when, with a more gentle note in his voice, he asked,
'Did I hurt you, Meredith, when I married you for those
shares?'

'Of course not,' she lied promptly. 'Though I'd have
appreciated a little more honesty from you before we got
that far,' she added, and realised, belatedly, that she had
left herself wide open to be challenged—what about her
honesty in pretending to care for him in order to get
away from her elderly relatives?

He did nothing of the kind, however, but, accepting
full blame for his actions, he owned, 'I could have been
more honest, I agree. I was wary, though,' he owned,
and explained, 'There was I, with the shares in Burgess
Electrical having dried to a trickle, searching all routes
to find some way of ultimately being in a position to
control that firm. Then one day, straight out of the blue,
and without so much as a word of prompting on my
part, a beautiful and totally unknown young woman
bearing the name-tag Miss M. Maybry buttonholes me
to blurt out that her father had left her thousands and
thousands of the precise shares I'm desperate to get my
hands on.'

Meredith sailed briefly up on a see-saw of delight to hear Ryan describe her as beautiful, only to plummet speedily at his factual 'buttonholes me'. Though since, in order to be strong, she thought it better to keep away from anything personal, she opted to keep her questions as impersonal as possible.

'You thought there was something fishy?' she asked.

'Wouldn't you, given the same circumstances?' he countered.

'Well, it didn't stop you from finding out where I lived and what my telephone number was, did it?' she retorted, her face unsmiling.

'Neither was too difficult to discover,' he replied calmly. 'Though, to be accurate, it was Monte Montgomery who set the wheels in motion to trace you, not I.'

Meredith did not like what she was hearing one little bit. 'The two of you wanted control of Burgess Electrical?' she questioned, remembering that Monte Montgomery had known, when she had not, that Ryan had married her for her shares, 'Confound it, Ryan,' she exclaimed, 'the pair of you must have laughed yourselves silly behind my back!'

'Don't be ridiculous, it wasn't like that!' he retorted sharply.

'Like hell it wasn't!' Meredith flew. But although she was feeling angry enough, and hurt enough, to march straight out of Ryan's apartment, she suddenly checked. She must not take everything he said so much to heart— she must not. She had to appear as if nothing he could say would hurt her. He must not gain so much as a hint of the extent of her caring for him. Yet, if she did not take control of her feelings and keep everything on that impersonal basis she was looking for, then he was much too clever to miss how things were with her. 'So,' she said, having gathered some control and hoping to make him believe she had just been taking what he said apart, 'why not tell me, if it wasn't "like that", how it really was?'

'I should like to,' he said simply, and when she had begun to doubt he would, he accepted her challenge and began. 'You'd spoken to me of your shares that Friday, as I mentioned, and I was still trying to work out what your angle was when later that day Monte Montgomery rang to thank me for my support at the opening.'

'An...' Meredith had been going to challenge his use of the word 'angle', but as she recalled that he thought she was ready to use the bait of her shares to get away from her relatives, she quickly changed what she had been going to say. 'Monte Montgomery rang to thank you for your support?' she queried—when she was not the slightest interested in Monte Montgomery.

'Believe it or not, even the most confident of us get nervous on some occasions,' Ryan replied quietly, his grey eyes steady on hers.

'I'll—believe it,' she mumbled, and he went on.

'Since Monte knew all about my aspirations regarding Burgess Electrical, it seemed only natural to tell him of my amazing encounter with you.'

'What did he say?' she asked, accepting that his amazement stemmed from the fact that, with everyone chasing around for Burgess Electrical shares, there she had been suddenly announcing that her father had left her thousands and thousands of them.

'Like me, he too wondered what your angle was. Though he was of the view that you'd read somewhere how most firms in the electronics field were showing an interest in Burgess Electrical,' Ryan replied. 'He thought, however, that it might be worthwhile getting in touch with his window-dressing section. In no time at all he had been on to some agency, and was back on the phone to me again.'

'This time to give you my address and phone number?'

'Precisely,' Ryan agreed, but without knowing it he made her heart race a little when he went on, 'I couldn't get you out of my mind the whole of that Friday night. Again and again, your face would come back to haunt me.'

A small sighing sound escaped her, but rapidly Meredith collected herself and got herself more of a piece. 'Well, it would,' she said, complimenting herself that in the circumstances her voice should come out sounding so even. 'Here was your chance to get your hands on those shares—if, of course, you played your cards right.' Her even tone started to falter, but she quickly dragged it back, as she reminded him, 'You made use of my phone number the next day, and rang asking me out to dinner.'

'And spent a good part of that dinner wondering if you really were as innocent as you looked and if I should tell you that the value of your shares had gone through the roof recently.'

'You decided against telling me, quite obviously,' Meredith put in.

'Let's say that my better judgement prevailed,' he commented, and, looking at him, Meredith was struck by the fact that his remark was not in any way boastful, but seemed to be said in a more self-derisory fashion than anything else. 'By then, of course, I'd been introduced to your family.'

'Hmm,' she took up, fully intent that he should not wander off the right track. 'That's when you realised what my "angle" was. You realised, almost at once, that I shouldn't at all mind living somewhere apart from my elderly relatives?'

Ryan nodded. 'If,' he qualified on her behalf, 'it could be done without causing them any pain.'

'You knew, then,' she made her face blank as she queried, 'that I was ready to marry you as a way out?'

'You didn't waste any time in telling me that those shares went to your husband on your wedding day,' Ryan confirmed.

'It's a wonder to me, what with you wanting those shares so badly,' Meredith said coolly, 'that you didn't propose to me on our first date!' Oh, lord, she thought, when Ryan gave her a sharp look, I'm getting personal again. 'Ah!' she said brightly, as hurriedly getting away from the personal. 'You hadn't seen proof then that my father had any shares to leave, much less that, as I'd told you, my husband was to inherit them if I married before my twenty-fifth birthday.'

'You were kind enough to "accidentally" leave the papers I needed in my car the second time we went out,' Ryan smiled, and Meredith smiled too because, quite plainly, he believed she had left the file containing the share certificates and her father's will in his car on purpose so that he could check them out. When in actual fact she had clean forgotten about the file until later. 'It soon became clear, since there appeared to be no way in which I could purchase those shares from you, that I was going to have to marry you,' he said, causing Meredith to have trouble with her smile.

'It's so tough at the top!' she said acidly, and thought, terrified, that she had completely blown her cover when Ryan looked at her sharply.

'Have I really hurt you so much?' he questioned quickly.

'Hurt me?' she scorned. 'Good grief, Ryan, you know better than that!'

Strangely, and to her surprise, he seemed more disgruntled by her reply than pleased, and he went on harshly as if he had suddenly got tired of telling her 'how it really was'. 'Once everything checked out,' he told her coolly, 'I again got on to Monte. You didn't look twenty, but if you were already twenty-five I'd have lost out on the deal.'

'And you couldn't have that!' she inserted, the pain he had caused her and was still causing her chipping away at the hard covering she was trying to protect herself with.

'No, I couldn't,' he agreed. 'I'm a businessman. For my company's future, I wanted those shares at any price. When I told Monte why I wanted to know your age, and he reported back that the agency records gave your age as twenty-two, he also advised that I shouldn't drag my feet. I invited him there and then to be my best man.'

'Before you'd asked me to marry you!' Meredith exclaimed, but quickly concealed her resentment that he should be so sure of her by saying evenly, 'though I suppose it was a foregone conclusion that I'd accept.'

'I thought so,' he replied. 'Though, frankly, I did feel some disquiet the first time I kissed you.'

'My apologies,' Meredith said drily, and loved him with all that was in her when he laughed as though she had amused him.

And then, quite electrifyingly, he said quietly, 'I think, Meredith, that that was the moment when you first started to get to me.'

'I did—what?' she asked chokily. But even while her heart began to race, scepticism was at work in her. She would not be led on a false trail—she would not. 'Oh, you mean because I—er—didn't seem to have been kissed before, or have too much experience of men?' she followed up aloofly.

'You hadn't *any* experience of men,' Ryan corrected, starting to look a little tough at her tone. 'But yes,' he admitted, 'that was part of it. And since it seemed you wanted a little romance in your life, I was prepared to play my part there too. Th...'

'How benevolent of you!' Meredith could not resist saying, and was ignored for her trouble.

'But everything seemed so easy,' he continued.

'Well, it was, wasn't it?' she tossed in, seemingly uncaringly. 'I needed an out, you needed the shares—the two fitted together perfectly.'

'*Too* perfectly!' clipped Ryan. 'As I was very soon to discover, there *had* to be a catch.'

'A catch?'

He nodded, and, looking at him, Meredith was reminded of his saying only a short time ago that even the most confident of men sometimes felt nervous. Because somehow Ryan, who had never been anything other than confident, suddenly seemed—as if he was a little unsure of his ground!

Shrugging away the notion as fantasy, she heard his voice as strong and as terrific as ever when he began to document, 'I'd thought it out all very carefully beforehand. I'd looked into every aspect of any marriage between us—or so I thought—and couldn't see any one problem that I couldn't handle. My bride, as I perceived her, was a young woman who, as well as being sweet, was, as you overheard me telling Monte, biddable into the bargain.'

'As you said,' Meredith murmured, keeping the tightest rein on her tongue, 'no problem.'

'Exactly,' he agreed. 'Were you ever to become a problem, though, or tiresome in any way, then I had the answer to that too. Quite easily,' he went on to openly admit, 'I would get a divorce.'

'Hmm,' Meredith murmured, as she tried to appear completely relaxed on the couch she was sitting on, when in actual fact she was suddenly as tense as a tautly strung bow. Because here, at last, with that word 'divorce', they had reached the purpose of her visit to Ryan's apartment. She somehow managed a smile, though, as she queried, 'I still don't see where the "catch" is?'

'It began, my dear Meredith,' he said softly, his words, his tone, threatening to ruin her determination never again to be weak, 'when, before we'd been married twenty-four hours, you were taking a furious swipe at me, and showing me quite clearly that I'd made the most serious misjudgement of character when I'd called you biddable.'

'I'm not sorry I hit you!' she found some stiffening to tell him hostilely.

'I deserved that slap, and more,' he undermined her again by agreeing with her. 'And more was what I got too,' he said slowly, 'when instead of telephoning you in Little Haversham to tell you your uncle was ill, I found myself making the journey to Derbyshire to come for you personally.'

'But you were in Derbyshire anyway—on business!'

'I agreed with you that I had business in the area,' Ryan replied, 'but I came especially—for you.'

With her blue eyes widening as she stared at him, all Meredith could hope as her heart suddenly gave the most tremendous surge of energy was that she would give none of her inner feelings away.

'You came because you believed my uncle to be most seriously ill?' she queried quietly.

'I came because, despite what I might at that time have been telling myself to the contrary, there had awakened in me a need—to see—you.'

Swiftly Meredith looked away from him. Oh, dear heaven, if only it was true that Ryan had felt a need to see her! But common sense soon quieted the wild clamourings of her heart. Had she not been ecstatic once before—on her wedding day, if memory served—only to receive the biggest let-down of her life a very short while later? It was not going to happen again, she resolved. Whatever Ryan said, she must listen to him with her head and not her heart.

'As I remember it, you didn't seem very pleased to see me,' she remarked as coolly as she was able.

'I was still mentally kicking myself for making the journey,' he said evenly, his eyes fixed on hers as he reminded her, 'As I recall it, your greeting to me was not over-effusive.'

The cheek of him! Meredith fumed. After the way he had shattered her dreams, he thought she should have been all over him! She bit hard on the angry retort that sprang to her lips, though, when caution prompted her that Ryan had had no idea of the dreams she had woven.

'There was no need for me to pretend any more, surely?' she queried, and left him to work out that, since they had both got what they wanted, she had no need to pretend that she even liked him if she did not want to.

'Perhaps not,' he replied stiffly. 'I was merely your husband. Not,' he said succinctly, 'your kissing friend.'

The nerve of him! Meredith thought, yet again, that he really was the limit. 'You can't make anything out of my friendship with Tessa's brother,' she told him shortly as it suddenly occurred to her that Ryan might in some obscure way be leading up to citing Aldo in his divorce petition.

'You've no feelings for him, other than those of a friend?' clipped Ryan, his eyes suddenly burning into hers as if the answer really meant something to him.

'No!' Meredith answered sharply, and because it upset her that he looked to be ready to soil her name to get his freedom, 'I might have had a crush on Aldo in my teens, but I was over that the one and only time that he kissed me on the mouth,' she told him woodenly—and was amazed at Ryan's reply.

'Thank the lord for that,' he said, and seemed so sincere that Meredith knew she must have got it wrong and that he had never meant to couple Aldo's name with hers in the divorce courts.

'That sounded rather heartfelt,' she remarked, and wished with all she had that she knew what sort of game Ryan was playing, when he said,

'It was heartfelt! You can have no idea of the jealousy I've had to endure on account of your friend's brother.'

'Jealousy!' she exclaimed, and could only stare, and wonder at her husband's powers of invention.

'I didn't know the meaning of the word jealousy until suddenly there you were introducing this man Wallace, who called you "pet", and who kissed you goodbye,' he told her. Remembering clearly how, when she'd introduced Aldo, Ryan had spoken to him curtly, and had seemed to have no time for him, Meredith felt her emotions were on a merry-go-round when Ryan, his manner wry, went on, 'And, if it wasn't enough that you should awaken that serpent jealousy in me, then, when all along I'd counted it as entirely my prerogative to make the decision with regard to a divorce, in less than no time you steal my thunder by talking to me about "when we divorce".'

'Shame!' Meredith mocked as she again took severe charge of the putty-like person she would be in his hands if she didn't do something about it. And even though she could tell from the sudden glint in his eyes that Ryan was finding her mockery very difficult to swallow, she went on to drawl insolently, 'We seem to have taken a very roundabout route, but at last we're back to the beginning. You want a divorce, and I . . .'

'That's just it,' he stopped her in her tracks, but paused, and again seemed nervous, before he added bluntly, 'I don't want a divorce!'

'You don't want . . . But . . . That's why I'm here!' she recovered from being winded to complete a sentence. 'I'm here to discuss . . .'

'You're here because I want, and need, and, quite simply, *have* to talk to you uninterrupted,' Ryan cut her off.

'You have—do you?' Meredith questioned warily, as she wondered which garden path he was taking her up this time.

'I do,' he confirmed, and set her heart thumping when, as if the space between them was too great, he moved quickly and before she knew it had come to share the couch on which she was sitting. 'I do,' he said again, and as she looked at him anxiously, 'Don't be afraid, Meredith,' he told her gently. 'If I've hurt you in the past, then I swear I'll never hurt you again.'

Sorely then did she need to scoff that, for goodness' sake, she had never been hurt by him for a moment. But the words to put any such idea out of his mind would not come, and she was left having to scrape up what intelligence his nearness had left her with, and to question, 'You—er—need to talk to me because you—er—don't want a divorce?'

'How I do *not* want a divorce,' Ryan said softly, and when she just stared at him, he went on, 'How or when you started to weave your spell over me, whether before our wedding day or afterwards, I cannot tell. Wh...'

'Spell?' she whispered.

'Yes, my dear,' Ryan breathed, and gently took her two hands in his as he told her, 'I don't know how or when; all I know is that, as suddenly as you came into my life, with hurricane force you were gone from it. And I,' he said quietly, 'discovered that I didn't like it.'

'You didn't like my—er—hitting you?' she asked chokily, thinking he must be calling the strength of her slap to his face a 'hurricane force'.

'I didn't like you leaving, sweet Meredith,' he replied, his grey eyes warm and serious on hers. 'I had told you that you were your own person now,' he continued, and had her staring at him open-mouthed when he ended, 'but when images of you began to penetrate my thoughts at all times of the night and day, I had to face the fact that anything you did as your own person from now on, I wanted to include me.'

'You're—not serious?' she just had to ask, when she could see for herself how serious he looked.

'I've never been more serious in my life,' he told her, and confessed, 'I hadn't wanted a wife, but, since I needed those shares badly enough to take a wife with them, a divorce seemed a most satisfactory outcome in due time. The catch, which I hadn't foreseen,' Ryan went on, 'was that I should start to miss my wife, and that, in missing this woman who had so recently become a part of my life, I should realise, when time and again I wanted to see her, how very much attracted to her I had become.' Meredith's attention was riveted on him when he brought out, 'The catch was that, ultimately, I had to accept that a divorce was the very last thing I wanted.'

'Oh,' Meredith said on a gossamer breath, and she very nearly smiled, and she was very nearly ready to do whatever he asked of her. Just in time, though, she recalled—with something of a jolt—the charm Ryan had used one evening when he had said to her 'You'd better marry me, without delay' and she had asked 'You love me?' He had never answered that question, and she had been foolish enough to believe that she had no need to put such a question to him anyway. But that was then— and this was now. It seemed to her then, though, that she would have only herself to blame if she asked the same question so foolishly a second time. However, if Ryan was as sincere as he would have her believe—then what were a few other questions between friends? But, because the feel of his skin against hers as he gripped on to her hands was doing nothing to aid her power of clear thinking, she hurriedly pulled her hands out of his hold. 'Forgive me, Ryan, if it seems that I've no great trust in y-your remarks,' she managed then, 'but, if I might be allowed to recap...'

'Ask anything you want to ask, and I shall answer honestly.' Ryan, she saw, seemed eager to have every one of her doubts brought out into the open.

'You said you came to Little Haversham that first time, especially to see me?'

'And the second time too,' he startled her by confessing.

'But—you had an elderly relative living that way; you told me you...'

'I lied,' he interrupted her gently.

'But you're not lying now?'

'I've done with lies and pretence,' he replied promptly.

'I see,' Meredith murmured, but she knew she was merely playing for time, because she could not see anything at all—and she was so desperately afraid. All her instincts were urging her to go along with everything he said, to believe he had no intention of telling her another lie. But, on his own admittance, he had lied to her before.

'I don't think you do see,' he said quietly. 'At least, if you do see, you're determined not to trust, nor to believe that you have me so much at sixes and sevens that I barely know where the hell I'm heading.'

'I seem to have—er—quite some—er—p-power over you,' she stammered, having meant it to come out sarcastically but discovering that there was not a shadow of sarcasm in her voice. And Ryan took her stammered comment seriously, when he replied,

'And then some! Without my even knowing it, something about you had started to get to me. I'd seen you sweet and gentle with your elderly relatives. Patient with your uncle, and guardian to him one early morning when, having spent the most restless night of my life in your bed, I came to your uncle's room to find you.'

'I don't think I could be called much of a guardian to him.' Meredith, on the lookout for further lies, found some will to oppose him.

'You were asleep when I came in to say I was going,' Ryan admitted, and defeated her opposition in one fell swoop when he added, 'You were asleep, and lovely, and as I looked down at you something so unexpectedly tender came over me that I just had to kiss your brow before I left.'

'I—w-woke up,' Meredith remembered, her voice more than a degree wobbly. That was before she recalled what had taken place only a very short while later. 'And I suppose you "just had to kiss me", too, when I went to the front door with you to see you out!' she exclaimed tartly. And, rushing on regardless of his surprised look at her harsh change of tone, 'Your kissing me then had nothing at all to do with the fact that Aunt Evelyn was standing there watching, I take it,' she added, and could have crowned him yet at the same time thrown herself into his arms when a smile of utter charm broke on his well-shaped mouth.

'Oh, Meredith—Meredith,' he breathed. 'I kissed you then, little love, because you were smiling so sweetly at me and I found you totally irresistible. I kissed you because I wanted to, and discovered that it was like kissing you for the first time. It was only after I kissed you that I saw your aunt,' he informed her. 'And at that time I was glad she was there, because I was striving for sanity and realising that I had made the right decision when, before I left your bedroom, I faced the fact that I needed to get away to try and get things into perspective.'

For a moment or two Meredith was too dumbstruck to say a word. Then, haltingly, while hating her weakness in asking, she just had to question, 'Did you g-get things into perspective?'

'Did I hell!' Ryan gritted, thrilling her. 'Logic was suddenly a thing of the past. I'd left you early that morning because I needed to think, and spent the rest of the day wanting to come back to you.'

'But you didn't.'

'I told myself I was being a fool,' he said, a self-derisory smile quirking his mouth. 'Which of course didn't stop me doing the next best thing.'

'You telephoned,' Meredith supplied.

'And you let me know—since I was supposed to be flying off somewhere that night—that you didn't want to hear from me for two weeks.'

'That's—true,' she said, refraining from telling him how much she had wished she had not said that.

'So can you wonder that I'm furious when, having spent over a week fighting the compulsion to ring you, when I do give in, as give in I must, I discover that you aren't cosily ensconced in your family home as I'd supposed, but cosily ensconced up in Little Haversham with your friend—and, for all I knew, your friend's amorous brother.'

'Amorous!' Meredith exclaimed, while wondering if her heart would ever beat normally again.

'Did I not mention that I've discovered myself a jealous man?' Ryan queried, and Meredith knew then that if she didn't take a firm hold on the situation, his charm was going to sink her.

'Yes, you did,' she said as coolly as she was able. 'Jealousy, instigated by my being friends with Aldo and...'

'And which friendship brought matters to a head for me last night,' Ryan quietly cut in.

'How?' she asked, wanting to run, wanting to stay, but above all trying to bury her instincts under the intelligence of her head.

'It was more than enough to have me want to physically rearrange his features when I saw that he was daring to escort *my wife* to the theatre,' Ryan replied. 'When, with him only yards away, you told me you wanted a divorce, to merely render him temporarily unconscious seemed mild to the murderous tendencies that awakened in me then. But, while I was able to outwardly conceal my inner feelings, I later knew that I'd have to take some action, or I would go demented for sure.'

'Which—is why you telephoned me tonight?'

'Which is why I rang and asked you to come where we could talk unhindered,' Ryan agreed, his phrasing, to Meredith's ears, slightly different from the way she remembered the telephone conversation going. 'Thoughts of you have had me sleepless more times than I care to remember,' he went on, 'last night having no equal. I've thought, eaten, dreamt you, Meredith Carlisle,' he told her. 'And seemed to have spent half of my life trying not to pick up the phone to ring you. But tonight, before I rang, I just knew that I couldn't endure another night without taking that action.'

Her breath caught in her throat, and Meredith desperately needed help from somewhere. But she was in this alone, and where her instincts were concerned she had learned a very hard lesson, a painful lesson. Indeed, she could still feel the pain from learning that Ryan had married her, not from love, but because of those shares. 'Ah!' she exclaimed when, on thinking of those shares, all her logic banded together to tell her that, whatever Ryan was up to now, it just had to have something to do with those shares. 'Those shares,' she said suddenly, and ploughed on through his look of surprise that she should bring them up when they had not been discussing them. '*Your* shares,' she corrected. 'Th . . .'

'They're not mine any longer,' he told her, and as it sank in that he must have sold them and—if the price he got was anything like the price she'd seen quoted— they must have realised a tremendous amount, Meredith

went cold from head to foot. 'With everything else happening, I forgot...' Ryan broke off, but even as he said,
'Just a minute...' and went swiftly from the couch to
stride across the carpet and up the three steps to dis-
appear round the hall in the direction of the bedrooms,
Meredith lost interest.

It was not the money. In fact, she didn't care then
that Ryan must have done a deal which had netted him
a colossal sum. It was the fact that he had deceived her
yet again. She had no experience whatsoever of what
went on with regard to the stock market, but as she heard
movements indicating that Ryan must be looking for
something, she was somehow sure that she was about to
be beguiled again. How it was to be done, she had no
idea. Why, since he had admitted to having sold his
holdings in Burgess Electrical, she knew even less. All
she did know, however, was that Ryan for some reason
didn't want a divorce, and that towards that end, though
of course without actually committing himself, he had,
for some nefarious business reason of his own, been
trying to get her to think he had some feeling for her.

Struggling hard not to cry out in her anguish at having
nearly been taken in a second time, Meredith was on her
feet when, with a folder in his hands, Ryan came swiftly
back into the room.

He seemed to take the three steps down into the sitting-
room in one as he noted that she was standing and that
she had a set expression on her face. 'Here it...' he began.

'Goodbye, Ryan,' she said frigidly, and as she realised
she should have done over the phone, 'My solicitors will
be in touch,' she told him icily.

'Your solicitors!' he exclaimed, for all the world as
though he had no clue to what she was talking of.

'About the divorce,' she told him hotly, and went to march across the carpet.

As she went to pass him though his hand shot out and he caught hold of her and spun her round. 'Divorce...' he grated, and Meredith knew that there must be something peculiar about the lighting in his flat, for he seemed to have lost some of his colour as he demanded, 'Have you not heard a word of what I've been saying?'

'I've heard every single word,' she replied, her nails biting into her palms as she fought for control. She had to get away. She had to go, and go now.

'It means nothing to you?' he retained his firm hold on her to ask, a hoarse note she could not allow herself to believe in coming to his voice. 'None of what I've said...'

'Means a thing to me,' Meredith told him, only by sheer effort of will managing to keep her tone hostile.

'You can't mean that!' he exploded. 'I thought... You seemed...'

'Would you mind very much taking your hand off my arm!' she told him coolly. 'I want to leave.'

'But you can't go!' he said in an anguished tone. 'I won't let you go!'

Oh, dear heaven, Meredith thought, and knew that if she did not get away now, he truly would walk all over her. 'What's the matter, Ryan,' she found enough strength to make a final effort, 'can't you take it when things don't map out the way you want them?' Watching through eyes which she was doing her hardest to keep cool and in keeping with her sarcastic tone, she saw a muscle move in his temple and observed that he seemed to be making gigantic efforts to get himself together. 'Do take your hand off me, there's a dear,' she went on to

drawl. 'As you once said, I'm my own person now—
and this person wants to go home.'

To her utter relief, she had no need to say more. Ryan
dropped his hand from her and, as though seeking to
grasp at what control he could muster, he abruptly turned
his back on her. Meredith turned too, in the opposite
direction, and made rapidly for the steps that led to the
hall.

Tears were stinging her eyes as she negotiated the three
steps, and although she felt certain that he would not
come after her, a flutter of panic made her take a side-
step along the hall. When she was out of his line of
vision, should he have turned about, she brushed an
emotional stray tear from her eye, and was about to head
for the apartment door when, for some unknown reason,
she flicked a glance to the right and along the hall. Ab-
sently she took in the fact that Ryan had been in such
a hurry to get back to her with that folder that he had
left his bedroom door open.

Her glance was still on the wide-open bedroom door
when she noticed something that was to instantly dry
any tears that might have been held back waiting to be
shed.

The swine! she fumed. The unmitigated, treacherous
swine! For there on his bedside table, positioned to face
his bed, stood a picture in a frame. Fury like none she
had ever known hit Meredith then. And as that fury
raged in her and mingled hotly with jealousy, she went
storming into the bedroom and snatched up the picture.

Quite what she intended to do with it she was not absolutely sure, though the desire to hit him over the head
with it for being able to talk as though lovingly to her
while he had the picture of some other woman on his
bedside came near to the top of the list.

But that was only until, expecting to see the face of Claudine Benetti, or someone sophisticated and beautiful like her, Meredith looked down at the framed picture in her hands. And then, as the world started to spin, she almost fainted from shock.

She did not faint. But as incredulity became credulity, she moved. With her heart banging away against her ribs, she went slowly from Ryan's bedroom and along the hall, until she was standing on the top of the steps. The folder that had been in his hand had been tossed down on to a low table near to one of the couches, but Ryan himself, still with his back to her, had moved to a drinks cabinet and appeared to be pouring himself a stiff drink.

'Ryan!' she called, and saw him freeze. Then she saw the bottle go down, and then the glass, and he turned. His expression by then, though, was a chiselled mask, and Meredith had an idea that this was how he would look when he was at his most unapproachable. She weathered his grim, steely-eyed scrutiny, but when he had not a word to say her courage momentarily faltered. She had the framed picture in her hands, though, and even if she still could not quite believe it, another glance at the laughing and carefree face sketched there made her grasp at courage and hold out the picture to him. 'Where—did you get this?' she asked him huskily.

For a moment she thought that Ryan was not going to answer. But, as though he had just sensed how vitally important her discovery of that picture by his bedside was, answer her he did, albeit curtly.

'I stole it.'

'Fr-from Tessa's kitchen dresser?' Meredith asked, nerves getting to her, because she already knew from where he had stolen it.

'While you went upstairs to get a jacket,' he confirmed, the gravity of his features remaining unchanged.

'Why?' she just had to ask then. And, when it seemed as if he thought he had told her all he was going to tell her, she pleaded, 'Please, Ryan, won't you tell me why you stole it, why you had it framed, and wh-why you wanted a picture of me on your bedside table?'

'I'm not in the habit of repeating myself,' he replied at long last. 'I've already told you why.'

Meredith's voice had dried up, but she regained it, only for her words to come out sounding more husky than ever when she told him, 'No, you haven't—actually.'

'I—haven't?' he enquired slowly.

She shook her head and, with her eyes fixed on his, she thought she saw that an alert look had come to his eyes as she asked, 'Couldn't you—just this once—repeat what you think I should have heard, but haven't?'

His answer was to take several strides towards her, as though he needed to read in return what there was in her eyes to be read. He stopped, though, somewhere in the middle of the carpet. 'It's—important to you?' he queried.

Meredith swallowed hard. 'Very,' she whispered, and nearly crumpled when the words she had been aching to hear, but never thought that she would, were suddenly there, floating from him to her.

'Then, dammit,' he rapped, 'I love you.'

'That,' said Meredith, as she stepped down one carpeted step, and then another, 'is quite the most wonderful thing you've ever said to me.'

'You—love me?' he questioned tensely.

Meredith nodded. 'Ever since I first saw you,' she confessed shyly, and, hearing his shout of elation, had no memory whatsoever of stepping down the last step.

She had memory only of Ryan coming for her and of being tightly enfolded in his arms as if he would never let her go. Then she had a sensation of minutes happily ticking by as they clung, and just clung to each other. Then his lips were over hers in a kiss of pure bliss and, still in his arms, she discovered that they were on one of the couches, with the picture she had held now down on the table to the side of them. Then, and only then, did they find space to talk.

'Oh, my little love!' Ryan breathed, and seemed to be having some trouble convincing himself that it was as she had said it was. 'Can it be true—that you love me?'

'I fell in love with you at first sight,' Meredith told him, never happier, and having the same sort of trouble herself.

'At that lift at...'

'Before that,' she said, and explained, 'I'd seen you at the opening ceremony, and I knew then, before I'd even spoken with you. That's why—later—at the lift, I just found myself speaking to you.'

'Oh, dear love,' he breathed. 'You're sure?' he questioned.

'I'm sure I'm in love with you, if that's what you're asking,'she told him. 'Though at the time I couldn't be-, lieve it. I went along to the staff rest-room to get over the shock, but it was when I decided that I'd better go home that I saw you at the staff lift.'

'And you still felt the same?' he asked, stretching out a hand to gently trace the curve of her face.

Meredith nodded, and she smiled as she told him, 'I've never accosted anyone in my life, yet before I knew it, there I was babbling on about my interests in the electrical field.'

'I'm so glad you did,' Ryan smiled, and with his hand still gentle on the side of her face, he leaned forward and tenderly kissed her, long and lingeringly.

'Oh,' she sighed when their lips parted, and her heart hammered away within her at what he could do to her. 'I know that it wasn't so immediate with you, but when did you...' Her voice tailed away, but it seemed that Ryan knew exactly what she was asking.

'All the signs were there that you were getting to me in a big way,' he told her lovingly, 'but I knew most definitely that I was in love with you on the night we shared your bed.'

'You knew then?' she queried.

'I knew then,' he confirmed, touching his lips to the side of her face when a faint flush of pink coloured her cheeks. 'I hadn't meant to stay in your bedroom with you, as you know, my shy darling,' he said adoringly. 'Neither had I meant to make love to you. At least,' he qualified as he gently kissed her again, 'thoughts of our making love were not in my head when I decided it was absolutely nonsensical for me to go through hell on that small chair in your bedroom while you had half a bed going spare. Anyhow,' he went on, 'in your anguish over your uncle you were restless in your sleep, and I had the most overwhelming need to try to comfort you. It seemed only the natural thing to do to take you in my arms.'

'I woke up once, and found myself in your arms,' Meredith told him.

'I know,' Ryan murmured.

'You know—knew!'

'I felt you go rigid in my hold, and knew you were awake and probably scared, so I thought it best for you to sort out for yourself that you'd come to no harm. All I wanted to do then was to hold and comfort you, though not from any sexual motive. It was then that I knew I was most definitely in love with you. The wonder of it was still with me when you later woke up, and what happened seemed meant to happen, only, on my part, with love.'

'Oh, Ryan,' Meredith sighed, 'it was the same for me too. But . . .'

'But?' he took up, wanting nothing held back, not now.

'But later I got to thinking that you'd made love to me, not from love, but because you had to be the boss. I thought,' she went on, 'in the days that followed, that, having had me "biddable" in bed, you had no further interest.'

'Great Scott!' he exclaimed, and stared at her in wonder at the way her thoughts had gone. 'I was aching to hold you in my arms again,' he told her. 'But you'd told me not to touch you, and I thought you must be going through some kind of guilt feelings that while your uncle was dying, you'd forgotten everything when the needs of your body were awakened.'

It was Meredith's turn to stare. 'Really?' she gasped, realising that Ryan was far more sensitive than she had given him credit for. 'Is that why . . . ?'

'My heart was aching for you, my darling,' he gently cut in. 'And each time I saw you I had a tremendous yearning to take you in my arms. Yet each time, rather than upset you with everything going on about your Uncle Porter, I managed to hide my feelings. By then I wanted desperately to bring you back here with me. I came specially to discuss our future one day, but . . .'

'But I told you I'd nothing to discuss with you!' Meredith remembered with more surprise. 'Though you did agree with me when I told you I would stay with my aunt,' she said quietly.

'Until we could make some arrangement to ensure that she wasn't left on her own now her brother had gone, I couldn't do anything else but agree,' Ryan told her. 'It was out of respect for your recent bereavement,' he revealed, 'that I had to let you walk away from me that afternoon when you reminded me of your recent loss by saying you'd return to sorting out your uncle's belongings. Though it was on remembering our conversation that afternoon, and how you'd told me that, if you'd ever been so idiotic as to have some caring for me, it would never have survived what you'd found out on our wedding day, that I began to hope.'

'Did I give myself away?'

Ryan smiled. 'Only in so much as, when I microscopically sifted through my knowledge of you, and of your endearing ways, I discovered that it just didn't tie up that, had you sincerely cared, you could be so fickle as to turn so immediately into someone who didn't care. The Meredith I thought I was beginning to know was the true sort who, once having given her heart, would give it forever. I, my darling, have spent this long day in an agony of uncertainty and hope.'

'Oh, Ryan!' Meredith cried, and as he hauled her close up to him they kissed, and kissed some more, until gently he pulled back from her.

'I think we've both known a little bit of hell, sweetheart,' he said. 'But, for my sanity's sake, do you mind if I don't kiss you again until I've cleared up every last whisper of anything I've ever done that has upset you?'

'I'm sure there's nothing else,' she smiled shyly.

'Forward baggage!' he grinned, and seemed utterly enchanted when she burst out laughing.

'The time we've wasted,' Meredith smiled, as she thought back over the weeks since her uncle had died.

'I thought it best to keep out of the way while you adjusted to your uncle's death,' Ryan owned. 'Though, had I met with a better reception on Monday, to have you act as my hostess to a visiting foreign buyer was to have been the start of my campaign to woo you.'

'Honestly!' she gasped. 'Oh, Ryan,' she mourned. 'And I told you that not only did I neither want to see you nor talk to you, but I didn't need you!'

'And I witnessed at first hand what a demon of a temper my biddable little wife has,' he smiled. 'You didn't mean any of it, did you?' he teased.

'I lied,' she confessed.

'As I lied when, to get you over here, I told you I was going away tomorrow.'

'You're not!'

He shook his head. 'Were you in any small way jealous of Claudine Benetti, by the way?' he wanted to know.

'I slipped up, didn't I?' Meredith said sheepishly.

'I thought I'd glimpsed a touch of green in your eye at the theatre last night. When I wasn't in a lather from my own jealousy of your companion, I took quite some heart at the idea that you might be jealous of mine.'

'Well, whoever would expect a woman as stunning as that to be on the board of some business or other?' Meredith excused herself, and was quite mystified when Ryan suddenly leaned to the table and picked up the folder lying there, and then asked,

'Have you looked in the mirror recently?' And, when she looked at him blankly, 'You're more than a little stunning yourself, Meredith, yet I'd say you've enough shares here to warrant you a seat on the board of Burgess Electrical.'

She opened her mouth in puzzlement, then closed it again. '*I* have?' she questioned, not taking in at all what

he was telling her, although there was some vague
memory tugging at her of him saying earlier something
about those shares no longer being his.

'I feel sure that your father always meant you to have
these shares,' Ryan told her, and added as he looked
with love down into her bewildered eyes, 'If you'd care
to take a glance inside this folder, you'll see that I've
had all the shares transferred to your name.'

'But—but . . . But those shares go to my husband on
the day I marry . . .'

'There's nothing in your father's will that says your
husband can't have them transferred back into your new
name, Meredith Carlisle,' Ryan smiled.

'But—but you wanted them!'

'I discovered that I wanted your love and trust more,'
he replied gently. 'If you want to vote your shares with
me when the time is ripe, you can. But you don't have
to. The decision,' he said, 'is all yours.'

Looking at him, her eyes were filled with her emotion.
'Oh, Ryan,' she said on a breath of sound, 'I do so love
you.'

'I'm glad about that,' he said softly, and tenderly he
enfolded her in his arms and kissed her.

Many long minutes passed, but finally they drew apart,
when Meredith, slightly delirious from his kisses, murmured, 'Did I—er—mention that I might soon have
nowhere to live?'

The grin that split Ryan's face was absolutely wonderful for her to see. 'You could try living with your
husband, Mrs Carlisle,' he invited.

'I think,' Meredith replied a shade breathlessly, 'that
I'd like to do that.'

His arms tightened about her, and again they kissed.

HIDDEN HEART

HIDDEN
HEART

BY
JESSICA STEELE

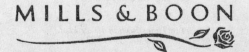

MILLS & BOON LIMITED
ETON HOUSE, 18-24 PARADISE ROAD
RICHMOND, SURREY TW9 1SR

MILLS & BOON, the Rose Device and Duet are trademarks of the publisher.

First published in Great Britain 1990 by Mills & Boon Limited

© Jessica Steele 1990

Australian copyright 1990 Philippine copyright 1990 This edition 1995

ISBN 0 263 78954 3

Set in Times Roman 10 on 11pt. 19-9502-59913 C

Made and printed in Great Britain

CHAPTER ONE

MORNAY HAYNES awakened on that June morning, saw
from the bedroom window in her small flat that the sky
was blue, and sighed contentedly. She closed her eyes
and snuggled down, intending to snatch another five
minutes before she prepared to meet the challenge of
another week.

Annoyingly, though, sleep eluded her. It was that word
'challenge' which struck a jarring note, she rather supposed. When she thought about it—and it didn't take
much thinking about—she was forced to acknowledge
that there was little that was challenging in her existence.

Mornay sat up in bed and contemplated the bed-
covers. She was twenty-two, and had a nice, safe secretarial job working for nice, safe Mr Probert in the nice,
safe surveyor's office at the town hall. She lived in a
small flat in a nice part of the town of Reefingham—a
flat found and approved of by her parents two years
previously—and she had a nice, safe boyfriend—'dull'
Claudia called him.

Torn between wanting to smile at pleasant thoughts
of her sister Claudia, and feeling that she ought to frown
at her sister's unflattering comments about nice and safe
Robert Naylor, Mornay pushed the button down on her
alarm clock before it could ring, and got out of bed.

Five minutes earlier, she mused, as she pattered to her
bathroom, she had been quite content with her lot. Now,
she felt decidedly dissatisfied.

Over her ablutions Mornay gave herself something of
a lecture on how she should thank heavens for her present
lot. Up until two years ago she had lived at home with

5

her parents, who had the strictest views on how their two daughters should be brought up. Was it any wonder that Claudia had rebelled?

Mornay climbed out of the shower and dried her slender body, with her thoughts gentle on her sister. Claudia was five years older than herself and had been seventeen when, having come in late from a date, she'd had that last terrible row with her parents, and had left home.

'It's like living in a strait-jacket living in this house!' she had declared angrily to an unhappy twelve-year-old Mornay, who'd watched her adored elder sister throwing a few of her belongings into a suitcase.

'Where are you going?' Mornay had asked unhappily.

'I won't tell you that, love, because they'll only get it out of you,' Claudia had replied, 'and I don't want them turning up to tell me how ungrateful I am after all they've done for me. But—I won't forget you.'

She hadn't either, Mornay reflected as she munched on her usual piece of breakfast toast. Claudia was forever mentioned in the house, though not in a loving way but as an example of what she would become if she did not take heed of what her parents were telling her.

For a few months Mornay had experienced the confusion of having it drummed into her that Claudia was bad while at the same time only being able to remember the nice things that her big sister had done.

Then, two months after Claudia had left, Mornay had come out of school to see her sister waiting for her at the school gates and her confusion had disappeared like magic. As happiness entered her heart at seeing Claudia, she had no longer fretted whether she should hate or love her sister.

'Claudia!' she'd cried joyously.

'Does Mother still have her hair done on Friday?' Claudia had asked, giving her a hug.

Mornay had nodded. 'I'm supposed to go and have a cup of tea and a scone at the Blue Bird Café and meet her in an hour,' she'd replied. She would by far have preferred to go home and wait for her mother there, but she was not allowed to.

'Good,' Claudia had smiled. 'I could do with a cup of tea myself.'

There had followed many months of Mornay now looking forward to her Friday afternoon cup of tea with a scone. For now, with Claudia working at a job which gave her Friday afternoons off, Mornay always had her sister's company.

Claudia was still held up as a model not to be copied, however, and though on one never to be forgotten occasion Mornay tried to stick up for her, the lecture she subsequently received was long and exhausting. At the end of that sternest of lectures, Mornay was left in no doubt that her parents considered Claudia wayward, and was in no doubt that they were going to take the gravest care that she did not go the same way.

'Have you told the folks that you see me every Friday?' Claudia asked some months later, seeming to Mornay to be positively glowing, she looked so happy. Quickly, though, Claudia was cancelling out the fact that she had asked anything of the sort. 'That was a dumb question,' she grinned. 'Of course you haven't, or you wouldn't be here now.'

'Do you want me to tell them?' Mornay asked, happy in her sister's company and feeling then that she could do anything she asked of her. But Claudia shook her head.

'No,' she said, and was grinning again when she asked, 'Will they be home tonight if I drop round?'

'You're coming back?' Mornay asked, wide-eyed.

'Not on your life!' Claudia promptly knocked that lovely idea squarely on the head. 'I'm getting married, and since...'

'You're getting married!' Mornay squealed, excited
and a week off her thirteenth birthday.

'Let everybody know!' Claudia laughed as a few
genteel heads turned to look at them.

'But... Oh...' Mornay thought she had the answer.
'You're coming to ask the parents' permission.'

'I don't need it, I shall be eighteen the week after your
birthday.'

Claudia then went on to tell her how Mr and Mrs
Overton, Gerry's parents, although in no way as re-
pressive in their attitude to their offspring as her own
parents, liked 'things' done properly, and were insisting
that the wedding was no hole-and-corner affair.

'Were it not for the fact that Gerry's parents have very
generously said they'll give us the deposit for the most
wonderful old house we want to buy over at Penny Dale,
I'd get married without letting Mother and Father know,'
Claudia revealed. 'But, as they do like things "nicely
done", and since Gerry *is* their only chick, he and I will
call round tonight to give my parents the good tidings.'

Five months after Claudia and Gerald Overton were
married, Claudia gave birth to baby Emily. Mornay was
delighted; Gerry's parents, after coming to terms with
the situation, were delighted. Claudia and Gerry were
supremely happy. The only people who were not overjoyed were Mornay's parents.

Nor were they overjoyed when, in direct contrast to
her own overstrict upbringing, Claudia's daughter went
through the first two years of her life without ever
hearing the word 'discipline'. Emily was two years old
when baby Alice was born, and once again everyone save
Claudia's parents were delighted.

'It's to be hoped that they bring this one up better
than that dreadful Emily,' Mrs Haynes sniffed, taking
no pleasure in being a grandparent to a child she considered to be a little hooligan and not at all mollified
that the blonde, curly-haired child looked the picture of

health and happiness. Two years later, baby Florence arrived, and when another two years had gone by baby Prudence made her arrival on the scene.

'Mother still carping on?' Claudia had asked of the nineteen-year-old Mornay who had taken the bus the five miles to Penny Dale to babysit her four nieces while Claudia and her husband went for a rare evening out.

'You know Mother,' Mornay said lightly, and was then slightly startled to find herself under Claudia's scrutiny.

'Why don't you leave?' her sister asked bluntly.

'It's not so bad.'

'Yes, it is, it's dreadful. For goodness' sake, I'd left home two years by the time I was your age!'

'But——'

'But nothing,' Claudia said crossly, and pressed on, 'What with your fantastic skin and your gorgeous blonde hair, not to mention your terrific big blue eyes, you're absolutely stunning, Mornay. No way should you be spending your Saturday nights babysitting, but with Mother and Father certain you'll come to a bad end "like your sister" and making you nervous to take home any gutsy flesh and blood male—not that I'd bother letting them vet my dates anyway——' she inserted hotly '—you might just as well start now to take a liking to knitting and stray cats.'

'What's wrong with knitting and stray cats?' Gerry Overton asked as he came into the room at the tail-end of what his wife was saying.

'Claudia's having a "go" at me,' Mornay told him, genuinely fond of her tall and thin shaggy-bearded brother-in-law who adored her sister.

'You know you're more than welcome to move in here any time it gets too much for you,' he told her seriously.

'Thanks, Gerry,' Mornay smiled, but she knew she would stay put.

'You're too soft,' Claudia told her. And life had gone on much the same for another year, the only difference being that occasionally in that year Mornay had experienced the stirrings of something akin to a feeling that she would not mind moving into a place of her own.

During that year, though, she had started going out occasionally with Robert Naylor. Robert was kind to old ladies and dumb animals, was keen on bird-watching—and was never going to set the world on fire. Mornay knew within half an hour of her first date with him any vital chemistry that would make them more than 'just good friends' was lacking. But, since Robert wasn't pushy and didn't want to be forever attempting to kiss her or hold her hand, he became her most regular boyfriend.

It was a bonus that her parents liked him, Mornay thought, and came out of her reverie to realise that she was locking the door to her flat and was on her way to work. She went down the stairs to the outer door, musing that she must have eaten her breakfast and, out of habit, tidied her flat and rinsed her cup, saucer and plate, all without knowing it.

As she walked over to the area where she garaged her car, however, her thoughts went back to how her parents' liking Robert had come in very useful when two years ago her father had been offered promotion which he felt he would be a fool to turn down. The only snag was that he would have to leave Reefingham in order to be within much easier commuting distance to his head office.

'There's nothing for it, my dear,' he had addressed his wife over the dinner table, 'we'll have to sell up and look for something nearer to Birmingham.'

'I rather fancy Solihull,' Dorothy Haynes had replied. 'Is Solihull close enough to Birmingham?'

Mornay was a quiet third at the table while Solihull was discussed. She knew that she would have to make the move with them, but knew also that, while she had nothing against Solihull, she wanted to stay in

Reefingham near to her sister, in whose erratic household she had known innocent fun and laughter.

'You're very quiet, Mornay!' Fifteen minutes into the conversation Dorothy Haynes suddenly noticed that her younger offspring had said not a word. 'Oh!' she then said, and, as though something had just occurred to her, 'I see,' she had gone on, and then, making Mornay stare at her wide-eyed, 'You don't want to come with us, do you?'

'I...' Mornay murmured, a feeling welling up in her that she must tell her parents exactly how she felt, but, against that, years of experience warning that if she didn't want her parents going on at her endlessly that she was going to turn out just like her sister, she had better stay quiet. Suddenly then, though, she grabbed at a strand of courage. 'I——' she began.

'Of course she wants to come with us, my dear,' Mornay's father interrupted when she had been on the brink of hauling down coals of wrath upon her head. 'Don't you, Mornay?'

Strangely, though, Mornay found that she had a streak of stubbornness in her. At any rate, she discovered that, whatever the outcome, whatever the extent of the verbal battering she might be letting herself in for, something in her was refusing this time meekly to acquiesce. Suddenly she was discovering that her 'anything for a quiet life' view of the past was starting to splinter.

'I—wouldn't mind—er—staying on in Reefingham,' she actually heard her own voice speak up.

'What did you say?' her father demanded heavily.

But before she could discover whether or not she had the courage to repeat it, her mother was putting a quick two and two together, and coming up with a totally erroneous five. 'Robert Naylor,' she announced to her husband.

'Robert N——' he repeated. Whether the fact that she had been dating Robert for a year now had been discussed by her parents, Mornay didn't know. But it seemed that her father was making the same error as her mother when he caught on. Mornay was little short of astonished however when, just as if she weren't there, he told her mother, 'Well, Robert won't be in a position to marry for a few years yet,' and, as she stared at her parents in amazement, the subject of the Solihull move was temporarily abandoned while they discussed Robert Naylor's prospects. Some while later, with Mornay having taken no part in the discussion, her parents had magnanimously agreed that, if a suitable apartment could be found for her in Reefingham, then if she really did not wish to move with them she could stay behind.

Hardly able to believe that her heart's desire looked like being achieved without an uphill battle where she would be shown up to be the most ungrateful daughter ever born, Mornay could see no point in ruining everything by telling her parents that she had no intention whatsoever of marrying Robert Naylor. Though while part of her was convinced that this way a lot of unnecessary fuss and bother could be avoided, there was another part which felt dreadfully guilty that—without his knowledge—she had used Robert so.

Which, she thought as she headed her Austin Metro towards the Town Hall that Monday morning, was probably why two years later she was still dating him.

Her thoughts were not upon Robert Naylor, nor her parents as she parked her car, swung into the Town Hall, and made for her office. They were on her sister, who was expecting her fifth child in a couple of weeks, and on how she did not suppose another little Overton in the scatty household was going to make it any less scatty.

There was a smile on her beautiful mouth as she reflected that, however frenetic, even mad sometimes that household appeared after her sedate upbringing, it seemed always, again unlike the home she and Claudia were brought up in, to be filled with love and laughter.

'How you can look so cheerful on a Monday morning beats me!' her nice and safe boss greeted her.

'Good morning, Mr Probert,' she replied, and smiled still. 'It's the weather,' she told him.

They discussed the present heatwave and the fact that, though May had been one of the wettest on record, another week of the hot, dry weather was bound to coincide with calls to conserve water. They then got down to work.

It was around mid-morning that a call came through that was nothing to do with work. 'Surveyor's Department,' Mornay answered the phone.

'It's me—Gerry,' the caller identified himself.

'Everything all right?' Mornay asked him. He sounded on top of the world, but it was more usually Claudia who rang her if she wanted her to babysit—not that she could see her wanting to go anywhere, with the baby due so soon.

'Couldn't be better!' Gerry cried exuberantly. 'I've got a *son*!'

'A son! But Claudia——!'

Over the next few minutes her brother-in-law related how, not waiting for two weeks, things had started to happen in the early hours, and how he'd phoned his father to drive his mother over to stay with Emily, Alice, Florence and Prudence while he'd driven Claudia to Reefingham General. Half an hour ago she had presented him with the son he had always secretly wanted.

'She's all right—and the baby?' Mornay asked urgently, feeling weepy but doing her best not to give way in the office.

'Fine—both of them,' Gerry assured her. 'You should see him,' he went charging on. 'Red face, red hair and—like his dad—handsome.'

'Clown,' Mornay laughed, and felt better and less like crying as she asked when could she go and see her sister.

'She's coming out of hospital tomorrow, but I'm sure she'd love to have a visit from you tonight,' Gerry told her.

'You don't mind?' she enquired, wanting quite badly to be at the maternity wing of Reefingham General that night, but not wanting to encroach on this special visiting time between husband and wife.

'Dope!' Gerry scoffed. 'My mother's staying with the girls all day, so I'm free to visit this afternoon *and* this evening.' He rang off, clearly overjoyed that the son he wanted was his.

'Do I gather from what I've overheard that you're an aunt again?' Mr Probert broke through the haze of Mornay's thought to enquire jovially.

'Isn't it super?' she beamed.

It crossed through her mind that she ought to ring her mother and pass on the glad tidings. The thought, however, that her mother would most likely shudder and look on Claudia's new infant more as her daughter bringing a fifth unruly monster into the world made Mornay decide that relating the news could wait until lunchtime.

Dorothy Haynes' reception of the news of her fifth grandchild was much as Mornay had expected when at a quarter past one she stood in a public telephone booth and made the connection to Solihull. Though it was fair to say that, even though her parents had—for the look of it—unbent sufficiently to attend Claudia's wedding nine and a half years ago, there had been little love lost between them since the day Claudia had left home. Which made it fairly predictable, Mornay realised, that instead of asking after mother and baby her mother's first comment was, 'It's to be hoped that she doesn't have any more!'

'Actually, I think both Claudia and Gerry like large families,' Mornay said on a flicker of anger. And, rather surprised at what was, for her, something of an outburst,

'I'm seeing Claudia tonight—can I give her a message from you?'

'I'll write to her when I have a moment,' her mother replied stiffly.

Mornay said goodbye and felt quite cross with her mother. She doubted then that her parents had ever loved either her or her sister. Normal parents, normal loving parents, would not talk in terms of writing but, she felt, in terms of getting to see the mother and new babe as soon as they could.

Mornay was busy that afternoon and was up to her eyes in work when she received her second personal call of the day. This time it was Robert Naylor.

'I'm afraid I'll have to cancel seeing you tomorrow night,' he apologised straight away.

It was on the tip of Mornay's tongue to quip, 'You love another?' but she knew Robert would think that she had gone crazy. 'Oh?' she murmured, wondering what on earth had got into her today. She had awakened contented, which mood had quickly changed to being dissatisfied, and she had mulled darkly over the repressions of her childhood which had seemed to be following her into adult life. She had then felt momentarily anxious over Claudia, and then tearful and then, for a rarity, she had felt angry with her mother *and* had let it show. She was not certain when so many moods and emotions had visited her all in the space of eight hours. 'You're off somewhere?' she guessed. Robert worked as a peripatetic stock-controller for a wallpaper combine, and visited most corners of the British Isles during the course of his work.

'I have to go to Wales at short notice,' he told her importantly. 'I may not be back before Friday.'

'I'll see you when you return, then,' Mornay answered non-committally and, because she knew more eagerness to see her new nephew than 'nice and safe' Robert, 'Don't forget to take your field glasses,' she injected some warmth into her voice to tell him. 'You might be able to fit in some bird-watching while you're away.'

'I always have my binoculars in the car, you know that,' he replied.

Mornay sat staring into space for some minutes after she had put the phone down. She owned then that she was feeling—and it had been coming on for some time, she acknowledged—a bit fed up with Robert. How, though, she went on to wonder, did one end a three-year relationship without causing hurt? Relationship, though, was hardly the word to use for the tepid sort of friendship she had going with Robert. And would he be hurt anyway? Did she even want to finish with him? What was there to finish, for goodness' sake? He was more like a brother than a lover. The thought of having Robert for a lover, though, was laughable. Yet she didn't want to hurt him.

Why, she began to wonder as she got on with some work, had she started to think in terms of telling Robert that she wouldn't see him any more? Unable to find an answer, she put the vagaries of her moods that day down to the heatwave that was at present scorching the country and absorbed herself in that which she was paid to do.

Back at her flat that early evening, she had a quick shower, a quick bite of something to eat and was dressed in a fresh summer dress with plenty of time to spare in which to get to the hospital.

That was, she did have plenty of time to spare until suddenly the phone rang to announce her agitated brother-in-law. 'Can you come and pick me up?' he asked urgently. 'Now, of all times, my car won't start. I'd ask Dad to run me to the hospital but it would take longer for him to get here than you.'

'I'm on my way,' Mornay told him, having quickly assessed the situation and anxious to get started so that they would not be late for the visiting period allowed.

Gerry, his mother and Emily, Alice, Florence and Prudence were all in the garden that ran along one side of the big old house when Mornay, the magazines she had brought for Claudia on the seat beside her, pulled up a short while later and got out of the car.

'Hello, Mornay,' Mrs Overton greeted her, looking strained as she came over to the three-foot-high hedge. 'It's ages since I last saw you—how are you?' she asked warmly.

'Fine, thank you, Mrs Overton,' Mornay smiled. 'Hello, girls,' she greeted the four who came tearing over, but anything else she might have said was lost when Gerry, clearly in a hurry, took a short-cut across the lawn and, charging out of the gate, held his hands out for her car keys.

'You can have a natter with Mornay when we get back,' Gerry told his mother when, knowing of old that her brother-in-law had a 'thing' about being driven by a woman, Mornay, in this instance of him being uptight about the possibility of keeping his wife waiting, handed over her car keys.

They drove off to the sound of Mrs Overton's, 'Really! The responsibilities of parenthood haven't improved your manners any, young man!'

When, having calmed down considerably, Gerry later relayed his panic of the last hour to his wife, Claudia broke up in giggles. 'Young man!' she hooted. 'Lord, I bet that pleased you. You haven't been "young man" since you were twenty and were carpeted by your father for having made me pregnant.'

'He did cut up a bit rough,' Gerry recalled. 'He's got a meeting tonight so he'll call to pick Mother up around ten.'

'Talking of mothers, did you ring mine, Mornay?' Claudia turned to ask her sister.

'I did, and...'

'And?' Claudia prompted.

'And she was very pleased about your news, and she's going to write to you, and she sent her love...'

'And you are the rottenest liar I've ever come across.'

'Have you decided on what to call the little chap?' Mornay abruptly changed the conversation, and Claudia looked to Gerry.

'I like the name Luke,' she told him.

'Which reminds me, if you'll excuse me, ladies, that it's about time I went and took a look at Master Luke Overton, my son,' Gerry said proudly, and with a peck on his wife's cheek he went from the ward.

Mornay would have liked to have gone to see baby Luke herself, but she sensed that Claudia, for all she wasn't showing it, was feeling a shade hurt that her mother cared so little that she could not be bothered to come and see her. Now, Mornay felt, was not the time to leave Claudia on her own.

'Are they really letting you home tomorrow?' she asked brightly.

'They'd better,' Claudia grinned. 'They only wanted me to come while I had Luke just in case of complications. Gerry, as you know, is having a couple of weeks off, so between us we'll soon have ourselves in some sort of routine.'

'Are you serious?' Mornay asked her, Claudia's household, even without the new babe, being the most disorganised she could imagine.

'Oh, shut up,' Claudia said rudely, and grinned, and they were both in happy humour when Gerry, cock-a-hoop after seeing his son, came back.

A little while later Mornay said goodbye to her sister and, leaving Gerry so that he could have some private time with his wife, she went out to the hospital car park. Only when she approached her car and made as though to take the car keys from her bag did she realise that Gerry still had them.

Still, it was a warm evening, not to say airless, and she would most probably have chosen to wait for him outside the car anyway.

Gerry was beaming from ear to ear when he eventually joined Mornay—a very different person from the tense and anxious not to be late person he had been earlier.

'Let's go and wet the baby's head!' he suggested as soon as he had let her into her car and had positioned himself behind the driving-wheel.

'Your mother will be waiting,' Mornay pointed out, aware that Gerry, understandably perhaps, was in a state of euphoria, but not wanting to be late if his daughters— who'd never heard of strict bedtime—were wearing their grandmother out.

'Your upbringing's showing,' her brother-in-law jibed teasingly.

'So mine's a half,' Mornay told him, realising that in the circumstances she was being extremely stuffy.

The sky had darkened and the heat was oppressive when, limiting 'wetting the baby's head' to one drink, they left the pub.

'We're going to have a thunderstorm,' Mornay said as Gerry turned on the headlights and steered the car out of the car park.

'Who cares?' he sang as he put his foot down and negotiated his way towards the centre of town prior to taking the road that led to Penny Dale.

Mornay smiled affectionately as she saw the traffic-light they were nearing change to amber. She was beginning to wonder if her brother-in-law would ever come down to earth again when, as the traffic-light changed to red, she saw a tall dark-haired man step from the pavement. He looked straight at them, and as his aristocratic features registered in her head—without her being fully aware of it—all thought in her suddenly ceased as she realised that Gerry was not going to stop!

'Slow down—brake!' she cried sharply. But it was too late!

The car lurched violently as Gerry suddenly became aware of what was happening and hit the brakes while at the same time he spun the steering-wheel frantically in a vain effort to avoid hitting the tall pedestrian. Mornay hung on as she saw the man collapse to the ground and the car lurched from left to right, thudded against a bollard, and bounced back to the road again.

By that time, though, they were halfway across the intersection. But to her astonishment, even as she unfastened her seatbelt and placed a hand on the doorhandle ready to go sprinting back to the injured man, Gerry was suddenly accelerating away.

'*Stop!*' she shrieked as, thrown back in her seat, she realised that he couldn't have seen the man collapse. 'We've knocked someone over!'

Her astonishment was total when, with a glance in his rear-view mirror, Gerry, instead of halting, kept his foot down and replied, 'He'll be all right. There's quite a crowd of people round him, they'll see to him.'

'But we have to stop!' Mornay told him forcefully. 'We might have killed him or something.'

'Grief, Mornay, I only tapped him—don't be so dramatic,' Gerry snapped, but he sounded all at once very agitated, and she formed a clear impression that he was trying to convince himself as much as her that he had only 'tapped' the accident victim.

He was turning on to the Penny Dale road, away from the direction of the nearest police station by then, but whether he was in a state of agitation or not Mornay felt she could do no other than remind him, 'We'll have to report it to the police, Gerry.'

'Don't you dare!' he replied, and sounded as shaken as she felt.

'But, Gerry, we——'

'Dammit, Mornay, I've enough points against me for silly driving offences—I'll lose my licence for sure if I have to go to court over this one!'

She had known that he had been caught for speeding a couple of times, and had last year been in a spot of bother for a small traffic accident, but in her view none of his previous traffic misdemeanours compared with the enormity of what had just happened.

'But you can't pretend it just—never happened,' she protested. 'It——'

'I can if it comes to a battle between my conscience about knocking a bloke over who in all probability was only stunned for a minute and then got up and walked away—and knowing that if I reported it, then my wife—*your sister*—can say goodbye to any feeling of security that I provide.'

'Why should doing what's right affect Claudia's security?' Mornay asked him sharply.

Gerry spent the time until they reached his home in telling her just how Claudia's security would be affected. He worked in the building industry as a site inspector, and it was his job to go around to any new building being erected to check that work was being completed to specification. A vehicle and a licence to drive were essential to his work, he highlighted. If he lost his licence and was banned from driving, he could say goodbye to his job and his wife and children could say goodbye to the standard of living which they now enjoyed.

'I can't do it to her, Mornay,' Gerry told her shakily as he pulled up outside his home. 'I've seen other women bowed down with worry about how they're going to feed their growing kids. I don't want that for my Claudia. And I'm sure you don't either.'

'Of course I don't. But...'

'Can't you see how idiotic you're being, love?' he asked. 'I'm sure that fellow's all right. Is it worth ruining your sister's happiness just because you've a nuisance of a conscience? You saw how happy she was tonight,' he applied more pressure. 'Could you bear to see her worn down with worry and unhappy?'

When it was put like that, Mornay supposed she was being idiotic. 'Are you going to tell your mother what happened?'

'I'm telling no one,' he answered.

It was no surprise to Mornay that she did not sleep well that night. Back in her flat, she went to bed with the accident to the forefront of her mind and lay awake for an age. When she did sleep, however, it was to be brief and she was to awaken at three in the morning from the most horrendous nightmare where she, at the wheel of her car, had shot the traffic lights and had mown down Claudia.

The sound of her own scream brought Mornay out of her nightmare. Bathed in perspiration, she got out of bed and went to the kitchen. She made a pot of tea and, feeling most disinclined to return to her bed, she sat for an age trying to get the nightmare out of her head. It was only natural that she should dream so violently, she mused shakily, and tried to put out of her mind the insistent prod of a thought that maybe her awful dream was meant to symbolise that she held Claudia's life in her hands. That should she follow the dictates of her conscience and report the accident, then, through her, Claudia's happy life would be over.

By the time Mornay returned to her bed an hour later, she knew that she was going to have to learn to live with her conscience. Claudia and her happiness were paramount.

Strangely, though, when Mornay lay down and closed her eyes, it was not the face of her sister that floated before her, but the face of a tall, dark stranger. A man she had never seen before that night, but a man whose strong, aristocratic features she suddenly had the most uncanny feeling that she would never forget.

When Mornay awakened from another restless sleep at six o'clock she was instantly wide awake and of the belief that it was not uncanny at all that she should feel she would never forget that man's face. She was of the opinion then that, in view of his having been knocked off his feet by her car, it would be most surprising if she *had* forgotten his face.

She sighed unhappily as she showered and dressed and hoped with all her heart that, as Gerry had suggested, the man had got up and walked away.

Proof, however, that the man had not 'got up and walked away' came when, with ages to go before she need leave for work, Mornay went over to her radio and twiddled the knobs until she was tuned into her local radio station. Tension began to mount in her while she waited for the disc being played to end. And then the announcer was saying, 'And now for some local news. Police are still looking for the hit-and-run driver who knocked over a man in Reefingham High Street around nine o'clock last night.' Her throat went dry as she sank soundlessly down on to a chair. 'Witnesses have described the vehicle as being brown or green and as being either a Ford Fiesta or a Vauxhall Astra.' Mornay was sitting gripping hard on to the sides of her chair, she and her brother-in-law alone knowing that the car involved had been a maroon Austin Metro, when the announcer came to the most important part as far as she was concerned. 'The injured man was taken to Reefingham General, where his condition was said to be comfortable half an hour ago.' Mornay was hovering between thanking God that Gerry hadn't killed him, and anxiety that even so the man had landed up in hospital when, to make her blood go cold, the announcer added,

'Unfortunately, when the hit-and-run victim regained consciousness, he was found to have lost his memory.'

Lost his memory! 'Oh, no!' Mornay gasped out loud. Stunned, she sat staring, horrified, at the radio. Oh, no, the poor, poor man!

CHAPTER TWO

MORNAY was still sitting in stunned silence, knowing in her heart of hearts that she was going to have to contact the police, when her telephone rang. Switching off the radio as she went, she ran into a towering wall of guilt when, wondering who could be ringing her at this early hour, she realised that it must be Claudia.

She picked up the phone, fully expecting to hear her sister giving forth on the unseemingly hour one was awakened in hospital, only to hear that it was not Claudia who was calling but her husband.

'I've just tuned in to the local radio station,' he began without preamble, 'and——'

'I caught the local news too,' Mornay told him flatly. 'So you know...?'

'Yes, I know,' Mornay told him, and, guessing why he was ringing—or so she thought, 'I'd better call in at the police station on my way to work. Do you want to meet me there?'

'Are you off your head?' Gerry exclaimed urgently. 'For pity's sake, Mornay, we had all this out last night! You agreed then that we could do nothing if we didn't want to jeopardise Claudia's happiness.'

'I know,' Mornay admitted, feeling miserable. 'But that was before I heard the news just now. The poor man didn't walk away from the accident but landed up in hospital without a clue to who he is, and...and it would be criminal for us not to...'

'It would be more criminal to let your sister and her babies suffer just because you've got a fidgety conscience!' Gerry declared, his alarm obvious. 'Would it make your conscience feel any better to know that through you my family will suffer?'

'No,' she said unhappily, and heard Gerry go on for another five minutes much in the same vein as the previous evening.

'They said on the radio that the man was comfortable, so he's not in a bad way,' Gerry came to an end. 'And you aren't going to make his memory return by going to the police and letting me in for a load of grief, are you?'

'No,' Mornay had to allow, but she felt her guilt no easier to live with after he had rung off, even if he did make it sound as though it would be a far bigger crime to report that her car had been anywhere in the vicinity of the High Street last night.

By the time she left her flat that morning Mornay had again managed to see the situation in the same light as her brother-in-law. That, however, did not make her feel in any way less jumpy. By the sound of it the police were looking for either an Astra or a Fiesta but, as she went to get her car out of its garage, she felt it would be some time before she would pass a policeman in the street without squirming.

Dismay hit her with a vengeance when, having reversed her car out of the garage, she went back to close the garage doors. There for all the world to see was a dent the size of a man's fist on the offside wing. Even without the dent, the fact that some of the maroon paintwork seemed to be missing struck fear into her heart. For certain daylight would reveal traces of maroon—not brown or green—paint left behind on the bollard her Metro had tangled with last night! Mornay drove her car back into its garage and decided to walk to work.

She had no sooner got to work however, than Gerry was on the phone to speak to her again. 'I haven't changed my mind,' she told him, while appreciating his nervousness, not really wanting him to ring her every five minutes of the day.

'I'm not ringing about that,' he told her. 'I've just rung the hospital to see what time I can collect Claudia, and they've said that she can't come home today.'

Immediately Mornay's heart lurched in panic. 'Why not? What's wrong with her?' she questioned quickly.

'Nothing to be too alarmed about, apparently,' Gerry quickly assured her. 'It's just that her temperature's rocketed for some reason, and they're insisting that she stays put until it comes down. Why I'm ringing, more particularly, is that my mother was a bit miffed as you know last night that the kids had been playing up, so I don't like to ask her to sit with them again so soon. Could you come and sit with them tonight for me while I go and visit Claudia?'

'Of course I will,' Mornay told him. 'Oh,' she suddenly remembered, 'have you got transport?'

She put the phone down having heard that Gerry had already had his car looked at and that the problem was nothing more serious than petrol pump failure, which had not taken long to sort out.

An involuntary sigh escaped Mornay as she got on with some work. 'Everything all right?' Mr Probert enquired.

She wished very much that she could confide in him, though knew that if she did he would only advise her to do what she knew she ought to do anyway. 'Claudia was supposed to be coming out of hospital today but her temperature's soared so they're keeping her in,' she told him by way of explanation for the fact that she was finding it very hard to find a smile that day.

'She'll be all right,' Mr Probert replied warmly. 'And she really is in the best place if she's not feeling quite up to the mark.'

'You're right, of course,' Mornay agreed, and spent the next couple of hours telling herself that, as he'd said,

of course Claudia would be all right, and wondering
whether she would, and what the penalty was for trying
to cover up a hit-and-run crime.

She had worked herself up into a state where she was
convinced that the next person who came through the
office door would be a uniformed officer to ask if she
was the owner of a maroon-coloured car, when the door
suddenly opened. The person who came in, though uniformed, was not a policeman, but the commissionaire
bringing a hand-delivered package. It was he, however,
who brought the news that there had been a hold-up in
one of the banks in the main street, and so unwittingly
gave Mornay a very small modicum of ease in the tension
she was enduring.

Surely a bank raid would have the local constabulary
using all their resources in chasing after the bank robbers!
The police were always short-staffed—weren't they? And
if they weren't—it went without saying that a bank
robbery would take priority over a hit-and-run episode
where no one had been seriously hurt!

Within minutes she was feeling dreadful again. That
poor man! She tried to visualise losing her memory and
thought it must be utterly ghastly. If he didn't know who
he was, then the hospital couldn't know who he was,
and the police couldn't know who he was—and that
meant that they couldn't tell anyone *where* he was.

Mornay went out on her lunch-break but felt too
churned up inside to be able to eat. That poor man, his
wife wouldn't know where he was, there'd be no one to
visit him—oh, how desperate he must be feeling!

She returned to her office feeling bodily weary from
her lack of sleep last night and mentally used up from
constantly having her mind on Claudia, the accident,
and the injured man.

Unbeknown to her, however, she had made several
mistakes in her work that day and, because this was such
an unusual occurrence, Mr Probert came from his office

to see her. She was staring into space when at around half-past two she became aware that her boss was standing at her desk.

'This...' he began, indicating some typing she had done and which he now held. Then he paused, and, giving her unsmiling expression a searching look, he changed what he had been about to say to tell her kindly, 'Why don't you take an hour off and go and visit your sister to see for yourself that she's all right?'

Mornay averted her eyes as it dawned on her that the anxiety she was going through must be showing. 'It's all right,' she mumbled, and experienced more guilt—this time at Mr Probert's misplaced kindness.

'Do me a favour,' he smiled, and, tapping the papers in his hands, 'Your work's suffering.'

'Oh, I'm sorry,' Mornay immediately apologised, and reached for her bag. Perhaps a visit to Claudia might endorse for her that by keeping quiet she was doing only what was right. 'I'll work late tonight,' she told Mr Probert as she got to her feet, and was stepping out the half-mile to Reefingham General before she recalled that she was babysitting that night. She'd have to go home for her car first, and if she wasn't at Claudia's house by a quarter to seven then Gerry would start to flap.

Realising that she'd have to back-track on her offer to work late, Mornay made a mental promise to work hard and pay closer attention to detail, and stopped by the hospital gates where an enterprising lady had set up a flower stall.

'I'll have two bunches of the red carnations, please,' she requested, thinking the bright colour would cheer Claudia up if she was down in the doldrums.

Having made her purchase, Mornay went through the main gates and up the drive of the hospital and through the main doors. Over the years she had become familiar with where each department lay, having at some time or another made a visit to someone or other in the various wards.

Apart from her visit last evening to the maternity wing—where Claudia had been delivered of her five babies—Mornay had many years previously visited the accident wing when Gerry—in those days the owner of a motorbike—had fallen off it.

She had no intention of visiting the accident wing, though. Indeed, had she thought about it, she would have determined to give that particular wing a very wide berth. But she suddenly discovered that, without any known volition, instead of turning right at the end of the long corridor, she had turned left. More, that in finding her feet were taking her along to the accident wing, she didn't seem able to stop.

Abruptly, as if to prove herself wrong, Mornay halted. Yet, having done that, there seemed to be someone else in charge of her, in that she found herself thinking that it wouldn't hurt at all if she went along to Sister's office to enquire how the man was whom she'd heard on the news had lost his memory. Slowly, as though compelled, Mornay resumed walking.

She knew where the ward sister's office was. The wards in this old building were all laid out pretty much the same, with double swing doors leading to another set of double swing doors. In between the two sets of doors, though, lay—to one side—a small kitchen, a walk-in linen cupboard and a side-ward big enough for two beds. Opposite lay a bathroom, a place where wheelchairs were generally parked and Sister's office, which had a window in it which looked on to the ward.

Pushing her way quietly through the first set of swing doors, Mornay took a few paces forward and was able to see through the glass of the other swing doors that it was visiting time, and that relatives and friends were seated by the various beds. Quickly she averted her eyes. The face of the man Gerry had knocked down seemed to be burned into her brain. She had enough guilt to be going on with without recognising him—or the fact that his would be the only bed without a visitor.

Nevertheless, she somehow still felt unable to go from the place where her feet had taken her, and she moved to where she knew she would find the ward sister, and tapped gently on the door. She then followed through by reaching for the door-handle, and turned it. She then took a step or two forward and stepped round the door— and knew, instantly, that she had made the most terrible mistake!

Sister's office must be on the other side of the connecting passageway. She, Mornay saw as she fought to hold down a sudden surge of panic, had entered a side-ward—a side-ward which had only one occupant, who was a man she would know anywhere! A man who, for all he was lying down in bed, she knew to be tall. A man who looked to be somewhere in his mid-thirties, and who had dark hair and aristocratic features—and whose dark eyes, as she nervously eyed him, were lazily assessing her.

'Come in,' he invited in unhurried tones.

He had a pleasant-sounding voice, she thought, but she was more inclined to make a hasty exit rather than go any closer to him. Then it was that she noticed that, although the man seemed to be free of bandages or plaster, there was an extreme look of exhaustion about him. Then it was that her conscience awakened with a vengeance and, as she saw how, all because of his having made contact with her car, his face was drained of colour and that he looked worn out, she could no more leave than fly.

'How are you feeling?' she asked, and so that he should not have to strain any sore muscles by turning to look at her she moved closer to him.

'There have been days when I've felt better,' he drawled in reply.

'Did you break any bones—or anything?' she wanted to know.

Relief started to rush in when he moved his head slightly from side to side in a negative reply. Then, 'Pull up a chair,' he invited.

As Mornay had had no intention of going any further into the room, she had no intention of pulling up a chair either. But, as her eyes again examined the exhausted-looking man, so she became guiltily aware that it might be causing him some effort to look up to where she was standing.

Hurriedly she found a chair and carried it to the bed. They were then on more of a level as she sat by the side of his bed. Suddenly though, as she became aware of his steady dark-eyed stare fixed on her features, Mornay all at once found that she was hurrying into a rapid false explanation of why she was there.

'I thought I'd come and see if there is anything you need,' she lied.

'You're some sort of voluntary worker?' he enquired.

'Oh, no, I'm a secretary,' she heard herself confess, and then, knowing full well that she hadn't much of a clue when it came to telling lies, she realised that if her innate honesty was not going to trip her up she would do well to think carefully over every word she uttered during what she was going to make the briefest ever visit. 'It was just that...' She hesitated and, having been about to tell him that she had heard about his accident on the radio that morning, she realised that that could get her into the realms of what sort of vehicle had hit him—a discussion on which was something she was anxious to avoid. 'It was just that—I was walking in the High Street last night when I saw the ambulance come and take you away.'

Hoping that her face did not look as pink as it felt, Mornay just then observed that, for all the man looked drained of strength, an alert sort of look had suddenly come to his eyes. She couldn't remember seeing it there before, at any rate.

His tone was easy, though, when he enquired mildly, 'You witnessed the accident?'

'Oh, no!' Mornay straight away denied any such idea, and, wanting to get him swiftly away from the notion, 'I arrived just in time to see the ambulance take you away, and today——'

'From what I hear,' the man butted in to remark, 'that ambulance broke all speed records to get me here without a moment's delay.'

'The ambulance driver didn't hang about, certainly,' she smiled, and, since someone must have told him of the speed and efficiency of their local ambulance service, 'No sooner were the rear doors closed than he was away,' she added for a touch of authenticity. Then she resumed, 'I was passing the hospital today, and——'

'You don't perform your secretarial duties on Tuesdays?' he interrupted her to question, and Mornay knew then that she had better tread very carefully. This man might be physically debilitated, but his brain was as sharp as a tack.

'I'm having an hour off—to go to the dentist,' she of the perfect teeth lied, and quickly took up again, 'When I was passing the hospital and I remembered the incident of last night, I wondered if—that is, if your—er—family—weren't able to—er...' She was floundering, and she knew it. She still felt that she had to keep quiet about having heard on the radio that morning the report which mentioned not only the speculation about the vehicle in question, but also his loss of memory. But added to that was an inner sensitivity she felt to the distress he must be suffering on account of his lost memory, and she just could not go on to make further reference to his family.

To her relief, he saved her from having to stammer on when, with a smile of some charm, he suddenly seemed to notice the red carnations she was clutching.

'You brought these for me?' he enquired.

Claudia, the intended recipient, was far from Mornay's mind when, in her relief, she grabbed at the suggestion. 'I thought they might cheer you up if you were feeling down,' she smiled in return, and got so far carried away that she began earnestly, 'If there's anything you need,' when he gritted one short and angry word that had her staring at him, wide-eyed. 'What...?' she asked, certain, for all there was no trace of a smile about him now, charming or otherwise, that she must have heard him incorrectly.

But she had not heard him incorrectly, she discovered. For he repeated that word again. 'Liar,' he gritted, 'was what I called you—and not a very good liar at that!'

'I... What...?' She struggled for a moment or two under his dark, forbidding stare. Then, as her common logic assessed that he could not possibly know the extent of her lies, she realised that his comment must have been made in connection with the flowers she had just said she'd brought him. 'I know some men don't appreciate flowers,' she surfaced to find a smile, 'but—— '

'Since it's through you that I'm cooped up in this damned place and likely to be for some days,' he cut her off harshly, 'to bring flowers is——'

'Through me!' Mornay choked on a whisper, fear entering her heart when, her brain seeming to seize up, she swallowed on a dry throat. With nothing very clever coming to her numbed brain, however, she could only attempt to bluff. 'I don't know what you're talking about,' she said and, trying for an aloof note, 'How on earth could I possibly have anything to do with you being—er...' her aloof manner started to slip under his harsh glare '...hospitalised?' she managed to finish.

'I'll tell you how,' he snarled, and did not waste any time in doing so. 'For starters, you weren't *walking* in the area of the High Street last night, you were driving! For——'

'Don't be absurd!' Mornay, inwardly in utter panic, tried to cut in.

'Nor were you paying proper attention to your driving,' he ignored her to rap.

'I always pay proper attention to my driving,' Mornay told him coldly, and could have groaned out loud when she realised that she would have been better to tell him that she did not drive at all.

'Which is why you shot a red light, hit me, and then, criminally, without stopping, drove on—is it?' he barked.

Mornay opened her mouth to hotly deny it. But then, suddenly, she was startled into realising that it was *her* he was accusing! All at once, it dawned on her that this man—having not so much as an idea that she had a brother-in-law, thought that it had been *her* at the steering-wheel of the car that had hit him last evening! Swiftly Mornay recalled the blue funk which Gerry had been in last night. Swiftly, too, she recalled all the arguments he had used for why she should stay quiet. And swiftly it came to her that, even though this man, despite looking as though to sleep for a week might do him some good, had still retained quite brilliant powers of deduction to have worked out what he so far had— Gerry might still get away with it!

Realising that she had been silent too long to make any scornful denial sound genuine, Mornay felt she had better hop on to the attack. 'You can't prove that statement,' she shrugged, hoping to convey that she did not believe him to be seriously accusing her anyway.

But, to make her insides churn with another helping of panic, 'I just did!' he grated acidly, and as Mornay's grasp of the flowers she still held tightened convulsively, he seemed about to add more acid when the door suddenly opened.

Her heart went into her mouth when she saw from the navy dress and white-bibbed apron that the person who had just come in was the ward sister. Only then did

Mornay realise that she must have secretly been hoping to leave the side-ward with no one being any wiser about her visit.

The plump ward sister was frowning severely though, Mornay observed as her heart plummeted to her boots and she realised that the man in the bed would lose no time in acquainting the nursing sister with his suspicions.

'Who——?' the ward sister began to demand, and Mornay had visions of being physically held down by the tough-looking lady if need be, while the police were called.

But no, to her surprise, not to say utmost gratitude, the man in the bed was suddenly cutting through whatever the sister would have said. 'Don't be starchy, Sister,' he smiled, the charm which Mornay had observed in him before—phoney charm, she now realised—there again. But, while she still expected him to repeat his allegations to the plump woman, 'I'm sure you wouldn't deprive me of my beautiful visitor.'

Mornay instantly switched her gaze from the sister to the man in the bed. She felt confused suddenly that the man who but a minute earlier had been all aggression, should a minute later describe her as beautiful and sound as though he meant it. Nor did her confusion end there. She was still trying to get to grips with the confusing fact that it looked as though he might keep his suspicions to himself when, having glanced back to the woman who had just come in, she saw the sister's look of curiosity to know who she was fade under her professional concern for her patient.

'You're supposed to be kept quiet,' she told him succinctly. And then, as though begrudgingly, 'Five minutes!' she allowed.

'If you're to be kept quiet...' Mornay murmured as soon as the sister had gone. In the next moment, she was on her feet.

Astonishingly, however, and with lightning speed, and all before she had taken so much as half a step away from the bed, his right hand had snaked out and had taken hold of her wrist in a grip there was no shaking off.

Mornay was still staring in amazement that a man who looked so drained of vitality should have such quick reactions and such strength when, 'Your visit isn't over yet,' he stated laconically.

Again her heart plummeted. But she took hope from the fact that he had not revealed his suspicions to the ward sister when she had been there. The same ward sister, she recalled without effort, had allowed five minutes' visiting time only. Surely she could find something to talk about in the time remaining before that fierce-looking woman came and insisted that, for the good of her patient, she must go.

Alas, the very thing which Mornay had not meant to refer to was the first thing that rolled off her tongue. 'Do you know who you are yet?' she found herself enquiring, and, wishing that the floor would open up beneath her, she felt impelled to gently go on, 'Have you recovered your memory?' His answer had her staring at him incredulously.

'I never lost it!' he announced forthrightly, and while she was grappling with that, 'And right now I'm more interested in knowing who you are.' Instinctively Mornay went to leave her chair. She had forgotten, however, the swiftness with which he could move. In one moment her wrist was once more manacled, and he was looking tough when he said, as she sank back on to her chair, 'You've got about three minutes before Sister comes back in which to tell me who you are.' Stubbornly Mornay glared at him. 'If you don't tell me,' he ignored her angry look to continue bluntly, 'then you'll leave me no option but to tell her that you're the woman who knocked me down

and who—despite calls for the driver to come forward—
has declined to do so.'

'You don't know it was me!' she challenged hotly. 'You
can't verify anything,' she went rapidly on, not seeing
how, with her maroon-coloured car hidden in its garage,
anyone could make the assumption he had. Convinced
that he could prove none of his deductions, Mornay
warmed to her theme as she went on stoutly, 'Just because I happened to be on the scene last night when the
ambulance arrived to——'

'I could,' he sliced in crisply, 'let you go on. But you've
already hung yourself with your lies—any barrister I
employed would make mincemeat of you inside two
minutes,' he inserted. 'However...' As Mornay stared
at him, and as her blood ran cold at that word 'barrister', he suddenly closed his eyes. 'However,' he went
on a second later, 'I've something of a thundering
headache and I think Sister might have got it right when
she indicated I should be quiet. So, since I wasn't brought
to this establishment by ambulance but by——'

'You—weren't?' Mornay gasped, and saw his tired
eyes open.

'As luck would have it,' he told her, 'one of the first
people on the scene was a passing doctor heading this
way. He stopped—you didn't. I'll have your name,' he
stated, and looked so decidedly groggy that Mornay was
tempted to go looking for someone on the nursing staff.
'Your name,' he repeated.

'Mornay Haynes,' she told him, and, as he closed his
eyes and seemed to her to have lost colour he did not
have, she was awash with guilt that she'd exhausted him
more by not telling him her name sooner.

The hold on her wrist slackened and, looking down
on him, she saw that he had fallen asleep. Leaving the
flowers on his bedside locker, she moved silently to the
door. She had the door open when she realised that he
was not asleep as she had thought.

'Come and see me tomorrow,' he suddenly commanded.

Mornay turned swiftly. 'But...' she tried to protest, and then saw that she was wasting her breath. It didn't matter whether he was asleep or whether he wasn't. What he was, was used up. She was doing him no kindness by staying there to argue.

She left the side-ward just as the sister hove into view. Mornay bade her good afternoon, but she was over-whelmingly relieved when she saw her go into the side-ward to take a look at her patient.

Mornay was going out through the hospital gates when she surfaced from being stunned by all that had so recently happened, to recall that Mr Probert had specifically given her some time off so that she could go and visit her sister. Turning about, Mornay made her way back inside the hospital.

For once she felt no heart to go and see Claudia, but since Mr Probert was bound to ask how she was when he saw her she aimed her feet in the direction of the maternity wing. She did not want to lie to Mr Probert and, since it had been proved that she was so awful at it, she began to wish that she had never embarked on a course of untruths that day.

That was not all she wished. Heartily then did she wish that she had not given the man in the accident wing her correct name. Where her brain had been then she had no idea but, away from the man and the panic he had caused her, it seemed to her that she had been particularly stupid. If she was going to give him a name at all, for goodness' sake, why hadn't she thought to give him a false one?

Perhaps he'll forget it, she mused hopefully as she neared the double doors of the maternity wing. He'd looked exhausted, she recalled, as she pushed through the first set of doors, so perhaps her name had not properly registered with him.

Mornay was going through the second set of double doors when she tried to come to terms with his astounding announcement that he had not lost his memory. How she wished she had known that before. Had she known in advance that there was nothing wrong with his memory, then she was certain that never would she have been so soft-hearted as to put a foot inside the accident wing.

She sighed as she circumnavigated a large table in the middle of the maternity ward and headed for the far end, where she could see Claudia with her head stuck in a paperback. She didn't know who the dickens the man was, for she had been too shaken to ask him his name, but, while he might never have lost his memory as he'd stated, it was clear that he had no memory of the actual accident. For had he had any memory of her car heading straight for him, since he had seemed to her to be looking directly into her car, he might well have remembered that the driver—with his bushy beard—was male.

'Mornay! What a nice surprise!' Claudia lowered her book just as her sister reached the end of her bed. 'I didn't expect any visitors until this evening!'

'I'm sitting with the girls tonight, so Mr Probert kindly gave me some time off so I could visit you this afternoon. Now,' she said cheerfully, 'what's this I hear about your temperature?'

'Wouldn't you know it? Just when I'm bursting to get home to show my daughters their new brother, my temperature has to go into orbit.'

'You could,' Mornay suggested, 'make the most of it. With five children and a husband, you'll have your work cut out when you get home.'

'I know,' Claudia agreed, and then, serious for once, 'but I do so love my home.'

'I know you do,' Mornay said softly, knowing full well how determined her sister was that her home would always be a warm, joyous and secure place for her family, and not in any way like the cold and strict home she had left at the first opportunity.

'I couldn't bear for anything to happen that would spoil it,' Claudia told her quietly.

At that point Mornay realised that her sister, because of her enforced stay, was on the brink of subsiding into the doldrums. 'Then we'll have to take jolly good care that nothing does,' she teased brightly.

'Promise?' Claudia responded to her teasing with a smile.

'I promise,' Mornay told her, and she was the more serious of the two at that time.

Claudia was much on Mornay's mind when for the second time that afternoon she left the hospital. So too, was the other person she had 'inadvertently' visited. Claudia's security was paramount, but he had looked so dreadful. Oh, what a muddle it all was. And she was in the middle of it.

There was she, freely promising—and meaning that promise even if it was in joking fashion—that she would guard Claudia's security for her, while at the same time the one person who was the greatest threat to that security was demanding that she pay him a visit tomorrow.

Mornay had reached the Town Hall when, her mind in a turmoil, she caught sight of a paper-seller at his usual stand. In an attempt to pin her thoughts on other things, she went over and purchased a copy of an early edition of the evening paper. Mr Probert was an avid bargain-hunter and liked to scan the 'Going for a Song' ads.

Intending to give the paper to him as soon as she reached his office, Mornay was just ascending the Town Hall steps when, as she glanced to the paper in her hand, a banner headline on the front page caught her eye— and she stopped dead.

With her heart beating ten to the dozen she opened the paper out. 'Industrialist recovers memory', the headline read. Quickly Mornay read the rest of it. Apparently the victim of last evening's hit-and-run accident had been staying at the Belvedere, one of the two prestigious hotels in town. It had been an extremely warm evening and he had left his hotel dressed in shirt-sleeves and trousers and without identification on him. The recovery of his memory, so the paper said, had been prompted when the manager of the Belvedere had that morning heard the news on the radio, and had come forward to report that one of his guests was missing.

Mornay clearly remembered that the man she had seen that afternoon had plainly told her that he had never lost his memory to begin with. But that didn't concern her then, because there was something else she remembered. Not an hour ago she had thought how she did not know the man's name. At the end of reading the report that covered most of the front page, she knew quite well who he was—and wished that she didn't. For the man who had last night been pole-axed by a hit-and-run driver was none other than the wealthy components manufacturer, Bradford Kendrick. Brad Kendrick, so it was said, had come up the hard way and was an 'eye for an eye' type. No man, according to the report, ever put one over on him without living to regret it.

Oh, grief, Mornay thought, did that go for women too?

CHAPTER THREE

AFTER another restless night, Mornay got up the next morning word-perfect with the report she had read in yesterday's paper about Brad Kendrick, thirty-six, industrialist, bachelor, and at present a patient in Reefingham General. So she should be word-perfect, she mused glumly—she had read the report often enough.

She had taken the paper with her to show Gerry when she'd gone to babysit, but he'd already seen it. 'Don't worry,' he'd advised. 'Just sit tight—it'll soon blow over. Now I must get going, Claudia will be watching the ward doors. Be good, girls,' he had instructed his daughters.

There hadn't been time then to tell him about the idiot she had been that afternoon, and when he'd returned he'd been a bit quiet because there had seemed some doubt that Claudia would be coming home the next day either, and Mornay had thought better than to worry him with a blow-by-blow account of how crass she had been.

Thinking over everything that had happened as she got ready for work that Wednesday morning, Mornay sorely wished that she could turn the clock back to two days ago. If she had known then what she knew now, there was no way she would have allowed Gerry to drive her car. No way she would have gone celebrating with him—be it only one drink. And for certain, she would have avoided Reefingham's High Street like the plague.

Guilt was her companion once more when for the second morning running she opted to walk to work. The other headline in yesterday's paper concerned the bank raid; thankfully the police were busy with that and had

43

not so far, made any headway with the 'hit and run'.
Mornay was grateful for small mercies, but she was not
of a mind to advertise the dent in her Metro by driving
it around in broad daylight—she'd done a detour of the
town to get to Penny Dale last night.

'Good morning, Mr Probert,' she greeted her boss with
every sign that she had nothing more serious on her mind
than what shade of lipstick to buy next. Then, remembering how she had barely earned her corn yesterday,
she put all her efforts into having a better work day that
day and for the first hour showed tremendous results.

Around ten o'clock, however, she discovered that her
concentration was wavering. Too often she found she
was having to pull her thoughts back from the fact that
Brad Kendrick was expecting her to pay him a visit that
afternoon.

As she had yesterday, she hoped he would forget her
name. But, as the hour hand on the office clock crawled
round, Mornay began to hope that he would have forgotten too that he had 'commanded' her, 'Come and see
me tomorrow'.

Oh, lord, she worried, and began to fret that if he
had remembered her name then—with him being an 'eye
for an eye' merchant and everything—if she didn't visit
him as ordered, all he had to do was to tell the police
her name and they'd find her inside two minutes! Since
her parents had left the area, the only person going by
the name of 'Haynes' listed in the telephone book as
living locally was her.

Mornay was starting to have horrifying visions of him
having called the police anyway, and of the police being
there at the hospital waiting for her if she did turn up
that day, when Gerry rang.

'They're not ready to let Claudia home yet,' he told
her. 'Can you do the honours and babysit again tonight? I sort of got the impression when I just rang my

mother that it will be many a long day before she'll come and sit again.'

'Of course I'll come,' Mornay said at once, mentally ruling out the evening as a time when she might have obeyed Brad Kendrick's summons.

She returned to her desk after lunch with the word 'barrister' in her head, the threat it implied making her feel quite ill. An hour later she accepted from the jitteriness inside her that she was fooling only herself if she thought she wasn't going hospital visiting that afternoon. Brad Kendrick had the upper hand. She, by virtue of going into the accident wing yesterday, had given it to him.

'Any chance of my having an hour off?' she asked Mr Probert.

'Want to go and see your sister?' he asked understandingly.

'I'd like to go to the hospital,' she replied.

Which, she thought as her feet trod the same path they had yesterday, must rank among one of the biggest lies she had told to date. She would not like to go to the hospital. No way did she want to go to the hospital. But, because she was having to jump to Brad Kendrick's tune, Reefingham General—and the accident wing in particular—was where she was heading.

Her fears that the police might be waiting for her were proved unfounded. Not that she had given serious thought to that alarming possibility. The person who was waiting for her when she went through the first set of double doors of the accident wing, however, was the ward sister who had been on duty yesterday.

That was to say that the ward sister's office door was open and, as Mornay paused prior to plucking up her courage ready to go into the side-ward, the sister came out from behind her door.

'Mr Kendrick's been transferred to the private wing, and has left word that you must be his only visitor,' the sister told her, plainly remembering her from yesterday. 'Do you know where it is?'

'I think so, thank you,' Mornay smiled, but thanked Mr Kendrick not for the privilege he afforded her. She turned about and headed for the more recently added-on wing, and asked the next nursing sister she saw, 'May I see Mr Kendrick, please?'

'I'm afraid he's not seeing visitors,' she was informed.

'Oh,' Mornay said, and had half turned away when a worrying thought struck her. 'He's not worse, is he?' she asked, while at the same time the lady in charge was asking her name. 'The sister in the accident wing said he would see me,' Mornay replied, having foolishly revealed her name yesterday and not likely to make that mistake a second time.

'You're Miss...'

'Haynes,' Mornay supplied resignedly, and received a smile for her trouble and an apology for not being allowed in without question.

'The world and his wife have been trying to get in to see him today,' the neat, professional woman told her. 'He's just not up to giving Press interviews yet,' she went on as she escorted her down a short corridor, took a right turn and, with the words, 'You won't stay too long, will you?' departed.

From choice, Mornay would have preferred to have made this visit the shortest on record. But, taking a deep breath, she tapped softly on the door, and went in.

'You took your time!' the man propped up on pillows gritted aggressively.

Very much wishing that she had never come at all, Mornay went forward to the bed. By the sound of it, his ill-humour of yesterday had not improved any. 'How are you feeling today?' she enquired politely, and, realising that she had to make the best of it, she pulled a chair up to the bed and sat down.

'How do you think I feel?' he grunted. 'It's not every day that I get mown down by an armour-plated truck.'

Strangely, the fact that he could so exaggerate having been knocked over by her car brought a smile to her lips. 'Austin Metro, actually,' she said quite without thinking and, even as she was inwardly wincing at the easy way he had extracted that piece of information from her, she was receiving yet another sharp edge of his tongue.

'I'm glad you find it amusing!' he bit out, his dark glance fixing on the upward curve of her attractive mouth.

Instantly Mornay straightened her expression. 'I don't find it a bit amusing,' she told him coolly. 'It was just that with you saying——' She broke off, irritated by him. How could she explain to this bad-tempered brute that something in his exaggerated comment had triggered her sense of humour? 'Are you in pain?' she changed course to enquire, thinking that the pain he might be enduring was responsible for his acerbic attitude—he looked more rested than yesterday but didn't have very much more colour.

'Had you been drinking?' he ignored her question to ask one of his own.

'I'd been celebr——' Abruptly she halted, wondering what it was about this man that had her speaking without first engaging her brain.

'You'd been celebrating!' he quickly caught on to what she had just bit back. 'You were *drunk*!' he accused harshly.

'No, I *wasn't*!' she denied vehemently. 'I had only one drink to——' Again she broke off.

'What were you celebrating?' he demanded to know.

'That's none of your business!' she rapped back smartly for his nerve, and ignored the narrowing of his eyes that spoke of him not caring very much for her tone. She was unrepentant though—she had already, unwarily, revealed more than she had intended, and had

no intention of telling him anything that might lead him
to speculate on anything connected with her sister—or
her sister's family.

'I could,' he threatened silkily, 'make it my business.'

Oh, dear heaven, Mornay panicked, and as that word
'barrister' popped up in her brain again, she was back-
pedalling fast. 'Er—there was quite a write-up on you
in the local paper yesterday, Mr Kendrick,' she pulled
out of a panicky nowhere, hoping to distract him.

'But nothing about you, I take it,' he drawled.

Mornay, who up until then had never known an
emotion as fierce as hate, suddenly felt that she hated
Bradford Kendrick. 'I'd hardly be likely to be here now
if there had been!' she snapped, and didn't care a bit
when she saw it register that, but for his blackmailing
her to come and visit him that afternoon, she would have
found something of a pleasanter nature to do.

He did not make further comment on it, however, but,
with a rapidly fired question that was at variance with
the still debilitated look of him, he abruptly asked,
'Where do you live?'

'In Reefingham,' she replied, knowing for sure that
he could find that much out for himself without much
help now that he knew her name.

'Where?' he further shot at her.

Mornay was getting a little fed up with him and, as
stubbornness paid her a visit, she felt she'd be hanged
if she'd volunteer her address.

'In a flat,' she replied coldly.

'With your family?' was his next cannon shot—and
Mornay sensed danger. She felt then that he must not
by any means know that she had a sister.

'My parents live in Solihull,' she told him, and wished
that she hadn't—but it was too late then. 'You live in
London, I belive,' she said in a desperate bid to get him
off a subject that was too close for comfort. 'According
to yesterday's early evening edition, you live——'

'For the moment, I live here!' he cut in in disgruntled fashion. 'Though not for much longer,' he added inflexibly.

From hating him Mornay swung to being afraid for him. 'Surely they're not thinking of letting you go?' she questioned, thinking it only natural that she should feel some disquiet, for he still looked far from well.

'They,' he retorted, 'have no option.'

'No option?' she queried, staring at him, at his firm chin, and even as she queried his remark she realised that it would be a brave man who tried to oppose him once he had made up his mind to anything.

'I've had it with this enforced incarceration,' Brad Kendrick told her in no uncertain terms, and caused Mornay to stare at him some more when he announced, 'I'm leaving tomorrow.'

Mornay had never received any medical training, but felt then that she needed none to know that he would be better for staying in bed for a week. In her view, even a person with limited vision would be able to see that by no chance was Brad Kendrick ready to leave hospital tomorrow.

'You can't!' she told him bluntly, and saw his right eyebrow shoot aloft at what he clearly thought her sauce.

'Watch me!' he mocked.

'But—you're not well! You need someone to look after you,' she tried to get him to see reason, forgetful when looking at the enervated state of him that she should be rejoicing that he was talking of leaving Reefingham and going back to London. Yet, suddenly, when she saw that a thinking look had come to him, she was beginning to doubt the evidence of her eyes. Something, she realised, had just occurred to him, and had given him an alert look. 'You have someone in your London home who'll look after you?' she enquired, wondering, since he was reported as unmarried, if he'd remembered he had a relation or a housekeeper who would look after him.

But no, he was shaking his head, and suddenly Mornay did not like at all the pleasant expression with which he masked his inner thoughts. Nor did she like in the least the solution which had just come to him when, his words more silky than pleasant, he softly drawled, 'Since you're responsible for the position I'm in, Miss Haynes, I'll— let you do it.'

'What?' she questioned, aghast, quite certain just then that her normally quite bright brain was having a day off and that she must be misunderstanding what it sounded as though he was telling her.

'I'll let you look after me,' he elucidated evenly. 'I'm sure——'

But, realising that she had not misunderstood him at all, Mornay wasted not a moment to cut him off. 'I'm not going to London with you!' she erupted hotly. 'You——' She was cut off this time.

'I never asked you to,' he told her forthrightly.

'But—but . . .' she stammered, and did not care for the phoney smile he bestowed on her.

'I'll come to your flat,' he announced, and while she stared, incredulous and disbelieving, 'A month's convalescence is the minimum you owe me,' he stated in a tone there was no arguing with.

But Mornay did argue. Convalescence! A month! A month with him in her tiny flat! 'That's impossible!' she told him shortly—and that was before she thought of the other complications.

Abruptly any sign of a smile, phoney or otherwise, left him. 'You have a "live-in" lover?' he demanded furiously, all too clearly a man who did not like to have his plans thwarted.

'No!' she flared, before she could think, and saw his anger fade.

'In that case you can come and collect me at ten tomorrow morning.' He had it instantly all worked out.

'But I can't,' she tried to get through to him. 'I've only one bedroom and——'

'Set your mind at rest, Miss Haynes. I——' he clipped '—shall not want to share it,' and for the first time in her life Mornay experienced an almost uncontrollable urge to hit someone. She was sure that she was more than gratified at this vitriolic man's point-blank assertion that he didn't fancy her, but that didn't stop her from wanting to box his ears just the same. She came even closer to wanting to set about him when, toughly, he added, 'Take my word for it, one more night here is all I'm putting up with.'

'But...' she tried to protest.

'Ten tomorrow morning,' he stated coldly, his blunt tone telling her that she would be wasting her breath in trying to get him to change his mind.

Mornay thought she might have had another try just the same, had the ward sister not chosen just that exact moment to enter the room, and with a smile to Mornay she came to take a closer look at her patient. 'You've got a bad head again, haven't you?' she declared. Mornay, taking the hint that in Sister's view she had overstayed her welcome, returned her chair to the spot from where she had collected it, and left.

Her mind was in such a ferment, though, that she was back at her office and Mr Probert was asking, 'How was your sister?' before she realised that she hadn't given Claudia a thought.

'About the same,' she replied and, not wanting to lie to him, she avoided any more questions by getting down straight away to some work.

The work she had chosen to tackle, though, was matter which did not require one hundred per cent concentration, and in no time Mornay was going over the same thoughts that had gone through her mind on the way back from the hospital. Despite Brad Kendrick's *deciding* to lodge himself in her flat for a month, it was just impossible. For so much as a week it was impossible—oh, what on earth was she going to do?

Aside from the fact of her flat having only one bedroom, the rest of it, with its sitting-room that did service as a dining-room too, and its poky kitchen and equally poky bathroom, was barely big enough for her—and he, though without spare flesh, was a big man.

Mornay had done nothing about asking Mr Probert for some time off the following morning when at five o'clock that evening he stopped by her desk and asked, 'Haven't you a home to go home to?'

'I'll just finish this,' she said knowing that she wouldn't be able to work too late if she were to be at Penny Dale for a quarter to seven. 'I . . .' she began, but because she did not honestly and truly want the time off she had to invent something else to say when he halted expectantly. 'It won't take me long,' she smiled.

When half an hour later she left her office, she knew full well that it just wasn't on for Brad Kendrick to stay with her for a month. She didn't have the first clue about nursing anyway—and somebody was going to have to keep an eye on him in the early days of his leaving the hospital.

She let herself into her flat, having time only for a quick cup of tea, and pondered that, just supposing that her flat were big enough to share with that six-foot-plus broad-shouldered individual, then—what about the other complications that would ensue? On an average of once a week Claudia would ring up for a half-hour chat—those chats had begun when she had first moved into the flat and Claudia had feared that she might be lonely. Mornay saw that she stood no chance of keeping from 'her lodger' the knowledge that she had a sister. Especially since it was not unknown for Claudia *and* Gerry and the children to call in at some time over any given weekend.

Shrugging aside the fact that Robert Naylor would be back from Wales on Friday if not before, and could well prove to be another complication, Mornay drove over to Penny Dale, racking her brains to think up some good reason for not presenting herself at the hospital in the morning to pick up Bradford Kendrick.

She reached her brother-in-law's home knowing the uselessness of hoping that the hospital would refuse to let him out. Even without what she had read about the wretched man and his determination in business, her instinct from what she personally knew of him so far told her that the hospital would not have a hope of holding him if he was determined to sign himself out.

'Everything OK with you?' Gerry queried, leaving the lawn where he had been watching his daughters playing on the swing he had put up, and coming to open the gate for her. 'You're looking a bit pale,' he commented.

That she looked a mite pale was no surprise to Mornay; she had barely slept since the accident, and what with one thing and another it was no wonder, she felt, that the strain should be showing. She felt near then to telling him what an idiot she had been yesterday and how, for her sins, she looked like having to put up with an unwanted convalescent for a month—starting to-morrow—unless she could think up something brilliant.

But, looking at Gerry, she could see that he didn't look as though he had slept much since the accident either, so, 'I'm fine,' she told him, and shooed him off to the hospital realising that, for all he wasn't outwardly showing it, he must be concerned to know how far he could trust her to stay quiet. On top of that, Mornay knew that he would not be truly happy until Claudia was back home.

'Are you going to read to us, Mornay?' Emily, who chose to do away with the title 'aunt', broke into Mornay's thoughts.

'What a good idea,' Mornay congratulated her, and, thinking to have the four girls bathed and in bed by the time Gerry returned, 'Have you had supper?' she asked.

'Daddy gave us "ghetti bol'naise",' three-year-old Prudence attempted.

'And told us not to tell Mummy that it came out of a tin,' Alice confided.

'I'll bet it was lovely,' Mornay murmured, and did not have another moment in which to think her own thoughts until an hour and a half later when Gerry returned. While he went upstairs to spend ten minutes with his wide-awake daughters, she went downstairs to make a cup of coffee.

Having decided against asking him how Claudia was in front of his daughters in case the sound of her name brought forth cries of 'I want Mummy', Mornay looked at him with the ready question on her lips when Gerry joined her.

'Terrific!' he told her before she could say a word. 'Claudia—with Luke, of course—is coming out of hospital tomorrow!'

'Oh, super!' Mornay exclaimed, and poured him a cup of coffee while he went into raptures about having Claudia back home and said how rudderless he had felt without her in the home.

Once coffee was out of the way he was then voicing the opinion that he'd better have a blitz round the place before the morning. 'You don't mind if I get the vacuum out, do you?' he asked.

Mornay enjoyed being a part of this family. 'Is that a basket of ironing I see?' she queried.

'Would you?' Gerry asked.

Mornay stayed in the kitchen and tackled the vast mountain of ironing while her brother-in-law went and cleaned the sitting-room. All too soon, though, her pleasing thoughts of her sister and her contented family unit started to get away from her, and into her head came the problem that had been with her since her own hospital visit that afternoon. What good reason could she find for not going to pick up Brad Kendrick in the morning?

She finished the last of the ironing having thought on the question for two solid hours. But, the best answer that had come to her was the answer she had already given—that there was no room in her flat for a guest—either wanted or, as in his case—unwanted.

She recalled how totally unimpressed he had been by her protestations that it was impossible for him to stay with her. 'Take my word for it,' he'd said, 'one more night here is all I'm putting up with.' Mornay unplugged the iron, and, deeply involved with her thoughts, she sighed, and did not hear her brother-in-law come in.

Only a few moments later did she realise that her expression must have revealed a lot of her inner tumult over the predicament she was in when he attracted her attention and looked at her worriedly. 'Mornay,' he said, 'you wouldn't do anything to destroy things for us, would you?'

From somewhere she found a smile, 'Rest easy, Gerry,' she told him.

A black cloud had descended on her thoughts as she drove herself home. Rest easy, she had told him—she wished that *she* could. The words 'One more night here is all I'm putting up with' were haunting her as she garaged her car and entered her apartment building.

She climbed the stairs to the first-floor landing, thinking disheartenedly that, if one counted baby Luke, then that was three people she knew who were coming out of hospital tomorrow—if she couldn't think up a way of ensuring that one of them stayed put. Petrifying visions then began to penetrate of her leaving the hospital with her unwanted guest tomorrow and coming face to face with Claudia and Gerry. It wouldn't take Gerry long to calculate who the stranger was by her side. Her brother-in-law would have a heart attack on the spot, she thought agitatedly.

But it wasn't going to come to that. Somehow, she must find a way of getting out of going to the hospital in the morning—but how? Oh, dear heaven, she began to panic as she made to turn the corner of the landing where she had her flat. If she wasn't at the hospital at ten to pick up Brad Kendrick in the morning then she didn't give much for her chances of not hearing from the police shortly afterwards. Oh, grief, Gerry... Abruptly, her thoughts stopped—frozen in shock!

No, her brain tried to deny what her eyes were telling her as she halted, horrified, in her tracks. Her thoughts then became rapidly chaotic, because evidence that there would be only two people to her knowledge leaving the hospital—not three—was there before her very eyes! Witness to the fact that one male of the species, with whom she was desperately wishing she had never come into contact, could not put up with even just 'one more night' in hospital was there in front of her.

'Oh, no!' she cried huskily, but, no matter how much she might want to protest, there was no getting away from it. All the proof she needed that she would not now be required to present herself at the private wing of Reefingham General tomorrow was there in the sound-asleep man who, with his long legs stretched out before him, was propped up against her flat door. Bradford Kendrick—with an expensive-looking overnight case by his side—had already left hospital!

CHAPTER FOUR

WONDERING how long he'd been there asleep on the landing outside her flat—for surely the hospital would have tried to dissuade him from leaving any later than eight, and it was going on for eleven now—Mornay realised that she just couldn't leave him there and, as was tempting, tiptoe away.

'Mr Kendrick!' she bent down to whisper his name, fearing to disturb the other residents, while quietly thinking that the gods must really have been kind if he'd been propped up outside her flat for a couple of hours and no one had seen him. 'Mr Kendrick!' she repeated, a little louder this time when he slept on. 'Brad!' she used his first name in an endeavour to get through to him when he slept on.

Abruptly his eyes opened and she found herself looking directly into a pair of intelligent dark eyes. 'What?' he asked.

'You can't sleep here,' she told him.

'I'm not returning to hospital,' he told her in that forthright way she was getting to know.

'I didn't mean that,' she told him and, observing that he was looking quite ill, 'Come on,' she told him more kindly, 'you'd better come in.'

'That sounds like a good idea,' he responded, but seemed so determined not to flinch as she stood back and he got to his feet that she felt certain that he must ache in every bone in his body.

She was convinced of it when, his face totally lacking in colour, he leant against the door-frame while she quickly found her key and unlocked the door. Somehow, though, when she experienced an urge to take a hold of his arm and help him into her apartment, she managed to resist it. One way or another, she instinctively felt that he would take exception to any such show of evidence that she was aware of his physical vulnerability.

'This way,' she told him, and did the next best thing, which was to pick up his overnight case and, leaving him to follow, carry it for him into her neat and tidy and pleasantly furnished, if small, sitting-cum-dining-room. 'Where did this come from, by the way?' she enquired as, holding out his case, she turned and saw that he had secured the door behind him.

'I had the hotel pack my few belongings and bring them to the hospital,' he muttered, and looked so rocky that Mornay thought that he actually swayed on his feet.

'You'd better sit down,' she told him, and whether he liked it or not she placed his case to the floor and went over to guide him to her two-seater couch.

She wasn't sure that a grateful grunt did not leave him as the couch took his weight, but he had his eyes closed and as she looked at him she wondered what the blazes she did with him now. He had said categorically that he wasn't returning to the hospital, and, since he'd got the hotel he'd previously been staying in to send over his belongings, she reckoned that she didn't need to ask how he felt about going to a hotel for the night.

As she looked at him, though, she was suddenly again smitten by guilt. He looked terrible and she felt partly to blame—how in creation could she think of sending him anywhere, the condition he was in?

Mornay stayed looking at him for only long enough to observe that, exhausted, he seemed to have fallen asleep again, and then she went quietly and quickly to her airing cupboard. A very short while later she had her bed stripped and remade with clean linen and had taken his case in her bedroom. She then returned to the man who was still sitting on her couch with his eyes closed.

'Mr Kendrick,' she awakened him gently.

'What happened to "Brad"?' he enquired as his eyes came open, showing that, if his body was temporarily broken, his brain was as alert as ever.

'When did you last eat?' she asked him.

'I'm not hungry.'

'Would you like anything to drink?' He shook his head and, catching his involuntary wince, Mornay knew that his head was bad. 'Did the hospital give you any medication?' she asked.

'In my case,' he replied.

'It's time you were in bed,' she told him, and had confirmation that he was done in when, not giving her the smallest argument, he left the couch.

With stiff movements he followed her to the bedroom. If he had any colour then as he sat down on her bed, it was grey. Oh, the poor man, Mornay thought, and was past caring then that by no means did she want him inside her flat.

'The sooner you're in bed, the sooner you'll start to feel better,' she told him, and began to help him out of his lightweight jacket.

'I'll take your word for it,' he mumbled as, used up, it seemed, he allowed her to unfasten the buttons of his shirt.

Mornay left him while he removed his shirt and went to his case and unfastened it. There was a phial of tablets on top which she removed and went to place on the bedside table. Then she returned to his case to hunt for his nightwear. 'They've forgotten your pyjamas,' she told him when her search proved fruitless.

'I don't use them,' he replied, and for no reason she could think of Mornay felt her cheeks go pink.

'Oh,' she mumbled and, unaware that his eyes had followed her and that he had been watching her, she got herself together, realising that there was more to this nursing of the wounded than she had bargained for.

Avoiding looking at his face, or his broad bare chest, she knew that, just as there was no way he was going to spend a comfortable night dressed as he was, there was also no way he was going to find the energy to shed his trousers without her help.

Attempting to appear matter-of-fact, she returned to the man sitting on the edge of her bed and extended a shaky hand to the waistband of his trousers. Though suddenly, with a quickness she had experienced before, he snaked out a hand to her wrist and was putting her hand away from his person. And when at the same time, 'Well, I'll be...' hit her ears, all the sensitive empathy she had for the way he must be feeling abruptly vanished as Brad Kendrick followed it up with, 'As I live and breathe—you're a virgin!'

Realising that there must have been something tell-tale about her actions, she snapped, 'What's that got to do with anything?'

'Don't be cross with me, Mornay,' he smiled, 'my head won't stand it.'

'Oh, I'm sorry,' she said, instantly contrite.

'Why don't you go and fetch me a drink of water?' he suggested tiredly, and as she grabbed at his suggestion and turned about he added, 'Let the tap run for five minutes.'

Seven minutes later Mornay returned to the bedroom to see that Brad Kendrick, his trousers on the floor, was in between the covers, and was once more asleep. As she looked at his pale but relaxed face, compassion stabbed at her and she watched him for some seconds, worried if she should wake him to see that he took his medication. Though maybe he had taken it while she had been in the kitchen. She watched him for a minute or so, then it suddenly seemed to her that, even without his tablets, to sleep soundly might do him as much good.

Quietly she placed the glass of water she had brought upon the bedside table in case he awakened thirsty in the night. Then she picked up his trousers and hung them tidily over the back of a chair, together with the rest of his clothes. Then, collecting her night things, she switched out the light and, leaving the door very slightly ajar so that she should hear him should he be in some distress during the night, she quietly left the room.

Her settee, Mornay discovered within a very short space of time, had never been designed with the comforts of sleep in mind. She tried sleeping on her back, then on her right side and then on her left, and a couple of hours later she estimated that if she'd managed to sleep for ten minutes, that was the sum total.

Think pleasant thoughts, she instructed herself, but within seconds her thinking was again centred on Brad Kendrick. The poor man had been worn out, she reflected, and guessed that he had used up what reserves of energy he had left by getting to her flat. The stairs up to the first floor must have seemed like a mountain!

Another two hours of totalling only another ten minutes of sleep, and Mornay's sensitive thoughts on the convalescent next door had undergone something of a change. Why did he have to come and park himself on her—he knew that he wasn't welcome!

Another tortuous hour went by and Mornay knew that somehow she was going to get him out of her flat. He'd stated quite unequivocally that a month's convalescence was the minimum she owed him, but she was beginning to feel that she'd be a nervous wreck before the end of one week, let alone four.

Dawn had broken when from pure fatigue Mornay at last got to sleep for longer than ten minutes. With Brad Kendrick forever on her mind, though, her last conscious and agitated memory was of reading that no man ever put one over on him without living to regret it.

She awakened a couple of hours later and found that her thoughts were instantly on the same treadmill. Anyone might call or phone and cause a slip which would alert that highly intelligent man who was now hogging her bed to the fact that she was not the driver who knocked him down. Somehow, she just had to get him out of her flat.

Knowing for sure that she was not going to sleep any more, Mornay moved the bedspread which had covered her during the night and, dressing-gown-clad, she went quietly to take a look at her 'guest'.

Having earned herself a few stiff joints from the awkwardness of cramping her fairly tall self on to her fairly short couch, she had some small inkling of the 'all over' ache Brad Kendrick must be enduring as she tiptoed into the bedroom.

He was asleep still, she saw, and as a wave of compassion once more smote her she wished with all she had that the accident had never happened. With warm, gentle eyes she stared at his high forehead, his straight nose, and his firm chin and, crazily, she suddenly felt the most absurd impulse to rest a hand on his forehead. Somehow she felt that by stroking his forehead she might stroke away any after-effects from the accident that he was still suffering.

A moment later she was never more glad that she had not given heed to that impulse, for abruptly his eyes opened and he was awake. Strangely then—when if she had expected anything it would have been for him to straight away be his usual acerbic self—to her surprise he smiled! She saw his glance go from her eyes, to take in her make-up-free unblemished skin and to her sleep-tousled blonde hair, and still he smiled. It was a slow smile, a gentle smile and, she was certain, genuine.

Feeling most peculiarly affected from seeing a first genuine smile on him, Mornay found her mouth curving upwards, and she was able to do no other than smile back. 'Good morning,' she bade him quietly, and then, realising that she must be smiling at him like an idiot, she turned swiftly about and was going through the doorway when she threw over her shoulder, 'I'll just go and get bathed and dressed.'

It did not take Mornay long, when in her bathroom she tried a spot of self-analysis, to realise that what had come over her a minute or two ago had been nothing more alarming than shyness. She was unused to having a male guest spending the night in her flat. In fact she had never had a male overnight guest in her flat, so it was hardly to be wondered at that she should feel a little peculiar about it—a little shy.

Pleased with her diagnosis, Mornay was quicker than usual in her bath that morning and was soon dressed in a summer dress suitable for the office, and had the tousled look brushed from her long hair.

For no known reason she took a deep breath and squared her shoulders before she went to take another peek at her 'guest'. To her consternation, however, he was not in the bedroom where she fully expected him to be, but, up and dressed, he was in her sitting-room.

'You shouldn't be out of bed!' she exclaimed in concern, seeing for herself how stiff his movements were when he came away from taking a look out of the window.

There was not so much as a glimmer of a smile about him now, she observed when, clearly taking exception to any idea she might have of bossing him around, 'I've had enough of bed,' he told her forthrightly, in 'end of subject' tones.

There was not a smile about Mornay either as, starting to get more than a degree fed up, and with thoughts of Claudia and how if she didn't go over to see her and the new baby tonight she reckoned she could be sure Claudia would be on the phone, she grew as forthright as him.

'If you're that well,' she snapped, as a hundred and one complications of his being there piled in, 'you're well enough to go home!'

If she was blunt, however, Brad Kendrick was blunter. 'I'm staying here!' he snarled, his chin jutting as though to say, argue with that.

'You can't!' Mornay tried.

'Why?' Ice was starting to glitter in his eyes as he challenged her to give him some good reason.

'Because...' she began hotly, and stopped. 'Because...' she attempted again, 'because I have to go to work, that's why!'

'You have a job—looking after me!' he informed her sharply, but as again Mornay felt the urge to physically lash out at him she saw the way he involuntarily rubbed a hand across his brow and, for all they were not quite yelling at each other, she realised that he was just not up to a shouting match.

Without another word she walked past him and into the kitchen. It was from there that she heard the bathroom door close, and she got on with the job of making a pot of tea and rummaging in her cupboards for something with which to feed the brute. She knew little about nursing, but it seemed to her that if he was to take his medication it would be best to have some foundation put down first.

She was in the dining-room part of the sitting-room, laying the table, when, showered and clean-shaven, Bradford Kendrick came from the bathroom and into the room.

'If you'd like to sit here, Mr Kendrick, I'll get you some scrambled eggs on toast,' she said, indicating one of the dining chairs, her tone even as she observed that just the action of shaving and showering seemed to have taken the stuffing out of him.

She turned away as he drew near to the table, and was on her way back to the kitchen when she heard him drawl, 'You can't call me Mr Kendrick for a month—make it Brad.'

Any kind feelings which might have surfaced were quickly banished as, thanking him not for his unsubtle hint, she was more concerned with getting him out of her apartment than putting up with him for a month. She glanced at her watch as she stirred eggs in the saucepan and knew that she didn't stand a hope of getting to her office on time.

But, 'Here we are!' she exclaimed breezily as she carried a tray containing both their breakfasts into the dining area. He did not seem at all impressed by her attempt to put a brave face on matters, though, and as she took her place opposite him she began to wonder if he was always such a bundle of joy or—was he in pain? 'You must take your tablets after breakfast,' she began as he picked up his knife and fork.

'I already did,' he grunted.

'Do you have a headache?' she queried kindly, and got a sour look for her trouble. Clearly Brad Kendrick was not the sort to down medication unless *he* considered it absolutely essential.

Silence reigned over the table as she set her mind to think up some tactful way to get him to leave without drawing his obstinate streak. She looked to his face, saw that he now seemed to have a trace of colour, and, cheered by that, she was about to launch into her tactful 'please go home' plea, when she suddenly became aware of how ham-fistedly he was cutting up his toast.

Then it was that she noticed the bruising on his left wrist and realised that he must have instinctively put out his hands to protect himself when her Metro had come at him—his left hand coming off worse than his right.

She was well and truly conscious-stricken when, 'To hell with it!' he suddenly grunted and, tipping the scrambled egg off the toast, he forked the egg up using his right hand, and downed toast which he held in his left.

'Where there's a will...' Mornay smiled, and when he glanced disagreeably across the table at her she asked, 'Have you damaged your wrists very badly?'

'According to the hospital they'll be as good as new within a few more days,' he condescended to answer.

'How about the rest of you?' she enquired, and realised when his reply came that he had not taken her question at face-value.

'Whatever,' he shrugged, 'I've still decided to take a month off work.'

Biting back the snappy retort of 'I hope it keeps fine for you', Mornay chewed on the toast and marmalade and sought afresh for some tactful way to tell him to be gone without his astute brain seeing right through her.

She soon realised, though, from the way he had looked beneath the surface of her question, 'How about the rest of you?', that she was wasting her time using tact. John Blunt here would see straight through her 'tactfulness' in two seconds flat!

He had finished his scrambled eggs and toast and was partaking of tea when, still the same needing a gentle way in, Mornay suddenly found it in a polite-sounding, 'I never thought, Mr—er—Brad—would you have preferred coffee?'

'Tea's fine,' he grunted.

'Good,' she smiled, and then embarked on a hurried and speedily put together suggestion. 'I've been thinking that if you'd like to go to a hotel—let me finish——' she inserted quickly when it looked as though he might chop her off '—I'd drive you there, of course,' she added, and weathered his look of acid, to go charging on, 'Then I could come and see you after I've finished work and...' He was shaking his head well before she had come to the end, and, suddenly infuriated by him, she erupted stormily, 'Well, you can't stay here!'

Furiously she glared at him. Mildly, his glance taking
in her sparking blue eyes, he stared back. Then, pleasantly, she heard again the question which she was beginning to believe he had been born asking. 'Why?' he
queried.

'Because,' she began hotly, when just then her glance
rested on the couch, 'because I'm *not* spending another
night on *that*!' she told him forcefully.

'For a virgin,' he drawled mockingly, 'you're rather
forward.'

'What does that mean?' Mornay flared. Somehow it
had never occurred to her, with the giant-sized headache
he'd had last night, that he would remember, let alone
refer to, his pronouncement that she was a virgin.

'Weren't you saying that you preferred to bed in with
me rather than spend another night——'

'I was not!' she hissed before he could finish, and it
was no wonder to her then that she should so often feel
like thumping him. He was the giddy limit—and that
was without the wicked gleam that had just joined the
mockery in his eyes.

'My apologies,' he offered insincerely, and, after some
moments of appearing to be thinking seriously, 'I have
it,' he murmured, and, looking straight into her wary
blue eyes, he announced, 'We must—both—move out.'

'Both!' she exclaimed, not crediting her hearing.

But there was nothing wrong with her hearing, Brad
Kendrick soon made that plain when he reminded her,
'You said yourself that I need someone to look after
me,' and added, 'Now, where would you like to go?'

She was asleep. She must be dreaming this, Mornay
tried to tell herself—though nightmare seemed a more
accurate description. But it did not work. For one thing,
she had her eyes open. For another she was looking
straight into a pair of dark eyes—the eyes of a monster
who was waiting—seriously—for her answer.

Though, even as she said, 'Scotland,' the furthest away spot she could think of, she just could not believe that he was as serious as he seemed with his statement that they should both move out.

'Anywhere in particular?' he enquired, and while as it started to get through to her that he jolly well was serious—deadly serious for all his former mockery—all she could do was dumbly shake her head.

She was still in a state of dazed shock when, her non-preference for a choice of destination in Scotland noted by him, she saw him flick a glance to his watch. As if he was now in charge of her, Mornay copied him. Her watch said five past nine, but she was feeling so shaken that it passed her by that she was already five minutes late for her office.

'Where's your phone?' was the next question Brad Kendrick asked, and Mornay started to come away from being shaken to note that he hadn't asked, 'Have you got a phone?' which seemed to confirm for her that he had found her address from the telephone book.

'It's plugged in in the kitchen at the moment,' she answered him, and sat staring after him when—his movements stiff—he left the table and headed for the kitchen.

From her seat at the dining table she heard sounds indicating that he was about to make contact with the outside world. Then, before she could start to panic that he might be ringing the police to identify her as the culprit who had knocked him over and who had driven on without stopping, she heard his voice, all authority, stating, 'Miss Boulter, please.' Then, 'Helen,' she heard him say, then a small pause when 'Helen' clearly recognised his voice and, obviously having been contacted by him previously, probably from the private ward, must have been asking how he was. 'I'm out of hospital now,' he told her and was then instructing, 'I'm having some time off—find me a hideaway in Scotland.' And while

Mornay, unashamedly eavesdropping, started to realise that maybe because he was so well known in the business world it was no wonder that he liked his privacy outside of it, hence his request for a 'hideaway', he was ending, obviously reading the digits of the telephone dial, 'Ring me back on this number.' And while Mornay realised too that 'Helen' must be his secretary, he gave her the number and promptly rang off.

And still Mornay could hardly believe it. 'Do you—*really*—intend to go to Scotland?' she just had to ask when he came back and retook his seat at the table.

'And that you should come with me,' he replied calmly and—obviously quite at home—helped himself to a slice of toast from the toast rack. 'So kind of you to offer to drive,' he murmured.

Mornay gave him a killing look, hoped his toast choked him and left the table to storm to the kitchen— where she began to tidy up. The man was a swine, she fumed as, not wanting him in her kitchen again, she unplugged the phone and went and plugged it into a socket in the sitting-room.

Without a word to him she cleared some of the used dishes from off the table and felt defeated when, catching a glimpse of the bruising on his left wrist, she realised that it would take some days before he was fit to drive himself anywhere.

Feeling, however, that she had not a thing that she wanted to say to him, she did some washing up and returned for the rest of the dishes to find that he had moved and was now resting on the settee.

She went back to the kitchen, torn between a desire to tell him to go and rest on the bed, and a desire to tell him to clear off. She busied herself with sudsy water, but was soon finished with her chores.

She felt disinclined to spend more time with him than she had to, however, and when she left the kitchen she went through to the bathroom to clean a bath that was already clean, and to generally give it a spruce-up.

It crossed her mind at one point to wonder what Brad Kendrick would do if she told him that it had been her brother-in-law who had been driving that night, and not her. But that notion did not linger for long. Hadn't the paper described Brad Kendrick as an 'eye for an eye' man? Wasn't he proving that now by insisting that in return for her injuring him she should pay by looking after him?

Whichever way she looked at it, it seemed to Mornay then that she had no option but to do everything that the wretched man said, because he'd find some other way of making Gerry pay—the obvious way: that of reporting him to the police.

Mornay was not at all certain why Brad Kendrick had not reported *her* to the police, anyway. But what she did know for certain was that somebody was going to be made to pay. Glumly she faced the fact that, if she did confess Gerry's part in the accident, when it came to the bottom line, it would be Claudia and her children who would ultimately suffer.

Mornay left the bathroom with a heavy heart—she had to go along with that monster—even if it meant going as far as Scotland. She was crossing the sitting-room and, she owned, not in the best frame of mind when, his voice light, Brad Kendrick halted her.

'Did you really sleep on this couch?' he enquired, having endured enough of it, it seemed, to be able to ascertain that its potential for ensuring a night of unbroken sleep was little short of murderous.

'Occasionally,' Mornay replied acidly, and would have gone on to the bedroom to tidy round when suddenly she was arrested by his laugh. She saw his face light up, felt a most peculiar sensation in her heart region, and realised, not only that her dry humour had amused him, but also that she must have eaten her toast too quickly.

Suddenly, however, her mind went a blank, and as his amusement faded she discovered that she was still standing in front of him, and that she was having to search really hard for something to say that would explain why she was still standing there looking at him. 'Er—what did the hospital say?' she pulled out of thin air.

'Say?' he enquired.

'When you told them you were leaving,' she enlightened him as she got herself together.

'What could they say?' he queried, and seemed so genuinely surprised by her question that she realised Brad Kendrick was a law unto himself. Quite plainly, when he decided to do something, he simply did not deign to consider that there might be any opposition.

Which, Mornay began to think a moment later, pretty well summed up what was happening with her. He had decided that, since she was responsible for his being incapacitated, she could jolly well look after him. When she, meaning a hotel locally, had hinted that she could look after him elsewhere, he, brooking no opposition, had gone to work on the idea.

'You said that your wrists will be as good as new within a few days,' she reminded him. 'What about the rest of you?' she enquired, wanting more of an answer to that than the one he'd given her before: that he'd taken a month off work.

'What about the rest of me?' he tossed her own question back at her, being deliberately obtuse, she felt sure.

Mornay gave him a look of hearty dislike—which bounced straight off him—and asked, 'Is it going to take long for you to recover completely?'

'No,' he replied promptly, but any joy Mornay found from that answer was negated when he added silkily, 'Especially with you right there to ensure that I rest.'

Gritting her teeth, Mornay ignored the first part of what he said and questioned him about the last part. 'Is that what they've said—that you have to rest?'

His reply was to give her a cool look. But, even though he seemed to have grown bored with discussing his health and had now clammed up, Mornay felt she could be fairly certain that to rest was the instruction his doctor had given him on leaving the hospital.

Since Brad Kendrick seemed to have nothing more he wanted to say, Mornay left him and spent some time tidying the bedroom—which was tidy to start with. She really ought to ring Mr Probert, she thought worriedly, though she supposed she was still hoping against hope that she might be putting in some time at her office that day. She next thought that maybe a phone call to her brother-in-law dropping a hint of what was happening might not be a bad idea. Though how she could ring Gerry with her 'guest' sitting so close to the telephone she'd no idea. Gerry would only panic anyway, if she did ring him, she decided, and forgot the idea totally when she realised that, since Gerry would not delay in going to fetch her sister home, Claudia would probably answer the phone—and no way could she tell Claudia what was happening.

She was standing staring into space when, at that precise moment, the telephone rang, and Mornay jumped like a scalded cat. In the next second, however, with thoughts of Gerry, Claudia and the telephone still in her mind, she was diving into the sitting-room to answer it.

To her horror, however, she made it to the sitting-room just in time to see Brad Kendrick in the act of picking it up. Worse, as she went to grab it from him—knowing that she was going to be hard put to it to explain why some strange man should be answering her phone, be the caller either Claudia, Gerry or indeed, Mr Probert—so the man who was using her home like

Liberty Hall, and who saw nothing wrong in answering her phone, was saying, 'Hello?'

Ready to snatch the phone from him, Mornay went forward to do just that when he suddenly put an arm out to bar her way. Then said, 'Ah, Helen, what have you got for me?'

Abruptly Mornay let her hands fall back to her sides, and as she saw him reach for the pencil and telephone pad and then start to make notes she began to fume, Trust him to have the most efficient secretary ever created!

She thereafter tried to ignore him as she realised that for the caller to have been either Claudia or Gerry, they would first have had to have telephoned her office and have discovered that she wasn't in work yet. When that thought began to trigger off even more horrendous thoughts—such as Mr Probert ringing Claudia to find out what was wrong with his secretary that she wasn't in work, and the consequences of that—Mornay decided that she would rather listen in to what Brad Kendrick was saying.

She tuned in as, giving his secretary a few business instructions, he then terminated the call by telling her, 'And, Helen—leave it twenty-four hours before you announce to anyone interested that I'm recuperating abroad.'

Mornay had time only for it to register that he really did value his privacy, then he was putting the phone down and had his eyes on her. He was starting to look tired again, she saw, though there was nothing tired about his voice when he addressed her. For his tone was firm and authoritative when, 'Are you packed?' he clipped.

'Packed?' Mornay queried, her thoughts more on how he looked as though a lie-down might do him more good than anything.

She was rapidly brought to earth, however, when he grunted tersely, 'If we're to make Scotland before nightfall, we'd better get started.'

CHAPTER FIVE

A CHILL struck at Mornay's heart. This was it, then—
he hadn't been joking! She looked at him and saw that,
for all he looked bone-weary, he still managed to wear
a 'not to be argued with' look. Biting back a torrent of
heated argument which threatened to burst forth anyway,
she turned swiftly about and returned to her bedroom.

As she threw some of her belongings into a case her
mood swung from being hotly furious, to one of defiance
which said, damn him, she wouldn't go, then to one of
defeat. She had to go and, when it came down to the
nitty gritty, she knew that she had no choice but to go
with him.

In between time, though, while she was fretting and
fuming and finally accepting, Mornay was desperately
wondering what she was going to do about letting
Claudia know where she was—or, as the case might be—
not letting her know where she was. As she loved her
sister, so her sister loved her. Claudia would worry herself
silly if, without explanation, more than a few days went
by with her not making contact. Visualising her sister's
hurt as day after day went by and she did not appear at
Penny Dale to view the new baby, Mornay grew yet more
desperate to know what to do.

It was out of that sheer desperation, however, that the
answer came to her. She was just visualising a whole
hornet's nest being stirred up if, say by tomorrow,
Claudia had thought it peculiar that she had not been
over, and rang her work, only to find out from Mr
Probert that he had not seen anything of her since
Wednesday evening. For sure, Claudia would be getting

75

Gerry to drive her to her flat on the instant. Mornay had just gone into visions of her sister's calling out the police when suddenly she thought—unless...and then she had it.

She was uncertain how long she would be away, but if Brad Kendrick insisted that the payment for her 'crime' be *a whole month* of looking after him, then she had packed a fairly large suitcase.

He was still on the couch when, toting her case, she entered the sitting-room. His eyes were closed, she noted, as though he was intent on getting what rest he could before the start of their journey. She flicked a glance to the phone and, guessing that beneath those closed lids he was not asleep, she was tempted to take the phone into the kitchen.

Her glance flicked to his bruised left wrist, the source of her present inspiration—her mother was left-handed— and she picked up the phone and dialled the Town Hall from where she was. What did she care? Let Bradford Kendrick know of the lies he had driven her to.

'Mr Probert, please,' she requested when her call was answered and, when put through to him, 'I'm so sorry to be ringing you this late,' she apologised, and then launched, not very comfortably, she had to admit, into how she was phoning from Solihull because her mother had sprained her wrist very badly and very much needed her to assist at her home for a while. 'I was wondering,' she ended, having presented him with a *fait accompli*, 'if I could have some time off out of my holiday allowance.'

She came off the phone renewing her previously held opinion of what a nice man Mr Probert was, for he had sounded more concerned that her mother's wrist would soon heal, when he could very easily have been most disgruntled at having to find a temporary secretary at such short notice. She had hated lying to him, though, but she felt that in that one call she had covered two possibilities. The possibility of Mr Probert's taking it into his head to ring Claudia when his secretary hadn't contacted him had been eliminated, as had the possibility of Claudia's contacting the police if she rang the office and spoke to him. From what Mornay knew of her sister, she felt that she could safely bet that, while Claudia might think her crazy to go dashing over to Solihull at a moment's notice, the one thing she could be fairly certain of was that she would not ring her mother. All that Mornay hoped was that, if her mother had not penned the letter which she had said she would write to Claudia, she did not take it into her head to do it today.

Mornay was just realising that, whatever happened, she must somehow or other get in touch with Gerry as soon as she could, when she suddenly became aware of a pair of dark eyes surveying her.

She was unused to telling lies, and guilt, she supposed, was the reason for her snappiness when, ignoring that his glance seemed to be taking in each of her delicate features in turn, she abruptly erupted, 'Thanks to you, Mr Kendrick, I'm now a liar!'

'Why thank me, Miss Haynes?' he drawled, his glance coming away from her mouth to look her in the eyes. 'If my memory is anywhere as near as good as it used to be, I'd say you were—without any prompting from me—lying your head off before now; within the first five minutes of our speaking to each other, in fact.'

More than ever wishing that she had never invented witnessing an ambulance coming for him after the accident, Mornay had to acknowledge the truth of what he said. That did not stop her from glaring at him just the same when, assuming that he had driven to Reefingham initially, and that he would want them to use his car, she questioned reluctantly, 'Do I have to go to the hotel you were staying in to pick up your car, or what?'

'Or what,' he replied shortly. 'When I contacted the Belvedere I told them to garage it for me until I either collect it or send for it.'

'What you're really saying is that you don't trust me to drive your car, isn't it?' she flared, and when he gave her a cool look as though to say that, if that was what he meant, he would have said it, she added tartly, 'It's a wonder to me that you're trusting me to drive you at all!'

'You can be sure if you hit anything that I'll be hauling you off to the nearest police station to report it,' he silenced her grittily, and Mornay, giving him a look of disdain for his trouble, picked up her case and went to the door.

At the door, however, she halted. Confound it, the man wasn't well, and as she turned and saw the stiff way he got up from the couch she realised that she could be more of a help to him than she was being.

'If you'd like to start on your way down the stairs,' she conquered her crossness to suggest, 'I'll bring your case.'

'I'm quite capable of carrying my own case,' he told her, his disdain beating hers into a cocked hat.

'Suit yourself!' she told him pithily, but was more fed up than angry when, fiddling about with the door lock when inner sensitivity hinted that it wouldn't be so obvious that she was waiting if she looked busy, she hung about while he collected his case and then joined her by the door.

Once her flat had been secured she went on a little way in front of him, her feet slowing at the bottom of the stairs so that it was together that they walked to where she had garaged her Metro.

Placing her case down on the tarmac, she left him standing by it while she unlocked the garage and drove her car out. Though on leaving the driving seat prior to stowing her luggage on board she caught him glancing cold-eyed at the dent in the wing.

'That's one you won't be claiming on your insurance!' he remarked sourly. 'Though, knowing you, I wouldn't put it past you!' he grunted.

'You know nothing about me!' Mornay flared, and received a cynical look from him for her trouble.

She had put her luggage in the boot and he had come round to the hatch and handed her his when she saw that he was looking a degree grey again, and suddenly her heart went out to him.

'Are you sure you're up to this?' she enquired, as yet having no idea of their exact destination but, at a quick calculation, guessing that it was going to take anything up to four hours just to reach the Scottish borders.

But his mockery was back, and despite his looking far from well there was nothing wrong with his tongue when, 'You care?' he drawled.

'Enough to hit every pot-hole!' she erupted, and, slamming the hatch down hard, she locked it and stormed to the driver's seat.

'Swine' was too nice a name for him—that was her considered opinion when, with Brad Kendrick beside her, she drove away from her garage and away from Reefingham and headed north.

Instinctively, however, she did avoid the pot-holes, and, for all she called herself weak for doing it, she drove with care so that no sudden movement would cause the aches in his body to protest more than they must be doing already.

She only realised that she had simmered down from being angry, however, when she noticed that her thinking was going along the path of not really blaming him, when she remembered him looking at the dent in her wing, and thought about the evidence *he* had, for not wanting her to drive his car. A few minutes later, and she found she had gone on to consider that maybe he wasn't so much bothered about his car but—since it appeared that he was a person who very much valued his privacy— that he was taking the precaution of not having his car recognised, his whereabouts pin-pointed—by using hers.

She had told him that he knew nothing of her, but there was, she considered, a tremendous amount that she did not know about him. It was around then that Mornay decided that, since it seemed she could not get out of going to Scotland with him—for, had there been a chance, she would not be with him now, heading that way—she was going to make the best of it. She had heard him laugh once, she recalled, so things couldn't be all bad. And for him to have laughed at all when he must be feeling as off-colour as he looked just had to be a plus—didn't it?

She took a sideways glance at him, and, seeing that his eyes were open, 'Where are we making for?' she asked him quietly, her tone affable.

'A place called Kilcaber in Renfrewshire,' he obliged in an even voice.

'Do you know it?'

'I've never been there,' he admitted, and added, 'We'll buy a map when we stop for petrol.'

Mornay was doing all she knew how to 'make the best of things' when not long afterwards they did have to stop for petrol. She came close to an involuntary eruption, however, when as she went to pay for the purchase she found that Brad, who had gone into the shop-cum-paying-area, had settled what was due at the same time as he had paid for a map he had selected.

Biting back her independent streak, she returned to her car, and when he got into the passenger seat she drove off the garage forecourt. He had decided to take a look at the map when, an hour later, thinking that his aching body must sorely be in need of a rest, Mornay decided to stop.

She stopped outside a huge motorway restaurant, and when he looked at her questioningly she lied, 'I need a rest,' and might have got away with that lie, had she not—in her search for tact—forgotten how quick-thinking he could be when she didn't want him to be. 'Do you feel up to having a meal?' she enquired with the best tact she could muster. 'Or shall I get something for us to eat going along?'

'Far be it from me to deprive *you* of your rest,' he replied coolly. He it was, then, who led the way into the restaurant.

They were seated in the restaurant however when, no matter what his private opinion of her might be, Mornay discovered that there was no way he would deliberately embarrass her in public. For when, if she had thought at all, she would have thought that he would either have ignored her, or, at the very least—especially in the instance of him not feeling so good—replied sharply to anything she had to say, he did nothing of the kind.

'Do you like your work?' he enquired when, he having ordered a curry while she opted for a salad, they were seated waiting for their meals.

'Driving?' she asked, her tone suspicious.

'Secretarial,' he replied, and suddenly smiled a gentle smile that sent her suspicions flying.

Just then the waitress came and Mornay, having chosen salad mainly because it was such a blisteringly hot day, watched as Brad picked up his fork. After telling him, 'Yes, I quite like my work,' she could not deny an inquisitiveness which she discovered she had about him when, in view of the baking heat, she just had to add, 'As you like curry.'

'Curry?' he replied, then, looking down to his plate, he actually grinned as he shrugged and revealed, 'It was about the only thing on the menu that I thought I could manage one-handed.'

'Oh, Brad!' escaped her involuntarily, as she guiltily realised that, after seeing the way he'd had difficulty at breakfast time, she should have been aware of his problems. 'I should have thought——'

'When I want you to cut my meat up for me, I'll let you know,' he interrupted, but there was still a trace of a smile about his most agreeably shaped mouth, she observed.

The day had started to cloud over when, back in the car again, they headed further north. Though it was still quite warm when, after an hour and a half of driving, Mornay considered that it might be an idea if she stopped to allow him to stretch a few of the creaks out of his body.

'I'm gasping for a cup of tea,' she lied. 'Joining me?' she queried as she drew the car to a halt.

'Wouldn't dream of disappointing you,' he murmured, and Mornay realised that quite plainly he had seen straight through her.

They stayed idling over a pot of tea for a good half-hour, and as before Brad Kendrick remained pleasant, and had no harsh comment to make that might have made her feel uncomfortable.

In fact so pleasant was he that, for all she was hoping against hope that a busy businessman such as him would get fed up with his Scottish exile well before the month he'd stipulated was up, she had started to think that maybe the time she had to spend looking after him might not be so completely untenable as she'd first feared.

They were back in the car and were motoring on when her new-found curiosity about him made her want to question what he had been doing in her part of the world that fateful night. She should, she later realised, have kept her curiosity to herself, but since his pleasant manner seemed to be still about him she plunged in— where angels feared to tread.

'Do you come to Reefingham often?' she queried, apropos of nothing.

'If you're thinking that when you've "nursed me back to full health" I shall again call on you—forget it!' he suddenly, and unfairly, she thought, snarled.

'The saints forbid!' she flared, wondering where the even-tempered being she had been before knowing him had gone; since knowing him, she had found she could go from calm to furious in less time than it took to blink. 'It's to be hoped that I never have to see you again! You can be darn sure that I'd quickly run the other way if I saw you coming!' she raced on angrily. 'It's——'

'Which is what I should have done,' he sliced in to chop her off. 'Foolish of me to suppose you would stop at a red traffic signal,' he added sarcastically.

The rest of the journey was completed in stony silence. Nothing in creation would have made Mornay speak to the vile creature again. When they reached Renfrewshire, she stopped the car and, without deigning to put a single question to him, leaned over and helped herself to the map, located the Kilcaber he had spoken of, and drove on.

She was feeling not one whit friendlier towards him when she saw the signpost saying that they had arrived at Kilcaber. Again she stopped the car, and again she said not a word. This time, however, she just sat perfectly still. It did not take but a moment for Brad Kendrick to catch on. In seconds, he had given her the address she was to drive to.

Mornay's spirits were in no way lifted when, arriving at the address he had given her, she saw that, though it was not a discreet hotel, neither was it a quiet boarding house—nor a house at all, for that matter. But, stuck in the back of beyond, the hideaway they had come to was a small, if modern-looking, bungalow.

More made speechless than not intending to speak, Mornay got out of the car and, not at all certain what

she had been expecting anyway, she realised that his
secretary had probably obeyed his instructions to the
letter. You couldn't, she thought dully, get more hidden
away than here!

'Are you going to stand there staring forever, or are
you going to unlock the boot so I can get my case?'

Mornay turned about and saw that Brad was out of
the car and that he was waiting by the back of her vehicle. She tossed him a look of intense dislike, but went
and opened up the boot, and was human enough to hope
it hurt him when—too impatient to wait for her to hand
his case out—he stretched inside to get it.

'I'll carry my own case!' she snapped when, as though
to prove that it had not pained him at all, he went to
lift out her much larger case, automatically, it seemed.

'Why shouldn't you?' he snarled, and left her to it.
Mornay was struggling up the path to a month's pur-
gatory with her case when suddenly the door to the
bungalow opened and a pleasant-faced sandy-haired lady
emerged, wearing a floral overall.

'I heard the car,' she greeted Brad, not yet seeing
Mornay who was passing behind an overgrown rhodo-
dendron bush. 'Come away in,' she beamed, in a beautiful Scottish accent, 'everything's ready for you!'
Mornay's depressed spirits had lifted a few degrees that,
by the look of it, she was not stuck with just that swine
of a man for company, but that there was a resident
housekeeper, when, 'Oh, gracious!' the woman declared, as she suddenly spotted Mornay. 'They didn't
say that you'd be bringing your wife!'

Wife! Mornay neared the door and was about to set
the woman straight without delay, but she did not get
the chance—for there was too much else going on.
Somehow or other they were all standing in the small
hall with the outer door closed and the sandy-haired lady
was introducing herself as Mrs Macdonald, and was
addressing them as Mr and Mrs Adams. About to again

try and interrupt to say that she was not married to the brute she had the misfortune to accompany, Mornay was distracted as she realised that his secretary had excelled herself when, in finding him his hideaway, she had also found him a name with which no one would associate him.

With the moment gone when she could have put Mrs Macdonald right, Mornay tuned back in to wonder why she should bother putting her right, and to hear that the woman was not the live-in housekeeper but was a lady who occasionally worked for the renting agent. She had apparently been called in to come and air the bungalow, purchase some provisions, and to prepare a simple meal for when a Mr Adams arrived that day.

'I didn't know what time you'd arrive, but because it's turned chilly I thought a casserole would be about the best. It's in the oven now,' Mrs Macdonald informed them, but fretted, 'But I don't know that it'll be enough for two.'

'I'm sure it will be, Mrs Macdonald,' Brad assured her, his charm, in view of his attitude five minutes earlier, startling Mornay. She was startled again when, not a second later, he went on, 'My wife and I ate a substantial lunch on the way here, so a small portion of casserole each will be ideal.'

'If you're sure...' Mrs Macdonald began, but had her smile flushed out by him, and when he asked how much was he in her debt, replied, 'I've put the receipts for what I bought on the kitchen table.' It seemed only polite to Mornay that she should leave her case in the hall and follow Brad and the woman into the kitchen.

Looking round the kitchen while 'Mr Adams' thanked Mrs Macdonald for seeing to things so well, and settled all accounts with her, Mornay observed that the kitchen was absolutely spotless.

'There's bacon, eggs, butter and milk in the fridge, and bread in the bin,' the woman who was such a tidy

worker drew Mornay's gaze. 'And I've left my telephone number on the pad next to your phone, should
you need me for anything,' she went on. And while
Mornay registered gratefully that the out of the way
bungalow had a phone—though when and how she was
going to get to use it to ring Gerry in private was another
matter—the wiry-looking woman was adding that she
lived but a mile down the road.

Mornay's gaze was then drawn to Brad when he courteously passed the time of day with the woman as she
collected her basket and cardigan from a chair and edged
towards the outer kitchen door. He was looking quite
exhausted again, she saw, and, as he went with Mrs
Macdonald and opened the door for her, so all Mornay's
animosity against him suddenly died.

'Goodbye, Mr Adams—goodbye, Mrs Adams,' Mrs
Macdonald smiled.

'Goodbye—and thank you,' Mornay smiled back, and
had more on her mind than to explain her single status.
From the kitchen window she saw Mrs Macdonald cycle
off down the road, then Mornay addressed the man
whom not long ago she'd have bitten her tongue rather
than speak to. 'If I may say so, Mr Adams,' she voiced
quietly, 'I'd say that you'd be better off in bed.'

He looked across at her, his expression unsmiling, and
she rather guessed that she was in for a repeated snarled
earful along the lines that he'd had enough of bed. But,
to her surprise, his reply was not snarled, nor was it in
any way what she expected. But, 'If I may say so, Mrs
Adams,' he replied, his tone as quiet as hers had been,
'you're something else again.' Quite what that was supposed to mean, Mornay wasn't sure, though she had an
idea that it might have something to do with the fact
that she seemed to be accepting a situation when she
must have realised that there was not a thing she could
otherwise do. He did not, however, take up her suggestion that he'd be better off in bed but decreed, 'Let's

take a look round,' and was on his way to the door that
led to the hall.

Mornay's respect for Helen Boulter went up in bounds
when she realised that his secretary must have worked
out that it might be better, in view of the trauma his
body had received, for him to live on one level rather
than have to climb stairs. Mornay had no complaints
about the furnishings either. The sitting-room, which she
quickly espied housed the telephone, was thickly carpeted, had fresh linen curtains, a quite luxurious-looking
three-piece suite, a television and a couple of highly pol-
ished occasional tables, as well as some quite liveable-
with pictures adorning one wall.

'So far, so good,' Brad commented.

The bungalow had a separate dining-room, and two
bedrooms, both of which, in addition to the normal
bedroom furniture, had a double bed, though only one
of the beds had been made up.

'Which room do you want?' he gave her the choice
as they stood in the room which Mrs Macdonald had
made ready.

'You have this one,' Mornay replied, and dared, considering that he seemed to be rocking on his feet, to
suggest, 'Why don't you get into bed now—it's been a
long day for you? I could bring your supper in on a
tray.'

'You're too good to me,' he mocked. His eyes went
to the bed. 'Give me a shout around eight,' he told her.

Mornay left him hoping that he would at least lie down
on top of his bed and have a rest, and went looking for
the airing cupboard. In no time at all she had rooted
out sheets, pillow-slips and a light blanket for the bed
in the room she would have, and, moving quietly so as
not to disturb the man in the room next door, she set
about making up her bed and doing some unpacking.

At a quarter to eight she was in the middle of laying
the dining-room table when Brad came and joined her.

She saw at once that he had more colour in his face, but not all that much.

'I was going to give you a call,' she told him.

'I've saved you the bother.'

She wanted to ask him if he'd managed to snatch a nap, but thought he might resent it. 'Have you taken your tablets?' she asked instead, adding hurriedly, 'Shall I get you some water?'

'I've taken them without,' he said easily. 'Can I do anything?'

'You can sit there,' she told him, a shade bossily, she had to admit. But to her surprise she saw him go and meekly take the chair she had indicated at the table. Before she left the room though, she glanced at his face and could have sworn that he was holding back a grin.

Now what had amused him? she wondered as she went to the kitchen and cut some bread to add bulk to their meal. Had it amused him that she should take it upon herself to boss him around—or was he amusing himself by humouring her and allowing her to give him orders?

'This is good,' he remarked when, insisting that the casserole be divided into two equal portions when she attempted to give him the lion's share, they sat opposite each other tucking in to Mrs Macdonald's excellent cooking.

'It is,' Mornay agreed, but very little else was remarked upon during the meal.

Though she was pleased to see that he had a good appetite. If his appetite stayed with him then day by day he would gain more and more strength. Mornay hoped that it was not wishful thinking on her part, but she felt that all looked fair for an early return to their respective homes.

'Have you had enough?' she enquired when he laid down his fork.

'Ample,' he replied.

'Mrs Macdonald has left an apple pie——'

'No, thanks,' he butted in, and Mornay's hopes for an early getaway took a dip.

She wanted quite badly then to tell him that he must eat, but, looking into his tired eyes, she refrained. 'Why don't you go and have an early night?' she suggested instead, and then found that, just as she was scrutinising his face, so he was scrutinising hers.

'You look as though an early night wouldn't come amiss with you, for that matter,' he observed.

It did not surprise Mornay that she looked a wreck, though she did not thank him for referring to it. She started to clear the table, of the opinion that, since she had barely slept on Monday night, and on Tuesday night for that matter, and that since one night on her couch last night was one night too many, the only wonder was that she didn't have bags under her eyes stretching down to her knees.

When, reaching for the cruet, she suddenly saw Brad reach for it at the same time, she realised that he was helping her to clear away—but she didn't thank him for that either.

In all honesty, she could not say that he was in a talk-ative frame of mind when he came into the kitchen and did the best his bruised wrists would allow to help with the washing-up. Thankfully, however, Mrs Macdonald had washed up after her cooking, and there was little of it to do.

Mornay had formed the opinion, as she cast a last tidying, inspecting eye around the kitchen, that she would be going to bed without another word passing between her and Bradford Kendrick.

But she was proved wrong about that. For, as she went to walk past him on her way out of the kitchen, she distinctly heard him comment, 'Cheer up—it might never happen!'

'Goodnight,' she said as civilly as she could muster, and carried on walking, not stopping until she was inside her bedroom with the door closed.

There it was that she sank down on her bed and sighed heavily. 'Cheer up,' he'd said. How could she? Here she was in Kilcaber, Renfrewshire with a man she had no liking for—and who certainly had no liking for her. What was there to be cheerful about, when she didn't want to be here but back in Reefingham? Or, more precisely, since she had a baby nephew she hadn't even seen yet, back in Penny Dale. At least in Penny Dale she would be with people who loved her.

CHAPTER SIX

ODDLY, Mornay slept exceptionally well that night, and awakened on Friday morning feeling much better about her situation than she had on going to bed.

Being careful not to disturb her 'patient', she went very quietly along to the bathroom, bathed and dressed in cotton trousers and, in view of the change in the weather, a lightweight long-sleeved sweater.

Then she returned to her room and brushed her long blonde hair prior to pinning it back in a simple plait which ended halfway between her shoulder-blades. By that time she was seeing nothing at all odd in the fact that she had slept so soundly last night. What would have been odd, she reflected, bearing in mind her scant sleep of the three previous nights, would be any chance she had of staying awake!

Mornay had left her room and had gone silently to the kitchen when she wondered what in thunder had come over her last night, that she had wanted to be loved—or at least be with people who loved her. Now that was odd, if you liked. Most odd.

She began opening cupboards and taking a mental inventory when, feeling so very much better-humoured for a good night's sleep, she determined that if her time with *him* had to be endured, then she would endure it in a more cheerful—yes, cheerful, mood.

Which was the reason why, when the kitchen door opened half an hour later and a clean-shaven Brad Kendrick walked in, she greeted him with a bright, 'Good morning!'

'Somebody obviously slept well,' he observed.

'How did you sleep?' she enquired, her eyes scanning his face as he came further into the kitchen. She was sure he was looking much more rested and a degree or two improved, but looks could be deceiving.

'Went out like a light,' he replied.

'Have you taken your pills?' she queried, and was made to suffer his baleful stare for her trouble.

'Hell take it!' he breathed. 'Are you going to go on bleating in this demented nanny fashion for the whole of our stay?'

'So don't take them—see if I care!' she sniffed huffily, and nearly died when, as the funny side of it hit her and her lips twitched, his sense of humour came out and met hers halfway and, against all odds, they were suddenly both laughing.

'So what's for breakfast?' he enquired when, the first to sober, he took his glance from the sweet curve of her mouth.

'I thought boiled eggs,' she replied, and then queried, 'How long are we staying?'

'Homesick already?' he rapped, his tone hostile and sounding every bit as though he resented that she had—briefly—had the power to make him laugh. 'Or,' he went on when she stared crossly at this change in him, 'is it that you're homesick for your boyfriend?'

Mornay tossed him a 'give me strength' look, and forced herself to remember that she had determined to endure her time with him more cheerfully. He must still ache here and there, she reminded herself, although by then she was under no illusion that one Bradford Kendrick was the best patient in the world.

'How could I possibly be homesick?' she bit back a hot retort to tell him sweetly. She waved an airy hand around as if pointing out the splendid isolation. 'Haven't you "brought me away from it all"?'

For a moment she thought she saw a smile trying to get through, but if it was he suppressed it. 'If you prefer, we can always drive to the police station,' he murmured silkily.

Mornay glared at him, not missing the underlying threat that one step out of line from her and he'd be hauling her off to the police station to make a full confession.

'How long do you like you eggs boiled?' she snapped.

'How the devil do I know?' he tossed back.

Clearly, he was a man who had never had to look after himself. 'We'll breakfast in here,' she told him, feeling sour enough to consider that it wouldn't hurt him to grow more familiar with what a kitchen looked like, and saw him shrug, it being apparently all the same to him where they breakfasted.

Strangely, however, as they sat across the table from each other, breakfasting on boiled eggs and bread and butter, she discovered that her thinking was dominated by the question of—who normally cooked for him? He wasn't married, she knew that. Did he have a live-in girl-friend? Mornay pondered that for some time, and came to the conclusion that surely, if he felt that deeply about any female, that female would be the one to be with him now.

'Something bothering you?'

Brad's voice suddenly penetrated, and Mornay blushed startled. 'I—er...' she murmured before she had got her thoughts together. 'If we're staying longer than today, I need to go shopping,' she told him.

'I'll come with you,' he at once stated.

Mornay stared at him, and was wide-eyed and in-nocent as she aloofly asked, 'You usually accompany your housekeeper when she goes into town shopping for provisions?'

He shook he head. 'But then, neither do I take Mrs Greaves with me when I go into town shopping for a change of linen.'

Mornay smiled, and even though she acknowledged that it was most peculiar, she realised that she was quite glad to know that he had a housekeeper. 'You're not worried that you might be recognised?' she queried.

'You're saying you want to go out on your own?' he questioned shortly.

'You must be getting better!' Mornay snapped. 'Or are you always such an irritable brute? It was you who wanted a "hideaway", not me!' she reminded him heatedly.

'No one around here will know Mr Adams from Jock,' he took the heat out of her by saying lightly. 'Unless you tell them differently,' he added, then spoiled it all by adding pleasantly, 'Which, of course, you won't.' Mornay glared at him, sensing the threat behind his words, and as she saw him transfer some stray eggshell from the table to his plate she hoped he grew warts. But she was mollified completely when he went on, 'But I've got double cover,' and, when she looked coldly at him without comment, 'Our friend Adams has a beautiful wife—Kendrick has no wife at all.'

Mornay bent her head as she got up from her chair and began to clear the table, and was certain that she wasn't at all flattered that, for a second time, Brad Kendrick had intimated that he thought her beautiful.

Again he helped her with the washing-up and, thinking that to dry a few dishes might be some kind of physio-therapy for his wrists, Mornay let him. Then, 'I'll just go and make your bed and tidy your room, then——'

'I've made my bed,' he interrupted.

'Then we'll go shopping,' she told him.

For all the skies had clouded over, there was no sign of rain, and it was still quite warm when Mornay drove into Kilcaber. There were two shops in the village— neither of which could even loosely be called a 'Gentle-man's Outfitters'.

'I'd better drive on,' she told Brad.

'What have we got to lose?' he replied, and seemed so content somehow to while the day away that Mornay suddenly had the oddest notion that he was starting to enjoy himself. That, there being nothing else for it, he had accepted the situation which being badly shaken up in an accident had caused, and was now—like her—making the best of it.

She was not terribly sure about what her intelligence had brought her, though, for she would have supposed that a man of his obvious sophistication would find little that was pleasurable in trundling along in an Austin Metro on his way to get the groceries and a couple of clean shirts. But suddenly she was feeling choked by an emotion which she could not define. 'Brad,' she involuntarily said his name, and when he looked at her she took her eyes off the road for a moment and turned her head, 'I'm sorry,' she said, and when he said not a word and she looked to the front again, she realised that her apology for being in her car that fateful night had been long overdue.

Mornay parked the Metro in the first town she came to that housed a supermarket and a men's clothiers, but as she got out of the car she was very much conscious of the fact that Brad still had some way to go yet to full recovery. His comment at breakfast about her 'bleating like a demented nanny', however, was in her mind too, so that when the impulse came to tell him to wait there while she went to the supermarket she held it down.

That did not stop her from keeping a watchful eye on him, even if she did pretend to be very much absorbed in the variety of ties on a tie display in the clothiers while Brad purchased everything he would need from the skin out.

'We'll take a trolley,' she told him at the supermarket, and, thinking that if he was tired that he could lean his

weight on it as they went round, she told him, 'and you
can push it.'

'You'll make someone a lovely sergeant-major,' he
murmured.

'Shut up,' she told him.

He was, she discovered, an extravagant shopper. Either
that or, shopping in a supermarket new to him, he found
pleasure in lifting things down off the shelves, exam-
ining them, and dropping them in the trolley. Or, she
realised, he was laying up stocks for a whole month's
siege.

The thought of a month away from her job, from
Reefingham and without a word to Claudia, who would
surely turn her back on her principles and phone their
mother if she hadn't heard from her in a whole month,
caused Mornay to come close to panic again. Her panic
did not stay around for long, though, for something else
was dropped into the trolley and she just had to ask,
'What, for crying out loud, do we want dried apricots
for?'

'Humour me,' he told her, and, looking up into his
dark eyes, Mornay could see laughter dancing there as
he added, 'I've not been well.'

What could she do? She burst out laughing and helped
him to push the trolley to the checkout. Fortunately, since
neither of them was equipped to carry a ton of shopping,
the supermarket had a system whereby they could collect
their purchases from the rear of the store and have them
loaded directly into the car.

Fortunately, too, there was a wealth of empty cupboard space when they unloaded the car at the other
end. 'Have you a preference for lunch?' Mornay asked
when, because he wouldn't have it otherwise, she'd had
to give way and allow him to carry the heaviest of the
boxes in.

'Anything will suit,' he replied, and sounded so indifferent to what he ate that Mornay could not help but

feel a degree of anxiety that his appetite seemed to have disappeared. She was therefore much cheered, however, when a moment later he commented, 'Though whatever we're having, can you make mine king-size?'

Realising that a boiled egg for breakfast was hardly likely to sustain more than a corner of his tall broad-shouldered manliness, she decided that, because of the difficulty he was still experiencing using a knife and fork, that they would have poached haddock for lunch. Brad could fill up on the delicious-looking apple pie Mrs Macdonald had made, and, Mornay thought, they'd have a more substantial meal for dinnertime when she'd have more time.

She was pouring milk into a saucepan when she began to wonder why she should worry whether his appetite had returned or whether it hadn't. Only a second later, she knew that anyone would have to be particularly heartless not to worry. It was only natural that she should be concerned, for goodness' sake—she was partly to blame for the state he was in. Anyhow, she concluded, the sooner he was fit, the sooner she could go home.

'Have you had sufficient?' she queried when, after a second helping of apple pie, Brad laid down his spoon.

'Plenty—it was delicious,' he said. 'All of it,' he qualified, just as though he knew that she was about to disclaim any credit for the apple pie. 'Who taught you the intricacies of slaving over a hot stove?' he brought a smile to her face by asking.

'My mother,' Mornay owned, and was so taken that he seemed to be semi-teasing her that she went on, quite unthinkingly, 'My sister and I...er——' she faltered and, there being nothing for it if she was not to draw his attention to what she considered a most gigantic gaffe '—both learned to cook from an early age.'

'How old are you now?' he enquired, and Mornay inwardly drew a sigh of relief that she was over that hurdle without his asking more about her sister.

'Twenty-two,' she answered.

'With that pigtail,' he smiled, and twisted to the side so he could see it, 'you look about sixteen.'

'I like it,' she defended her plait.

'Did I say I didn't?' he queried, and Mornay experienced the most peculiar tingling sensation that he must be saying that he liked something about her.

'The newspaper said you were thirty-six,' she said hastily. 'Did they get it right?'

'For once,' he replied, but suddenly any sign of friendliness in him had gone—and Mornay knew she was to blame.

She began to clear the dining-room table, and went to the kitchen reflecting that she should be used by now to the way Brad's attitude cooled whenever anything remotely connected with that car accident came up. That report about him would never have been in the paper had her car not knocked him down—and plainly, being reminded of the accident brought back to him her guilt in it all.

Mornay washed dishes at the sink and with her thoughts on the newspaper article she again remembered—and wished that she hadn't—that it had stated how no man ever put one over on him without living to regret it. She swallowed hard as she thought of the one she was putting over on him in that it was her brother-in-law, and not she, who had knocked him down.

At that moment Brad entered the kitchen and she flicked a · glance to his grim-looking expression. She somehow knew that his thoughts were on the accident too, and felt then that the best she could hope for was that he never discovered the truth.

Which thought made her jumpy when he came near, and before she could stop herself she had snapped, 'I'll do that!' when she saw him reach for the tea-towel.

'Please yourself!' he gritted, his arm falling back to his side, but to her displeasure he did not go from the room but took a seat on one of the kitchen chairs.

Mornay carried on with her chores, not glancing his way once, but wondering all the while if he was watching her or, with his long legs stretched out in front of him, was studying his toes.

When the tea-towel was hung up to dry and, having wiped down all the surfaces, she had draped the dish-cloth over the washing-up bowl, Mornay, on her way out of the kitchen, did take a glance at him. Was it the light, she pondered, or was he not looking as improved as he had at breakfast?

Whether he was or not, however, she suddenly discovered that it was just impossible for her to walk by without a word. 'Why don't...?' she began, but the words to suggest that he go and rest for an hour or two on his bed were suddenly beaten back by the memory of his 'demented nanny' comment that morning. Which, since she had stopped bang in front of him and was standing looking into a pair of disagreeable dark eyes, left her with little alternative but to snap aggressively, 'Are you going to sit there all day?'

She saw his eyes narrow, and, catching a glimpse of the ice that was starting to form as his aggression came out to meet hers, she was hard put to it not to swallow on a suddenly dry mouth. Then he was standing up, and from his superior height he was looking down his superior nose and barking aggressively, 'No! I'm going for a walk, and you're coming with me!'

Mornay had no intention of going for a walk, or so she thought. But that was before she remembered that he had the upper hand—and she knew then that she was in no position to do other than to jump to his black-mailing bidding. Stubbornly hostile, though, she stared mutinously up at him. Then, to her annoyance, when she saw that he did indeed seem to have lost some of his

earlier improved colour, her mutiny began to fold. She
had no idea how far he intended to walk but from the
look of him somebody had to go with him, if only to
make sure that he got safely back.

But, 'Who,' she snapped, not wanting him to think
she was going under anything but protest, 'could resist
such an invitation, *and* one so charmingly put?'

Their walk was not overlong, nor was it filled with
scintillating conversation, for just as she had nothing
she wanted to say to him, so he, it soon became apparent, had nothing he wanted to say to her.

And so it continued for most of the weekend. Mornay
coped as best she could with her inner anxieties about
getting back to Reefingham before her sister rang her
parents' home in Solihull to enquire why her mother's
sprained wrist was taking so long to heal, and in between times set about making the most delicious meals
to tempt Brad Kendrick's appetite.

But by Monday, although his health seemed to be tremendously improved in that he was now moving with
very little sign of stiffness, and was most definitely
looking much better, Mornay had fresh worries on her
mind.

How she had come to overlook the fact that, since
Robert Naylor knew where her parents lived, he might
well telephone them, she couldn't have said. Though in
all likelihood it was probably because she had so much
else on her mind that, with Robert—up until last
Friday—safely away in Wales, it just hadn't occurred to
her that her lie to Mr Probert could well reach his ears.
If Mr Probert had passed her lie on to Claudia then there
was nothing to prevent Mr Probert's or Claudia's passing
that lie on to Robert if he rang trying to contact her.
Mornay blanched when she realised that, by now, Robert
could have phoned her mother to hope that her wrist
was mending while at the same time asking to speak to
her younger daughter.

'Oh, grief!' Mornay groaned when she got out of bed on Tuesday morning—somehow, she was just going to have to phone Gerry to find out what was happening. Though how she was going to be able to do that with that surly brute Brad Kendrick forever being within earshot, she had no idea.

Or rather, she thought she had no idea. But that was before she'd done an after-breakfast reconnoitre of the kitchen cupboards. In particular she was anxious to note what—of the many purchases made—they did not have.

Brad, his wrists virtually no longer a problem now, was giving a solemn hand with the washing-up and was putting plates away in a dresser while Mornay investigated the plentiful supplies available. They did not have any asparagus, she saw. Nor, in truth, did they actually need any—but the lack of it represented a chance for her to get to a telephone booth.

'We're having smoked salmon and asparagus flan for lunch,' she addressed Brad aloofly over her shoulder, putting all her faith in the hope that his one taste of supermarket shopping had been enough to last him a lifetime. 'I'll have to take the car and get some asparagus,' she added.

She could have happily crowned him when, dealing her high hopes a mortal blow, he loftily replied, 'I'm ready when you are.'

Swine! Mornay dubbed him when, having gone completely off the idea of making a smoked salmon and asparagus flan, she drove, with Brad in the passenger seat, to get the rest of the ingredients to do just that.

She was aware of his brooding silence all the way to the supermarket, just as she was aware that, with him as her shadow, she was not left alone for a minute in which to try and get to a phone.

Which was why she was probably as brooding as him on the homeward journey when, quite suddenly, he abruptly asked, 'How long have you lived in Reefingham?'

Having almost blurted out straight away that she had lived in Reefingham all her life and that he should mind his own business, she suddenly grew wary. She had no idea what—if anything at all—lay behind his question, but with his being so quick on the uptake she thought she might do well to watch anything she told him, no matter how innocent that question might be. So, having made a point of looking in her rear-view mirror as though concentrating on something that was happening behind, 'Er—why do you ask?' she questioned evenly.

From the corner of her eye she saw him shrug as though to say that if she was going to make an issue of it, he wished that he had never asked. 'No particular reason other than idle curiosity as to why you should want to leave your home in Solihull.'

'I've never lived in Sol...' Damn. Feeling intensely irritated with herself that for all her being so wary she had walked straight into that when it was clear that he thought she had moved from Solihull to Reefingham, Mornay had to confess anyway, 'I've lived in Reefingham all my life.'

'Ah,' he said after a moment, 'your family moved to Solihull fairly recently, but you didn't want to move with your parents and sister when they went.'

She felt she could have kissed him for that 'sister' bit, and her heart suddenly lifted, but there was no way she was going to tell him he had made the wrong assumption about her sister. It was far better for him to believe that Claudia lived many miles from Reefingham.

'No,' she replied, and could have added more, but decided that the less she volunteered, the less she had to worry about.

She went on to realise that perhaps his mistake in thinking her sister had moved from the Reefingham area was maybe a natural one in the circumstances of her not having given her a ring to say that she was leaving town. For surely he must be of the opinion that, if she told *anyone* she would not be around for a while, then a sister living locally—if she had one near—would be a far more appropriate person to telephone than even an employer.

Mornay was just taking another relieved breath that it seemed he would never now put two and two together about her sister living so close, or about her sister's having a husband, or any of the rest of it, when, ever a man to question that which needed tidying up, Brad Kendrick put another enquiry.

'Why,' he asked, '*did* you stay behind?'

'I—didn't want to go.'

'Why?'

'You must have driven your mother mad when you were a child!' Mornay snapped, thinking he must have gone around all and every day asking 'Why?'.

'She has the patience of a saint.

'She'd need it!' she said tartly, but, oddly, she felt curiosity begin to stir about his mother. So much so that she almost turned the questioning round to ask him about his family. He, however, got in first.

'Is it such a secret?' he asked.

'What?'

'Your reason for wanting to stay in Reefingham. Don't you get on with your parents?'

'Of course I do!' she snapped stoutly, but suddenly she wanted him off the dangerous subject of her family when who knew, he might start asking questions about her sister. 'It was just that I've got a good job, a good boss——'

'One who's so good that you don't mind lying to him,' Brad cut in coldly, knocking on the head any idea Mornay had that he had started to thaw a little.

'Whose fault is that?' she flared, not thanking him for the reminder that, while he had been in earshot, she had told Mr Probert that awful lie about her mother's sprained wrist.

Brad ignored her question, just as he ignored the reason she chose to give him for staying behind. 'There's some man involved, of course,' he growled.

Mornay was about to deny any such suggestion—then wondered why the dickens she should. 'What if there is?' she questioned, but found that question ignored.

'When did your family move to Solihull?' he wanted to know.

'Wh...it...' Mornay gave a fed-up sigh. 'A couple of years ago!' she answered, becoming resigned, while still wary of some of his questions, to the fact that his 'water wearing away stone' tactics were getting the answers from her that weren't of such great importance.

If she thought, however, that his comments might be done with and that she might be allowed to give her full concentration to her driving—not that there was any traffic around to speak of—then she very quickly was made to realise that she was not going to be allowed to have the last word.

For no sooner had she given him the impression that her major reason for remaining in Reefingham when her family had moved away a couple of years ago was some male of the species than Brad was curtly snarling, 'And you're still a virgin!'

'What the heck has that got to do with anything?' she erupted.

'A hell of a lot, I'd say!' Mornay decided thereafter that she would ignore him, but she had driven only a half a mile further when, 'Do you still see him?' he questioned.

It was on the tip of her tongue to ask what that had to do with him, but she was fast suspecting that when he started out on a course of questioning that sort of a reply would be batted out of the way if he was intent on being answered. She took a deep and restraining breath. 'Regularly,' she told him tightly, and, having hoped that that would shut him up, she was left holding fast on to the steering-wheel—at the next question he found to fire.

'Had you been with him a week ago yesterday when, after your "celebration", we—"met"?' he asked acidly.

'No, I hadn't!' Mornay answered promptly, as she fought not to panic that it seemed he might latch on to the idea any minute now that she had not been alone in her car. 'For your information,' she went on trying to head him swiftly off the scent, 'Robert spent the whole of last week in Wales.'

'Let's hope he didn't spend too much time at the weekend looking for you,' Brad replied silkily, and Mornay could have hit him—she drove the rest of the way to the bungalow in a state of agitation in case Robert, after a call to Claudia, had taken it into his head to ring her mother.

Lunch was eaten in morose silence. Mornay felt she had nothing she wanted to say to Brad—he quite obviously had nothing he wanted to say to her. Which was just lovely, she thought, for if he got fed up enough with her perhaps they could both go home.

The sooner, the better, too, she mused as she washed dishes and he dried them. She then became irritated with herself that she should feel something akin to a small sensation of regret that he plainly took not the minutest bit of pleasure from her company.

For goodness' sake! she inwardly exploded and, impatient with herself, and with the washing-up done, she went without a word to him to the outer door. He had joined her for what was now a habitual after-lunch walk before she had the door open.

After fifteen minutes of walking, she thought they had better turn back. Brad was improving all the time but he still wasn't up to a marathon, she felt. As she expected, he turned about with her, but when they had walked for

another five minutes so a weakening appeared in her resolve not to say another word to the wretched man.

Another five minutes further on and she grew conscious that, since he had made that 'demented nanny'
crack, she had not once asked him how he was. He
looked improved, but, as she had thought before, looks
could be very deceiving. Perhaps he was such a miserable devil because despite appearances he was feeling
very far from up to the mark.

It was touch and go then that she did not ask him
how he was. She did open her mouth as the bungalow
hove into view, but fear of a rebuff, and knowing that
she was going to feel like hitting him over the head if
he made another 'demented nanny'-type crack, caused
her to close it again.

She could not resist a quick glance at him, however.
But, when she had meant only to check on how well or
otherwise he was looking, so as she looked up she saw
that he had his glance on her. Hurriedly she looked away,
but was certain that he must have seen her open and
close her mouth as though she had changed her mind
about saying something—that, or she was doing her
goldfish impression.

Mornay saw very little of him once they were back in
the bungalow. He took himself off to the sitting-room
with the newspapers and paperbacks he had purchased
while they had been out that morning, while she stayed
in the kitchen. She made some cakes, prepared the vegetables for dinner and in between leafed through a couple
of magazines she had purchased.

Half an hour before they normally ate, she went into
the dining-room intending to lay the table, only to find
that Brad had not spent the whole while since she had
last seen him with his head stuck in a book.

Somehow, the fact that he had laid the table softened
her. She might have got it wrong, but it seemed to her
that his attempt to help was a very nice way of saying

'I'm sorry I'm a grouch, but I'm not feeling quite fit yet'.

She consequently felt much more sensitive to him than she might otherwise have done when, the meal ready, she went into the sitting-room and broke her silence of the past six hours. 'Dinner,' she said quietly, and went to the dining-room.

Brad followed her into the room almost immediately, but seemed no more talkative than he had been. But that was all right by her; he had tried to make up for being such a taciturn monster by laying the table, and he couldn't help it if he wasn't well.

When the pudding stage had been reached, however, and barely a word except a request for the pepper had left his lips, Mornay started to wonder if she had got it all wrong after all. Perhaps he'd had no intention of making amends when he'd laid the table—perhaps he'd just been bored with his book.

She flicked a glance to his face, thinking that she might better judge his mood from his expression. But again she found that his glance was on her, and she opened her mouth. This time, however, she felt that to close it without saying anything might give him cause to believe that she was afraid to voice an opinion on anything that came to mind.

'Er—do you know Reefingham well?' she asked the first question to pop into her head, forgetting entirely that the last time she had attempted to question him about what he had been doing in her home town that never-to-be-forgotten Monday she had regretted giving her curiosity its head.

But to her relief, this time, instead of hurling something short and sarcastic at her, he replied civilly enough, 'Not at all,' but pleased her by adding, 'Which is why I motored down the day before a scheduled meeting in connection with some industrial development that might or might not take off.'

'You're thinking of building a factory on the Springfields Industrial Estate?' Mornay cottoned on fast to ask, and felt enormously proud of her brainwork when he nodded.

She was not so pleased a few moments later, however. For, though Brad's glance went from her eager parted lips to her eyes, and she expected that whatever he said next would be said pleasantly, instead he suddenly frowned darkly.

At once Mornay's spirits started to dip, and that was before he toughly stated, 'In view of the millions ultimately involved, I decided to take a look round Reefingham prior to that meeting. I didn't get very far—just as far as from my hotel to a set of traffic lights in the High Street. You,' he accused harshly, 'know the rest.'

Feeling just as though he had physically slapped her, Mornay stared at him in anguish. And then, with her bright blue eyes huge in her face, to her utmost horror she felt the prick of tears at the back of her eyes.

In an instant she was on her feet, but so too was he. Mortified, she felt the shimmer of those tears come to her eyes and abruptly she raced for the door. 'Mornay!' she heard him call, but she was not waiting for anything.

In seconds she had reached the sanctuary of her room. It was many seconds later, though, before she had got herself under control. What for heaven's sake was the matter with her, that he could hurt her so? He was only stating the facts, the facts as he knew them, for goodness' sake. Those same facts that she knew.

Mornay did not venture from her room again that night. She knew full well that the dining-room table was waiting to be cleared. Just as she knew that the washing-up was waiting for her. But the fact that she could easily have burst into tears not so long ago had unnerved her. And since Brad was the cause of that, she was not yet ready to face him again.

She then started to feel that she was his prisoner. True, there were no bars anywhere, and if she cared to leave her room she was free to wander anywhere in the bungalow. Outside of it, though, he was her shadow, she thought glumly.

She went to bed certain that she hated him, and fretted so much about wanting to return to Reefingham, yet knowing that she was forced to stay in Kilcaber until *he* said differently, that it took her an age to get to sleep.

Consequently she overslept the following morning. Indeed, she was sleeping soundly way past the time she was usually up and about. And in fact she was only just drifting up to a lighter plateau of sleep when the sound of someone tapping at her bedroom door started to penetrate.

By the time she had surfaced enough to open her eyes, however, the person who had been knocking at her bedroom door had opened it and had begun to enter into the room.

She had started to come rapidly awake by the time Brad, with a cup and saucer in his hand, arrived at the side of her bed, and placed what she suspected was a cup of tea upon her bedside table.

She looked from him to the cup of tea and, as she remembered the acrimonious way he had been last night, she struggled to sit up, taking the bedclothes with her.

'What's got into you?' she questioned as she eyed him dubiously.

'I thought it wouldn't come amiss if I did something—nice—for you for a change,' he told her, and, if she could trust it, he seemed to be wearing a genuine smile. And, while her heart felt most peculiarly carefree suddenly that he must be saying that the way she cooked, cleaned and generally kept a weather-eye on him had not gone unnoticed, he was parking himself on the edge of her bed and to her amazement was owning, 'I've been a cantankerous devil, haven't I?'

Mornay looked at him stunned for several wide-eyed moments, and discovered that her voice came out sounding quite husky, when she replied, 'You need to ask?' and felt quite swamped with emotion when he pinned her glance to his and would not let her look away.

'Are you going to forgive me?' he questioned quietly, and all at once Mornay felt all of a tremble inside.

'You haven't been—at all well,' she excused every one of his bad-tempered moments—and the next thing she knew, as her heart suddenly started to flurry wildly, was that he was bending his head, and that his face was coming nearer.

Gently, he saluted her lips with his, and Mornay knew as he drew back that his light kiss had been his way of making up—of making friends. All at once, because she hated to be bad friends with anyone, she just had to smile—her forgiveness complete.

She had thought then that he would get up from her bed and leave her to drink her tea, but as his glance went from her eyes to her smiling mouth he was suddenly still. Then, a kind of groan escaped him, and in the next moment he was reaching for her.

Her heart racing like an express, Mornay had time only to give him a completely unafraid look, and then she was in his arms, and his mouth was once again over hers—only this time his kiss was different.

His mouth was warm and giving, but a hint of growing passion was there that had been entirely absent before, and Mornay, to her surprise, began to experience emotions that caused her to want to meet his passion with her own.

'Brad!' she murmured his name when for a brief moment his lips left hers. Then he was kissing her again, and she was delighting to feel through the thin cotton of her nightdress the strong manliness of his arms.

She delighted even more when, as his mouth left hers and he traced tender kisses down the slender column of her throat, so his hands warmly caressed her back.

'Mornay!' It was he this time who murmured her name, and, as his lips once more took hers, so his hands caressed to her shoulders. Slowly then he began to slide the cap sleeves of her nightdress down her arms.

Mornay felt her cheeks begin to flame. But a fire had started to burn in her for him, and even though she knew that once he had slipped her arms out from her sleeves the low front of her nightdress would drop lower, and that her breasts would be naked, she did not back away.

She wanted him, and as he started to pull back from the passionate kiss they shared she knew that he wanted her. She knew, as he moved the sleeves of her nightdress lower down her arms, that her face was a warm crimson.

But then, while her heart was pounding furiously against her ribs, Brad looked passionately into her eyes and then at her normally creamy complexioned skin, and abruptly she felt all movement in him suddenly cease. The hands that, in caressing movements, had been on the way to leaving her front uncovered, were suddenly still, clamped hard on the material of the cap sleeves of her nightdress and her upper arms.

Then, 'Hell!' he muttered throatily. Then, the sound clearer, though still with that husky male sound, 'I didn't mean this to happen, Mornay, believe me,' he said.

'I ...' she murmured chokily and, accepting that what had just happened had been as entirely spontaneous for him as it had been for her, she fought desperately hard to rise over what had just been the most earth-shattering emotional experience of her life. Never had she been stirred to want any man before! 'Perhaps,' she found a light note from some amazing somewhere, 'perhaps—Mr Adams—you'd better go.'

She thought she saw a look come to his eyes that seemed to be admiring of the way she was trying to treat

the matter lightly. But, as he pushed the sleeves of her
nightdress up on to her shoulders and then glanced down
to check his handiwork, so Mornay looked down too,
and saw, as he must have done, the way the hardened
tips of her breasts were peaking against the thin cotton
of her nightdress.

Abruptly, he stood up. 'Perhaps—Mrs Adams,' he
murmured in a light tone, although Mornay wasn't sure
that there was not an undertone of strain there, 'you're
right.'

He did not stay after that, but went quickly from her
room, leaving Mornay staring after him. Five minutes
ticked by and she was still staring—had that been her?
Had that warm, feeling, vibrant woman really been her?
She had not known that she was capable of such intense,
passionate feeling.

CHAPTER SEVEN

THE memory of the way she had been with Brad accompanied Mornay as she bathed and dressed and returned to her room. She was still thinking—had that really been her, had it really happened?—when her glance caught sight of the cup of tea which Brad had brought to her.

Oh, yes, it had happened, she thought, and somehow she felt that she would never again be the person she had been before. Leaving her room, she was in a state of confusion and shyness as she went up the hall, and she had no idea of how she was going to greet Brad when she saw him again.

That problem, however, was solved for her when, as she reached the open sitting-room door, she saw him, standing with his back to her. He was on the telephone, she observed, and she was about to walk on when suddenly she was transfixed to the spot. For quite plainly she heard his clear, clean unaccented tones state, 'She likes roses—send her two dozen with the message "I'll see you soon".'

His call was finished, but he had not so much as put the phone back on its receiver before Mornay was being assaulted by a pain so dreadful it was almost physical. She knew Brad wasn't sending *her* roses—why should he?—and anyway he had no idea whether she liked them or whether she didn't. And the message could hardly apply either, could it, since they were both living in the same property?

Rocked to her foundations by another new emotion which had that morning surfaced in her, Mornay was not certain that she would not have crumpled under the weight of it when, to her undying gratitude, great face-saving quantities of pride arrived.

The phone went down. Brad turned and spotted the blonde-haired woman who was eyeing him coolly. 'How——?' he began, but she was already coldly cutting him off.

'If we don't have breakfast now,' said she who felt she could not swallow so much as a crumb, 'it'll be time for lunch.'

With that Mornay marched on to the kitchen, where she set the kettle to boil and put bread in the toaster while most of her energies were engaged in keeping her thoughts at bay. Yet she was aware of Brad the very moment he entered the kitchen—even though she did not look up.

'Can I help?' he enquired levelly, and she knew then— if she hadn't known it before—that he didn't give a damn about her, or her emotions, and never would.

She shook her head and while keeping her expression entirely indifferent, she made a pot of coffee and put the toast in the toast rack. He carried the coffee-pot to the table while she carried the toast, but though they had shared many meals without a word being said on previous occasions, the silence at this mealtime grew into an unbearable strain for Mornay.

Not that she let it show; she'd have died sooner. Though she was to discover, as Brad sat aloofly opposite her, that he wasn't even aware of the taut, stretched silence. There was nothing strained in his manner anyhow when, obviously not aware that there was any silence to break, he finished the last of his coffee, and casually asked, 'May I borrow your car?'

Biting back an angry retort to the effect that there might be just enough petrol in it to take him a yard past the cliff-edge at Beachy Head, Mornay hid her hurt at his first indication since they'd left Reefingham that he wanted to do something without her. She raised cool eyes—to find that he was regarding her equally coolly.

'You expect me to be here when you get back?' she asked with lofty acid, and knew that neither her comment, nor her arrogance were being kindly received when his eyes narrowed.

'You were thinking of going somewhere?' he challenged icily, and, before she could form a reply, 'With the evidence I have on you—I doubt it,' he rapped, and got up from the table.

Mornay got up from the table too, feeling defeated in more ways than one. She could have saved her breath—she wasn't leaving—she dared not, and he knew it. She went to her bag and extracted her car keys.

'Don't hurry back!' she said sweetly, only she knowing how much that sweet tone had cost her as she placed the keys on the worktop. She turned her back on him, the sound of the outer door opening and closing telling her that he was in a hurry to be away.

She moved to the sitting-room doorway and, standing where she could not be seen, she watched as he drove off down the road. She went back to the kitchen. She was glad he was gone—she hurt, and she wanted to be alone.

So this, she mused dully, was what being in love felt like. Collapsing on to a chair, Mornay was as staggered by her new-found knowledge as she was by the riot of emotions that had raged through her from almost the first moment of opening her eyes that morning.

Though, as she thought about it, she realised that the love which she now acknowledged for Brad Kendrick had been coming on for some time. Her head had been filled with thoughts of him since that very first moment she had seen him. That, of course, was not so surprising in the circumstance of her involvement in his accident, but she doubted that she would have thought so constantly about him had he not had that particular magnetism for her.

This—this love she felt for him was at the base of why he had the power to hurt her. This love she had for him was the reason why she had so recently experienced that emotion, jealousy.

She wanted to believe that she didn't give a hoot whom he sent roses to—but she did. She wanted to believe that she didn't give a light where he had gone to—in her car!—but she did.

Damn him, she thought, and loved him. This, she now plainly saw, was why he had been able to arouse the response he had aroused in her that morning! Never in her life before had she ever experienced such wild, wanting emotions. Lord knew what would or would not have happened had he not called a halt to their love-making. She had little conviction that she would have put up any resistance—and that was before she had actually been aware that she loved him.

Which, she realised, made it imperative—now that she did know that she was in love with him—that she resisted with all she had. Not that he was likely to take her in his arms again. Indeed, from the frosty way they had *not* said goodbye just now it wouldn't surprise her if they never so much as spoke to each other again while they remained in Kilcaber.

Mornay got up from her chair and, thinking that she had herself together again and that Brad was never likely to gain so much as a whiff of an idea that she cared for him, she began to collect up the used dishes prior to doing the washing-up when she was stopped dead in her tracks as something suddenly struck her. She had gone to her room last night and had left the washing-up undone, yet there was not a sign of even one of the various saucepans she had used.

Swiftly she left the kitchen and went to the dining-room. She opened the door and, looking in, she leant against the woodwork—there was not a sign of a used pudding plate or anything to be seen.

Weak tears came to her eyes that Brad, who although improved still wasn't fully recovered, had cleared the table and taken all the used china and cutlery out to the kitchen. 'Oh, Brad!' she whispered softly, for, though kitchens and washing-up were all alien to him, he had washed, dried and put away the dishes, leaving everywhere immaculate.

A few moments later Mornay realised that, while she and Brad stayed antagonistic towards each other, he was more likely to think that she hated him than loved him, and that she was going to have to watch those moments when he did something unexpected and kind.

She half wished that she was back in Reefingham when, with her time with him over, and her pride still intact, he would never know... Abruptly her thinking came to a full stop. But only to start up again.

Grief! She had been so engrossed, so taken up with the astonishment of discovering that she was in love with Brad that she had forgotten entirely that with him out of the way she was free to make that urgent telephone call to her brother-in-law.

Wondering at the time she had wasted in getting to the telephone, Mornay hurried to the sitting-room—Brad might come back at any moment. Swiftly she picked up the phone and dialled the Penny Dale number, hoping against hope that it would be Gerry who answered. She didn't want to lie to Claudia, and realised that she was going to have to pretend that she was still in Solihull if luck was against her and her sister picked up the phone.

'Hello.' It was her brother-in-law.

'Hello, Gerry, it's Mornay,' she told him quickly, 'I...'

'Hello,' he greeted her cheerfully, 'we were beginning to think we were never going to hear from you again. How's your mother?'

'Is Claudia there?' Mornay asked urgently.

'She's upstairs seeing to Luke—hang on, I'll give her a shout.'

'No!' Mornay rapidly stopped him, and hurriedly asked, 'Are you still there?'

'Yes,' he replied to her relief, and, seeming to twig that she was a bit agitated about something, 'What's to do, Mornay?'

'I only asked about Claudia because I didn't know whether she was in the same room as you or not, but first—are the police still...?'

'Everything's gone quiet on that front,' Gerry quickly assured her, and Mornay gave a sigh of relief and then went on to break the news of where she was—and who with. Five minutes later, with nothing but, 'You didn't...' and, 'You mean...' and, 'I can't credit it, Mornay,' coming from her brother-in-law, Mornay had told him most of what there was to know.

'The thing is,' she went on, 'that I just don't know when I'll be able to come back. Brad—Kendrick,' she added, 'intimated it would be a month, and...'

'He's treating you all right, Mornay?' her brother-in-law forgot his own panic for a moment to enquire. 'I mean, he's not—er—making you do anything you—er—don't want to do——'

'No,' she quickly assured him, 'apart, that is, from making me stay here to look after him until he's fully recovered. As soon as he's completely well again, I'll be able to return to Reefingham, but meantime I go into a cold sweat whenever I think of Claudia ringing my mother and Mother telling her that she's got a perfectly sound wrist.'

'I'll cover for you there,' Gerry said promptly.

'Can you cover if Robert Naylor rings too?' she queried. 'I've been more than half afraid that he'll ring my mother too, and——'

'Don't worry about it any more, there's a love,' he quickly comforted her. 'I'm only sorry that through me you've been through what you have—even if I do think you were quite nutty to go anywhere near the accident wing of Reefingham General. I'll sort things out this end,' he told her. 'You just keep that man up there until he's fit enough to want to be driven back to London.' Mornay forbore to tell him that Brad's own car was at present being housed at the Belvedere Hotel, Reefingham and was about to ring off when, a little less comfortingly, Gerry was saying, 'You'd better give me your phone number in case I need to get in touch with you.'

'I'd rather you didn't—it's not easy for me to talk . . .'

'I'll not ring you unless it's absolutely essential,' Gerry promised, and Mornay read him the number off the telephone dial.

Having made what she had considered quite an essential phone call herself, and all before Brad had returned, Mornay went to the kitchen and got started on the chores. Again and again, though, as she washed and dried dishes, she could not deny a compulsion to keep glancing out of the window to look for Brad's return.

He was much on her mind as she wiped work surfaces and then swept and mopped the kitchen floor. When the kitchen was back to being presentable, however, and with Brad nowhere to be seen though still to the forefront of her mind, she tried to pin her thoughts on something else.

Should she ring Mr Probert, she wondered, and tell him that she wouldn't be back next week? She ought to, she mused. If by chance she and Brad did leave Kilcaber and she was able after all to go to work next week, then she could always say that her mother's wrist had improved dramatically.

Mornay thought seriously about it for a few minutes and then decided that, since Brad might come back at any moment, and it might be an age before she had another opportunity to make free with the telephone, she would ring Mr Probert. As ever, he was kind, and sent his best wishes to her mother, and Mornay came off the

phone a little crimson-cheeked—this time because she
hated lies of any sort and had just spent a couple of
minutes in evading the truth.

Then she decided that she might as well be hung for
a sheep as a lamb, and, with a view to preventing Robert
Naylor from inadvertently stirring everything up, she
rang his place of work. To her relief, however, she was
not called upon to tell any more lies. For, 'Mr Naylor's
been trying to contact you,' Vicky, who worked in the
stock department of his head office, told her, and went
on to say that a decision at higher management level had
been made to update their stock-records procedure.
'Which means that everyone, Mr Naylor included, will
be working flat out to get everything stock-taken ready
to enter on the new system,' Vicky explained. 'I know
it's inconvenient, but it looks as though quite a few of
them will be working weekends too. Is there any message
I can give to him when he rings through?'

Mornay rang off having left no message other than to
tell him that she had rung, but felt it couldn't be more
convenient as far as she was concerned that the powers-
that-be in his firm had taken a decision to restructure
their stock procedure. At least it took one worry away
from her.

Her anxieties were plenty, however, when lunchtime
came and went, but Brad did not. By four o'clock, when
he had still not appeared, she had undergone a whole
range of emotions that went through fear that he might
have had an accident and worry that he might have come
over unwell. She then grew angry with herself that she
could be so stupid, then angry with him that he hadn't
said what time he'd be back. And when she was not in
turmoil over him in general, she was beset by jealousy
in particular. Damn him, him of the 'send her two dozen
roses', and damn his 'I'll see you soon' messages too.
The way things were going, she of the two dozen roses

fame would see him before she of the Kilcaber prison infamy.

By nine o'clock that evening, however, Mornay's anger and jealousy had departed and she was close to tears in her anxiety about him. She was almost certain then either that he'd been involved in an accident or that his health had suffered a sudden set-back.

At half-past nine she was torn between ringing the hospitals thereabouts and ringing the police, when suddenly the sound which her ears had been straining to hear for most of that day started to appear faintly. When the sound grew louder and she then definitely heard a car pulling up, Mornay was in a highly emotional state, too scared to go and see if it was Brad, in case it was the police who had somehow found out where he was staying, and had come to tell her some dreadful news. Loving, she realised, was hell.

She was hovering in the hallway when, half expecting there to be a ring at the front door, she heard the sound of the rear door into the kitchen being opened. Weak tears of relief sprang to her eyes that it was Brad. Then, even while she conquered her tears, she was suddenly furious with him.

'Where have you been?' she demanded, charging into the kitchen. She wanted more than anything to box his ears that he could so casually stand there, and without a mark on him, while she had been in the throes of a mental breakdown for the past eight or so hours.

She saw his right eyebrow shoot aloft at her demanding manner. But though she fully expected him to take exception to it he was, perhaps because he could see that she was exceedingly het up about something, by contrast extremely calm.

For all that, however, he did not answer her question but, like a conjurer bringing a rabbit out of a hat, he brought his right hand from behind his back and handed her the most beautiful bouquet of roses. 'For you,' he told her, and gently smiled.

Mornay was not one bit mollified. 'You give roses to every female of your acquaintance?' she snapped, knowing full well exactly where his roses were going—in the bin. In the meantime, she placed them down on the worktop.

But Brad, even as an alert light entered his eyes and he carefully scrutinised her expression, was shaking his head. Mornay was well on the way to realising that she had better calm down and fast if she didn't want to give herself away when, with his eyes still quietly on her, he murmured, 'Only to my best girls.'

But whatever he meant by that, Mornay was rapidly coming down from her initial 'hitting the roof' reaction to seeing him casual and unharmed after all the mental agony she had been through that day. So, 'Huh!' she muttered, and left him to sort out what she meant by that while she quickly endeavoured to cancel out any glimmer of a notion he might have received from her outburst that she felt anything at all out of the way for him. 'You weren't looking so well when you left,' she lied without a qualm. 'I couldn't help being worried that you might have collapsed behind the steering-wheel.'

She saw a warm look enter his eyes, and her heart somersaulted when, 'You were worried about me?' he gently asked, and, just as gently, he reached for her and gathered her in his arms.

'S-surely it's only natural I should worry?' she tried to get her head together to tell him. 'What sort of human being would I be not to worry when I know how recently you've been in hospital, and how you're even now still convalescing?'

'I think you're a rather sensitive kind of human,' Brad told her softly, and, looking down into her eyes, he quietly added, 'Perhaps I should have told you that I was going to Perth to pay my mother a visit.'

'Your mother lives in Perth?' Mornay questioned, re-alising that Perth wasn't too far away. 'You've been to see her?' she asked, not waiting for him to answer her first question. But, with his arms still about her, she realised that she in all probability wasn't thinking straight, and it seemed to her that it was most likely that he was an even bigger liar than she was. 'And if I believe that I'll believe anything,' she remarked tartly.

'You—care?' Brad questioned, but Mornay was certain that there was mockery in his tones. Although in any case, the fact that she did very truly care was the last thing he was going to hear her admit.

'You must have shaken your brains up in that ac-cident!' she scorned, and might have said more on the same theme, only just then Brad took the opportunity of having her in his arms to silence her by placing his mouth over hers.

He did indeed silence her. Or at least, as he broke his gentle kiss and pulled his head back from hers, Mornay was so all over the place that she could not remember a word of what she had been saying.

What she did know, however, was an instinctive feeling that she should not be responding to him for some reason. By luck, as she flicked her glance away from him, her eyes fell on the roses he had brought her.

'I'd—better put these flowers in water,' she told him as she eased herself out of his arms. She had hunted up a vase and filled it with water, and was arranging the roses to their most attractive advantage, when it sud-denly dawned on her that she seemed to have changed her mind about throwing them in the bin.

Brad's kiss when he'd taken her in his arms proved to be an isolated incident. Thursday and Friday came and went and the weekend passed in an unruffled kind of way. By Monday Mornay had fully recovered her equilibrium and even if she was still being battered by emotions, all connected with her love for him, then she was swiftly learning how to cope without letting it show.

She sometimes had a feeling that his eyes were on her, but when, casually, she would glance over at him, he was either looking nowhere near her vicinity, or, more often, had his eyes glued to a book, or glued to something of interest outside the window.

They were having breakfast in the kitchen on Tuesday when, again feeling that his glance was on her, Mornay looked quickly across the table at him and discovered that for once she was right.

He didn't seem put out in any way at having been caught staring at her, however—and Mornay later realised that he hadn't been staring at her anyway but more looking her way while he thought his own thoughts, for his manner was quite easy and relaxed as he enquired, 'Isn't it—er—about time we went shopping again?'

Mornay reckoned she knew what his hesitation had been about, too. He was reluctant to go shopping, but recognised that shopping was a necessary evil. This time, however, she had no intention of trying to get to the shops alone—she had made all the phone calls she wanted to make.

'You're a devil for punishment,' she smiled, her smile turning into a laugh when he gave her a pained look, acquiescing to go with her.

She thought it must be over a week now since she had driven her car. Brad had driven it last Wednesday, though, she remembered, and she wondered if she should ask him if he would prefer to drive them to the shops. He, however, unlike her brother-in-law, didn't seem to have any hang-up about being driven by a woman.

With her shopping list complete, Mornay took her car keys from her bag and, leaving Brad to lock up, she went over to her car. Perhaps it was because she'd had Gerry in her mind, and his driving, that as she went round to the driver's side she glanced especially to where he had managed to put a dent in the offside wing. She then had the shock of her life for, fully expecting to see a sizeable dent, she saw instead that there was none!

'It's gone!' she exclaimed in surprise over the top of her car to Brad who had arrived and was ready to get into the passenger seat. 'The dent's gone!'

'Fairies,' he replied.

'You,' she said. 'You had it done! You had it done on Wednesday!' she accused.

'Come round here and say that,' he challenged, and Mornay burst out laughing.

Given all that was happening, all that had happened, and not forgetting that Brad could and probably had spent some time with some female who was not his mother last Wednesday, Mornay felt the happiest she had ever felt in her life as she drove with him to the shops that Tuesday.

There had been absolutely no need for him to have that dent in her car seen to, nor to have it resprayed so that no one would ever know that her car had been in an accident, but he had, and she loved him for it. She realised, of course, that he most likely had a receipt which said something to the effect that there had been a dent there, so that if it ever came to a prosecution he had all the evidence, but she was beginning to think that it would never come to that—not at his instigation, anyhow. And she loved him for that too.

In fact, she loved him so much just then that when she got round to wondering how much longer they were going to stay in Kilcaber she experienced a tremendous pang of regret that it could not be for much longer now. For, although she realised that Brad must still be feeling not one hundred per cent fit yet, outwardly he seemed as if there was nothing wrong with him. She felt she knew, regretfully, that the moment that he did feel one hundred per cent again, he would want to return to London—and that they would part.

It was then that she decided she was going to make the most of her time with him. She felt happy. She wanted to have some happy memories for when that dreadful day dawned that they parted, and she had to accept that their paths would never converge again.

Tuesday went on being a happy day; so, too, did Wednesday. Thursday also was a day when she and Brad got on well without either of them getting cross with the other about anything. On Friday, however, as it was getting on for the time when Mornay usually began to prepare the evening meal, the phone—which had remained silent all the time they had been there—suddenly rang. Mornay made a startled movement from the unexpectedness of it, and Brad smiled at her as he went over to the instrument and, in his firm voice, gave their telephone number.

Mornay realised that someone was taking their time in answering him when, 'Hello?' he queried, and a moment later told her, 'Somebody must have misdialled,' as he replaced the receiver.

She smiled, and said, 'I'll go and make a start in the kitchen.'

She might then have forgotten all about the wrong number call of Friday. But when at around the same time on Saturday the telephone rang, and with the same result—that when Brad answered it in his all-masculine voice no one replied—she began to have edgy thoughts. She hoped it was just her guilty conscience that was making her have such thoughts, but—was Gerry trying to get in touch?

That possibility fidgeted away at Mornay all the next day—and caused her to wonder at her chances of getting in touch with him to see if everything was all right. There was no chance, however, for every time she went anywhere near to the telephone that day Brad seemed to appear.

He was in the sitting-room with her, reading from the pile of Sunday papers they had that morning driven to purchase, when at around six-thirty that evening the phone went again.

Oh, no, Mornay thought worriedly, and became more worried when Brad went to answer it. Her worries rapidly increased when this time, having picked up the phone, Brad said not a word.

It was then that she knew he was suspicious. Two consecutive phone calls when he'd answered the phone only to hear the dialling tone a short while later, followed by a third consecutive phone call at more or less the same time, was enough to make him so, she realised.

She calculated that a full half-minute went by with Brad just standing there, saying nothing, and as her anxiety peaked it was in her mind to call loudly—loud enough for any caller to hear—something along the line of, 'Who is it, Brad?' in an endeavour to warn the caller—if it was Gerry—that it was not she who had picked up the phone.

But the caller, forced by the silence coming from the other end, must, it seemed, have decided to risk a query. Because, before Mornay could call out anything, a grim sort of look was setting on Brad's face, and she heard him grate tersely, 'Who wants her?' She saw Brad's expression go thunderous, then, without comment, he was handing the phone to her.

Mornay took the phone and with a fast-beating heart hoped against hope that Brad would leave her to take her call in private. He did no such thing, but, giving her a look of intense dislike, he turned his back on her and went to look out of the window.

Momentarily, fully aware that his ears would be flapping, Mornay hated him. Then, 'Hello,' she said, and discovered that she had been right to fear that her brother-in-law had been trying to make contact, for as soon as he heard her voice, so she heard his.

'I know it's difficult for you, Mornay, and I know I haven't helped by ringing, but I had to risk it.'

'Is——?'

'Don't say anything but yes or no,' Gerry broke in quickly to stop her before she could say anything that might incriminate him. 'Everything's fine here,' he went on to quickly assure her, 'it's just that Claudia's a bit—er—fretful.'

'Fretful?' Mornay straight away forgot his instructions to query.

'She's not in post-natal depression, or anything like that,' Gerry quickly assured her, 'but Luke's proving more demanding than any of the others were, and she's worrying herself silly about how she's going to cope with the four girls and Luke when I go back to work tomorrow. I've already had an extra week off, so I just have to go in tomorrow,' he told her.

'I—see,' Mornay said slowly.

'The thing is,' he went on, 'with Claudia thinking that you managed to get time off easily enough when your mother needed you for such a simple thing as a sprained wrist, she's got it into her head that you wouldn't hesitate to have another week off to come and give her a hand.'

'I—er—don't see how I can,' Mornay replied, starting to feel wretched as her heart went out to her sister.

'I knew it was a long shot,' Gerry sighed, 'but I felt I just had to ask.'

Mornay put the phone down after the call with her thoughts on how devoted her brother-in-law was to her sister, and how worried he had sounded. Though she was not thinking of anything in particular in the next second, for suddenly Brad, in furious mood, was standing in front of her, and instinctively she knew that there was going to be trouble!

And there was. Before she could so much as draw another breath, 'Who was that?' he snarled threateningly.

It took Mornay all her time not to swallow apprehensively at his foreboding expression, but she hoped she had more spirit than to let him or any man browbeat her, so she snapped hotly, 'I thought you'd asked?' only just remembering in time that the only thing Brad had said down the phone this time had been, 'Who wants her?'

'You told me Robert was your boyfriend's name!' he rapped, clearly not taking kindly to her nerve in answering back.

'So it is!'

'So who's Gerry?' he demanded, and suddenly Mornay was starting to panic.

'Just—a friend,' she replied, knowing, whatever else she did not know, that she must not let him know that Gerry was her brother-in-law.

'How did he know where to contact you?' Brad charged, his mood not getting any sweeter as he pursued his interrogation.

'I rang him,' Mornay told him defiantly, but was able to see then that Brad wasn't so much mad that she had made the call but, valuing his privacy, was incensed that she had risked his 'hideaway' cover. 'I rang him,' she repeated, just to let him know that she wasn't afraid of the fearsome glint that came to his dark eyes, 'on the day you went to visit your "mother"!' Immediately she wanted those defiant words back, for with an enraged growl Brad took a furious stride forward. 'Don't you dare touch me!' she yelled, fearing she knew not what, but, as her hands went out as though to push him away, knowing with yet more instinct that the time for brave heroics was not now.

'Why the...?' Brad began, but by then he had taken an angry hold of her hands. And then, it was as though the touch of her had inflamed his temper some more. At any rate, there was perhaps half a second when if she'd any sense she had a moment to snatch her hands free and race out of there. But—she didn't.

Because, oddly, when she knew full well that there was the very devil riding on his back, just the touch of Brad's skin, of his hands on hers, was affecting her. Her lovely blue eyes were wide in her face as she stared at him in a stunned kind of a way—and then Brad was pulling her to him.

Half a second later, and she was in his arms. Furiously, he kissed her. With his arms iron bands around her, he pulled her closer to him, moulding her body to his, while he claimed her mouth again and again.

Mornay tried to struggle against him. Quite desperately she attempted to tell herself that this was not right. But, as passion began to rage in her, she started to press her body voluntarily closer to him—and at her response he no longer had to use his superior strength to bind her to him.

'Mornay!' he cried on a ragged sound, holding her to him with one arm as one hand undid the top two buttons on her blouse, and Mornay knew more delight when, bending his head, he traced kisses to the V of the satiny skin he had revealed in the cleavage of her breasts.

Her arms were around him when he moved unhurriedly with her to the settee. 'Oh, Brad,' she moaned his name, and was lost to everything but him when he lay down with her on the settee and caressed her and undid the remaining buttons on her blouse.

She had no idea that her breasts were totally naked until, as one of his hands caressed warmly from her waist, he gently but unexpectedly moved that hand until he had captured that naked, swollen globe.

'Oh!' she gasped, and knew her colour was crimson as, sending her into ecstasies of rapture, Brad moulded that breast tenderly in his hands.

Wanting to feel his body too, she tried to undo his shirt buttons with her trembling fingers, making a hash of it until Brad, suddenly smiling down at her, undid his shirt for her.

She almost said thank you, but by then Brad had come to rest his uncovered, hair-roughened chest over her satiny breasts. And, 'Oh!' she breathed again. For suddenly he wasn't angry any more. Suddenly, all the fury seemed to have gone out of him and he was being gentle with her, and she loved him.

She wasn't sure that she did not call his name again when his mouth left hers and he traced warm, virile kisses down her throat and to her breasts until his lips stayed at one pink, hard peak. Then he was kissing her breasts and moulding her to him again, and one hand left her breasts and moved to the waistband of her skirt.

Mornay knew then that she would deny him nothing. Never had she been in the grip of an emotion such as this, one which knew no holding back.

Or so she thought. Though even afterwards, she was never sure whether she was making a protest or not. But, feeling the need to take a deep breath in all this that was so new, she suddenly placed a nervous staying hand over the one that was already pulling down her zip, and Brad took the opportunity to study her burning face.

What he read there she had no idea, although she felt that he must see that she wanted him, and would not hold back once she had got over her moment of nervousness. But, after staring into her all-giving blue eyes for some tense seconds, suddenly, and to her utter bewilderment, he groaned, 'Oh, my...' and left her and— as if the devil himself were after him—went from the room!

Quite how long she sat staring after him, Mornay could not have said. Nor could she have said how long it took her to come to an awareness that she was half sitting, half lying, partly naked, looking to the door as if hoping he would come back. When that realisation did hit her, however, she moved.

In next to no time she was in her bedroom, properly dressed, with the door firmly closed while she leant against it and tried to get her head back together.

Oh, dear heaven, how was she going to face him again after her wanton display just now? Again she was set to wonder—had that person who had clung to him so passionately been her?

She moved away from the door and for the next hour went through agonies of thinking that she should have fought Brad all the way, while knowing that what she should have done and what she had done were two entirely different things. Her head might initially have put up some resistance, but she had been weakened from that first moment of him taking hold of her hands.

Having gone through agonies, however, Mornay knew that if Brad was not to gain so much as a whisper of how deeply she cared for him, then she was going to have to show him a very different person from the one she had all that week.

No more smiling or laughing at any amusing quip he made, she was in the middle of instructing herself firmly, when, to make her spin round in startled anguish, there came a tap at her door.

Wanting badly not to answer, Mornay knew without thinking about it that Brad would see nothing wrong in coming straight in if she kept him waiting too long. Feeling torn between a desire to hide and a desire to yell at him to go away, Mornay grabbed at what courage she could and went to the door.

Opening the door, she saw him tall, dark and steady-eyed as he studied her face. She knew, even as she renewed her resolution to be cold to him, that her colour was high, but she held his gaze unflinchingly as she waited for him to announce the purpose of his visit—which, when he did, caused her to stare at him some more.

For, 'Dinner's ready,' he announced. All thought of preparing an evening meal had completely passed her by. Oh, Brad, she wanted to murmur softly as it penetrated that, though she was only too well aware that he was practically helpless in the kitchen, he had made a meal for her.

But she did not murmur anything of the kind. From somewhere she was remembering the importance of showing him that he meant less than nothing to her. 'Thank you,' she told him coldly, and, throwing his efforts back in his face, 'but I'm not hungry.' She saw at once from the way any gentleness in his expression suddenly and instantly evaporated that he liked neither her tone nor what she said, so, in case he might get round to thinking that his rejection of her had taken away her appetite for dinner, she added more for good measure. 'In fact,' she tossed in arrogantly, 'I'd like to go back to Reefingham if——' It was as far as she got, for, his expression all at once as black as thunder, Brad was wasting no time in cutting her off.

'Panting for Gerry?' he snarled, and then, very nearly paralysing her with the savagery of his tongue, 'Why bother?' he sneered. 'From your response to me not too long ago, I'd have said any man would have done!'

A shocked gasp left her, then, 'You—swine!' she choked, and had to look away lest he saw the sudden, mortifying tears of hurt that suddenly sprang to her eyes.

Whether he had seen them before she could blink them away, though, Mornay didn't know. But suddenly, as if taken by instant remorse, he groaned, 'Oh, hell!' and in the next moment he had taken her gently in his arms. 'That was a foul thing to say,' he apologised, and sounded sincere. And, as if realising the effect he had on her, 'You're so damned confused you don't know where the hell you're at, do you?' he asked of her quietly.

But as fear hit at her heart she was too agitated to know what he was referring to. Was he merely referring to the state of confusion he must know she was in from their lovemaking—and the response he had awakened in all that was so new to her? Or was he referring to the confusion he might be thinking she was feeling if he guessed at her love for him? Mornay realised that she had better act—and quickly.

Pride rose in her over the joy and comfort she experienced at being in his arms, when, grasping at every ounce of strength, both mental and physical, she pushed him away hard and pulled out of his arms.

'I know where the hell I *want* to be!' she told him furiously—and saw that that hadn't met with his favour either.

She saw his chin jut at an aggressive angle as his arms fell down to his sides. Then he had taken a step back, and she could see his eyes were glinting with ice when he barked, 'Tough!' and walked away.

CHAPTER EIGHT

WHEN, Mornay wondered when she awakened the next morning, had she ever felt happy to be sharing this isolated spot with Brad? She felt far from happy as she left her bed and started to get ready to face the day. Any happiness she had thought she'd known had completely gone.

She returned from getting bathed and dressed, and knew that she still loved Brad with all her being—but she found no joy in that. Thank goodness for pride, she mused dejectedly as she brushed her long blonde hair and tucked it behind her ears prior to going along to the kitchen. Pride, if nothing else, would get her through this day.

'Good morning,' Brad greeted her courteously enough, coming in as she was preparing scrambled eggs on toast.

'Good morning,' she replied in kind, but felt that there was a definite strain in the atmosphere.

She was sure of that strain when not another word passed between them, but a taut silence ensued while she did a collection of other jobs which included taking a freshly made pot of coffee to the table.

In silence she left the scrambled eggs keeping warm while she seated herself at the table. From beneath her long lashes she noted that Brad had followed suit, and she tucked into half a grapefruit with every appearance of having a healthy appetite. Then she left the table to put scrambled egg on freshly buttered toast. She was conscious as she did so that Brad too had left the table. From the corner of her eye she saw him clear their place settings of the dishes they had so far used. He was back in his place at the breakfast table, however, when, without a word, she placed a plate of scrambled eggs on toast in front of him.

Silence reigned, and Mornay was halfway through her scrambled egg when she suddenly realised that she had been so busy with her other thoughts that she had forgotten to remember her usual care about what she placed before Brad. In view of that first breakfast she had given him of scrambled egg when he'd had the utmost difficulty in cutting up his toast, she had been particularly careful not to ever again give him anything on toast.

She took another glance beneath her lashes—at his hands this time—and saw that, as well as coping magnificently, he was holding his knife and fork in a quite normal manner. Indeed, so normal were his actions, there was no sign that there had ever been anything the matter with him.

It was that thought—that there was no sign that there had ever been anything the matter with him—which caused Mornay to raise her eyes to his face. Her heart began to beat a little faster as she took in his normal healthy colour, and the rested look of him. Quite suddenly then, she was ready to swear that he was once again a fit and healthy man.

And for that she was enormously grateful. Though abruptly, as Brad all at once looked up, so Mornay, who had been studying him, found herself caught out. What could she do? For a split second as his dark eyes looked straight into hers she was stumped—which left her only one method of defence available.

Her voice was challenging when, 'You're well again now, aren't you?' she smartly attacked—and saw the angry glint that came to his eyes at her tone.

She was not, therefore, particularly surprised when he retaliated in harsh kind, 'If you mean, have I recovered from the injuries I sustained when you drove your car at me and then, like a coward, drove on without stopping,' he attempted to shoot her down in flames, 'then I've been *fully well* for over a week now!'

His remarks about her cowardice hurt, even if he had got the wrong person. But she was beginning to think that there was little he could say when he was in acid mood that wouldn't hurt. So, tilting her chin an angry fraction, she favoured him with a cool, unsmiling look of her own. 'Then perhaps you wouldn't mind telling me what the blazes I'm doing here looking after you,' she questioned stiffly. 'You don't need me!' she told him for good measure—and was straight away slapped down for her trouble.

'You're being repetitious,' Brad told her curtly, and, while Mornay started to grow indignant at his insinuation that her talk of wanting to return to Reefingham was getting boring, he went on to lay it on the line. 'My good health may have returned, but nothing else has changed.' His voice had taken on a silky edge when, leaning back in his chair, he threatened arrogantly, 'I'm sure I don't have to remind you that the police will still be looking for the low-down hit-and-run type who rendered me unconscious one night last month.'

And at that, something in Mornay snapped. 'It's a pity you ever woke up!' she hissed furiously, and, throwing down her napkin, she was off her chair and halfway out of the kitchen when he mocked,

'I adore you too, sweetheart.'

Mornay spent a lot of time over the next few days wishing that Gerry Overton had never telephoned. So, OK, maybe she had, prior to that call, been in a fool's paradise, thinking that she was happy, but surely that had to be better than what she had now? The atmosphere between her and Brad was more strained than ever. She supposed she should apologise for her 'pity you ever woke up' remark, but he hadn't apologised for his threatening remark which had provoked it, so why the hell should she?

Thursday morning dawned dull and cheerless. Great, Mornay thought—it matched her mood. 'Good morning,' Brad started the day right anyhow as he tossed her a civil greeting when he came into the kitchen.

'Good morning,' Mornay responded coolly in kind, and wondered just how much longer they were going to go on like this. Though Brad didn't seem to be showing any sign that he felt anything to be amiss, and she was darned sure she wasn't going to be the one to suggest that there might be.

As on Tuesday and Wednesday, breakfast was taken in total silence. Mornay munched her way through toast and marmalade that tasted like chaff and knew that the only thing that prevented her from again suggesting that they returned to Reefingham was Brad's acid implication that such a topic of conversation was boring.

She finished her toast and took her plate to the sink. She heard Brad move, but did not turn round. She was aware of him, tautly aware of him standing somewhere behind her, and suddenly her nerve-ends seemed more stretched than ever. Needing some action then as never before, she extended a hand towards the kettle, intending to fill it and set it to boil, but her hand never reached that far. Because, as she pushed out a hand, a long arm came from behind her and, as if yanked by some puppeteer, she jumped back in nervous tension.

Too late, she saw that it had never been in Brad's mind to touch her. Too late, she saw that he had merely been reaching for a teaspoon which was by the side of the kettle, and which she had missed putting in his coffee-saucer. Too late, she saw, as he must have done, that the way she had jumped back from him must have seemed as though she was afraid he was going to take her in his arms.

'Oh, for lord's sake!' she heard him grunt grimly, and the next sound she heard was the sound of him slamming short-temperedly out of the bungalow.

He had never done that before, and it upset Mornay. It was clear that he was upset too, but it was too late then to wish that she'd had more control of her reflexes. She hadn't meant to jump back like that, but she knew that there was no way she was going to explain that her unguarded reaction had been brought about by the uneasy tension between them.

Ten minutes later, with no sign of Brad returning, Mornay was starting to rebel and wonder why she should want to explain anything anyhow. If he'd asked for a spoon she'd have passed one over to him. No wonder she'd jumped. It served him right for coming creeping up behind her. Perhaps he'd be more careful in future.

Thoughts of the future brought to mind thoughts of a return to Reefingham, which in turn brought a reminder of Penny Dale and her sister and her family.

As on the only other occasion when Brad had left her in the bungalow on her own, Mornay wondered at the time she had wasted in getting to the telephone. This time, though, as she went to the sitting-room Mornay knew an odd reluctance to dial that number in Penny Dale, though why, she had no idea. She still loved her sister as much as always, and as always she wanted to help her—if she could.

The words 'if she could' played back in her mind as she dialled. Claudia wanted her to go and stay with her to give her a bit of help with the children, but how could she? Mornay didn't even know why she was ringing Claudia, though as she waited she supposed it must be something to do with the bond of love that had been forged in their growing years.

'Mornay!' her sister gave a glad cry when she heard her voice. 'Oh, I knew you wouldn't let me down—how soon can you get here?'

'Er—I'm not in Reefingham,' Mornay thought she had better explain.

'You're not still away with the parents!' Claudia exclaimed. 'Good heavens!' she went on. 'I could hardly believe it when Gerry said that because of Mother's wrist you were going on holiday with them. Although,' she conceded, 'you being you, perhaps I can. Anyhow,' she went rushing on, 'Mother's had you for long enough now, so you just tell her you're coming to me and——'

'But—er—my job!' Mornay cut in, clutching at straws and still trying to keep the truth—the truth that would threaten Claudia's security—from her.

'Oh, Mr Probert's an old softee; if you've used up all your holiday allowance he'll give you some more time off, I'm certain. Especially when you tell him how much you're needed here.'

From clear memory, it seemed to Mornay that there always had been a certain amount of pandemonium in her sister's happy home, but, 'Are things really that bad?' she gently asked.

'Chaotic is an understatement!' Claudia replied, and to Mornay's horror she was sure she heard a catch in her sister's voice as she told her shakily, 'Luke never stops crying from morning to night, the house is a tip and Gerry's had to work late the last three nights to compensate for having all of last week off. I'm telling you, Mornay,' she went on, and there was a definite break in her voice, 'I t-tell you I'm getting so depressed, I-I just can't cope!'

Mornay stayed trying to calm her for another five minutes. Then a tearful Claudia was telling her she'd have to go, that baby Luke was screaming his lungs off, and begging her to come and give her some help.

'I'll see what I can do,' was the best Mornay could promise, but she came away from the telephone feeling exceedingly worried. In normal circumstances she'd have been over at Penny Dale like a shot.

But, she sighed as she returned to the kitchen and got busy with the chores, these were not normal circumstances. Nor, though, was it normal for Claudia to be depressed, and Mornay found that very worrying.

Having finished in the kitchen, she went to the sitting-room with a duster and fretted that, when Claudia had always been there when she had needed her, she should be letting her down at this time. Not that she could recall ever having any major problem that she hadn't been able to work through for herself, but it pained Mornay that the best she could tell her sister was 'I'll see what I can do'.

She was entirely forgetful, as her concern increased, that, far from letting her sister down, she was in fact, by being so many miles away from Penny Dale, doing what she had to to ensure the future security of her sister and her sister's offspring.

Her anxieties, though, had reached a climax by the time she heard Brad return. Immediately she wanted to go to him and plead for him to let her return to Reefingham, but she was still smarting from the 'boring' label he had given the subject.

She guessed, however, that her anxiety must have been showing when, a minute or so later, he stepped into the sitting-room, took one look at her and instantly frowned. Then, flicking her an annoyed look, he turned abruptly about and, as if he thought himself the cause of her anxiety, he showed her just how much he wanted to touch her again—by striding out again.

But, 'Brad!' she called urgently, as she swallowed on the realisation that any passing desire he might have had for her was just that—passing. She saw him halt by the door, and saw him slowly turn, and she fought frantically for something to say that would not give away any of what had to be kept most secret from him.

'Well?' he barked when, instead of telling him why she had called his name, she continued to stand there looking huge-eyed and worried.

'I . . .' Mornay began, and then, finding her powers of invention were suddenly in hiding, 'My sister wants to see me!' she blurted out in one go.

'Your—sister wants to see you?' he questioned, one eyebrow raising aloft as he took a couple of casual steps back into the room.

'I rang her while you were out,' she confessed, and was made to suffer another dark look for her deceit in using the phone only when his back was turned.

But, 'Naturally,' was his only comment, sarcastic though that one word was.

'The thing is,' Mornay continued slowly, feeling her way as she went, 'my sister—well, she's a bit depressed, and—and I think it would cheer her up if I—if we—she and I,' she pressed on, starting to flounder at his look that said he thought she was lying about the whole of it, 'if we could see——' She broke off when his look became totally sceptical. 'She *is* depressed!' she snapped, starting to get angry. 'You didn't hear her. . .'

'What's she depressed about?' Brad questioned her toughly, and Mornay glared at him.

'If you must know,' she flared, 'she had a baby—some while ago,' she tacked on hastily, and backtracked over what she had just told him, but could see nothing in what she had said that would link Gerry in as being the driver of her car that particular night. 'Some women can feel low for ages afterwards,' she enlightened him for extra emphasis, even though she was fully aware that Claudia's problem was not one of a hormonal imbalance, but the fact of Luke's being more demanding than his sisters, and that of Claudia's finding difficulty in getting into a routine.

'She doesn't get on with your mother?'

Brad's bald statement caused Mornay to stare at him in some surprise. How on earth had he known that? She was sure she hadn't said... 'No,' she confirmed, 'that is—what's whether she gets on with my mother got to do with anything?' she flared.

'You tell me!' he grunted. 'It seemed to me an obvious question since, according to what you've told me, your sister lives with your parents. I could only assume, with your sister wanting to see you, that things can't be too amicable in the Solihull household.'

'Oh,' Mornay murmured, and, fully aware that a pair of dark eyes were firmly fixed on her creamy complexion which, as heat washed over her, she was sure had turned to a 'found out' pink, 'Er—Claudia—er—doesn't live in Solihull—er—actually,' she was made to confess.

'She doesn't?' he questioned, a grim light starting to enter his eyes.

Grief, thought Mornay, hoping, since it seemed that he took great exception to being told lies, that this was the last lie he ever found out about. 'I never actually said that she did,' she told him, but could see he had awarded her no merit marks for pointing that out.

'Where—*actually*—does she live?' he questioned.

'With her husband—and five children,' Mornay stalled.

'Surely not in a shoe,' he commented drily, and Mornay was suddenly struck by a feeling of wanting to laugh.

Nerves rather than amusement were the cause for that, she quickly decided, and as quickly realised too that in trying to avoid telling him what it seemed he was determined to know, she was drawing greater attention to her reluctance—which was only going to make him wonder his famous 'Why?'.

'She lives in a house, as a matter of fact,' she told him, 'in Penny Dale,' and since if he'd never heard of

Penny Dale it wouldn't take him long to find out where it was, 'It's near Reefingham,' she told him.

'How near?'

Damn you, Mornay fumed, feeling suddenly irritated with him and his mind that left no question unasked. 'About five miles,' she shrugged, as though carelessly.

'On your doorstep, in fact,' Brad commented.

'If you like,' she said coldly, and weathered his long, level look which told her as clearly as if he'd said it that he was remembering the morning they had left Reefingham and how the only person she had telephoned had been her employer.

Mornay half expected some acid comment from him to the effect that it would not have surprised him had she told him that she and her sister didn't get on either, since she had gone away without a word despite their living on each other's doorstep. Or, she thought, perhaps some acid comment on the lines of being surprised that her sister wanted to see her when, apart from living near to each other, they did not otherwise appear to be close at all.

But, whatever Mornay expected, it was she who was surprised when, taking her back to that morning three weeks ago, he suddenly and abruptly clipped, 'Are you packed?'

'Packed?' she questioned witlessly.

'If we're to make Penny Dale before nightfall, we'd better get started,' he replied loftily.

There was more to be done than pack their belongings, however. But, in less time than she would have thought, the beds—at her instigation—had been stripped, and Mrs Macdonald, the woman who had greeted them on their arrival, had been contacted and asked if she would mind coming to clear out the cupboards. Then, with Brad doing the driving this time, and stopping at Mrs Macdonald's home to drop off the key, they were heading back the way which three weeks ago they had come.

As an aching pang of regret took Mornay, she was glad that Brad had opted to drive. It seemed odd, when she had known joy and sadness, happiness and dejection, that she should feel such regret at having left that bungalow in Kilcaber. But, now that she knew that her time with Brad Kendrick was at an end, regret, a very real regret, was what she felt.

She knew full well that she should be glad he had shown himself to have a heart when she had told him of her sister's depression, for, as he once had before, he could have easily answered 'Tough'. But, he hadn't, and she loved him, and after today she was never going to see him again and—she wanted the journey never to end.

'Are you hungry?' Brad suddenly enquired, and Mornay had to quickly choke down weak tears that were at that moment threatening.

'A bit,' she lied, and realised as they stopped for lunch that what she was doing, even while part of her knew that she should be hurrying to get to Claudia, was trying to delay the hour when she must say a final farewell to the man who held her heart.

Once lunch was over Brad drove for a further three hours without stopping. By then Mornay thought that she had got herself more under control so that, had he asked whether she would like to stop for tea, she would have told him no.

But he did not ask, and, perversely, she started to worry that he might need a rest. 'Shall we stop for a cup of tea?' she asked, and as he pulled in at a service area she could only wonder at the contrary person she had become since love had fired its blunderbus of varying emotions at her.

They did not spend long over their tea, but when, still thinking that he might appreciate a rest, she suggested that she would drive, he would not hear of it. 'It's not

far now,' he told her evenly. It was about that time that
Mornay awakened to a sense of danger.

They were on their way again when, racking her brains,
she felt certain that, when asking if she was packed, Brad
had then followed up with—not 'If we're to make
Reefingham before nightfall...' but, 'If we're to make
Penny Dale'!

Penny Dale! she thought alarmed, and at the thought
that he intended to drive her to her sister's home her
alarm started to turn to panic. She couldn't let him drive
her to Claudia's, she just couldn't! If Gerry wasn't
working late and, having worked late three nights on the
trot she thought that there was a fair chance he might
finish work on time or even early that night, then he
could well be there by the time she and Brad drove up.

With her head swimming with endless complications
which might conceivably ensue, Mornay felt too het up
to leave it to see whether Brad took the Penny Dale turn
before she said anything.

'Er——' she said in a strangled kind of way, and then,
plunging straight in, 'We—er—should have rung the
Belvedere to let them know you were coming to pick up
your car tonight.'

'I don't suppose they'll have parted with it,' he replied
evenly, which, frustratingly, told her absolutely nothing
about his intentions once they reached the borders of
her home town.

'I don't suppose they will,' she agreed carefully, and
left it a moment or two before she added casually, 'Will
you be driving back to London tonight, do you think?'

'I hadn't given it any thought,' he annoyingly let fall.

Then damn well give it some thought, she wanted to
yell at him, but didn't. For the next ten minutes her
thoughts were taken up with knowing that it was out of
the question for him to take her to Penny Dale, while
at the same time she wondered how the dickens she was
going to stop him if he was decided upon doing just

that—and, how in creation was she going to handle it if she couldn't stop him?

The sign said 'Reefingham,' and they went by it with Mornay racking her brains while her stomach churned within her. Then 'Penny Dale 5 miles', said a sign, and as, to her horror, Brad steered the car in that direction, she broke into speech.

'There's no need for you to drive out of your way!' she told him urgently. 'Th——'

'It's no bother,' Brad told her easily. 'After the miles we've come today, another five miles is neither here nor there.'

'Yes, but—but, you must want to get to the Belvedere to reclaim your car and...' Her voice petered out when he gave her a sideways, eyebrow-raised look. 'You've been so good already,' she hopped hastily on to another tack. 'It doesn't seem fair that you should...' Her voice faltered when, as he flicked her another all-seeing glance, she realised he must have seen that she was in a stew about something.

'You've said many things during our time together,' he murmured sardonically, 'but never, Mornay, have you accused me of being "good".'

Go to hell, she wanted to tell him, but instead, she sighed defeatedly, and told him ungraciously, 'I shall only have to leave Claudia to run you back.'

'I wouldn't dream of permitting it,' Brad answered suavely. 'I'm sure the local taxi service will be more than adequate.'

Apart from giving him directions to her sister's home, Mornay had not another word to say to him. In relative silence she fumed for the rest of the way, and put her faith in Gerry's not being home from work yet, in Brad's not staying for longer than it took to summon a taxi, and in everything's turning out all right.

Fate, Mornay soon realised, was laughing up her sleeve. For from the very start everything began to turn

out all wrong. From the instant Brad pulled up outside
Claudia's home and Mornay saw that her sister was in
the garden taking advantage of the sun's rays that late
Thursday afternoon, one tearing-apart emotion after
another flooded through Mornay.

'Mornay!' Claudia cried in delight as, with Brad following, Mornay went over the path and on to the lawn,
and Claudia came over to greet them.

Hugging her sister, Mornay was pleased to see that
she was looking far more cheerful than she had feared
she might. Though, knowing something of her sister's
character, it was highly probable that she was putting
up a show in front of the stranger she had brought with
her.

Which reminded Mornay—not that she could have
forgotten him. 'Claudia,' she smiled, and turning to the
tall, dark, watchful-eyed man standing silently by her
side, 'this is Brad Kendrick,' she introduced him, hoping
against hope that Claudia had been so taken up with her
family that she had not chanced to hear his name mentioned anywhere in connection with an accident in
Reefingham's High Street. 'Brad,' she continued smile,
'this is my sister, Claudia Overton.'

As soon as her sister's surname had left her lips,
Mornay was wishing it hadn't. Far better, she thought,
as the two shook hands, not to feed him any information which he didn't absolutely have to know; was it
too soon for her to make noises about ringing for a taxi?

'Where are the girls?' she questioned, guessing that
perhaps Gerry's mother must have taken them for an
hour to give Claudia a break, and again wished that she
had not said something when she heard Claudia's reply.

'Gerry's taken them for ice-creams,' she announced
sunnily, and as Mornay caught the look in Brad's eyes
that plainly told her that Gerry's name had registered,
'Gerry's my husband,' Claudia smilingly explained, 'and
the girls are my four daughters. And this,' she said

proudly, leading the way to the pram which was situated close to where she had been sitting, 'is my son.'

Luke was beautiful, and at any other time Mornay would have peered into the pram and have crooned over the little mite. But her nerves were starting to feel stretched to breaking-point, and all she had in mind to do just then was to get Brad away from Penny Dale before Gerry returned. She doubted very much that Gerry would give anything away, but just the two being introduced to each other represented a risk, and yet more complications.

She was making a show of admiring the sound-asleep babe just the same when, to make her heart sink, she heard Claudia offer Brad some sort of refreshment. At any other time she would have been surprised had Claudia not done so, but this time she could have wished that her sister had forgotten her good manners.

'Brad isn't staying!' she found herself hastily refusing for him, and when she glanced from her sister to a pair of dark, all-seeing, all-thinking eyes, 'You said something about taking a taxi back, didn't you?' she queried, forcing a smile.

'So I did,' he replied levelly. 'Perhaps...' he hinted.

'May I use your phone to ring Ibbotson's taxis?' Mornay asked, starting to feel a trace of relief that it wouldn't be much longer now before Brad went.

'Of course,' Claudia replied, and added with a smile, 'they're all male drivers on that firm.' Then, before Mornay had taken a footstep in the direction of the telephone, she promptly sent any trace of relief flying, and very nearly caused her heart-failure, when by way of explanation for her last remark, 'I noticed when you arrived that you were doing the driving,' she addressed Brad. And brightly she went on to suggest, 'Perhaps you, like my husband, can't abide to be driven anywhere by a woman.'

An almost soundless cry, half strangled at birth left
Mornay, who was unable to prevent it. Unfortunately,
one of the two people standing near picked it up. It was
the one person she would have preferred not to have
heard. Because suddenly Brad had pinned her gaze with
his, and dark eyes were looking straight into panicking
blue ones.

She knew at once that he had sensed that there was
something amiss, and she panicked some more when she
saw an alert, considering look enter his eyes. She had
seen that alert look before and she knew, where Claudia
didn't, that Brad Kendrick had been born asking,
'Why?', and that he was about to start asking questions
any minute now.

Rooted to the spot, all thoughts of going to ring for
a taxi forgotten, Mornay tried to get in first to say something, anything to detract him from his purpose. But her
throat was dry and nothing would come, and anyway,
Brad had got in first.

'Mornay never mentioned that your husband shares
my aversion,' he smiled, full of charm, to Claudia.

Don't! Don't answer him! Mornay wanted to shriek,
knowing full well that he had no such aversion. But her
sister was taking the man she had brought to her home
on face-value, and was responding warmly to his charm,
and did answer—openly. 'I'm not surprised,' she smiled
back at him. 'Mornay's probably still peeved at him over
the last time he asked her to hand over her car keys.'

'No!' Mornay tried to get in, but her sister merely
took it that she was denying that she was still peeved
with Gerry, and hardly needed the invitation Brad gave
her to continue.

'What happened?' he seemed pleasantly interested to
know, and, while Mornay was striving to control her
panic by telling herself that Claudia couldn't tell him
anything because Gerry wouldn't have told her about
the accident, Claudia blithely continued.

'I was in hospital at the time, having Luke,' she said, glancing to the babe in the pram. 'Both Gerry and Mornay were coming to see me when Gerry's car went on the blink, so Gerry rang Mornay to come and pick him up. But Gerry, being Gerry, wouldn't allow her to drive him. Cheek, I call it,' she smiled to Mornay, 'especially after you'd taken the trouble to come and pick him up.'

'You were in hospital recently?' Brad took up when Claudia seemed to have momentarily lost her thread.

Mornay felt herself growing paler and paler and could hardly believe that this nightmare was happening when she saw Brad look over to the babe as if to gauge how old he was, then heard Claudia proudly tell him, 'Luke's four weeks old next Monday.' And as Mornay wanted to groan out loud that her sister was telling him *everything*, her limbs suddenly seemed to have seized up, causing her to feel powerless to move. Then Claudia went on to add yet *more*! 'It was over that young scamp's arrival that I wouldn't have been surprised if my sister never spoke to my chauvinistic husband ever again.'

'Oh?' queried Brad politely.

'I'm sure Brad isn't interested,' Mornay found vocal release to put in hastily and huskily.

'But of course I am, Mornay,' he replied gently, and Claudia needed no more encouragement than that to reveal all.

'According to Gerry, Mornay was in quite a state that, after they went for a celebratory drink to wet Luke's head, Gerry afterwards put a dent in her car when he missed his turning and ran her car into a brick wall.'

At that point Mornay murmured a quiet, 'Excuse me,' and went into the house to telephone for a taxi. There was nothing that Brad 'eye for an eye' Kendrick did not know now, and nothing she could do to stop him from using as he would the information which Claudia had so eagerly supplied.

Mornay made her call and went back out into the garden wondering what on earth Gerry had been thinking of to have told her sister any of it anyway. It did not take her long to find out about that, however. For, as if she was starved of adult company and conversation, Claudia was still giving forth about the wretched dent Gerry had put in her car when Mornay—avoiding looking at Brad—joined them.

'Gerry was really worried, Mornay,' her sister told her sincerely. 'I don't think he was going to tell me about it, but when I could see that something was on his mind and badgered away at him to tell me what it was—he just had to confess that he didn't think he was your second-best friend any more.'

'Dope!' Mornay murmured, and was grateful that Luke at that moment awakened and seemed bent on impressing the neighbourhood with the prowess of his lungs.

Fortunately, a short while after that, the taxi arrived. Courteously, bearing in mind that Luke was yelling his head off, Brad said goodbye to Claudia then, without a word to Mornay, went striding to retrieve his belongings from her car. Without a backward glance he then went to the taxi.

Quickly Mornay followed. 'Brad!' she urgently called his name. He turned and, waiting for her to state what she wanted, looked at her with grim hostility. 'You—you won't . . .' Her voice faltered. 'Please,' she rephrased what she had been going to say, 'please don't—d-do anything to . . .' Her voice faded when she saw the murderous glint in his eyes. Without a word of farewell, he turned and got into the taxi, and Mornay watched the taxi drive off with fear entering her heart, certain in her knowledge that Brad Kendrick was not the sort of man to sit back and do nothing.

Mornay began to be aware that she was not on her own when, despite the fact that Luke was refusing to be pacified, her sister came over to her, and as if she had been having the most tremendous battle in holding down her curiosity ever since they had arrived, yelled over the top of Luke's cries, 'Who—was *that*?'

Mornay sought for words, looked away from her, and replied, 'Here's Gerry.' She had a small breathing space when Gerry drove his car on to the drive, braked, and Emily, Alice, Florence and Prudence tumbled out, and came rushing over crying her name.

'That's enough!' Claudia laughed, not very authoritatively, it had to be said. 'Mornay doesn't want your ice-cream-sticky fingers all over her clothes.' She was shooing them inside for an all-round hand-washing session when, 'Hello, Mornay—how's things?' Gerry greeted her, bestowing a brotherly kiss on her cheek.

He looks worried, Mornay thought, and told him, 'Fine.' What with four young ladies all wanting individual attention, and young Luke making his presence known, all was bedlam, and there was little chance of more than bitty conversation.

By the time a bed had been made up for her, and the children were safely tucked up and all was quiet, however, Gerry had been acquainted with the fact that a man named Brad Kendrick had driven her to his home and, staying only a few minutes, had left by taxi. Mornay had not missed the worried look that had again come to Gerry's face, and even though she feared that there was a great deal of trouble ahead she doubted—had it been possible to have a private word with him—that she would have confirmed she thought he was right to look worried.

She knew she was wrong not to warn him, but if Claudia, seeing him worried about something, had ferreted out of him that he had dented her car, then she would soon get from him that Brad Kendrick had cause to, and might well, bring a case against him. And that, together with the realisation that a driving ban spelt doom to her security, would do nothing whatsoever to improve Claudia's state of depression.

So Mornay smiled and did her best to appear as though she was in the best of spirits—and she guessed she had succeeded in making believe that there was nothing at all wrong in her world, for the worried look left Gerry, and Claudia seemed far from depressed.

'You're feeling better now than when I rang this morning, aren't you, love?' Mornay asked her.

'Yes, thank goodness!' Claudia replied with a heartfelt sigh. 'Everything seemed to be on top of me earlier today,' she added, and apologised, 'I'm sorry about being such a pain when you rang. I felt terrible about it after I'd put the phone down——'

'It's understandable,' Gerry cut in, and Claudia sent him a loving look for his understanding.

'Did anybody ever tell you that you're the best husband any woman could ask for?' she teased him.

'I'm going to make some coffee before Mornay gets the impression that you're glad you married me,' Gerry grinned, getting to his feet.

'So,' said Claudia the minute he had gone, '*who* is he?'

'I thought you'd forgotten,' Mornay played for more time, having had plenty in which to try to think up something convincing to explain the total stranger whom Claudia had never even heard her mention.

'Is that likely?' Claudia queried, and added, 'I purposely didn't ask you about Brad Kendrick in front of Gerry in case you felt a bit—um—shy about telling about him in front of anyone.'

'Oh!' Mornay exclaimed, and realised at once the track her sister's mind had taken. She supposed then that, given that apart from Robert Naylor she had never brought any other man-friend to her sister's home, and given her reluctance to talk about Brad, her sister's conclusions were perhaps only natural ones. But as if it were

manna from heaven, Mornay grabbed at the explanation
Claudia had offered her. 'Brad's—er—a bit—er—
special,' she confessed, and was not lying.

'I thought so!' Claudia replied.

'It didn't show in my face, did it?' Mornay asked in
sudden panic.

'Of course not,' her sister assured her stoutly, but had
Mornay panicking again when she asked, 'Where did
you meet him—while you were away with the parents?'

'I...' Mornay said, and, knowing that she was on
tremendously shaky ground here, 'I...' she said again,
and ducked the question entirely by saying, 'I'm a bit...
Do you mind if we talk about something else?'

Mornay hated herself when Claudia, her look fully
comprehending, murmured gently, 'Poor love, you've
been knocked for six, and don't know yet how Brad feels
about you.'

Mornay went to bed that night and reckoned she'd got
a very good idea of how Brad felt about her. Never would
she forget that murderous glint that had been in his eyes
before he had left in the taxi.

She spent a most dreadful night, when she would
waken again and again to find Brad's face with that
murderous glint in his eyes swimming in front of her.
Curiously, though, at the self-same time, there was an
ache like a void within her that Brad was not there in
the room next to hers. She missed him, and wanted him
near.

Unable to sleep as she was, she could have wept from
the pain of knowing that she would never see him again.
It was during her wakeful hours, though, that it came
back to her how the newspaper had said that no one ever
put one over on him without living to regret it.

She was awakened by the baby crying on Friday
morning and remembered how she had hoped Brad
would never find out that she, by virtue of not telling
him that Gerry had been the one driving her car that

night, had put one over on him. What, she began to panic, would Brad do?

Leaving her bed, Mornay hastily washed and dressed and went down the stairs, still feeling rock-bottom at the thought of never seeing Brad again, while at the same time she was inwardly a mass of agitation that the next piece of Royal Mail to drop through Claudia's letterbox would be a summons addressed to her brother-in-law.

How much or how little Claudia had told Gerry of their brief conversation about Brad last night, Mornay had no idea. But with Gerry wanting to get to a particular site by eight, and with the rest of the early-rising household a thriving multitude of activity, there was no time as the day got under way for any sort of private conversation with him.

She spent a busy morning giving the house a blitz while Claudia, with three daughters at school, in between keeping three-year-old Prudence amused and attending to the whims of baby Luke, tackled a mountain of ironing.

Mornay still had plenty of space in her thoughts for Brad, however, and he was much on her mind when Claudia broke through her thoughts, and queried, 'Penny for them, Mornay?'

'My thoughts are worth more than that,' Mornay returned lightly, but realised then that if she didn't want her sister to begin to conjecture about her, she had better buck her ideas up.

By three that afternoon, though, as Mornay walked with Claudia to collect the children from the village school, her head was again in turmoil. What was Brad going to do? Would the weeks she had spent in Scotland with him count for nothing? She had thought him a fair man, but she kept remembering his aversion to having one put over on him, and felt that she was going crazy wondering whether his fairness would stand the test of her having done just that.

Back at the house an hour later, her doubts and fears had grown worse instead of better, and Mornay knew then that she was going to have to take some action or go potty. 'Can I use your phone?' she asked Claudia while the courage to do what she must was fresh about her.

'Of course. Come on, you lot, we'll go out into the garden and see if we can find a shady spot for a picnic,' Claudia at once prepared to make herself and her family scarce.

'There's no need...' Mornay began.

'There's every need,' Claudia replied. The very fact that she hadn't asked with her usual sisterly familiarity whom she was going to ring told Mornay that she knew something was troubling her, and that she was going to ring Brad Kendrick 'You can't even think when they get going, much less make yourself heard.'

Five minutes later, Mornay, after at first shying away from making that call, had given herself a short lecture and had then proceeded to find out the office number of Kendrick Components. Taking a deep breath, she then dialled that number, and while she waited for her call to be answered she renewed her lecture which had gone along the lines of the fact that, with Brad's office likely to close in an hour or so, not to make that call would mean that she would have to sweat it out until Monday to make contact—if by then he had not—through the legal system—made contact first.

'Kendrick Components, good afternoon,' said a pleasant voice.

'Miss Boulter, please,' she requested, feeling fairly certain that she'd have been wasting her time in asking for Mr Kendrick direct.

'Helen Boulter,' said an efficient-sounding feminine voice.

'Ah, Miss Boulter,' Mornay said quickly, 'It's Mornay Haynes here—can I speak with Mr Kendrick?'

'I'm afraid he isn't available at the moment,' her call was instantly blocked. 'Can I take a message or can anyone else help you?'

Mornay calculated that this was perhaps normal office procedure for anyone unknown to the secretary trying to get through to speak to Brad, and she put a light laugh into her tone as, 'Oh—I should have said, this is a personal call—if you'll tell Brad that it's Mornay, I'm sure that——'

'I'm sorry, Miss Haynes,' Mornay found herself blocked again, 'but Mr Kendrick is abroad on holiday.'

Mornay came away from the telephone feeling utterly defeated. For a few moments then she got angry—it hadn't taken him long to pick up his passport and fly off, had it? As swiftly as her anger had come, though, it as swiftly died when she began to wonder—had he stopped by at his lawyer's on the way to the airport?

She spent the next hour having a picnic with her sister and her offspring and in trying to appear as though she felt loads better for having made her phone call. In actual fact she felt worse than ever, because suddenly she was jealously certain that, as well as stopping by at his lawyer's on the way to the airport, there was every probability that Brad had stopped by to pick up the recipient of the two dozen roses.

A short while later Gerry came home, and as his daughters made a fuss of him Claudia made him a cup of tea and asked him how he felt about taking the family *en masse* to the late-night-opening supermarket.

'En masse!' he jokingly shuddered, and asked, 'Is it essential?'

'The cupboard's bare,' Claudia informed him.

'Then supermarket it is,' he agreed cheerfully, and, indicating the cup of tea in his hand, 'Just give me a minute to recuperate,' he added, 'and I'll be there.'

'Do you mind if I don't come?' Mornay suddenly piped up, that word 'recuperate' suddenly stirring a memory to life.

'Chicken!' Gerry teased.

Fifteen long minutes were to elapse before Mornay waved her sister, brother-in-law and their five children off, and was able to sit down and quietly think through the idea which that word 'recuperate' had suddenly sparked off.

Hurriedly she went back over her phone call to Helen Boulter, in which Brad's secretary had told her that he was abroad on holiday. But, Mornay then wondered—was he? Hadn't she been in the same room with him when, prior to their going to Scotland, he had instructed his secretary, 'And Helen—leave it twenty-four hours before you announce to anyone interested that I'm recuperating abroad'?

But he hadn't been abroad, he'd been in Scotland, and his secretary had known that because it had been she who had arranged Brad's 'hideaway'—so where did that leave her now? Mornay wondered anxiously.

Quite clearly Helen Boulter was an efficient secretary who would obey her employer's instructions to the letter. Had she, Mornay had to ask herself, merely been obeying his instructions to tell anyone interested that he was abroad, and was Brad, in point of fact, actually still in England?

Three minutes later, Mornay knew that there might be a way of finding out. Her stomach was churning away inside her when, the telephone number of the bungalow in Kilcaber indelibly imprinted on her mind, she found the area code and proceeded to dial. She swallowed hard as she waited—and then discovered that she had no need to be nervous, for Brad wasn't there—at least, if he was, he wasn't answering the phone.

Replacing the receiver, she sighed, feeling quite fatigued with the emotion and trauma of it all. It seemed imperative that she contact Brad, but by then it was becoming hazy in her mind whether she wanted to contact him because her top priority was to prevent him from doing anything that would jeopardise her sister's security—or if she felt it so urgent to contact him because she was desperate for the sound of his voice.

Mornay knew Brad would not still be at the Belvedere when she looked up their telephone number. He hadn't even booked in for so much as last night, she knew that as, feeling compelled by she knew not what, she began to dial. All he'd done was to stay long enough to settle for the garaging of his car and then he'd been off, and headed straight back to London.

'The Belvedere Hotel.'

Quickly Mornay got herself together. 'Would you put me through to Mr Bradford Kendrick, please?' she requested—and got the shock of her life when the receptionist told her to hold the line a moment.

Mornay surfaced from her shock to realise that the receptionist would come back at any moment now and tell her that she was sorry but that Mr Bradford Kendrick was not registered.

But the receptionist did no such thing, and Mornay was left dumbstruck when she came on the line again and told her, 'You're through now.'

Mornay opened her mouth, and then closed it when no sound came. But no sound was coming from the other end either, and that alone forced her to try to get some sound out of her vocal cords. 'B-Brad?' she eventually managed to query, and very nearly collapsed when he replied,

'What kept you?'

'I—d-didn't know where you were,' she told him, stupidly, she rather thought, for his tone had been more toughly sarcastic than genuinely enquiring. But silence was all that came from the other end and, forced to go on, 'What—are you going to do?' she made herself ask.

'About what?' he asked, sounding terse and unbending.

'About Gerry,' she replied, and felt her nerves tensing as the silence from the other end stretched.

Then, clearly and quite distinctly, he arrogantly told her, 'You'd better come and find out.' Then the phone went dead.

CHAPTER NINE

TWENTY minutes after putting down the phone after her call to Brad at the Belvedere, Mornay was still trembling. Her first instinct had been to get to her car and to get over to the Belvedere as fast as she could. But life wasn't as simple as that. For one thing, she was not in her own home, but in Claudia's, and since her sister and her family were out and she didn't know if they had a house key she realised that she would have to wait for their return.

In any case, she realised an hour later, she didn't think she was ready to face Brad yet. She wanted to be calm when she saw him again, but she was far from being cool and collected. She looked down at the cotton shirt and trousers she had worn all day, and in the next moment she was haring up the stairs to take a quick shower and change into a smart linen two-piece. She then applied a small amount of make-up and pinned her blonde hair into a classic knot, and then she stood back to observe in the mirror that the cool female who stared back at her and who wore just a hint of sophistication bore no resemblance to the totally all-over-the-place person she was inside.

Mornay was human enough to be pleased with her appearance as she went downstairs to wait for Claudia and Gerry to return. She had taken the two-piece with her to Scotland, but had not worn it, so Brad had never seen her in it, nor, so far as she could remember, had she worn her hair this way while they had been together.

Not, she thought a moment later, that he'd give a fig what she looked like; he was more interested in her nerve in daring to lead him up the garden path over who had been at the wheel of her car that one particular night.

Agitatedly Mornay flicked a glance to her watch. Should she ring Brad and tell him that she couldn't leave the house until her sister and brother-in-law returned from shopping? On the grounds that he would think her an idiot, she decided against ringing him.

In all, though, she had to wait over two hours since she had made her call to Brad before she could obey his command that she 'come and find out'. She was at the window when she saw Gerry's car approaching, and she was out of the house, her car keys in her hand, by the time he had pulled up.

'I've got to go out,' she went to Claudia's open window to tell her.

Whatever Claudia felt like saying, one look at Mornay's solemn expression made her hold back. 'I'm sure it'll be all right, whatever it is, love,' she said quickly, and earned Mornay's gratitude for not prying.

Mornay was driving off down the road before the children had been released from their safety harnesses. The nearer she got to Reefingham, though, the faster her heart began to pound.

She was hoping with all she had as she pulled into the parking area of the Belvedere that she still looked as outwardly cool now as she had looked in the mirror in her bedroom at Penny Dale—because never had she felt in such a haywire state of agitated turmoil.

Leaving her car, she tried to keep her expression impassive as she went into the plush interior to the hotel and approached the reception desk. 'Could you tell Mr Kendrick I'm here?' she asked of the smart male on duty, and was just about to add her name when she discovered that that wasn't necessary.

'Miss Haynes?' the man enquired with a charming smile, and, when she murmured that she was, 'Mr Kendrick is expecting you. I'll get someone to show you up.'

In next to no time she, who had assumed that her interview with Brad would most likely take place in the

hotel lounge, was in the lift being escorted upwards.
Mornay had time only then in which to feel most
relieved—since she had a fair idea that she was in for
some of Brad's acid—that she was to be spared having
that acid heaped on her in public. Then the lift was
stopping, and before she was ready for it her escort had
taken her to one of the doors in a long corridor, and
with a pleasant smile departed.

With a shaking hand Mornay tapped on the door in
front of her and, when a feeling of wanting to run away
presented itself, she had to firmly remind herself that
her purpose in being here was to ask Brad what he proposed to do about Gerry.

Then the door opened, and there, tall, dark-haired,
dark-eyed and arrogant—and just as she remembered
him—stood Brad. She saw his glance go from her face,
flick over her slender linen-clad figure, then up to her
smooth hairstyle and back to her face. He looks tired,
she thought, and was not conscious of thinking anything for many minutes after that when, the first to
speak, 'Did you walk it?' he enquired sarcastically as he
stood back to allow her into his room.

She knew he was referring to the length of time in
which it had taken her to get there. 'Claudia and... I
had to... They went to the supermarket—I had to wait
until they got back. I didn't know if they'd got——' She
broke off, realising that she was babbling in her nervousness, and walked past him to discover that she had
crossed the threshold, into not an ordinary hotel room,
but a suite of rooms.

'Take a seat,' he invited laconically, as he closed the
door, walked across the carpeted sitting-room of the suite
and indicated one of the two settees drawn up before a
fireplace.

'Thank you,' she murmured politely, and was glad to
sink down into its padded depths. With her ankles neatly
draped one over the other, her long legs at a slanting
angle, Mornay endeavoured to look doubly cool to make

up for her show of nervousness earlier. But, aware that the utmost tact was called for, she hardly knew where to begin. 'You—said to come over,' she reminded him for starters.

'Which—in due time—you did,' he replied gravely, which, as he availed himself of the settee opposite her, was of absolutely no help at all.

'You know why I'm here,' she told him.

'Remind me,' he suggested, quite infuriatingly, Mornay fumed, because he had a brain, more of one than most, and she doubted that he ever forgot a thing.

But she felt better to feel angry; it took the edge off her nervousness at any rate, as she coolly told him, 'I want to know what you're going to do about...' Her voice started to fade as her anger fled and nerves started to bite again, '...about G...my brother-in-law,' she made herself finish.

'Ah, yes, Gerry, the man who rang you when we were in Kilcaber,' he drawled.

'He rang to see if I could come back to give Claudia a hand,' Mornay explained.

'Which was after you had rung him to let him know where you were.'

'I had to ring him—don't you see that I had to?' she began earnestly. 'No one knew where I was—well, except Mr Probert—he's my boss,' she inserted, and saw then Brad had not forgotten that call from her flat to her boss, and went on, 'Well, he thought I was with my mother. Anyway,' Mornay rushed on, not seeming able to stop now she had started, 'it was important that Claudia didn't guess that I wasn't at my mother's, which she might have done if Robert Naylor had rung her——'

'Rung your mother?' Brad cut in, right there with her so far, Mornay was glad to see.

'Yes,' she nodded. 'Actually, had I known that Robert was and probably still is in Wales, I wouldn't——'

'You've not seen him since we got back yesterday?'

Mornay shook her head; in actual fact she could not remember giving Robert so much as a thought since she had returned. 'No,' she told Brad, and thought she saw an easing in the aggressive way he had been looking at her. She knew herself mistaken about that, though, for his aggressive look was there in full force as she resumed, 'If I'd rung Robert first instead of Gerry I'd have known——'

'You rang Naylor too from Kilcaber?' Brad sliced in to snarl.

'I...I...' Her nerves were back with a vengeance at the furious glint that came to his eyes. 'I—er—rang his firm—but he wasn't there for me to speak to——'

'What did you want to speak to him about?' Brad fired, and suddenly Mornay started to get just a bit fed up with his constant, questioning interruptions.

'Because he's my boyfriend, that's why!' she snapped, but when Brad glared more fiercely than ever, and indeed seemed as though he would leave his seat on the settee to more forcefully press some point home, she went rapidly on the defensive to tell him, 'I just wanted to prevent him from ringing my mother.'

'Why would he do that?' Brad gritted annoyingly, and Mornay had a feeling then that he was being obtuse on purpose. Though what any of this had to do with why she was there, she failed to see.

Though, because Brad was the piper and he was calling the tune, there was nothing for it but that she should reply to each and every one of his questions—no matter how annoying. 'Because,' she began stiffly, 'I could see, if Robert tried to contact me at home and I wasn't there, that—as Claudia would have done similarly—he'd either ring me at work, in which case Mr Probert would tell him I was staying with my mother, or he'd ring Claudia, who would tell him the same.'

'Which would see him ringing your mother and sub-sequently setting the fox among the hens when your mother told him you weren't there,' Brad took up, more than able, as she had known, to work it out for himself.

'Exactly,' she replied.

'Weren't you afraid Claudia would ring you in Solihull for a chat? From what I've seen I'd have said you and your sister are very close.'

'We are,' Mornay confirmed, and was a degree or two softened by his insight. 'But Claudia and my parents have—er—grown apart over the years, and I thought I was safe for a little while there. When Gerry knew where I was he told Claudia that I'd gone away with my parents on holiday—and that—er—stopped Claudia from trying to contact me in Solihull.'

'Now why, I wonder,' Brad suddenly changed tack, 'would a husband lie to his wife?'

'You know *why*!' Mornay exclaimed.

'No, I don't,' he denied. 'I'm not even sure I know why you've lied your blonde little head off from the first moment you and I came into contact—verbal contact, that is,' he added drily.

'I—that...' Mornay stopped and started again. 'Gerry couldn't tell Claudia the truth about that accident. Don't you see, it would have worried her silly?'

'Why?' he asked, as at some stage Mornay knew deep down that he would. 'He didn't hold back from telling her of the dent he put in your car when he "hit a brick wall". So where's the difference—given that I got carted off to hospital and that he was the coward, not you, for not stopping.'

'I'd have said that what you've just said is enough reason,' Mornay muttered coldly.

'Why?' he repeated. 'No one got killed, and since it seems your drinking spree stayed at the one drink level, he wasn't likely to get summonsed for driving with excess alcohol in his bloodstream.'

Stubbornly Mornay kept her lips sealed. He had more than enough to hang Gerry now—surely, much as she loved Brad, she couldn't be expected to tighten the noose.

But, when about ten seconds of her stubborn silence had ticked away, she was suddenly discovering that she had no need to tell, or not tell Brad anything, for he had it all worked out anyway.

'Of course!' he said, and she knew then that, whatever he had been thinking about since the last time she had seen him, it certainly was not Gerry, or he'd have worked it out before this. 'Your brother-in-law's been up before the magistrate on a driving charge before, hasn't he?' Mornay still stubbornly kept her lips sealed—much good did it do her. 'Quite obviously,' Brad went on, his dark eyes boring into hers, 'Overton has sufficient points against him to know that another driving misdemeanour would mean the certainty of having no driving licence at all!'

'He needs to be able to drive to get himself to work!' Mornay uncrossed her ankles and leaned forward to tell Brad urgently. Then she sat back in her chair and could have groaned that, in her urgency, she had just about confirmed all he had just guessed at. Which left her with nothing but to beg, and plead if need be, for him not to give that information to the police. 'Can't you see that for the sake of Claudia's peace of mind, her security, for her and her five children, it would be almost as much criminal to report Gerry?' she said quickly.

'Criminal?' Brad questioned toughly, and Mornay could see that, since he had been the victim, perhaps her powers of tact were less than they might have been.

'Can't you see that, with my sister's security at stake, I should never have ventured anywhere near the accident wing of Reefingham General that day after the accident?' Mornay tried a different but still crucial approach. 'C——'

'But you did,' Brad reminded her levelly.

'I hadn't intended to,' she got side-tracked to let slip. 'That is,' she went on to qualify, 'I'd hardly slept the night before, and when I heard on local radio that you were in hospital and had lost your memory, I felt dreadful.'

'So you should!' he grunted toughly.

'I'd wanted to stop when we hit you,' she hurriedly told him. 'I was sure Gerry was going to stop, but he...' Her voice faded as she realised that she so wanted Brad's good opinion of her that her tongue was running away with her again.

'But he refused,' Brad finished for her.

Having brought herself up short, Mornay declined to confirm that, and said quickly instead, 'Anyway, when because of everything that had happened I couldn't concentrate properly on work the next day, Mr Probert thought it was on account of my worrying over Claudia, and——'

'She was having problems?'

'Nothing too great,' Mornay replied. 'She had a soaring temperature which caused her to have to stay in hospital for a couple of days longer than she'd expected. Anyhow, when, because of you, my work began to suffer, Mr Probert, thinking it was Claudia I was so anxious about——'

'You were anxious about me?' Brad asked quietly.

'Of course I was!' Mornay exclaimed. 'Anybody would be! What do you think I am?' she charged, and, realising that she would rather not know, she went rapidly back to what she had been saying. 'So Mr Probert told me to take an hour off to go and see Claudia. First, though,' she slowed down to continue, 'although I knew quite well where the maternity wing of Reefingham General was—I found myself in the accident wing.'

'Your conscience had brought you there to see me,' Brad suggested, not unkindly, she thought, but though she had lied to him before, she discovered most oddly just then that she could lie to him no more!

'I didn't intend to come and see you,' she found herself confessing. 'I got my geography wrong and thought the side-ward you were in was Sister's office. I—er—got the shock of my life when I saw you there.'

'You knew me straight away, didn't you?' he questioned, and even if Mornay could have denied it she saw that there was little point. He'd remember from the way she had straight away started talking about the accident that she had recognised him—when it later became plain, by virtue of the ward sister's appearance, that no one had told her where he was.

'You looked directly at me,' she told him. 'Just before my car hit you, you looked straight at me—I . . . I knew that I'd never forget what you looked like,' she said shakily, but felt more shaky than ever when Brad, as if the initial nightmare she had gone through showed in her face and had stirred him to feel compassion, suddenly left the settee he was occupying, crossed the carpet in a couple of strides, and came to share part of the settee she was on.

Then, as if that wasn't enough to totally unnerve her, he looked deeply into her wide blue eyes and murmured softly, 'Poor Mornay, you've been to hell and back, haven't you?'

'I—er——' she choked, and just couldn't believe the gentleness which she suddenly thought she saw in his eyes. It must be, she realised, that, having been aggressive to start with, Brad had decided to use a softer tactic before he delivered a death-blow to her hopes of getting him not to prosecute Gerry. 'Er—did you recognise me straight away?' she asked, that being the only question to come into her head that had any sense to it since she had just mentioned that Brad had looked directly at her. 'You—er—said, at the hospital—that you'd not lost your memory at all,' she belatedly recalled.

'Neither I had,' he replied, his tone evening out as any genuine softening there might have been in him faded, and he adjusted his position to move a few inches away from her. 'Though of the accident I remember nothing. All I can remember is waking up in hospital and the nursing staff telling that I'd been the victim of a hit-and-run driver. Then, while I'm still trying to sort my head out, along comes a most beautiful red-carnation-carrying blonde.'

'Oh,' escaped Mornay on a little gasp. Then, fearing that he might have caught a glimpse of what it meant to her to hear that *he* thought her beautiful, she sought hurriedly for some sensible remark. Though the only thing to come to her was, 'Er—actually I bought the carnations for Claudia.'

'I realised that a few minutes ago,' he stated, his tone entirely unoffended. 'I thought about you a great deal after you'd gone.'

'You—did?' she questioned warily.

'And then some,' he confirmed quietly, and, as she warily eyed him still, Mornay began to receive the oddest notion that Brad was holding himself in check. Somehow, she began to get the strangest feeling Brad was a man with a lot on his mind, a lot which, although it involved her, had little to do with the accident.

'It's—er—natural, I suppose,' she replied to what he had said, while at the same time she could not help but wonder if being in love with him had given her an extra sensitivity to his thoughts and feelings—or were her senses playing her entirely false? 'I'd—as you thought—just put you in hospital; it would be only natural that you'd—er—give me some thought,' she added nervously.

'Which is exactly what I told myself,' he murmured. 'What would be more natural than that I should be angry with your lies about seeing the ambulance come for me? Wasn't it only natural that I should be furious—when I cannot tolerate being ill or incapacitated, and have a particularly strong dislike of being in hospital—that through you, hospital was where I ended up?' he asked, but went on, not waiting for her to answer, a hint of warmth entering his voice, 'But why then, furious and angry with you, should I find myself also intrigued by you?'

'In-intrigued?' Mornay questioned chokily.

'What else?' he questioned in return, and effectively stilled any wild beating in her heart when he itemised matter-of-factly, 'How could I not be intrigued when, having run me down and seemingly driven off without conscience, this beautiful woman who stands every chance of getting away with it then turns up at my bedside when there's a great chance that someone will start asking questions?'

'I was—a bit stupid, wasn't I?' she mumbled.

'Not stupid at all,' he denied. 'Just basically a caring person, as I realised very early on.'

'Oh,' she murmured, trying to quieten loud, clamouring bells of alarm that warned he must not see just how 'caring' she felt where he was concerned.

'Though I rather think that your second visit to me in hospital would not have been so voluntarily made,' Brad went on.

'You ordered me to come and see you!' she reminded him.

'And you turned up later than I thought you should,' he inserted.

'And you were horrible to me,' she said without thinking.

'How should I be...?'

'I'm sorry,' she swiftly apologised. 'You were hurting, and——'

'It wasn't just that,' he cut across what she was saying, and then astonished her completely by adding slowly, 'I thought you weren't coming. I thought that you'd re-alised I'd no intention of having you prosecuted over the accident. I——'

'You weren't going to prosecute!' Mornay gasped. 'But—but... You mean I went to Scotland with you for nothing! You...'

'Hardly for nothing!' Brad told her sharply.

'Well, I suppose not,' she had to agree, remembering how rocky and without colour he had been when he had come out of hospital. 'You needed someone to look after you, so why not the person whom you thought had put you in hospital?' fairness made her agree.

'My sentiments exactly,' he concurred. 'Though, to be fair in return, I'd been ill before my meeting with your car saw me hospitalised.'

'You'd been ill!' Mornay echoed, unable to hold down her concern. 'What was wrong with . . .?'

'Nothing to worry about,' Brad told her, sending her a smile, a warming smile, at the concern in her voice. 'I was halfway to recovering from a quite severe bout of flu when I suddenly woke up to find myself in hospital.'

'This was after the accident?' she asked, and when he nodded, 'But you were in Reefingham working,' she said, clearly remembering him saying that he had come to her home town the night before a meeting to have a look round the place. 'You shouldn't have been working . . .'

'I'm used to working,' Brad said softly, and for some reason she could not fathom he seemed encouraged by her anxiety over his health as he went on, 'I'd worked more or less on and off all the way through flu, so I suppose it wasn't so surprising that when I woke up in hospital where I was forced to rest, I was also forced to face the fact that I felt exhausted.'

'You could have had pneumonia!' Mornay cried in alarm as her imagination took off. 'The shock of the accident together with your flu, could have brought on pneumonia!'

'You did a splendid job of looking after me,' he said gently.

'Oh, Brad,' she cried, and wished then that she'd known more about his health, and that she'd done more for him—though, since he wasn't at all keen on fuss, she doubted he'd have let her do more than she had.

'You're sweet,' he said, and suddenly, as if he could not resist it, he sent her heart wildly racing by leaning forward and placing a gentle kiss on her mouth. Then he pulled back and, looking into her eyes, he quietly told her, 'Don't feel too badly about what happened, Mornay, for I have to confess that one or two good things came about from that accident.'

'What good could possibly come from you being knocked over?' she exclaimed, and entirely missed the fact that she had moved from her defensive position where her brother-in-law was concerned to being quietly indignant on behalf of the man she loved.

Silently Brad studied her ruffled expression, then a warm look came to his eyes. Then, 'Perhaps I needed a few days' enforced incarceration in hospital,' he said softly. 'I should never otherwise have taken time out to pause and wonder why I found it impossible to let up.'

'You're a workaholic?' Mornay questioned.

'Let's say that, with my father's shiftless attitude to work before me, I determined from a very early age that I was going to be different.'

It was the first time Brad had mentioned his father, and Mornay loved him more than ever that he was letting her take a glimpse into this personal side of his life. 'I shouldn't think anyone could call you shiftless,' she told him gently, knowing for sure that no one got to the top the way he had without working jolly hard.

'I'll let you run my fan club,' he teased, and she loved him for that too. In love with him, and loving this time of suddenly being in tune with him, she was in no way going to spoil it all by taking exception to anything he said.

'When did you last have a holiday?' she asked him as the question popped into her head.

'Apart from Scotland——'

'Which was convalescence,' she put in.

'Which was convalescence,' he grinned, 'I can't remember the last time I had a holiday.'

'So being made to rest in hospital was probably just about what you needed,' Mornay suggested.

'That's more or less what I realised when I woke up feeling shattered, but not knowing whether it was from the flu, overwork, or if it could all be put down to my being knocked unconscious. When the idea came to me that perhaps it might be an idea if I let up a little, I promptly dismissed any such idea—and went to sleep. I seem to have done a lot of that—sleeping—in those first days after the accident,' he commented.

'You said yourself that you felt exhausted,' Mornay reminded him.

'Which is most likely why I couldn't be bothered to tell anyone who I was. I rather enjoyed being anonymous,' he owned. 'Not that it lasted long.'

'The manager of this hotel soon let the cat out of the bag,' Mornay remembered.

'True,' Brad agreed, 'And I spent some time sleeping and then waking to find that the notion I was dismissing, about letting up a little, kept returning. By the time you'd come to visit me that first time I must seriously have been thinking in terms of taking a rest—or at least I must have been on the way to realising that the time seemed right for me to take a distanced view of my life.'

'You'd never had time before,' Mornay commented with sudden empathy.

'It was for certain just then that I wasn't going anywhere in a hurry,' Brad replied, 'so what better time than the present to accept that I needed some time out from work to take stock?'

'You made a conscious decision to review your life?'

'I think it was more that, feeling flattened, the decision was more or less made for me. I knew that my company could run smoothly without me for a month—so began thinking in terms of finding a hideaway.'

'You didn't want any attention from the Press,' Mornay put in, and he nodded.

'But where to go?' he murmured, and added, 'I wasn't feeling fit enough to drive any distance.'

'So you thought of me.'

'It seemed logical,' he answered. 'Though I have to admit that you gave me the idea when the natural, caring you came through, and you began to protest that I couldn't leave hospital because I needed someone to look after me. I soon began to think—who better than you? And I was sure that, under the circumstances of your wanting to keep quiet your part of my being below par, you wouldn't be inviting the nation's newshounds round for a Press conference.'

'I made it easy for you, didn't I?' Mornay stated, and started to feel very mixed up inside suddenly—on the one hand she felt a chump for being so naïvely open with him, yet on the other she knew that she would not have missed knowing him for anything.

But, 'Easy!' Brad exclaimed in denial. 'You're joking!'

'But—you came to my flat and...'

'The alternative, when I decided to leave hospital, was for me to return to London, where it was fairly certain that my instinct to put my nose to the grindstone and keep it there was bound to surface. I felt at the crossroads in my life, Mornay,' he warmed her heart by confiding. 'I had a thriving business, I'd worked hard and got where I wanted to be by my own efforts—there was nothing left to prove.'

Mornay was silent for a few seconds, but, warmed that he had confided what he so far had, she glanced away from him in fear that he might read in her eyes how she reacted inside to his every entrusted word. 'So,' she got herself a little together to start questioning, 'you signed yourself out of hospital and came to my flat, and began to take stock, and...'

'That,' Brad said, 'was the trouble. I didn't begin to take stock.'

She turned her head to hurriedly look at him, 'You—didn't?' she asked, and saw him move his head slowly from side to side.

'Before I knew where——' Abruptly he checked, and quickly looked away, and Mornay had the clearest impression that he had been about to say something totally different from what he did say when he resumed, 'Before I'd been in your flat more than a few hours you were getting tough and telling me that I couldn't stay there.'

'Me—getting tough!' Mornay exclaimed, and could have hugged him from the sheer joy of it when he blatantly lied,

'I was frightened to death of you.' He paused, arrested by the amused smile that came to her mouth, and then went on, 'Your idea of Scotland suited me fine.'

Mornay's amused smile quickly departed. Scotland would have suited him fine, wouldn't it? she thought jealously, as she instantly recalled how he had visited his 'mother' in Perth while they had been in Scotland. 'Because it then gave you the time you needed to review your life?' she enquired, her tone grown cool.

'Review—hell!' Brad replied, and, when she looked away from him he sent her heart stampeding along by placing a warm hand under her chin and turning her head round so that he could see into her face. Then, quite distinctly, as her heart drummed rapidly away inside, 'Don't blow hot and cold with me, not now, Mornay,' he asked of her urgently, and indeed, he seemed to be experiencing something of the same inner turmoil that she had been in when, 'I didn't even begin to take stock,' he told her in such a restrained kind of way that Mornay again had the feeling he was holding himself very much in check.

'You weren't feeling well enough,' she suggested, her cool tone suddenly gone.

'Physically, I'd started to improve minute by minute,' he hit that theory on the head. Then, to make her stare, 'But how could I begin to sort myself—my life out,' he went on, 'when I discovered—that I was a total wreck about you?'

She felt utterly amazed by what he had just said, and
her eyes went saucer-wide in her face. She tried, as nerves
began to attack, to turn her head away from him. But
Brad still cupped her chin in a firm, warm hold, and she
could not turn her head away. 'W-what—are you—um—
saying?' she asked croakily.

'I'm saying, my dear, dear, Mornay,' he answered, to
make the blood course round in her veins even faster,
'that when, without exception, I've always had the ability
to view everything clearly, objectively, within hours of
meeting you my clear perspective had vanished—clouded
by emotions which I didn't begin to understand. While
my objectivity was likewise distorted.'

'By—er—emotions?' she asked faintly, having been
pummelled remorselessly by her own emotions since she
had known Brad.

'That's what I said,' he confirmed, and, looking into
her agitated eyes, he took his fingers away from her chin
and caught hold of her trembling hand. 'Before I knew
what had hit me, there I was in the grip of emotions
which I have never experienced before.'

'What sort—of emotions?' she just had to ask.

Without her knowing it, she was gripping his hand
tightly. 'Jealousy, for one,' he confessed.

'Jealousy?' she whispered.

'Furious jealousy,' he agreed, 'at the thought that you
might have a live-in lover.'

'Live-in...' Her voice faded in astonishment at what
he was saying.

'I was still in hospital,' Brad took over to elucidate.
'I barely knew you, yet when you started to argue the
toss about me not coming to your flat, and I realised
you might have a live-in lover, I was staggered by the
energy in the jealousy I experienced—until you denied
my charge.'

'Good heavens!' Mornay gasped.

'If you're shaken, think how I felt,' he murmured. 'In
less than twenty-four hours I'd met you and told you to

come and see me the next day. Then, when you didn't come at the time I'd decided you should come, I'd grown angry with myself that not seeing you had the power to irritate me. And, all before I knew it, I was roaringly jealous over you and discovered—when you'd gone— that I was wasting no time in coming to find you.'

Mornay swallowed hard; she wanted with all her heart to believe what she thought Brad was telling her but, because it was so unbelievable, she was afraid. 'You were over-tired, ill,' she found excuses to put forward for his emotional state.

'Which of course is exactly what I told myself when I got out of bed early in the morning after that one night I spent in your flat.'

'I didn't hear you.'

'You were dead to the world,' Brad told her, adding, 'I suspect you'd been awake most of the night on that most uncomfortable of couches. Anyhow, I stood looking down at you and, as the most staggering emotion took me, and my heart began to thunder, threatening to fracture my ribs, I knew then why I had checked in the telephone directory for your address, and had taken a taxi to come looking for you.'

Quite desperately then did Mornay want to ask him her own 'Why?', but the sudden fear in her that he might be turning the tables on her and leading her up his garden path as her punishment caused her to hold back.

'You . . .' she cleared a constriction in her throat '. . . you—hmm—felt better when you went back to bed. You were back in bed when I got up to come and take a look at you,' she remembered. 'You smiled,' she said, quite without thinking, and could have died from the inanity of her remark.

'You looked so lovely standing there with your blonde hair all anyhow,' he murmured, casting a sideways glance at the classic knot into which her hair was now confined. 'But,' he went on, 'by the time we saw each other again at the breakfast table I'd realised that, while this new emotional side that had awakened in me must be put down to my still being affected by the accident, and I must therefore counteract it by checking any feelings of—pleasantness I felt towards you, I could not deny that it didn't suit me at all to have you suggest, as you did, that I was well enough to go home.'

'Oh?' Mornay queried cagily.

And Brad smiled. 'I wanted time with you, Mornay,' he told her softly. 'You'd told me I knew nothing about you, and I realised that I wanted to know all there was to know about you. So much so,' he went on when, dumbstruck, she just stared at him, 'that on our journey to Scotland, when you were so solicitous about how I was standing up to the journey, I began to realise that I was being more "pleasant" to you than I'd intended, and that I was starting to feel totally vulnerable where you were concerned.'

'Vulnerable—you?' Mornay asked.

'It was all so new to me,' he explained, but it explained little to her, and she was afraid to ask for a fuller explanation. 'Then in no time we're laughing with each other, and I'm trying to remember that I don't want to be vulnerable. But I am, because again I experience jealousy over your boyfriend. And then, suddenly, for the first time in years, I'm relaxing, and starting to feel great.'

'I'm so glad,' Mornay said simply, sincerely, and saw that Brad seemed to take heart from her simple statement.

'So am I,' he said, and caught a gentle hold of her other hand. 'I've suffered in more ways than one since I've known you, dear Mornay,' he went on softly. 'Will you not end that suffering for me?'

'I...' she said, and faltered. His eyes were fixed firmly on hers and she had to take a steadying breath. 'I'm not sure—that I know what you're asking,' she told him huskily.

'Have you not reasoned, from what I've been telling you, how things are with me?' he asked her, his voice gone as emotional as hers. Dumbly Mornay looked at him, afraid to blink, afraid to say a word. Then, 'My love,' Brad said, and, raising her hands, he placed a gentle kiss on each in turn. 'I've seen tears in your eyes when I've hurt you, and been afraid to follow you for fear I might take you in my arms to comfort you. I've subsequently spent the worst night of my life wanting to come to you, but settled for bringing you in a cup of tea the next morning when I was up and about, but could hear no sounds of you astir.'

'That was the morning after you'd been all—er—brutish—when you'd reminded me of the accident,' Mornay said nervously.

'That's right,' he agreed, 'and I so badly wanted to make up for being such a swine, I kissed you,' he reminded her, 'and then knew hell when, having torn myself away from you, the next time I saw you you had changed from being the warm and vibrant woman I'd held in my arms to being cool, cold, and giving me the "I wouldn't care if I never saw you again" treatment.'

'It—er—bothered you?'

'It sure as hell did,' he replied without hesitation. 'I just couldn't fathom what had happened in between our sharing of ourselves in your bedroom and your giving me the cold shoulder the next time I saw you. So,' he said, 'I had to ask myself—why?'

'You—would,' Mornay murmured, and felt her heartbeats speed up again when Brad leaned forward and gently laid a kiss on her cheek.

'The only conclusion my question brought me, even though nothing too alarming had taken place in those moments of our mutual embracing, was that you must be regretting that anything at all had taken place. That,' he said, and paused, and then, his eyes watchful on hers, 'or, could it be, dare I hope, that you had heard me sending roses to a lady and—were jealous?'

'I——' Mornay said, and had been ready to deny that she had ever experienced a moment's jealousy where he was concerned. But she hesitated. Brad could be leading her up some most dreadful garden path but—had she learned nothing of him in those weeks in Scotland? Oh, Brad, she wanted to say, please help me. Please tell me in words what you're saying. She had flicked her glance away from him, but suddenly she looked back at him, and could see nothing but sincerity in the dark eyes that held hers—sincerity, and a look that said: trust me. She swallowed hard once more, then asked him, 'Did you really go and see your mother that day?'

'Yes, Mornay, I did,' he replied at once. 'The roses were for her, too. It was her birthday, and I hoped to brighten for her what, prior to my getting on my feet financially, had not been too sunny a life.'

'Oh, Brad,' Mornay said softly, and was rewarded by a warm smile.

'My mother doesn't have the best of health,' he went on, 'but even so, I'd not intended to be away from you for so long.'

'Hadn't you?'

He shook his head. 'Having that dent filled in your car took forever to dry, and then it had to be sprayed over.'

'Oh, Brad,' Mornay sighed again, and at the loving look he bestowed on her it wasn't a question of trusting him any more, for it seemed quite natural that she was able to tell him, with only the smallest shy hesitation, 'Then—I was jealous all that day, and since then, for nothing.'

For perhaps two ageless seconds Brad studied her with a stunned look in his eyes. Then, suddenly, the most wonderful smile she had ever witnessed spread across his features. Then, 'My darling!' he cried triumphantly, and before she had taken another breath he had hauled her into his arms, and she was held fast against his chest.

Moments turned into minutes as, with Brad's arms iron bands about her, he held her as though never intending to let her go. Then, as if, like Mornay, he could not believe what was happening was real, his hands went to her shoulders, and he moved her gently from him and, keeping his hands secure on her shoulders, looked long into her loving, beautiful blue eyes.

Then, 'My darling,' he breathed again, and suddenly she was in his arms once more, and more bliss was hers when he laid his lips gently over hers, and then pressed tiny kisses over her face. 'My dear love,' he whispered, and again his mouth claimed hers in a long and loving kiss.

'Oh, Brad,' Mornay murmured shakily, held firmly against his heart, when his mouth left hers.

'You're all right, Mornay?' he asked, looking down at her, and she loved him more for his concern.

'Fine—now,' she told him, and saw him smile.

'Has it been the same hell for you that it's been for me?' he asked.

'I—think so,' she answered shyly.

'From the start?' he wanted to know.

'I . . .' she began and, when she hesitated, she saw him frown. But even as his frown arrived, he scrutinised her face and she realised that he must have read her shyness there, for like magic his frown cleared.

'For a man who's spent his life paying attention to detail, I've just slipped up very badly, haven't I?' he queried, and, not needing an answer, 'Forgive me, sweet Mornay, but I've been in such a hell of a state since your phone call that it's no wonder to me that I forgot to tell you the most important thing of all.' Mornay's eyes were glued to his when, first bestowing a tender, almost reverent kiss to her mouth, 'My heart, my world,' he said throatily, 'I love you—with everything that's in me.'

'Oh, Brad!' Mornay cried trembly.

'And it's the same for you?' he wanted to know.

'Y-yes,' she told him shakily, and was hauled tightly up against his heart for many long seconds.

Then Brad was putting some daylight between their two bodies, but he still had his arms around her when, looking nowhere but at her, he wanted to know, 'When did it start, this love I don't deserve, but need so badly?'

'I'm not entirely sure,' she answered as truthfully and as honestly as it now seemed she could only do. 'I can remember feeling quite glad to know that you had a housekeeper rather than a live-in girlfriend, so I think jealousy must have been at the root.' Mornay just adored him when he grinned in delight at her confession. 'And I can remember being most definitely jealous of the lady you were sending roses to. I knew that day that I was in love with you.'

Again Brad drew her close to his heart, and delicious moments passed for Mornay where Brad saluted her with tiny kisses and told her of his love for her and how he'd been afraid of frightening her off, while at the same time he'd been trying most desperately to gauge what, if anything, she felt for him.

'Honestly?' she questioned, wide-eyed.

'Honestly,' he confirmed. 'I came back from Perth and took you in my arms. When you didn't immediately push me away, I kissed you because I'd missed you, and spent the next few days in a state of wanting to take you in my arms again, but being too anxious in my love for you to risk it.'

'But you did—take me in your arms again, I mean.'

'Don't think I've forgotten,' he smiled warmly, and went on, 'Never will I forget the fury that raged in me last Sunday when Overton rang, and you had the nerve to tell me that you'd dared to ring another of your men-friends.'

'I couldn't tell you that he was my brother-in-law,' Mornay told him softly. 'Though I thought at the time the reason for your fury was because you thought I'd given away your hideaway.'

'Hideaway, nothing,' Brad growled, mock ferociously. 'My jealousy had just gone over the top, and I was hearing nothing more, seeing nothing more than my crazed belief that you'd cheated me by ringing some man behind my back. Only when you began to respond to my kisses, to being in my arms, did a modicum of sanity start to stir. Then, my love,' he told her quietly, 'when I looked down into your shy face, full sanity returned, and I knew that I had to leave you while I still could.'

'You knew then that I—er—wouldn't have—er—opposed you?'

'Forgive me, my love,' he breathed, 'but, yes, I did. But I also had to think past that moment. What if we'd made love and, when that time of sharing of each other was gone, you maybe got round to thinking that I'd seduced you, or worse, that I'd blackmailed you into giving yourself? What if you ended up hating me? What could I, who wanted you to give yourself in love, do then?'

'Oh, Brad, I could never hate you,' she told him from her heart.

'Now you tell me!' he teased, and hugged her to him, and reminded her of the grim days that had followed when she had wanted to get back to Reefingham. 'You'd said, "You don't need me!",' he backtracked, 'and I knew then that I needed you more than I needed anything in my life. That for me there was no life without you.'

'Oh,' Mornay sighed, and Brad kissed her hair and, as if he quite liked her present hairstyle, but wanted his Mornay back, he gently removed every one of the confining hairpins.

'Do you mind?' he asked, as he ran his fingers through her long blonde tresses.

'Not a bit,' she smiled.

'Good,' he said in a satisfied kind of way, and then went on to tell her how the strained atmosphere that had grown between them had really started to get to him.

'Then one day you jumped in alarm, I thought, when I came near you, and——'

'You slammed out,' Mornay clearly remembered.

'I went for a walk to try and get my thoughts together,' he confessed. 'I knew you wanted to return to Reefingham, but I was afraid that if I allowed that, then I might never see you again once we had parted. I still hadn't sorted out in my head what your jumping like that might mean. Were you afraid of my touching you? Were you scared of your own feelings if I did touch you? It was something of a relief, sweetheart, to find that the anxious state you were in when I returned had nothing to do with me.'

'I'd rung Claudia and she'd sounded tearful and said that she couldn't cope with everything, with a new son who never seemed to stop crying.'

Gently, Brad placed his mouth over hers, and pulled back to murmur, 'What could a man do when faced with his love being unhappy about her sister?'

'I'm sorry I lied to you,' Mornay told him quietly.

And knew how exactly they were on each other's wavelength when he replied, 'By implying that the new son and heir was older than he is?' He smiled wryly as he went on, 'I knew, of course, by the time I'd been acquainted with the actual age of that young man, pretty much all there was to know.'

'I'm sorry,' Mornay murmured again.

'So you should be!' Brad told her mock severely. 'It was so obvious that you'd got the jitters about my going any further than Reefingham that day that I began to suspect you didn't have a sister.'

'Really?'

He nodded. 'Our old enemy, jealousy, began to make me fairly certain that there must be some man involved somewhere. Which of course made me doubly determined to accompany you to the very last yard of your journey. And,' he added softly, 'am I glad I did!'

'You are?'

'Now I am,' he smiled. 'At the time I felt—to put it mildly—slightly murderous.'

'You—er—looked it,' Mornay remembered.

'How else should I look?' he enquired. 'I'd just met your sister, and within minutes I knew exactly why you hadn't phoned her to tell her you were leaving Reefingham. Within minutes, while you were losing some of your colour, I was hearing all there was to hear, all that in the weeks we'd been together you hadn't learned to trust me enough to tell me yourself.'

'I—couldn't,' she had to confess. 'Claudia means a lot to me. I'd gone with you to Scotland hoping that by doing so I'd sort of settle the bill for my car's having knocked you down. But the newspaper, the local one that gave an account of the accident, described you as a man who didn't like to have one put over on him, and—well, to be truthful, I thought you might see what I'd done in that light. I was still fearful about what you proposed to do about Gerry when I drove here tonight,' she owned. 'Even when I saw you—when we began to talk—I still wasn't certain, for all you said you'd no intention of prosecuting, that you weren't leading me on while you prepared to exact full retribution.'

'Ye gods!' Brad erupted explosively, and Mornay was seeing a coolness in his eyes again when, his arms dropping from about her, 'Do you still think that way?' he demanded.

But Mornay was no longer afraid. 'I love you, and trust you,' she told him simply, and was straight away hauled back into his arms.

'I once referred to the fact that you didn't know where the hell you were at,' Brad murmured against her ear. 'But those words have returned again and again to describe what I've been like. When I left in that taxi yesterday and booked in here I went through the hell of knowing that I'd fallen in love with a marvellous woman, and spent a long, tortured night, with half of me feeling that you should have known I wasn't going to prosecute, and the other half going through the nightmare of wondering if you had any feelings for me at all—other than fear. The thought that you might fear me, my dear, was worse than a nightmare. All I could do,' he ended, 'was to sit tight and hope with all I had that you would come to me.'

'You knew I'd ring?'

'I didn't know anything of the kind. I just hoped that if you were missing me a tenth of the way I was missing you then you'd phone. I just hung on, praying that, as I felt compelled to stay near to you, you, on whatever pretext, would feel compelled to get in touch with me.'

'By the time I did make contact, I was too confused to know if I was ringing to ask you not to do anything that might harm Claudia's security, or,' Mornay had to confess, 'if it was because I was getting desperate to hear the sound of your voice.' Tenderly Brad leaned forward and kissed her, and Mornay sighed from the beauty of it when he pulled back and looked adoringly at her. Then, softly, 'You wouldn't have contacted me?' she asked.

'I would never have allowed you to go out of my life,' he replied most definitely. 'But while I've been in hell all today, and wanting to contact you, I have at the same time been furious with you for what you've done.'

'What I've done?'

'You could have gone away with just about any man,' he told her severely, and when she just had to burst out laughing at his biased reasoning, he grinned too, and told her, 'You see what you do to me? I've waited and waited all this long, endless day for you to ring, and then for you to come to me. Then, when I'm fully determined before you get here that I'm going to remain aloof with you, you, within minutes, just by virtue of being with me, send all my pre-planning up in smoke.'

'Serves you right,' Mornay laughed.

But she sobered rapidly when, leaning back from her, Brad studied her solemnly for a few seconds, and then quietly let fall, 'Are we going to have your four young nieces as bridesmaids?'

'B...' Mornay opened her mouth, and had to swallow as a wave of emotion took her. 'Are—we—g-getting married?' she asked him chokily.

'Are you saying no after all you've put me through?' Brad asked, his expression unsmiling.

'I—wouldn't dream of it,' Mornay answered lovingly, and saw his wonderful smile start to break through again.

'Come here,' he growled gruffly, and then their lips met.

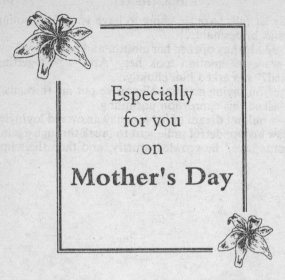
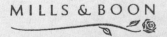

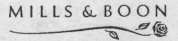

Temptation

Lost Loves

'Right Man...Wrong time'

All women are haunted by a lost love—a disastrous first romance, a brief affair, a marriage that failed.

A second chance with him...could change everything.

Lost Loves, a powerful, sizzling mini-series from Temptation starts in March 1995 with...

The Return of Caine O'Halloran
by JoAnn Ross

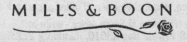

MILLS & BOON

Forthcoming Titles

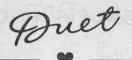

❤

Available in February

The Emma Darcy Duet

**THE ULTIMATE CHOICE
TOO STRONG TO DENY**

The Jessica Steele Duet

**FAREWELL TO LOVE
HIDDEN HEART**

LOVE ON CALL

❤

SMOOTH OPERATOR   Christine Adams
RIVALS FOR A SURGEON   Drusilla Douglas
A DAUNTING DIVERSION   Abigail Gordon
AN INDISPENSABLE WOMAN   Margaret Holt

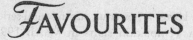

❤

A LOVE AFFAIR   Lindsay Armstrong
BLIND PASSION   Anne Mather